FURY

A GABRIEL WOLFE THRILLER

ANDY MASLEN

TYTON PRESS

For Jo.

Heaven has no rage like love to hatred turned, nor hell a fury like a woman scorned.
William Congreve, 1670-1729

1

PARTNERSHIPS

LONDON/MANHATTAN/VENICE

The woman who called herself Erin Ayers didn't feel like riding in the back of the white Rolls Royce Phantom this evening. She motioned Guy, the chauffeur, to close the rear coach door, stalked round to the other side of the car, and climbed into the passenger seat.

"How was the dinner, ma'am?" Guy asked as he settled himself beside her and buckled in.

"For a start, you can knock off the *ma'am* bit. I'm not the fucking queen. You can call me Erin or boss, I don't care which. And since you ask, it was a fucking train wreck. That smug bitch Simone Berrington told me moneymaking was one thing, but that 'politics is best left to those who know what we're doing'." Erin's mimicry of the foreign secretary's Home Counties accent was wickedly accurate, even down to the trace of a lisp her party-appointed speech therapists had all but erased.

"I'm sorry to hear that, M—boss."

"She even gave me her card in case I ever want to talk about donating to the party."

"There must be others you could approach."

"Oh, don't you worry. Berrington will rue the day she turned me down."

They cruised through the streets of Mayfair, quiet now evening had fallen.

Erin looked idly out of the window to her left at the artworks and designer dresses displayed in the windows. Suddenly, the Rolls jerked to a stop and Guy swore under his breath as a Lycra-clad cyclist swerved in front of them. The lights ahead changed to red, and they drew alongside the cyclist, who turned out to be a middle-aged, bearded man bearing a hostile scowl. Rather than taking a foot out of his pedal clips, he stretched out his right hand and rested it on the car's roof.

Erin buzzed her window down and spoke.

"Get your fucking hand off my car, you moron. And while you're about it, learn some manners."

The cyclist whipped his head round and down, and spat into the open window.

"How's that for manners, you Tory cunt?" he shouted. Then he gave her the finger and jumped the light across to the next quiet stretch of road leading towards Park Lane.

Guy looked sideways at Erin, eyebrows lifted fractionally.

She nodded back. He returned his eyes to the road and once the lights turned to green, accelerated smoothly across the junction, using the full might of the car's V12 engine to catch the cyclist. He drew level and slowed to match the man's speed. Then, with a sudden wrench left of the steering wheel, he slammed the two and a half tonnes of car into the cyclist's right side, crunching man and bike into the side of a removals van, parked for the night.

He pulled into the next available space. Erin got out of the car and walked back towards the fallen cyclist, her high heels clicking on the tarmac. He was unconscious, his legs twisted beneath him at unnatural angles. Two bright shards of bone protruded through the flesh of his right calf muscle, and blood was pooling beneath his head.

She stooped and placed a small rectangular card with a Foreign and Commonwealth Office crest on his fluttering chest, then sauntered back to the Rolls.

"Home, James," she purred. "And don't spare the horses. We have to be in Manhattan tomorrow and I haven't packed."

* * *

A sheet of pale-blue, lined notebook paper swirled high above Central Park's Jacqueline Kennedy Onassis Reservoir, snatched by the wind from a home office desk by an open window in the Fifth Avenue penthouse belonging to Erin Ayers. Written in elegant, sloping calligraphy was a partially completed list:

Friends
    Car
    Comrades
    House
    Business
    M

A gust of gritty, fume-laden air rose up from the street and carried the list south. It whirled away, over the spire of St. Paddy's, then shifted eastwards onto Park Avenue. Caught in a vortex of air moving around the stainless-steel cladding of the Chrysler Building's terraced crown, it fluttered over and over, traveling southwest towards Mott Street in Chinatown. A downdraft like a cold, wet hand pushed it out of the thermals so that it dropped from the grey sky into a cobbled alley running between a vacant lot and the back of a row of Chinese restaurants. It landed in a puddle of week-old cooking oil. Moments later, a rat darted out from a pile of rotting cabbage stems, sniffed at the paper and, perhaps deciding it would make good nesting material, sank its long, yellow incisors into it and pulled it free from the oil before trotting off to a grating and disappearing. The list had vanished. Its consequences would begin two weeks later.

* * *

In the kitchen of a flat in Chiswick, West London, Gabriel Wolfe and Britta Falskog were drinking Pol Roger champagne. She held the flute in her left hand; her right was bandaged.

"So, what's the special occasion?" Britta asked.

Gabriel raised his glass to his lips, sniffed the stewed-apple aroma of the wine and took a brief sip.

"There's something I want to ask you."

"What is it? If it's a trip anywhere except to bed, the answer's no."

He smiled and shook his head.

"I want to ask you if you'll marry me."

Her blue eyes popped wide with surprise. She put her glass down. Then she turned to face him. His breathing was steady, but as she opened her mouth to speak, his heart was racing. He didn't bother slowing it.

"It would be tough on our kids, you know," she said.

It wasn't either of the answers Gabriel Wolfe had been playing in his mind.

"What?" the ex-SAS Captain asked. "What kids? You're not …?"

"No, idiot! But can you really see us as a cosy married couple with a couple of, what is it, ankle-biters? Daddy off to kill bad men in Africa for the British government's black-ops hit squad, Mummy going undercover to defeat a terrorist plot? I mean, it's not exactly home sweet home, is it?"

Gabriel scratched the back of his head and ruffled his short, black hair into spikes. He had just proposed and somehow hadn't been expecting a logical analysis of the pros and cons. More fool him for not knowing how the redheaded Swede standing opposite him would react.

"No, I guess not. But we don't have to have kids." He noted her eyes flashbulb in surprise, the whites showing all the way round the irises. "Not straight away, anyway. Do we? We could just be … unconventional."

"Well, for one thing," Britta drained her champagne and started counting off points on her fingers. She'd picked up the habit from Gabriel, who in turn had adopted the mannerism from his boss at The Department and former CO in the SAS, Don Webster. "Yes, we do have to have kids. Otherwise, what's the point of getting married? Two, *unconventional* doesn't really begin to cover it, does it? Children need stability. You of all people should know that." Gabriel's eyes fell, and his mouth compressed into a thin line. "Oh, Jesus, sorry, my darling. I didn't mean about Michael."

Michael Wolfe was Gabriel's younger brother. Had been. Until very recently, Gabriel would have sworn he was an only child. Then a series of events had led him to realise that not only was that untrue, but he had been responsible for his brother's death, by drowning, when Michael had been just five years old.

"It's OK," Gabriel said, then smiled a small, sad smile. "You're right. Kids need a stable home. Somewhere safe. But couldn't we provide that? Surely, there's a way? And why can't you give an answer to the main question? It's not the most romantic way to respond to a proposal of marriage."

She closed the two-foot gap between them and wrapped her arms around his waist. "Okay. Answer time. I can't think of anything I'd like more. So, yes, please. But," she added hurriedly as his face broke into a wide grin and his dark-brown eyes crinkled at the corners, "it's a 'yes, please' with conditions."

"Fine! Tell me. SAS and Swedish Special Forces guard of honour with fixed bayonets? Knife throwing at the reception? Tell me."

"Give me till the end of the job they're sending me on next. Just to work out some of the practicalities."

* * *

The gondola seemed like a tourist cliché, but the assassin was happy enough to trail her fingers in the cold water as her muscular gondolier poled them along. She looked up at him. *You look good enough to eat*, she thought, a smile on her black-cherry lips. He caught her expression and smiled back, puffing his chest out a little further and sucking in his stomach. *That's my boy. Maybe I'll invite you back to my hotel after we're through.* A buzz on her left hip switched her frame of mind back to business. She had few friends, and those she did have never contacted her on this phone.

She pulled the phone from her pocket and glanced at the display. Unknown caller. Well, this should be interesting. Not one of her regulars.

"Sasha Beck," she said. Then waited.

"Ms Beck, my name is Erin Ayers. I have a job for you, but I don't know whether I should come to you or have you flown out to meet me here. I'm in Manhattan."

Sasha looked up at the gondolier, who had adopted a comically macho pose – all bulging biceps and jutting jaw that almost made her laugh – then turned away from him so that she was facing in the opposite direction. "Well, *Mizz* Erin Ayers, you're going a little too fast. If you don't mind, we'll slow things down. One, I'm a Miss. Two, nobody flies me anywhere, unless I tell them to. Three, I don't know you from Adam, or Eve for that matter, and I want to know how you got this number."

"I'm so sorry, *Miss* Beck." The caller's clipped English accent laid heavy emphasis on the title with unmissable sarcasm, further piquing Sasha's curiosity. "Let me begin again. I was given your number by a Kazakh gentleman named Timur Kamenko. He spoke very highly of you. And, of course, I should be quite happy to come to you. Wherever that might be. Is that splashing I hear in the background? Are you on the water? Ooh, church bells. And those acoustics – all that stone and water. You must be in a gondola. I do love Venice."

"Bravo. So you're a distant relative of Sherlock Holmes, and you

6

know Timur. Meet me at Caffè Florian at eleven o'clock the day after tomorrow. If you're late, you won't find me waiting."

"Very well. I'll pack extra euros – my treat."

Assuming that anyone with the connections necessary to gain access to her business number would also have no problems making the rendezvous or recognising her, Sasha ended the call and smiled hungrily up at her gondolier.

2

A SLAP

LONDON

"What's the mission, then?" Gabriel asked.

He and Britta Falskog were walking down Piccadilly. It was ten in the evening, and they'd just had dinner. The air was unseasonably warm, and the arm he had round the redheaded Swede's waist she had drawn there purely for pleasure.

"Let's find somewhere for a nightcap, and I'll tell you."

Gabriel scanned ahead and behind, spotted a street he knew and whirled Britta around, not releasing her, as if they were dancing.

"This way, milady," he said. "I know a nice little bar where they serve excellent champagne cocktails."

They turned down Eagle Place and ran across the narrow street, incurring the wrath of an oncoming taxi driver, who leaned on his horn for a comically extended time and swore at them through his open window for good measure. They were still laughing when they pushed through the door into the interior of Bar Toulouse.

Inside, the place was busy, the drinkers several deep at the bar. One corner was filled by a large group of people in office wear – suits and ties, smart but sensible dresses.

Two champagne cocktails procured, they found a corner table and set the tall, sparkling drinks on its engine-turned aluminium surface, the overlapping circles glittering like fish scales in the light from the wall lamps.

"Cheers!" Gabriel said.

"*Skål!*"

Gabriel sipped the cocktail and uttered an involuntary moan of pleasure. "Mmm. Best in London. Yours OK?"

"*Jävla fantastiskt!*" Britta lapsed into Swedish at moments of heightened emotion. She laughed. "Oh, shit, Wolfe. I've had too much to drink. How come you never seem to get drunk?"

"British Army training. They wouldn't let you pass out of Sandhurst unless you could put away four pints, a bottle of wine and a couple of stiff whiskies without throwing up. And being on parade at six the following morning."

"Well, in Sweden we were much more civilised. Now," she looked around, as if she were an old-time police informant selling street secrets to a gumshoe for a tenner, "the operation. You remember that people trafficker you helped me deal with?"

She was referring to a Lebanese gangster called Omar El-Hashem. He was no longer a problem for British law enforcement, or for the very young east European blondes he'd been keeping prisoner in his house in Kensington. Mainly on account of being dead of a 9mm gunshot wound to the head.

"How could I forget?"

"We're working on rolling up the rest of his network. He mentioned that guy in Chelsea, remember?"

"Yes, I do. What was his name?"

"Dmitri. Full name Dmitri Torossian. A charming gentleman from Armenia. I'm part of the team tasked with collecting intelligence on his operation. It's a nasty business. Trafficking, drugs, guns, Islamist terrorist groups. Think of an angle, and Torossian has his finger in the cake."

"Pie."

"What?"

"His finger. It's in the pie. Cake's what easy things are a piece of."

Her eyes widened in mock anger and she punched him on his right bicep.

"Fuck off, Wolfe! You're so … so, fuck, what's the English word? In Swedish we say *pedantisk*."

Gabriel laughed. "Pedantic."

"Yeah, well, that's you. I notice you don't speak Swedish among that babel of languages you picked up."

"*Jag visste nog svensk att charma dig i säng, inte jag?*"

Her mouth opened into a perfect O, revealing her gappy teeth. "Is that what you think? You charmed me into bed by cooing in Swedish to me? Let me remind you, I was the one who made the move on you. In fact—"

Britta didn't get to finish her sentence.

In the far corner of the bar, someone was shouting. A high-pitched, aggressive, man's voice, the accent from somewhere in Essex.

"Where's my fackin' coat? I put it down 'ere and now someone's fackin' taken it."

Another man's voice answered. It was one of the office workers.

"Leave her alone. She's with me. Nobody took your coat."

"Oh really, sunshine? Well it ain't 'ere, is it? That's a fackin' Burberry I'm talkin' about. Not some cheap piece of chain-store shit like what you probably wear. I'm talkin' quality. Fourteen 'undred quid it cost me. And one of you lot's got it."

Gabriel stood. Britta looked up at him.

"Need any help?" she asked, nodding in the direction of the shouter.

He shook his head. Smiled. And began to make his way over to the other corner of the bar.

On his way past the knots of drinkers, who had started, in that wary way big city dwellers instinctively possess, to smell trouble and establish a *cordon sanitaire* between themselves and the troublemaker, Gabriel conducted a swift combat appreciation.

The aggressor was a short, little man, maybe five-five or six. Slight build, mid-thirties. Not an obvious candidate to be throwing his weight around. Then Gabriel noticed the source of his confidence. Behind the shouty guy stood two men cut from altogether different cloth. One was Gabriel's height, five nine, or maybe a shade taller. He had a muscular build only marginally disguised by the cheap two-piece suit he'd stuffed himself into. But the real threat stood beside him. An ogre: six four, minimum. Constructed seemingly from blocks of muscle. No gym-built pecs or swollen biceps, just large and very solid. His face was impassive as he watched his boss insult the hapless office worker, whose own face had turned pale and whose colleagues were uneasily watching as the scene unfolded before them.

Something was wrong with the bigger man's features. The ridge of bone and muscle above his deep-set eyes was grotesquely oversized, giving him the hooded gaze of a large primate or even a textbook illustration of "early man." His nose was huge and misshapen, and his lips were thick and wide.

From somewhere deep inside him, it appeared the office worker had discovered a thread of primal aggression, and he was drawing on it now.

"You can't talk to her like that. Leave her alone. We haven't got your coat."

To his left, Gabriel saw the barman, a moustachioed hipster with tattooed arms, shaking his head frantically at the office worker, eyes wide. His meaning was clear to Gabriel, if not to his intended recipient.

Don't do this! It's a really bad idea.

Too late.

The ogre slid round his boss and slapped the office worker. Not hard. Not enough to put him down or knock him out, though Gabriel was sure he was more than capable of it with those slab-like hands. No. Just enough to deprive him of his dignity, and the small measure of courage he'd displayed so far.

"Told you so!" the little boss-man crowed, as he pulled a tan Burberry trench coat from a chair off to one side of the group. "Some facker chucked it over 'ere. Come on, boys. We're going."

The bar was silent as the little gangster and his two minders left. While the office worker's colleagues gathered round him, offering comforting hugs and, in the case of the woman he'd been defending, a kiss on the slapped cheek, Gabriel followed the trio out into the street.

They turned left after twenty yards, into a dark side street, at the end of which Gabriel could see a black Lexus parked on a double-yellow line.

On silent feet, he closed in on the big man, who trailed his boss. The second minder led the way along the greasy pavement.

3

"ONE OF DON'S BOYS"

Closing the distance between them to no more than an arm's length, Gabriel leaned forward and tapped the giant on the left shoulder. As the giant turned, Gabriel crouched and drove his knee upward into the man's groin, simultaneously clamping his right hand across those oddly distorted, fleshy lips, and punching the straight fingers of his left into the soft flesh under his Adam's apple.

The man was screaming in pain; that was clear to Gabriel from the outrushing air that leaked between his fingers. But it was a silent scream. As he folded to his knees, hands scrabbling at his wounded throat, Gabriel stepped back and then kicked him hard on the side of the head.

Had it been delivered by a bare foot, the kick would still have been devastating. But Gabriel was wearing a pair of handmade Oxfords, bought from a shoemaker's not a hundred metres from where he now stood poised over his victim. The heavy, leather sole connected with the man's thickly muscled skull with a sound like a cricket bat smacking a ball for six. He went down and stayed down. Neither of the other two had heard him fall, and they were now pulling away.

As a teenaged boy – an *unruly* teenaged boy – Gabriel had been

15

raised for the most part by a friend of his parents. A wise and tolerant Hong Kong Chinese named Zhao Xi. The English diplomat and his half-Chinese wife, a private tutor, had despaired of their older son's increasingly hostile and antisocial behaviour. They knew it had been caused by his shock and grief when a misplaced rugby kick had led to his younger brother's drowning in Victoria Harbour. But still they needed to find a way to live with him. Zhao Xi had taken the young boy in and begun to educate him. Alongside academic subjects, languages being Gabriel's favourite, Xi had schooled his charge in ancient arts both martial and spiritual. They included karate, meditation and hypnosis, and a tradition handed down by the Shaolin monks of the island: *Yinshen fangshi*. Translated into English as "the Way of Stealth," it enabled practitioners to enter another's personal space unnoticed, even to the point of physical touching.

It was the martial arts skills he had learned from Master Zhao, as he called Xi, that Gabriel was now employing.

Silently disabling the ogre had taken barely five seconds, and ahead of him, the gangster and his remaining minder were still walking, oblivious to the one-third cut in their forces.

Gabriel fell into step behind his quarry, heart beating fast, but not uncomfortably so, seventy-five, maybe eighty beats per minute. He shifted his weight, took a skip step forward and swiped his right foot at the gangster's trailing shoe. As the man stumbled with a shouted, "What the fack?", Gabriel hastened his fall with a shove between the shoulder blades. Minder number two spun round at the sound of his boss's oath, only to catch Gabriel's right fist in the throat. He gasped, eyes wide, trying to bring his hands up, then doubled over, retching, as Gabriel leaned back and kicked him in the stomach.

"What are you doin', you fackin' cant?" the gangster yelled from his prone position, twisting round to stare up at Gabriel over his shoulder. He tried to rise, but Gabriel knelt in the small of his back and dealt him a punch to the left kidney that brought forth a scream of agony.

The second minder was on his hands and knees, vomiting a

thin, stringy stream of yellow bile into the gutter. Too easy, Gabriel thought.

He stepped over the squealing gangster and punched down hard onto the second minder's neck. The point of impact was an imaginary target drawn on the skin just above the nerve junction his SAS instructors – and those in the Parachute Regiment before them – had referred to first as the basal ganglion and then as, "a bloody good place to hit someone you don't want to get up. Sir." The second minder went down onto his face in his own vomitus. Gabriel pushed his face sideways so he wouldn't drown and then turned to the gangster, who was pulling himself to his knees and fumbling with his phone.

"I don't think so," Gabriel said, snatching the phone from the man's fingers. He turned and dropped it down a drain grating that led to the sewer beneath the street.

"Listen, what do you want?" the little man said, catching on at last that he was alone with this apparently unstoppable attacker. "I got cash, right? There's a monkey in 'ere," he said, pulling a darkly gleaming wallet from an inside pocket. Crocodile skin, it looked like. "Five 'undred, yeah? Take it. It's yours."

"I don't want your money," Gabriel said, dusting his hands together and standing over the man.

"What then? Don't hurt me, OK? Who are you, one of Deano's boys? You are, aren't you?"

Gabriel shook his head. "No. I'm one of Don's boys."

The man started snivelling. "Oh, fack! The Don? You mean the fackin' Mafia? I never done nothing to them. I only operate 'ere, up west, I mean."

In Gabriel's case, Don was a name, that of his boss at The Department, not a rank, but he wasn't about to spoil the man's illusion.

"That's right," he said, improvising. "We're here and we're taking over. The Don says if you're seen anywhere in the West End, we're to bring you to him. Or part of you. He doesn't care which. My advice? Leave town. Go and play cops and robbers somewhere quiet. Somewhere far away from London. Capiche?"

The guy was scrabbling backwards through the muck now, smearing grime and grease from the pavement over his fawn raincoat.

"Yeah, yeah. I get it. Capiche, mate."

Gabriel grinned, then lunged at the man. The thug ran out of room, backed up against the slimy brickwork of a rundown warehouse building, eyes wide, lip trembling.

Gabriel turned and left, shaking his head. Cowards. They were the same wherever you found them.

4

ROCKET MAN

Inside Bar Toulouse, the noise had returned to the clamour of after-work drinking. A warm gust of alcohol-scented air breezed out at Gabriel as he entered the crowded space.

He returned to the corner table, where Britta was scrolling through emails on her phone. She looked up at him, her freckled face enquiring but not worried or even relieved.

"Everything OK, Sir Lancelot?"

"Uh huh. There's at least one local thug who thinks the Corleones are taking over the West End."

"How come you hate them so much, Gabriel?"

"Hate who?"

"Bullies." She took a sip of her drink. "You're always diving into some trouble just because you see someone throwing their weight around. You could get into trouble, you know. With the police, I mean. What if you killed someone?"

He drained his glass. "I didn't kill anyone. There'll be a few bruises, maybe a thick head for a day or two, but that's all. Anyway, those guys are the last people to go to the cops."

"I know that, dummy. But like I said, why do you go after them?"

"Buy me another drink and I'll tell you."

Five minutes later, Britta returned from the bar with two more cocktails. Gabriel noticed the way a couple of guys at the bar, and several of the women, checked out his fiancée as she shimmied through the gap they left for her. From her flame-red hair to her neat little rear, she was quite the looker, and over the years he'd known her, he'd watched as she'd playfully deflected the attentions of both sexes in clubs and restaurants, markets and even officers' messes, around the world. And what was that he'd just called her? His fiancée? Jesus! He was going to be married.

She placed a drink in front of him.

"So, spill the peas."

"B—"

"I know, fool! I was just testing your *pedanteri*."

"Fine. It was back in Hong Kong. In the last school I attended, there was a gang. Rich brats, mostly. I don't know where they got their attitudes from—their parents, I suppose. They needed people to pick on, and they chose me. Because my mother was half-Chinese. Used to call me a half-breed, a mongrel, things like that. The name-calling I could take, for the most part. But one boy always took it too far. His name was Bruno Valdosta."

Britta snorted. "Hardly a purebred English name, that?"

"No. Claimed they were descended from Portuguese royalty. One day, he came up to me, smirking. Crooked his finger and beckoned me over. I wasn't going to go, but there were four of his friends behind me and they frogmarched me over to him. 'I've finally figured it out, Wolfe,' he said to me. He pushed his face right into mine. His breath stank. Like rotting meat. 'Your mother's not a whore at all. But hers was. Must have got knocked up on the game and she was too stupid to get rid of it. Your mother was the result, and you're the result of her and your father breeding. Fancying Chinese food must run in your family.'

"So I hit him. Butted him, actually. I broke his nose. His friends panicked and tried to run, but I caught one in the corner of the yard. They pulled me off him in the end but not before I'd knocked him out against the concrete. He was in hospital for two weeks. That was it. The headmaster summoned me with my parents to a meeting after school and expelled me in front of them. He pretty much took Valdosta's side. Said it was just 'part of the normal horseplay young gentlemen can expect to meet within the precincts of a schoolyard.' Those were his exact words, but it was clear he didn't consider me to be a gentleman. Sanctimonious prick.

"It left me with, what shall we call it, a strong sense of injustice? Basically, I don't like to see people throwing their weight around."

Britta had remained silent throughout this story, her right hand resting lightly on his thigh.

"That's why you went into the Army? To right wrongs? Prevent injustice?"

He laughed. "Me? No! I did it to spite my father. He wanted me to go to Cambridge and then the Diplomatic Service. I loved the old man dearly, but he had this vision for me, and it just wasn't mine. So I went into the Paras. We patched it up in the end, and he came to the ceremony when I got my MC."

"Well, I still think you should call the cops from time to time instead of taking the law into your own hands."

"I know you do. And your Swedish moral rectitude is one of the things I love about you."

She grinned her gap-toothed grin. The one that could reliably set his pulse ticking just that little bit faster. "Take me home, and I'll let you see the other side of me, if you like. The one that's not so upright."

Gabriel's phone rang. He slid out of bed and grabbed the phone, leaving Britta snuffling somewhere in a dream where she kept calling out for "*Farfar*" in a quiet but insistent voice. According to the backlit blue display on his bedside clock, it was two thirty.

He answered as he left the bedroom and settled in a chair in his office next door.

"Mr Wolfe. My name is Carl Mortensen. I apologise for the late hour. I am the CEO of a company called SBOE, Incorporated. I doubt you'll have heard of us."

It was spoken as a question, in an accent Gabriel found hard to place. Maybe Dutch originally but with a transatlantic twang that suggested its owner had lived in the United States for a while.

"I'll be honest, Mr Mortensen, I haven't. What can I do to help you?"

"Please, call me Carl. We're a new company, but we have substantial financial backing. Our field of endeavour is space research. SBOE stands for—"

"Surly Bonds of Earth?"

"Impressive, Mr Wolfe. Very Impressive. You know your Reagan."

"I know my Magee. It was his poem Reagan quoted when Challenger blew up. Now, it's late, Carl. Or, rather it's early. You have something you need help with?"

As well as freelancing for The Department under his old boss from the Regiment, Gabriel maintained an independent business, troubleshooting for companies, governments, and foreign intelligence agencies that needed a tough, resourceful individual to help them deal with what one client in the banking industry had described as "non-standard operational threats." In that case, it had been ex-Iraqi secret police trying to shake down his bank over a foreign investment in that country's burgeoning reconstruction.

"I'm sorry for the late hour, Mr Wolfe. Or Gabriel, may I call you Gabriel? I've been travelling tons recently. My internal clock is shot, to be honest, I have no idea what time it is! I may have some work for you. I have to take a trip to Kazakhstan. I'm researching potential sites for a launch facility. Only problem is, we're hearing some unsettling tales about bandits there and, frankly, I'm scared. I want someone with me who'll act as my personal security detail."

"Why me?"

"Why you? Very modest. I did a little digging, asked a few friends in DC, and your name came up. Twice. So I figured if you were good enough for Uncle Sam, you were good enough for me."

"OK, look, Carl. In principle, it sounds fine. But as I said, it's late. Can I call you tomorrow?"

"Sure, sure. Glad to have you aboard. I'll be in my office from ten, so that's what, oh, jeez, let me think for a second, three p.m. your time?"

5

AN AMERICAN IN VENICE

VENICE

Two days later, at 10.30 a.m., Sasha Beck took up position at a table outside Caffè Florian on the Piazza San Marco. It was at the end of the row nearest the front wall of the caffè itself. It gave her a view not only of the people strolling in the piazza, but also everybody sipping or nibbling at the expensive treats ferried to them by the self-important waiters bustling between the tables, their white jackets as spotless as the tablecloths.

As a matter of habit, Sasha tended to wear all black, although when circumstances demanded it, she might lighten the look with white or gold. Or camouflage, either military or improvised. She had once completed a job disguised as a homeless person, camping in a cardboard box outside a bank headquarters for two weeks. *That* had cost her client dear. Today, with the sun beating down from a clear blue sky that might have been painted by Titian, she had reverted to her signature look. Tailored trousers in a silk and cashmere blend that flattered her athletic limbs without being so tight as to impede her should she need to run. A black silk blouse. A black leather biker jacket with sterling silver buckles, zips and press studs in the shape of skulls, and pockets stuffed with banknotes in a range of currencies including dollars, euros and sterling. Her feet were shod with black-and-silver Nike sneakers. They looked unimpressive. Just another pair of high tops with a few decorative flourishes. The price had been anything but. On her most recent trip to New York, she'd visited a sneaker store on Broadway in Lower Manhattan. Flight Club, it was called, and her momentary misreading of the sign as Fight Club had appealed to her.

The place looked more like a shrine than a shoe shop. Around the walls, from floor to ceiling, single sneakers were displayed like relics in Lucite cases. In front of them, on tiptoe if they were young, or interested in the topmost shoes, or genuflecting in front of the models at knee-level, were the worshippers. Mainly black kids, although a good smattering of white youngsters, too, most with eye-rolling parents in tow, a few on their own, whispering oaths at the prices quoted.

"How may I help you today?" a slim black girl with braces and heavy-framed glasses had asked Sasha.

"Tell me, darling, which are the most expensive sneakers here?"

"Oh, right," the girl said, beaming her silvery smile at Sasha. "Come over here."

She led her to a second room, down the centre of which ran a single-width Lucite case. The sneakers within were even more garish than those in the main part of the store. Some appeared to be caught in their cuboid plastic boxes in mid-metamorphosis from pupa to some exotic insect, the colours unimaginably bright, laces replaced with fittings whose workings Sasha could only guess at.

The girl pointed at a dull-looking black sneaker sandwiched between a shoe the iridescent blue of a Kingfisher, and a gold number mounted on a translucent sole in which crystals appeared to float.

"That's it."

"How much, darling?"

"Um, well, it's thirty thousand. It's a collaboration with Eminem. Only two pairs in each size."

"My, my, what a clever chap Mr Mathers is," Sasha said, before buying the shoes.

Beneath her table at Florian's, leaning against her right calf, was a black ostrich-skin handbag. She had shot the bird herself while on safari in Kenya. It had been her second two-legged kill of the day. The raised circular bumps where the feathers had been – quills, the leatherworker in Nairobi had called them – reminded her of small-calibre bullet holes. Inside the handbag were the usual items a woman of means might carry.

Her phone was bespoke, its case milled from a single piece of billet aluminium at the same factory that produced switchgear for Spyker, an exclusive Dutch manufacturer of hand-built sports cars. It never left her side, containing as it did the numbers of her clients. One of them had confided in her that he believed there were combined bounties of over three hundred million US dollars on the heads of the fifty-five or so people in her contacts. The FBI, Homeland Security, NSA and CIA in the US; the French *Sûreté*; the British Metropolitan Police Service and MI5; the *Bundespolizei* in Germany; the Kremlin and its internal security agency, the FSB: all these and a dozen other security and law enforcement agencies around the world had the faces of the men – and occasionally women – on Sasha's phone on their "Most Wanted" lists.

There were a few cosmetics – including a Chanel lipstick in Ultraberry – that Sasha applied each morning before leaving whichever of her residences or favoured hotels she was staying in at the time.

And there was her gun.

No, not her gun.

One of her guns.

Sasha Beck, as befitted a woman in her trade, owned a great many weapons. Most were simply collectors' items, much as trout fishermen might collect antique bamboo rods, or antiquaries might collect first editions. Some were gifts from grateful clients. One African ruler had presented her with a gold-plated Browning Hi Power 9mm pistol in a box made from mahogany harvested from his own forest. The grips, chequered and engraved with her initials, were fashioned from the tibias of a man she had killed for him.

The weapon in the ostrich-skin handbag was one of her working weapons: a Smith & Wesson M&P 40 Shield. Not a big pistol. Not a flashy one, either. No gold or camouflage, no gaping maw designed to spit out bullets half an inch in diameter. But it worked. Every time she pulled the trigger. It had a snub snout, a narrow body and a squat grip. They were all features that made it perfect as a concealed carry weapon – at once easy to hide and easy to draw – without the risk of one of its protruding parts snagging on the suede lining of her bag, or her pocket. It was fitted with a single accessory: a green laser sight by Crimson Trace, snug in the angle between the underside of the barrel and the front of the trigger guard.

In front of her was a small cup of exquisitely well-made coffee, its flavour a mixture of spice, chocolate and dried fruit. To its left, a white side plate bore a swirl of buttery, flaky pastry filled with a mixture of ground pistachios, chocolate and sour cherries. Trapped under the plate was a small slip of paper generated by the till. The amount, excluding service, was forty-three euros. Roughly the cost of the eight .40-calibre hollow point rounds in the magazine of the Shield, plus the fifty in her hotel room.

She checked the time. Quarter to eleven. She paused to admire the elegant black-and-white face of her watch, a Limited Edition Christopher Ward C9 D-Type, made in England. Some of her contemporaries favoured the more obvious bling from Rolex, Tag Heuer, and Patek Philippe. Sasha, in her way, was a patriot. Yes, she'd killed British targets. And yes, some, though by no means all, of them had been pillars of the establishment. But the country itself and its institutions, *those* she held in high regard. And she tried to buy British whenever she could. Sadly for Sasha, although Accuracy International – the manufacturer of what it claimed were the world's finest sniper rifles – was based on England's south coast, the firm's supply chain was locked down tighter than The Bank of England's gold vaults. There being no other British manufacturers, she used a Knight M110C in the US, a SIG Sauer Tactical 2 in continental Europe, and in the UK, a Remington MSR.

Across the piazza, a movement caught her eye.

Amongst the tourists, with their stupid selfie sticks and brightly coloured rucksacks, a dark-haired woman was striding towards Florian's. Sasha narrowed her eyes and observed her progress.

"Hello, darling," she whispered. "You wouldn't happen to be Erin Ayers by any chance, would you?"

6

SASHA BECK, ERIN AYERS

The woman wove expertly between the milling groups of picture-takers, gawping at themselves as they posed in front of Florian's or tried to capture themselves with Saint Mark's Basilica in the background. A scowl made her otherwise beautiful face turn ugly as an overweight Asian teen in a lime-green windcheater backed into her. She stopped to say, "Watch where you're going, you idiot," Sasha decoded from her lips, and the boy put his hands out in a "sorry" gesture. Then she arrived at the perimeter of Florian's rectangular arrangement of white-framed wicker chairs and began scanning the customers.

I could stand and wave, Sasha thought. But that's terribly gauche, and besides, darling, you said Timur referred you to me, so let's see if you can find me.

Sasha remained sitting, watching with a half-smile on those deep-red lips. The woman she was waiting for was dressed simply, but in that effortless style that only the very rich and the very stylish manage. A cream silk blouse, cut to accentuate her breasts, which, Sasha admiringly noted, were magnificent: large and high. Navy trousers cut high on the waist and fastened at the front with two parallel vertical rows of three brass buttons. A sky-blue cashmere sweater draped over her shoulders and knotted so that the sleeves covered her cleavage. And Louboutin stilettos in navy suede, their scarlet soles the giveaway.

Erin Ayers was sweeping her gaze methodically along the rows of affluent punters scooping gobs of cream from the tops of their hot chocolates, or dabbing crumbs of smoked salmon club sandwiches from the corners of their lips. Then she stopped.

Ooh! Target acquired, darling?

The woman's smile appeared to Sasha to be full of genuine warmth. Ayers came over, turning sideways to slide between a pair of chairs creaking under the weight of their obese German occupants, then stood in front of Sasha, hand outstretched.

"Miss Beck, I presume," she said.

"Mizz Ayers. Delighted. Please, sit. I'll find a waiter."

Ayers sat. "I wouldn't bother. They're a bloody law unto themselves here. They come when they're ready."

Sasha smiled, then lifted her eyes and locked on to a young woman on the far side of the tables. She lifted her chin a fraction and raised one dark, arching eyebrow. Twenty seconds later, the young woman arrived at their table.

"Thank you, Jelena, darling," she said in flawless, unaccented Serbian. "Would you bring me another of these delightful coffees, and whatever this lady is having."

The woman smiled and turned to Ayers, speaking in English now.

"Yes, madam?"

"A Bellini, please. And a *croissant al prosciutto crudo di San Daniele.*"

The waitress's face fell, then brightened again, as if a cloud had flitted across the sun. "I am so sorry, madam. Bellinis only when peaches are in season and as it's April ..."

"Please tell Signor Rafi that it's for Erin Ayers. He likes to oblige me."

Confused, but wilting under the hard stare of this supremely confident customer, the woman turn on her heel and scooted off towards the kitchen.

Sasha tilted her head to one side, smiling at the other woman's display of confidence.

"So we both know Florian's. How delightful for us. Tell me, Mizz Ayers, how do you know Timur?"

"I think we should drop the formalities first, don't you? You call me Erin, and I'll call you Sasha."

"Very well. Erin. Irish? You don't have the colouring. More of an English rose complexion, though those emerald eyes are straight out of the land of the Blarney Stone."

"Not Irish," Erin said, her nose wrinkling, just for a split second. "English, as you say. My family goes back to William the Conqueror."

"French, then." Another smile. *How much needling can you take, darling?*

"And you, Sasha. You sound very county, but is that breeding or Saturday morning elocution lessons, I wonder?"

"Touché! I think we'd better stop fencing before one of us gets wounded, don't you?" *And as I know my edged weapons better than you do, darling, I have no fears for* my *safety.*

Erin nodded. "I think we've established we're both women of the world, so yes, by all means. After all, I intend to hire you."

"Well, let's not jump the gun, no pun intended. In my line of work—or should I say, at the level at which I operate *within* my line of work—it is I who takes on clients, not the other way around. So, as I asked, how do you know Timur? He is not the easiest man with whom to get acquainted."

"He and I go way back. I helped him set up his business and then his party. Ultra-nationalism is very fashionable in Central Asia right now, but it wasn't always so. Without the financial backing I provided, Kazakh Purity would have remained a little club of disgruntled fascists firebombing mosques."

"Is that your interest? Politics?"

"You could say that. I had ambitions once before, but at the moment I am focusing on my business interests."

"And that's what brings you to me, is it? Business?"

Jelena appeared then, bearing a silver tray aloft on the tented fingertips of one outstretched hand. From the tray she took a champagne flute filled with a pale-yellow liquid, topped with half an inch of white froth. It smelled of peaches.

"Your Bellini, Madam," she said with a smile, placing the tall glass before Erin. "Chef Rafi says he is most pleased you are back."

She then arranged Sasha's second coffee and the croissant filled with cured ham on the table, tucked the second till receipt on top of the first, placed them both under Erin's plate and removed the empty cup and plate from in front of Sasha.

Erin took a sip of the Bellini. "Oh, God that is excellent. Now, is it business? No. Not precisely. I think you could say this is more of a personal commission."

"Oh, good," Sasha said, sipping her coffee and then replacing the small, white cup carefully in the saucer with a quiet *clink*. "Personal is so much more fun. Tell all, darling."

Sasha watched as her prospective client sipped delicately at her Bellini then nibbled at her croissant. The woman was attractive, but had she had some work done? The forehead seemed suspiciously wrinkle-free for someone who, from her voice, attitude and sophistication, Sasha judged to be in her thirties. To a casual observer her almond-shaped eyes would simply be pretty, with long lashes accentuated by black mascara, expertly applied. But Sasha's observational skills were anything but casual. Over the years she had honed them to an edge as sharp as any of the blades in her possession. She applied them now to the woman in front of her.

Yes. There were ultra-fine silver scars, almost invisible, just inside the line of her eyebrows. Two more at the corners of her mouth, which was accentuated with a frosted pink lipstick. The dark-brown hair looked real enough, but wigs, Sasha knew, were so good these days. An Orthodox Jewish friend of hers, whose religious views necessitated her wearing a wig over her own clipped scalp, had confided in Sasha one day that her wigs were made with real human hair collected from women in India who were paid for their locks. Or it could simply be the work of a good colourist. *What are you hiding from, darling? You're far too young to need it.*

"There is a man," Erin said.

34

"There usually is," Sasha said, winking.

Erin's brow did, finally, crease a little as she frowned at the interruption.

"He caused me a great deal of trouble. I had plans that were almost perfect and he came along and fucked them up for me. Now I want him to suffer for it, the way I did."

"Are you sure this really needs *my* services? Dealing with interpersonal," Sasha paused for a beat, "*friction* is hardly a job for a woman like me. Perhaps you two could talk it out?"

Erin's green eyes flashed. Sasha enjoyed watching the younger woman struggle to control her emotions.

"Forgive me, Sasha, I didn't fly from Manhattan to meet you to receive a homily on the need for truth and reconciliation. This man wronged me in ways you cannot begin to imagine, and I want him to pay."

"What on earth can he have done to you, darling? You're clearly a very affluent and powerful woman."

"It doesn't matter."

"It matters to me. I like to know at the very least the rough outlines of the project I'm taking on." Another pause. "*If* I take it on."

Erin inhaled slowly, then let it out in a sigh. She appeared to have reached a decision.

"Very well. Some years ago, I had political ambitions. I suppose you might call them grand ambitions. And at the eleventh hour, after many years' planning, this man, whom I had trusted, betrayed me utterly."

"And now you want payback."

"And now I want payback."

"If I," another pause, indicating that Erin should follow her example and adopt a code, "*take care* of him for you, it will cost."

Erin Ayers smiled, her lips widening and hiding those silvery scars in natural creases at the corners of her mouth.

"I don't want you to *take care* of him."

Sasha took a sip of her coffee. Not hot enough. She frowned with displeasure.

"Then, forgive me, darling, but why are we sitting here?"

"I want you to help me take away from him everything he cares about. When you have done all that for me, I will take care of him myself."

Intrigued now, Sasha sat forward.

"We should discuss this further. In private."

Erin smiled again. It was the smile of a woman used to getting her own way and who believed she was about to again.

7

FUNERAL RITES

SALISBURY

Back in his cottage in a village outside Salisbury, Gabriel felt an odd sense of emptiness. Living on his own since leaving the army, he'd become used to solitude. He'd deflected questions about whether he was lonely with a stock answer, "I'm alone, but I'm not lonely." And until recently, it had been the truth. For a time, he'd had the company of a brindle greyhound called Seamus. He'd taken him home from a rescue centre a few years earlier, and they'd become used to each other's company. Then, while Gabriel was in the US working on the mission that was to lead him back to a job with Don Webster, his old CO in the SAS, Seamus had been killed by a car while chasing a rabbit. Gabriel hadn't replaced Seamus. His work took him away too often for it to be fair to a dog. And he always had the option of a dog walk with Julia and Scout.

Now things had changed. He could look into the future and see a different sort of life to the one he'd always imagined for himself.

One with a wife. And children. That was what Britta'd said. "Otherwise what's the point?"

He checked the time. His Breitling, a gift from his father, told him it was 2.00 p.m. An hour before he could call Carl Mortensen, whose website and biography had checked out. He made some tea, taking his time to measure out teaspoons of Earl Grey, Kenyan Orange Pekoe and English Breakfast – the house blend, as he called it. Once it was poured, after timing it to exactly four-and-a-half minutes, he took it through to the sitting room and squatted in front of his music hard drive.

With Frank Zappa singing "Joe's Garage," he sat in a brown leather armchair, its cushion still scarred from Seamus's long claws, and sipped his tea, wondering about the threats he might have to deflect in Kazakhstan.

Bosnia was the furthest east he'd ever fought in mainland Europe. An unholy place where atrocities were committed in the name of God, of land, of national identity. Where a three-hundred-year-old vendetta was seen as a short-term argument between families. He and Britta had fought side by side there. Their mission had been to capture a Bosnian Serb militia commander and transport him to a UN holding facility from where he could be brought before the International Criminal Court and charged with war crimes.

Gabriel's eyes drooped. Mortensen's call the previous night had disrupted his sleep, and he'd only dozed fitfully between then and six, when Britta had woken, demanded one last bout of athletic sex, then showered and left.

He placed the mug of tea beside the chair on a low table made from an African tribal drum, set an alarm on his phone for 2.50 p.m., and closed his eyes. His PTSD often caused nightmares, but the daylight hours seemed to bring fewer of them, and he'd found himself favouring catnaps as a way of recovering from the broken nights when he awoke, screaming, sweating and, on one memorable occasion, attempting to strangle Britta.

He was at a funeral. A pall bearer. But the coffin was ridiculously small, a little bigger than a hat box. Together with the other five men, he stumbled through ankle-deep mud to the graveside. They could each only manage to keep a single hand under the box, and Gabriel was anxious lest the whole thing should tumble from their grasp, spilling its contents into the mud.

He looked over to the minister and the mourners gathered by the edge of the neat, rectangular hole, edged with what looked like Astroturf. There among them stood Smudge Smith, the lost SAS trooper whose body Gabriel had finally managed to retrieve from Mozambique just a few weeks earlier. He was smiling, his handsome brown face whole and unblemished.

"But if you're there, Smudge," Gabriel said, "who's in the box?"

"Take a look, boss."

The other pallbearers stood back, respectfully. Holding the box by himself, Gabriel looked over at them. They were grinning widely, revealing mouths lined with bullets instead of teeth: sharp-pointed 7.62mm rifle rounds that glinted evilly in the sun.

He placed the box on the ground and opened the flaps. Inside was a rough, undyed cotton carrier bag the colour of bone. He lifted it clear. He could hear sniggering from the mourners and when he looked over at them, they were pointing straight at him with long, yellow fingernails.

The bag was growing heavy in his hands. He reached into its cinched neck and spread it open with his fingers. Peering out at him was a face. His own face. The neck was a bloody tangle of sinews and torn blood vessels. A black hole, crusted with blood, formed a third eye in the dead centre of his forehead.

The cracked lips opened, and the head — his head — spoke to him.

"Every soldier meets his Maker in the end, captain. Some sooner than others. Be careful. You get too close to her, and you'll only have to leave her."

Then it coughed, and a fine mist of blood sprayed into Gabriel's face.

"No!" he shouted, and dropped the bag, staggering back into the muscular arms of a group of teenaged boys who'd surrounded him while he was mesmerised by his own disembodied head.

"Hey, Wolfe!" the tallest of the boys jeered at him. "My father told me he had your mother in a brothel. Said she was cheap at the price."

Then they shoved him hard, pushing and jostling him towards the open grave. He struggled, but the ringleader pulled a long-bladed knife and held it to Gabriel's throat.

"Don't struggle, Wolfe, or I'll slit your throat like a pig." Then he shouted, "Now! In he goes, the little mongrel."

The boys flung him into the open grave, one sticking a rugby-boot-shod foot out to trip him so that he toppled headfirst into the dark. The last thing he saw before his head smashed into the hard soil at the bottom was Britta's tear-streaked face, peering over the edge.

He jerked awake with a moan of dismay. It was 2.45 p.m. He reached for the tea – cold – and swigged it anyway. He felt sick, and wiped his palm across his forehead, which was clammy with greasy, cold sweat. What had his shrink told him about dreams? "I don't go in for that Freudian bullshit," she'd said, which shocked, coming as it did from that friendly, brown-skinned face framed by a bright, fuchsia-pink hijab. "If you want to interpret your dreams, think of them as your subconscious trying to tell you something really simple: what you want, or maybe what you're afraid of. Like your hallucinations, they're just the you that senses things on a deep emotional level trying to get a message through to the you that pretends everything's about facts, and reason, and analysis and planning."

"So, basically, I've laid Smudge to rest, and his ghost, only now I'm scared of losing Britta. Of dying on a mission and never getting to have a life with her. Is that it, Fariyah?" he asked the empty room.

He shook his head and went to the kitchen for a glass of water. He drank it at the sink. A bottle of single malt whisky – Laphraoig – sat off to one side, in front of a row of tall Kilner jars, each one containing a different type of flour. He reached for the bottle, unscrewed the cap, poured an inch of the smoky, seaweedy whisky into a tumbler sitting on the draining rack, swallowed half, then took the remainder upstairs to his office.

Mortensen answered on the third ring.

"Gabriel, good of you to call back. Thank you. So, what do you want to know?"

"There are three criteria I employ when accepting new clients, Carl. One, they can afford me. Two, they pay a deposit in advance. Three, they brief me fully. In my line of work, the last condition is the most important."

Mortensen chuckled. "Fair enough, and, may I say, unusually frank for a Brit. You guys are normally so busy being polite, you forget to talk about money. I appreciate your frankness, so let me repay you in kind. One, I don't know what you charge, but I am fairly confident I can afford your services. I own SBOE outright and every test launch costs me personally one-point-five million US. So what's your day rate?"

Gabriel was just about to quote the rate Don Webster paid him: £1,000 a day. Then he clamped his lips together for a second and recalibrated his response.

"£2,000 a day plus expenses."

"Which is fine. Hell, let's not make life needlessly complicated. Why don't we call it £3,000 a day all in?"

"That's very generous. Thank you."

"Good. It's no more than you're worth, I'm sure. My trip's for four days, so I make that twelve grand in total. Send me your bank details after this call and I'll wire you the money. And finally, the briefing. Like I said, the big picture is my upcoming trip to Kazakhstan. I know to you Special Forces guys, that's probably a cakewalk. But for me? A tech guy? I'm not afraid to admit it − it frightens me. I can give you more detail, but I'd prefer to do it face to face. Can you meet me? In London? I'm staying at the Ritz."

They agreed to meet for lunch two days later.

8

A CONTRACT

VENICE

That evening, at 8.00 p.m., Sasha opened the door of her suite at The Gritti Palace on Campo Santa Maria del Giglio. Erin stood there, her weight on one hip. She had changed for their second meeting and now wore a different pair of tailored trousers. They were black and silky, the wide hems covering the toes of her shoes. Her emerald-green blouse was open at the neck to reveal a thin gold chain that descended into the space between her breasts. She carried a slim, black, leather, clutch bag fastened with a gold clasp.

Sasha had changed into a long, black, halter neck dress. Both women were showing they meant business, but in different ways. Both wore clothes that displayed their bodies. But where Erin's was all curves and sex appeal, Sasha's was a muscular, panther's build, with rounded deltoids and sleek biceps and triceps, the results of many hours of training from the age of nineteen, when she'd first embarked on her chosen trade. She looked Erin up and down, taking her time.

"You look good enough to eat," she said, finishing her appraisal. "Come in. Drink? I have some champagne on ice."

"Thank you. You look good, too."

The room was painted a beautiful shade of duck-egg blue and finished in high Venetian style as imagined by the hotel's owners. Gold was a predominant theme, painted, layered and gilded onto almost every surface. Four reproduction Louis XIV side chairs, resplendent in gilded carving and watered silk upholstery the colour of sunflowers, gathered like courtiers around a similarly ornate table topped with swirling walnut inlaid with ebony and more gold. Beside the table was a low chaise longue, upholstered in gold velvet. Set in gold candlesticks were a couple of dozen tall, white candles, their wicks trimmed perfectly so the flames were smooth-sided yellow tulips.

The table was laid with two places. To one side, a smaller table was crowded with silver chafing dishes. Their gleaming, domed lids permitted tendrils of steam to curl out, carrying delicious aromas of seafood, herbs, wine and garlic. The centre of the table bore a gold ice bucket from which the foiled neck of a champagne bottle protruded at an angle.

Sasha poured Erin a glass of champagne and topped up her own. The glasses, engraved with twining ivy leaves, were the shallow bowls known as *coupes* rather than the tall flutes served at Florian's.

They clinked glasses. Sasha held hers up to the light.

"Much prettier, don't you think?" she asked. "More decadent, somehow. People claim they were modelled on Marie Antoinette's breasts, did you know that?"

Erin smiled. "Not much to get hold of, was there?"

Sasha beckoned her guest to the table.

"I hope you like lobster."

The lobster was served out of its shell and dressed in a pale broth of white wine, cream and butter, in which delicate, green fronds of fresh dill floated. Erin spoke.

"Perhaps we should clear the way for a more substantive discussion by getting the subject of money out of the way. Timur wouldn't enlighten me as to your fees."

"No. He wouldn't. Mr Kamenko is a very discreet man, bless him. Well, my fees start at three million US dollars."

"That's fine. And by 'start' you mean?"

"Adult male. No political office above regional or state government. National pols, heads of state, women, celebrities and younger targets cost more."

"Scruples?"

"Publicity."

"And you do children?"

"I've never been asked."

"That's not a proper answer."

"Are you asking me to kill any children?"

"No."

"Then, it's not a proper question."

Erin laughed. "Fair enough. I anticipate a maximum of five human targets, at least one of which will be a woman. Plus help with the destruction of property. Why don't we call it twenty million for the package?"

Sasha put her cutlery down. She looked Erin in the eye.

"You're something of a mystery woman, aren't you, Erin?"

"What do you mean?"

"I Googled you. Do you know how many hits I got?"

"Enlighten me."

"None. Not a single reference. Which struck me as peculiar. People in my line of work aren't on Google, though some advertise on the dark web. Trailer trash aren't on Google. African nomads, with whom, by the way, I have travelled, aren't on Google. But women with sufficient wealth to jet about having coffee in Florian's at two days' notice, women with grand political ambitions, women with twenty million to drop on an assassin: those people *are* on Google. So tell me, Erin Ayers, what's going on?"

Erin took a mouthful of the succulent lobster meat and took her time chewing it. Then she sipped her champagne. She dabbed her lips with the white and gold damask napkin, and smiled.

"I enjoy my privacy, what can I say? My wealth is inherited, and such business dealings as I have, I conduct through intermediaries.

It isn't difficult to hide oneself away from prying eyes, especially if one has dirt on the CEOs of the big internet companies. Which, believe me, I do. Now, shall we discuss business, or do you want to continue interrogating me? Perhaps this will establish my bona fides."

She reached over to pick her clutch bag up off the sofa beside her. Twisting the overlapping arms of the clasp, which unfastened with a muted *click*, she opened the bag and withdrew a thin rectangular package, wrapped in black tissue paper. From the way she gripped it, it appeared to be heavy. Erin offered the package to Sasha.

"Well, well, what do we have here?" Sasha asked, moving her plate to one side and placing the package in front of her, though she was fairly sure she knew. It wasn't the first time a client had tried to impress her this way.

Using her fingertips, she separated the leaves of tissue paper and spread them apart with a soft rustle. As the slim ingot of gold became visible, she smiled. It was the approximate dimensions of a mobile phone, but much heavier. The gold gleamed in the candlelight. On its face were stamped the words:

PAMP
SUISSE
1 KILO
FINE GOLD
ESSAYEUR
FONDEUR

"You know," Sasha said, "in the old days of the gold rush in California, they used to bite coins to check they were really gold."

"Be my guest," Erin said. "Although you don't want to damage a tooth."

"No need. In the entire time I've been pursuing my profession, only one person has ever tried to cross me. Can you guess what happened to him?"

Erin raised her eyes to the ceiling. Then brought them back to bear on Sasha. '

"Did he have an accident?"

"He did!" Sasha clapped her hands as if Erin had solved a particular thorny logic problem. "He fell into a wood chipper." She took a mouthful of the champagne. "Twice."

"Did he really? How careless of him. Me, I like my life. The bar's worth a smidgeon under thirty-eight-and-a-half thousand dollars at today's spot price. Call it a gift to seal the deal."

Sasha rewrapped the ingot and placed to one side.

"Fine. And thank you. You're a woman of means. You dress well. And I like your style. So who's this unfortunate man who came between you and your political ambitions?"

Erin leant forwards.

"His name is Gabriel Wolfe."

9

HOW TO MAKE A KILLER

VENICE

Sasha threw her head back and laughed, a full-throated sound that made the champagne glasses ring.

"Oh, dear God, will that boy never stop causing trouble?"

Erin frowned. "You know him?"

Sasha nodded then dabbed her eyes with her napkin. "You could say that, darling. I've been hired to kill him before."

Erin raised her eyebrows. "And yet he lives."

"It's complicated." As she said this, Sasha thought of the trick Gabriel had pulled in a Hong Kong nightclub belonging to a Triad boss. Doping her, then hypnotising her into thinking she'd already fulfilled the contract on him. As he'd then gone on to kill her client, she'd decided to walk away. *Oh, come on, sweetheart,* her inner voice teased. *You fancy him, plain and simple.*

"I hope I'm placing my faith in the right person, Sasha. Three million is a lot of money to spend on somebody who misses."

Sasha placed her glass in front of her. Looked Erin in the eye, and spoke.

"I have completed sixty-one contracts since I embarked on my chosen profession. In my training, I put down four men, for whom I wasn't paid. And the event that pushed me into this line of work saw two men lose their lives. That's sixty-seven occasions when I haven't missed."

"And one where you did."

"And one where, owing to some exceptionally unusual circumstances, the contract was nullified before I could complete it."

Erin nodded. "You said, 'pushed you' into your line of work. What happened?"

Sasha looked away from Erin, closed her eyes and thought back twenty-five years. She sighed, then opened her eyes. "Do you have time for a little story of what happens to nice English girls when they're too trusting?"

Erin reached for the champagne, refilled their glasses and leaned back in her chair. "I love stories."

Sasha's voice deepened fractionally and lost its playful tone as she began to tell her story.

"Picture an eighteen-year-old girl from a little rural village in Kent. Awkward, socially isolated, homeschooled by her hippie parents, picked on by gangs of girls from the local comprehensive whenever she gets away from her tofu-eating mummy and daddy for a couple of hours at the weekend. Passed around by a gang of bikers she falls in with. Eventually, she's raped by one of them, beaten badly, but still goes back to them.

"An aunt leaves the girl some money, and she buys a plane ticket to LA. Just like that. She's never been out of the country before and after eleven hours on a jumbo jet, she arrives at LAX with a few pairs of knickers, a couple of T-shirts and a spare pair of jeans in a bag, a few hundred dollars in cash, and a massive sense of liberation.

"The girl gets through immigration, baggage reclaim and customs, and finds herself in the arrivals lounge with so many stars in her eyes it's like a galaxy in her head. She's looking around for a taxi when this big, handsome guy – leather jacket, Gucci loafers, designer stubble – comes up to her.

"'Hey, darling,' he says, 'just got in? First time in LA?'

"She's just dazzled by everything. 'Yes,' she says. 'I can't believe it.'

"So the guy says, 'Where are you staying?'

"The girl hasn't booked anywhere and she only knows one street in the whole of LA, so she says, 'Rodeo Drive.'

"The guy offers her a lift and five minutes later, she's throwing her bag into the trunk of a bright-red, shiny, Mercedes convertible. And she can't believe her luck. They're driving along a road lined with palm trees, and the sun is shining, and the girl is basically just in heaven. After a while, she notices that the shops and houses have changed a little. Not so upscale, you know? A few pawn shops, a few sex shops, cheque-cashing joints, junky kinds of places. The guy seems relaxed, though, and he hasn't tried anything so she figures, well, OK, maybe this is a shortcut to Rodeo Drive.

"Then the guy pulls in at a bakery, more of a factory, really, and says, 'I have to get some keys to my sister's place. You could stay there while she's out of town.' And the girl is starting to feel like maybe this isn't such a good idea after all, but her bag is locked in the trunk. She says, 'I don't want to do that.'

"But the guy shakes his head and says, 'No, I think it's a good idea.'

"She can't cut and run, so she waits, and sure enough he comes back out and he's got two sets of keys and he gives one set to her and says, 'Look, I got you your own set so you can come and go as you please, just till you get settled, OK?'

"So now the girl is a bit more reassured and pretty soon, he turns off the road and down what is basically a building site track to this really scuzzy apartment building.

"They get inside and take the stairs to the second floor, past a guy bringing boxes up to an apartment down the hall, moving in, she guesses. And when he lets her in, she gets a real surprise, because she's been expecting some kind of crack house or whatever, shit all over the place and cockroaches, and it's actually really clean. Spotless, like a show home.

"'Look,' he says, 'I have to go out and do some shopping,' just for an hour or so. Lock yourself in.'

"He goes out of the front door and closes it. Now, the girl is thinking, well, I can just pretend to lock the door and then after he's gone I'll just take off and find that normal-looking guy down the hall who was just moving in and get him to help me. So she sticks her key in the lock but doesn't turn it, and twists the knob but doesn't lock it. Instead she leans against the door with all her weight. The guy tries the door and it doesn't open. Then she hears his footsteps getting fainter as he walks away from the door.

"Now she's alone in the flat and she needs the toilet so she goes in the bathroom and it's clean and tidy, but there's nothing in the cabinet. No pills, no toothbrush or moisturiser. Nothing. Then she pulls the blind up and guess what? There's foil over the window. Which is odd, she thinks, like maybe they have damp problems or something.

"Then she goes into the kitchen and pulls a few drawers open: nothing in them. Not so much as a teaspoon. And when she opens the curtains? More tinfoil. Finally she checks out the bedroom and it looks fine, except there are no clothes in the wardrobe. She pulls the curtains: more foil. The bed looks clean enough and she's starting to get really tired from the flight, almost out on her feet, and she's just thinking, maybe I'll have forty winks and I can still be gone before he gets back, when she sees something peeping out from under a corner of the pillow.

"She pulls the pillow away. Underneath it is an axe. The guy must be into snuff movies, is what the girl is thinking. And now she is truly losing it. Shaking. Sweat pouring off her. Thinks she might wet herself even though she's just been to the toilet.

"She grabs her bag and runs to the front door and twists the doorknob but it's locked from the outside or stuck or jammed or something, and she is well and truly freaking out because now she is convinced the guy is coming back with a couple of friends, going to party hard with her, film the whole fucking thing and then they're going to off her on camera.

"But then, something really odd happens to the girl. She goes very, very calm and cold inside. She isn't going to be a victim. Not this time. Not ever again. She puts her bag down and walks back to the bedroom, lifts the pillow aside and picks up that axe. Hefts it in her hand. Takes a couple of practice swings. Then she smacks it down onto the bed as hard as she can. It doesn't do any damage, just puts a dent in the bedclothes that she smooths out with her hand. Then she just sits on the bed and waits. About an hour later she hears the guy's key in the door. Very calmly she slides in behind the bedroom door.

"He calls out, 'Hey, little Miss England, where are you?'

"And she calls out to him, 'I'm in the bedroom.'

"There are two voices, both male. They're laughing, but it's a cruel laugh, like before they do something bad. Then in steps the guy who picked her up at LAX.

"'What the fuck?' he says, because there's nobody there.

"But it's the last thing he ever does say, because the girl slams the door back on its hinges, which catches guy number two in the face, and swings the axe down on guy number one's head. It's not a good shot, because she's shaking so much. It goes wide and takes a slice out of his scalp and his right ear off. Then guy number two bursts back into the room, only now his nose is pouring with blood and he is swearing and cursing. He's got a camcorder too, a professional one, which is hanging from his left hand. The girl turns and she hits him in the face with the axe. This time it *is* a good shot. Right across the eyes. He screams and goes down. The first guy is moaning and crying, clutching his head. She goes to him and rests the blade of the axe on his neck.

"'You were going to kill me,' she says. 'You were going to rape me and kill me and film it and sell it to perverts on the internet.'

"He starts to say something, but like I told you, he'd already said his last words. The girl lifts up the axe and brings it down on his neck and cuts right through the spinal cord and all the blood vessels and shit in there. The second guy is on his knees, hands over his eyes and he is screaming, over and over again. Really high pitched. So she whacks him in the centre of his skull. There's this cracking sound, and a little bit of brain comes out round the edge of the axe blade. It's stuck, so she just leaves it in there.

"There's a ton of blood. The bedroom carpet is sticky with it, and it's sprayed all over the walls and the ceiling and right across the bedlinen, which was white, with these little spriggy blue flowers, forget-me-nots, maybe, I'm not sure. The girl goes to the bathroom and strips off and climbs in the shower and stands there under the hot water, rinsing all the blood off her. Then she pulls out her only change of clothes from her bag and gets dressed.

"Then she leaves. The door is unlocked now. Bastard must have given her a dummy key or something. She runs down the hallway, past the guy who's still humping his boxes into his new apartment. He gives her a funny look, probably he heard the screaming. But she doesn't stop. Out on the street she looks around for a cab, but this neighbourhood? It's not so good for hailing a yellow cab. Then, and she thinks maybe someone is looking out for her after all, a minicab – they call them gypsy cabs – turns a corner at the end of the street and comes towards her. She jumps right out in the middle of the street and puts her hands out in front of her. The cab stops and she races around and jumps in.

"'You all right, miss?' the driver asks. He's an Indian guy, middle-aged, paunchy. 'This very bad neighbourhood. You shouldn't be out on the street on your own.' And he seems okay, you know? First impressions.

"She just says, 'Take me to LAX. Now! I need to go.'

"So he shakes his head and just takes off. Thirty minutes later, she's at the airport. She uses her cash to buy a ticket back to England. An hour and a half after that, she's sitting in Economy with a double vodka on the rocks, still shaking."

Sasha stopped speaking, emptied her glass and refilled it. During the whole story, Erin had sat motionless, not even sipping from the glass of champagne at her elbow. Now she spoke.

"Was there ever any trouble with the police?"

Sasha shook her head. "My fingerprints must have been all over the place, but I wasn't on any databases. Never been arrested or in any kind of trouble. No motive. By the time the cops would have been asking around, I was back in London."

"And after that?"

"And after that, I did in London what I would have done in LA. I found somewhere to live. Found a job. Got on with my life."

"The job?"

"Started off working in a bar. Ended up managing it. A punter got leery one night and I chucked him out. The boss got to hear about it. I ended up working in his personal security team. Things just snowballed from there."

"To being an assassin?"

She nodded. "He had me trained. In Serbia. My master was a man called Stefan Zcilowic. We did firearms: pistols, assault rifles, submachine guns, shotguns, sniper rifles. We did knife-fighting. Unarmed combat. Some other, more, how shall I put it, refined techniques. When I was ready, he sent me back to London. I worked for my first boss for two years, then we fell out over pay and conditions. So I went freelance."

Erin raised her glass. "Then I salute you. And I'm sorry for my remark about missing. But in any case, I don't want you to kill Gabriel Wolfe."

"No?"

"No. I intend to perform that particular act myself. But I want his life dismantled first, then you can lure him to me or march him at the point of a bayonet for all I care. Here's the brief." She pushed a sheet of notepaper across the table to Sasha. It was a new version of the list snatched by the wind from her desk in Manhattan. She'd reordered a couple of the items but in every other respect, it was the same.

Sasha read in silence, nodding at each item and then breaking into a wide smile at the final line. She made up her mind. *Good. Gabriel stays alive. With his old life gone, perhaps I can make him see sense.* Sasha raised her own glass. "I am at your service, Erin."

10

PUTTING ON THE RITZ

LONDON

For his meeting with Carl, Gabriel decided to play up the English gentleman act. Carl had referred admiringly to Gabriel's un-Brit-like willingness to talk about money, yet he'd clearly been won over by some Washington contact's description of his skills and experience.

"Was it you, Lauren?" he asked the mirror as he dressed. He was thinking of a Department of Defense agent named Lauren Stevens-Klimschak, an African American woman with whom he'd worked on his first mission after leaving the world of advertising behind. "I bet it was. Some space exploration CEO knows people in Washington, there's bound to be a defence angle, and the DoD would be his first port of call."

He'd selected a lightweight, three-piece suit in a Prince of Wales check. The soft, wool-cashmere blend was black and silver-grey with burnt-orange. The shirt was white poplin in a herringbone weave with a cutaway collar that exposed the neat, four-in-hand knot of his tie, knitted silk in French navy. He looked down. His freshly polished black monkstrap shoes gleamed in the light streaming through his bedroom window. A burnt-orange silk pocket square and lapis lazuli cufflinks set in eighteen-karat gold completed the outfit.

At 12.45, he was nodding to the frock-coated doorman outside the Ritz and leaving the hubbub of Piccadilly behind for the tranquillity of this most famous of hotels.

Inside, it was as if the golden age of luxury had never ended, which, Gabriel supposed, it hadn't for the world's super-rich. As he crossed the marble floor to the reception desk, itself a masterpiece of overblown woodcarving, with classical buttresses and decorations, he took in the gold, the cut glass, the chandeliers; huge vases full of tropical flowers; uniformed porters and bellhops with flat-topped hats; and a cocktail pianist in white tie and tails, competently working his way through something Gabriel thought was probably Mozart. *Not a patch on Oscar Peterson.*

He paused at the door to the restaurant. An elegant young woman was standing behind a lectern. She might have been Iranian, to judge from her colouring: olive complexion, dark-brown, elliptical eyes, full lips enhanced with a plum-coloured gloss. She, too, wore a tailored suit in the hotel's signature colour scheme of midnight-blue and gold.

"Welcome to The Ritz Restaurant, sir. Do you have a reservation?"

Gabriel smiled. "I'm meeting a friend at one. His name is Carl Mortensen."

She bent to the leather-bound bookings diary on the sloping top of her desk, running a burgundy fingernail across and down the neatly squared paper.

"Here we are." She ticked against the name and turned to her left. She signalled to someone with the merest hint of an eyebrow-raise, and a few seconds later, a waiter, sixtyish, trim build, appeared at her elbow. "Jean-Pierre, would you show Mr ...?"

"Wolfe," Gabriel said.

"Would you show Mr Wolfe to table eleven, please?"

Table eleven turned out to be a secluded perch in a corner of the restaurant. It sat on a low platform that raised it by six inches. The seating comprised a three-quarter circular booth with the opening positioned so that those seated within its soft, leather confines would have an uninterrupted view of their fellow diners. A screen of potted plants meant that Gabriel and Mortensen would be neither overlooked, nor hemmed in by other tables whose occupants might easily overhear their conversation.

"May I bring you an aperitif, sir?" the waiter asked, with a smile. His accent was French, Parisian, Gabriel judged.

"*Un martini, s'il vous plaît. Fait de Tanqueray Numéro Dix. Pas trop sec. Avec trois olives.*"

The waiter beamed. "*Bien sur, monsieur.*" He spun on his heel and stalked away through the tables to the bar.

Five minutes later, he returned bearing Gabriel's drink aloft on a silver tray. A martini made with Tanqueray No. Ten gin, not too dry, and garnished with three pimento-stuffed olives, threaded onto a plain cocktail stick.

Gabriel took a mouthful of the ice-cold drink. Perfect. As the alcohol hit his stomach and spread its warming fingers through his gut and into his bloodstream, he began to relax. He looked around.

Here were London's super-rich. Not too many Londoners, though, to judge from the babel of languages being spoken at the white-linen-dressed tables. Plenty of Russians, the men all wearing ostentatiously well-cut suits in fabrics too heavy for the time of year, the women in designer dresses, furs slung carelessly over the backs of their chairs, despite the best efforts of the waiters to remove them to the cloakroom. Chinese, too. Gabriel was fluent in both Mandarin and Cantonese, and here was an opportunity to listen in on the newly wealthy mainlanders as they paused for a break in their shopping. Arrayed at the feet of these eager capitalists were glossy paper bags with twisted silky ropes for handles, bulging with merchandise from Prada, Rolex, Tiffany's, Ferragamo and a dozen other brands unreachable for the remaining ninety-nine percent of the capital's population.

"You would have loved this, Dad," Gabriel muttered, taking

another pull on his drink. His father had been a diplomat in Hong Kong. Had assisted in the handover of Hong Kong to the Chinese. From time to time, as a boy, a teenage rebel, and then an adult, Gabriel had wondered whether there was more to Dad than met the eye. Was he simply a diplomat, or were there times when his work involved more clandestine activities than hosting embassy cocktail parties and shepherding visiting politicians from Britain around the colony? It was too late to ask him. He'd died of a stroke while sailing.

His musings were interrupted by Carl's arrival. Gabriel stood as his prospective client approached. They shook hands and then Carl slid onto the leather banquette seating so he was sitting at an angle to Gabriel, neither facing him nor next to him.

"Gabriel, it's my pleasure," Carl said with a broad smile, once he'd ordered a drink – bourbon on the rocks – from the waiter who'd brought Gabriel his martini.

He was tall, six three or four, and with the lean look of a man who'd seen action and kept himself in shape. His hair was cut short, blond with flecks of silver. Gabriel estimated his age at mid-forties. Hooded eyes with crinkles at the corners that showed white through his even tan. The nose, long and with flaring nostrils, had been broken at some point. Whoever had set it had done a good job, leaving no boxer's kink to it or lump of crooked bone, just a zigzag scar across the bridge.

Gabriel smiled back. "It's good to meet you, Carl. Are you over here on business?"

"Mm-hmm," the older man said, before pausing to accept his drink from the waiter, swallow half of it, then put the cut-glass tumbler on the table. "Finance guys. Bunch of money men in three-thousand-dollar suits at some fancy merchant bank over there in the City." He nodded at the back wall of the restaurant, roughly eastwards.

"You're not a fan of bankers, then?"

Carl shook his head. "Ever since I was a kid, I've been fascinated by space travel. Apollo 11 landed on the moon the year before I was born, and I grew up with that. My dad was an engineer at NASA as well. The old man used to take me to work with him. I grew up, put away childish things for a while, made my money on Wall Street. Then, a few years back, I started SBOE. Put all my money into it. We're doing OK, but like I said on the phone, it's an expensive business, and we need additional investors from time to time." He paused, finished his drink, then signalled the waiter for a refill. "You need another drink?" he asked, gesturing at Gabriel's glass. Gabriel nodded. "Would I rather be talking to bankers or rocket designers? What do you think?"

As he was talking, Gabriel was listening with half an ear, but also thinking. *You grew up in the States? So where's that northern European edge to your voice coming from, then? Parents were immigrants? And you own it outright but you also need finance?* He answered, even though Carl's question had been rhetorical.

"I'm guessing rocket designers."

"Damn straight!"

They ordered steaks and French fries, and continued talking over their lunch.

"Tell me about Kazakhstan," Gabriel said, as he sliced off another piece of the 21-day aged sirloin that was falling apart under his knife.

"We need a new launch site. Their government is really working hard to pull in western investment. They don't care whether you're setting up a drug manufacturing plant, a branch office for a bank, or a chain of language schools. Generous grants, tax breaks, minimal red tape. Compared to what you have to go through to even get to talk to the right civil servant in Europe," he wrinkled his nose, "well it's kind of a no-brainer. But it's also a pretty lawless place. Armed bandits literally riding around on horseback with Kalashnikovs, demanding protection money, bribes, whatever. So, I need someone with me who'll have my back."

He reached down and pulled a thick, brown envelope from the black, leather briefcase at his side. "Everything you need is in there. Full workup on SBOE, our operations, key staff, and my itinerary over in Kazakhstan."

The lunch ended with the two men agreeing with a smile and a handshake that Gabriel would take the job and meet Carl at Heathrow Airport two days later.

Walking towards Trafalgar Square, Gabriel called Britta.

"*Hej*! What's up?"

"Nothing. Just wanted to hear your voice. Also, I just got a new client. He bought me lunch at the Ritz, no less."

"The Ritz, eh? Very swanky. What's he like?"

"Really nice. Following his childhood dream to send rockets into space. He wants me to go to Kazakhstan with him for protection. We really got on."

"Ooh, fancy restaurants then a trip abroad together. You are having a bromance!"

Gabriel laughed. He loved being teased by Britta.

"No! But OK, it's not often I have a client whom I genuinely like."

"Well, make the most of it, lover boy. Maybe your next job will be for a corporate sleaze bag. Or shooting up terrorists for Don."

* * *

Erin was standing at the picture window of her Fifth Avenue apartment. She looked down at the trees in Central Park. They were coming into leaf, pale-green and deep-red pom-poms stuck into the ground that made the park look like an architect's model. A white porcelain mug of coffee steamed in her hand, and she smiled as the aroma – strong, nutty and dark – brought back a memory of drinking coffee at her father's dining table, planning together. The smile disappeared as quickly as it had arrived, replaced by downturned lips clamped together.

As the yellow cabs streamed along the street beneath her, she drained her coffee and set the mug down with a *clink* on the glass-topped side table to her left. Oh, he would pay. He would pay with everything he had. But in instalments. She was in no hurry to collect on the debt in full.

11

A COLD COUNTRY

KAZAKHSTAN

On landing at Karagandy International Airport, they were met by a swarthy, stubble-cheeked man whom Carl introduced merely as "my go-to guy here." Despite the sun, the air was bitterly cold, and their fur-lined parkas and thick, woollen trousers were only just up to the job of preventing their freezing to death. The spring sunlight was strong, and both men wore Ray-Bans to cut the glare.

They drove to a warehouse on a bleak, Soviet-era industrial estate, where the go-to guy produced what appeared to be a brand-new SIG Sauer SIG516 assault rifle.

"You know gun?" go-to guy asked Gabriel.

"This gun? Or guns in general?"

The man frowned. "This gun."

"Never used one. But I know AR-type rifles. I used to shoot M16s."

The man nodded his approval. "OK. All same except this one semi-auto. Chambered for 5.56mm NATO rounds, yes?" He handed it to Gabriel. "Passed NATO Over the Beach test. Very fine weapon."

The man also brought out a spare thirty-round STANAG magazine, and a box of 500 rounds of ammunition.

"What about the pistols?" Carl asked.

"Yes, is coming." Go-to guy turned and retreated into the open door of the warehouse, emerging a few minutes later with two Czech-made CZ 75 pistols.

Gabriel frowned at the mismatch between state-of-the-art, American, semi-auto rifles and these serviceable but dated pistols. He hefted one in his hand, turning it this way and that, then turned away and aimed at a sign on the far side of the road.

"Is fine combat pistol. Chambered for 9mm Parabellum."

Gabriel nodded. "Ammunition?"

Go-to guy handed over another heavy carton.

"So, we good to go?" Carl asked Gabriel, stuffing his pistol into the side pocket of his parka.

"Do you need to pay?"

"All done on account."

Go-to guy took them for a short walk to a small hangar. Inside the sliding doors loomed a huge, angular, silver SUV.

"Wow! Look at that. What the hell is it?" Carl asked as they approached the side of the vehicle.

"It's a Lamborghini LM002," Gabriel said.

Go-to-guy nodded his head. "Very good truck. Not fast as Ferrari, but maybe keep you safer." He grinned, showing strong, yellow teeth like a horse's.

Gabriel smiled back. No sense upsetting the man who'd just supplied your gear. Then he turned to Carl. "Ferruccio Lamborghini started out making tractors before getting the notion to go up against Ferrari. This was his attempt to crack the military market."

"So you ever use one of these in combat?"

Gabriel shook his head. "Our pinkies were Land Rovers. The Saudis and the Libyans had some, though. And places like this."

"Wait a minute," Carl said, smiling. "What did you just say? 'Pinkies'?"

Gabriel laughed. "In the desert, we started off painting them pink. It was excellent for camouflage. We ended up going back to traditional camo, but the name stuck."

Inside the four-wheel-drive, with the heater turned up full, the cab gradually filled with diesel-scented hot air, and they slung their parkas into the back seats.

"There it is," Carl said, pointing to a spot off to the west of the single-track road that ploughed on in an arrow-straight line through the unchanging landscape of low scrub, hard-baked earth, and the odd patch of thin, scrappy grassland. Carl was using a handheld GPS. Gabriel had already identified it as a military-spec device. He'd used them himself in theatres of war from the Horn of Africa to the Gulf. They were easy enough to get hold of if you knew the right people, or visited the right places. Which, as he'd recently learned, included the fathomless depths of the dark web, that part of the internet where drugs, guns, people, data and technology were available to the highest bidder. Gabriel swung the four-by-four off the road, and they jounced and bumbled across the rough ground for half a mile before he brought the four-by-four to a stop.

They had come to rest in the centre of a vast plain. In the far distance, Gabriel could see mountains, their peaks white against the clear, blue sky.

They left the warmth of the Lamborghini's cab for the icy blast of a wind that was blowing, uninterrupted, all the way down from the Russian steppe and the Arctic Circle beyond that. Above them, Gabriel caught the faint and plaintive cry of a bird of prey. He looked up, shading his eyes. High above them was the bird, just a tiny black shape. He had no idea what species of raptor might find a living out here – eagles, vultures, buzzards, kites? It was big, he could tell that. His scrutiny was ended by Carl.

"Hey, Gabriel. Come on. I didn't bring you out here to go bird watching. Stay focused OK? This is bandit country."

Gabriel turned through a full circle. Not a building, a pylon, a tree or even a bush more than knee height as far as he could see in all directions. He nodded.

"Sorry. You're right. We're clear, though."

"All the same, go get your weapons."

Not guns? Weapons? Odd choice of words for a banker-turned-space-entrepreneur.

Gabriel walked round the back of the truck and opened the tailgate.

With Carl wandering around kicking at stones, then stopping to peer at the horizon, Gabriel stood guard by the four-by-four, cradling the SIG in the crook of his arm. He caught a movement in the corner of his eye. He turned. Way ahead on the road, a couple of miles from their position, he could see a plume of dust drifting off to the south. Too big for a single vehicle, it was throwing up the classic shape of a convoy moving at speed.

12

COMPANY

Gabriel called out.

"Hey! Carl. We need to move. We have company."

Carl turned to look in the direction of Gabriel's pointing finger.

"Do you think it's trouble? Could be a trucker or something?"

"Out here? It's hardly a motorway, is it? It runs between the arse-end of Astana and the middle of bloody nowhere. Look, you hired me to protect you. Well, I'm telling you we need to go. Now!"

Carl trotted back to the Lamborghini, and they climbed in. Gabriel fired up the engine and slammed the unwieldy vehicle into first, spinning the tyres in the loose, gritty surface as he slewed round in a circle and shot away from the launch site. He looked up at the rearview mirror. The plume was still there, but it wasn't closing, or not fast. He kept his foot down hard on the accelerator and rammed the truck up through its gears until he maxed out the speed at just over seventy.

He looked across at Carl. The man seemed unbothered by the possibility that the bandits he'd spoken of now seemed to be on his tail.

"You all right?" he asked.

"Hey, we've got guns, right? You're ex-SAS, which is why I hired you. So keep driving." He looked down at the side mirror. "They're not gaining. Must be in some shitty Soviet truck or something."

It was true. Their pursuers, if that's what they were, weren't gaining. Gabriel's heart rate, which had jumped to ninety, slowly returned to sixty, above his normal resting rate but comfortable enough. He checked the mirror again. The plume of dust was drifting further south and had decreased in size even as it climbed into the air.

"Maybe they were trucks after all," Gabriel said. "Sorry. Just a little twitchy."

"Don't apologise, man. That's what I'm paying you for, isn't it? To be twitchy on my account? Let's head back to Astana, grab a beer. The site's perfect anyway. I checked it out on Google Earth, but you have to see the ground with your own eyes, know what I'm saying? Substrate looked good. No settlements, so no people to whine about noise or anything. Why don't you tell me about your military service while we're driving? It's a couple hours and there's no radio in this thing."

"What do you want to know? I don't really make a habit of going over old missions."

Carl shook his head. "I didn't mean that. I'm not some weekend warrior with a subscription to Soldier of Fortune and a garage full of assault rifles. But, I mean, the life. Your buddies. You must have made some good friends in the Army."

Gabriel thought back to his time in the Paras. Hundreds of jumps all over the world, some for training, some in anger. Comrades he'd fought alongside. Parades, medals, life on base, deployments to Belfast, the Gulf, secondments to struggling states in Africa and Latin America to train their own ragtag armies of conscripts and dope-fuddled regulars. And then of his time in the SAS. The patrol he'd led. A tight group of four men who'd saved each other's lives on more than one occasion, as they were depriving others of theirs. He'd lost one man, buried him just a few weeks earlier after retrieving his remains – skull, a single vertebra and identity discs – from Mozambique. Of the two others, one, Trooper Damon 'Daisy' Cheaney, had lost an arm to a .50 calibre round and left the regiment. The other, Corporal Ben 'Dusty' Rhodes, was still a serving member of the armed forces, though he'd rotated out of the Regiment and was now back with the Paras himself.

"I did make some good friends, you're right." *Now I come to think about it, apart from Daisy and Dusty, I'm not sure there are any other men I'd really call my friends.*

"They were guys in your squad?"

"Patrol, yes. Ben and Damon. I saw them recently." *At Smudge's funeral.*

"You guys close?"

"I guess so. We don't go out for beers every week. Live too far apart for that. But we keep in touch. Regimental dinners. Occasional nights out in London, you know the kind of thing."

Carl nodded, staring out through the windscreen. Then he peered at his side mirror again.

"Speaking of friends, I think we're on our own again."

"I know. They disappeared about ten minutes ago."

"You have many friends who aren't military? I know a few guys back home who are kind of loners. I mean they might be married but they pretty much keep to themselves."

"Not many. I used to have a dog and met a friend for walks."

"Oh, yeah?"

"Yes. Julia. We call her 'Angell by name, demon by nature.' Fight arranger in the movies. She punches hard. She says it's because she likes me." Gabriel smiled as he thought of his friend in the village with the hazel eyes and the salty laugh. The friend who'd had to text him the news of Seamus's death while he'd been away in the US.

"Tough lady, huh? So is there someone special? A lady who maybe doesn't punch you?"

"I just got engaged, actually."

"Wow! Good for you." Carl turned in his seat and clapped Gabriel on the right shoulder. "Me? I'm single. You know, I have female company from time to time, but the business pretty much sucks up all my time. So what's she like?"

"Britta? God, what to say. Well, she's Swedish. Works in

government." *MI5 in fact, but you don't need to know that.* "Funny, direct like all Swedes, good company."

"Looker?"

Gabriel nodded. "Red hair, nice figure. And she's got this smile that just, you know, does something."

"I know what you mean. I used to date a girl from Minnesota. Linda. Lot of Swedes and Norwegians immigrated there. Had this long, blonde hair and this unpronounceable surname. Like, I don't know, Berda-langs-something, some crazy Scandinavian name anyway. What's your fiancée's name? Hope it's easier to say than Linda's."

"It's Falskog. Nothing too complicated."

"Good news is, she'll be Wolfe soon, so you won't have to worry."

"I'm not sure she will. And I don't worry. Languages are my thing."

"Hey, you want something to eat? I got coffee and some rolls when we gassed up in Astana. They're in back."

Gabriel realised he was hungry. And a break from Carl's cheery conversation would be good, too.

"Sure. Let's stop." He brought the LM002 to a halt by the side of the road, even though, since their brush with the convoy, they'd seen not a single vehicle, or living thing, come to that.

With the cab filling with steam from the hot coffee from Carl's flask, and chewy bread rolls stuffed with smoked ham filling his belly, Gabriel spoke.

"So, Carl, tell me about you. What do you do when you're not conquering space?"

Carl took a gulp of coffee and swallowed hard on the mouthful of roll he'd been chewing noisily.

"Me? Not much to tell. Like I said," he scratched at his nose, "I made some money in finance. Selling CDOs, know what they are?"

Gabriel did, but decided to feign ignorance. He shook his head as he chewed the delicious smoky ham. "No," he said.

"Collateralised debt obligations. Just money-jargon for a kind of bet on whether some poor fool with no visible means of support is going to pay his mortgage every month. You package them up and buy and sell them like shares, only to other banks and some rich investors. I made a pile and cashed out before I burned out. Started SBOE because that was my thing. Now we launch satellites for other folks with deep enough pockets. The big media outfits, governments. You know. Those childhood passions, they stay with you. Buried maybe, for a while, but they never go away. How about you? What were you into when you were a kid?"

"Fighting, mostly. I was what you would probably call a disruptive influence. I took an air gun into school once and shot pigeons off the roof."

Carl barked out a laugh. "Jesus! You get into trouble for a stunt like that?"

"Expelled. It wasn't the first time. Or the last."

"But you must have turned things around? I mean, we did our background checks on you. Sandhurst, all that British officer training shit they put you through. Where did you find the self-discipline?"

"I didn't. Not exactly. My parents handed me over to a friend of theirs. He brought me up. Taught me how to respect myself, and others."

"Sounds like a hell of a guy."

In the face of Carl's relentless enthusiasm, Gabriel told him about Zhao Xi. Carl shook his head from time to time, as Gabriel explained some of the things he could achieve with the skills he'd acquired from Master Zhao, finishing with, "I sure could have used a guy like him when I was growing up."

They finished the coffee and the rolls, and then Carl took a turn at the wheel, speeding back towards Astana with the four-by-four's V12 engine roaring.

13

ABSENCE OF THE NORMAL

Waiting for the lift at the hotel, Carl turned to speak.

"I have some calls to make, but then what say we head out and find somewhere to eat?"

"Sounds good. It was a long day. Did you learn what you were hoping to?"

"Oh, yes. Everything looked real good out there. Apart from your little freak-out about the *bandits*." Carl grinned and put air quotes around the final word and Gabriel reflected inwardly that it was Carl himself who'd hired a personal bodyguard because of his own fear of just such an eventuality. *Never mind. The money's OK. And it's only for a week or so, then you can be back with Britta.*

Inside his room, a rectangular box with a functional bathroom built into a corner, Gabriel stripped down to his underpants and sat on the bed. He texted Britta.

Kazakhstan very flat. Minor alarm today. Turned out to be nothing. Carl fine. V talkative. Hotel OK. How are you?

·   ·   ·

His finger hesitated.

I miss you.

He backspaced.

I love you. G x

Then he set an alarm on his phone, lay back on the bed and closed his eyes. He'd agreed to meet Carl in the lobby at seven thirty and it was six now. Sleep wouldn't come, though. He got to his feet and spread his towel on the floor. Took some deep, lung-filling breaths, in through his nose, then sighed them out through his mouth, squeezing his abdominal muscles and lifting his diaphragm until his lungs were empty. With his eyes closed, he began working through a series of yoga moves known collectively as a sun salutation. As he stretched, bent, jumped back into a press-up position, slid to his belly, arched his back, folded himself into an inverted V and started again, he let his mind settle and clear, repeating the sequence over and over again.

He heard his phone buzz as, hopefully, a reply from Britta came in. He ignored it. For now, the meditation was more important. A thought rose to the surface of his mind like a bubble plopping in a mud pool.

Death follows you around, Wolfe.

With his breathing synchronised to his movements, he continued his yoga practice, not trying to interrogate the thoughts that began piling in on themselves.

· · ·

How many is it now? How many since you left the Army?

Meeks and his Hells Angels. Bart Venter. Sean Cunningham. Toby Maitland. Gary Granger and his skinhead friends. Vix and Lizzie Maitland. Kasym Drezna. Elsbeta Daspireva. The other Chechens. Yuri Volkov. Christophe Jardin. Diego Toron. The Children of Heaven. All six hundred of them. Philip Agambe. His wife. Her brother …

… you are not the Archangel Gabriel. You are the Angel of Death. You deliver it or you bring it.

Gabriel was holding a press-up position as this last accusation swam up from his subconscious. With his arm muscles shaking he maintained the pose, eyes open now and observing the drops of sweat that fell from the tip of his nose to the white towel beneath him, darkening the twists of cotton to a translucent pale-grey.

He shook his head, flipping a final drop of sweat off to one side and jumped forward into a squat then stood and reached for his phone, which had just buzzed.

The text wasn't from Britta. It was from Fariyah Crace, his psychiatrist.

How are you Gabriel? Come and see me soon, yes? Fariyah

He grunted. "Huh. Perfect! Were you listening in, Fariyah?" he asked the blue rectangle containing the eleven words, and headed for the shower. He stood motionless, letting the hot, faintly ammonia-smelling water stream over his face as he tried to argue with himself about that last, devastating comment from his subconscious.

"I don't mean to bring death. It's a consequence not a purpose," he said out loud as the water drummed on the plastic floor of the shower stall. "I'm righting wrongs. It's what I do. It's all I *can* do."

The inner voice replied.

And still they fall.

"Better them than me," he said grimly, stepping from the shower and towelling himself dry.

Carl was waiting in the lobby when Gabriel emerged from the lift. He'd dressed in that classic style Gabriel had come to think of as Exec-At-Play: navy blazer over a pale-blue button-down shirt, no tie; khaki chinos, razor-sharp crease; polished, nut-brown deck shoes. In a nod to the temperature outside the oven-like confines of the hotel and its central heating, Carl also had on a puffy, scarlet hiking jacket. Gabriel himself was less smartly dressed than his client for once, in black chinos, a denim shirt with pearl press studs and a forest-green crew neck sweater. A heavy, black, military-style greatcoat completed the outfit.

"Good to go?" Carl said, as Gabriel approached him, nodding to the two pretty receptionists as he passed the front desk.

"Ready when you are. Find somewhere good to eat?"

"You better believe it. Zagat recommended this new place on Daraboz Street. Chinese-Kazakh fusion. Sounds pretty interesting."

Sounds pretty disgusting, Gabriel thought, but didn't say.

It was growing dark. Carl led the way, keeping up a stream of small talk that left Gabriel free to maintain his situational awareness as they traversed virtually deserted road junctions and meandered through the dimly lit streets of Astana.

"Should be around the next corner," Carl called over his shoulder. He'd been striding ahead for most of the walk, and Gabriel had been happy to hang back a few steps, the better to keep his client and potential threats in view.

They turned into a street where the first three streetlamps were out. Gabriel looked past Carl's right shoulder down to the end of the street. No lighted shopfronts. No neon. No A-boards on the pavement. No marquees. No doormen. No sign of any retail or commercial premises at all. The absence of the normal.

14

STREET-FIGHTING MAN

A movement caught his eye. Across the road, a shadow had detached itself from the deep pools of black in the lee of a black-windowed office block. A six-foot-tall shadow that resolved itself into the shape of a man as it took a diagonal path across the road towards Gabriel and his charge.

Gabriel's pulse ticked up a notch and he closed the distance between himself and Carl. The shadow divided, amoeba-like, and one became two. The distance between him and them was no more than thirty yards.

He began to run a combat appreciation. *Two opponents. No sign of weapons … correction.* From the right hands of the two men, long shapes had appeared to extrude, sliding almost to the ground. *Clubs. No, baseball bats.*

Carl seemed oblivious to the threat and was bleating on about some restaurant he'd visited in Beijing. Gabriel tapped him on the shoulder.

"Be quiet. I need you to get behind me."

"Why? What's up?"

"Company. I can handle them, but if I say run, you run."

"Oh. OK. Got it."

Carl backed away and stood against the empty shop window behind them.

"Shit!" Gabriel hissed.

Ahead, two more figures had materialised under the sickly yellow glow of one of the functioning streetlamps. Then another three came strolling down the centre of the road. Flashes of yellow light blinked at him from the waists of a couple of the men approaching. Reflections. In steel. Gabriel reached into the right-hand pocket of his greatcoat, drew his CZ 75 and held it up where they could all get a good look at its satin-black contours. He called out, first in English, then again, in Russian.

"Stop! We don't want any trouble. Back away!"

"Stop! My ne khotim nikakikh problem. Otoydite!"

It had no effect. The men didn't even check their progress. One man was dragging his bat along the ground, so that its end scraped and clanged, a nasty metallic sound.

"Shit, man. Do something!" Carl hissed from behind him.

Gabriel pointed the pistol at the man in the centre of the gang, who were now less than twenty yards away. In the gloom, at least two of the others on his left and right would also feel the gun was pointed at them. A small psychological advantage, but better than nothing.

A flash of silver lit the corner of Gabriel's right eye. Then a jolt of pain like electricity leapt from his hand to his shoulder as a hard object smashed down onto his gun arm. The CZ 75 fell from his grasp and he saw it kicked to the gutter.

Gabriel whirled round. Three more men stood there grinning. Bad teeth, bad breath, bad hair. Bad men. One looked like a pirate, with a black patch over his left eye.

Two of them set to work on Carl, punching him to the ground and then raising the bat. Somehow, Carl scrambled back to his feet and took off down the street, back in the direction of the hotel.

Gabriel feinted to his left, then leant back and kicked the man closest to him high in the chest, on the left side, directly over the heart. He dropped to all fours, groaning and gasping. With his right arm useless, for now, Gabriel danced to his left and struck out at the other man. His left hand held stiff like a blade, he chopped him across the throat and snatched his bat as he toppled backwards. A backhand swing caught the man on the right temple. A high-pitched *crack* told Gabriel he'd smashed the man's temporal bone.

As Gabriel had begun his counterattack, a shout went up from the main group of attackers. Now he ran, with the seven remaining men pursuing him, cursing in Kazakh.

"Choose and shape the battlefield, even if you can't choose anything else," one of his war course instructors had advised his group of trainees early in Gabriel's service with the Parachute Regiment, before his transfer to the SAS. Now he took that advice to heart, sprinting into a side street that was darker and narrower still. In a confined space, a single man has an advantage over a group – he has full freedom to act while they must close ranks and either impede each other or wait in line.

Ahead, he saw an iron fire escape zigzagging down the side of an apartment building. Without breaking stride, Gabriel leapt for the lowest rung of the ladder and hauled himself up. He groaned with pain as his battered arm almost failed, but his grip held, and seconds later, he was swinging himself up and onto the first platform of the escape.

He looked down. His leading pursuer had a hand on the topmost rung. Gabriel stamped down on the man's knuckles, drawing forth a scream as his heavy, cleated boot sole smashed the man's fingers against the cold steel bar. Then he was climbing, breathing hard, heart racing, the adrenaline flooding his system doing the job nature had intended and flooding his skeletal muscles with additional oxygen to increase their power.

On the second floor, he glimpsed a dark narrow rectangle halfway along a walkway, and ran for it. The passage was cut between two parts of the apartment block, presumably to allow residents access to the rear of their flats. Gabriel darted down it, reached the far end, and flattened himself against the wall to the right

Five seconds later, one of the gang popped out from the entryway, to catch Gabriel's bat across the bridge of his nose. He crumpled, screaming, blood spurting from between his fingers. Almost instantly, a second man tripped over his fallen friend's inert form. Gabriel stamped down on the back of his neck, then skipped back and kicked him, hard, on the chin. Gabriel turned and sprinted down the walkway that ran round the inside of the hollow square of the apartment block.

He headed for another dark rectangle. A passage through to another side of the block. He hoped it would lead to another fire escape. Then either up and away over the rooftops, or down to the ground if the men were still pursuing him. He couldn't hear footsteps. No cursing, either. He stopped, just for a second and turned round. Nobody. Even the residents were wisely staying indoors, with their blinds drawn and their curtains closed. Gabriel permitted himself a grim smile. *Weren't expecting much of a fight were you boys?* he thought.

Then his right kidney exploded with agony.

Gabriel cried out and slumped to his knees.

He glimpsed a man built like a bull wielding a leather cosh before the incoming blow to the back of his skull lit a painfully bright star in his field of vision.

Then it, and all the other lights, went out.

15

INJURIES

Someone was shaking his shoulder. Gabriel opened his eyes and winced as pain flared behind them. He was lying on his back, legs twisted beneath him. His lower back ached from the blow to the kidney, and the pain had seeped like dark oil into his bladder. Looking down at him with an expression of curiosity and concern was a small child. A girl, maybe eight or nine. She had pink cheeks, flushed as though from a hot bath, and startling blue eyes. She looked over her shoulder and called out.

"Mama!"

Gabriel pushed himself up on his elbows and instantly cried out as a blade of pain stabbed into the back of his head. The girl flinched and drew back, then patted him again, softly on the cheek. She said something in Kazakh that he didn't understand, but could translate:

"Lie down."

He did, thankful for his coat. He didn't know how long he'd been out, but his muscles were stiffening in the cold. He untangled his legs.

A woman appeared at the door of the flat outside whose red-painted front door he'd been coshed. She was skinny, with ash-blonde hair pinned up into a bun. She knelt by Gabriel's side, and spoke, in English.

"You are hurt. You must come inside. We will help you."

"Thank you. I would like that very much."

Together, the girl and mother helped Gabriel to his feet. He ground his teeth to stop himself crying out again and frightening the girl. The awkward trio manoeuvred through the narrow doorway and into the flat, which was mercifully warm.

The woman spoke to her daughter, and together they half-pulled, half-pushed Gabriel through an internal door to a small sitting room where he collapsed onto a squashy couch upholstered in some sort of grey suede-effect fabric. Now he did groan.

"Where are you hurt?" the woman asked.

He leaned forward, gingerly, and pointed to his lower back. "Here." Then he touched the back of his head. "And here." His fingers came away sticky with blood and he leaned forward lest it stain the back of the sofa.

The girl sat beside him on the sofa, mouth set in a determined line, and took his hand in hers and patted its back. She spoke to him again in Kazakh. The tone was soothing, and he wondered if she liked to play doctor with her toys.

The woman returned and sat on Gabriel's other side. She carried a glass bowl half filled with water with a few grains of salt swirling in the bottom. In her other hand she held a pale-pink washcloth. With the bowl set on the coffee table front of her, she began to clean the wound at the back of Gabriel's head. He inhaled sharply with a hiss as the pressure sent a fresh dagger of pain into his head. She dabbed away, not stopping, and murmuring in Kazakh as she worked. Each time she dipped the washcloth in the bowl and then squeezed it out, it added a fresh swirl of pink to the water. But it was only pink, not scarlet, so whatever damage had been caused by the blow was superficial. He'd seen enough scalp wounds to know they bled like fountains, so this must have been little more than a nick.

"You have a small cut," the woman said. "It has, er, I do not know this word. When blood goes hard. Dark."

84

"Clotted?"

"Yes. It has clotted already. No need for stitching. Your back now. We must take off your coat and clothes."

With slow, gentle movements, she and her daughter helped Gabriel to wriggle out of the greatcoat. Then, as he held his arms up, they pulled his jumper off over his head and unbuttoned his shirt, before removing that too. Gabriel felt a sudden sharp memory of his early childhood: he was a little boy, being undressed by his mother for his bath. And there, lying on his back on a folded towel on the bathroom floor, was a baby. Michael.

"Turn, please," the woman said.

Gabriel shifted his weight cautiously and twisted to his right, away from the woman and towards the daughter. He smiled at her. Now, at last, she smiled back.

He jumped as the woman's fingers found the site of the punch, over his kidney, the soft, vulnerable spot between pelvis and ribcage where any trained fighter knew to hit an opponent.

"Bruised?" he asked.

"Coming. It will be very pretty colours. But not too serious, I think."

He looked round at her. She was smiling and he noticed the way her eyes were the same shade of blue as her daughter's.

"Thank you for helping me," he said, as he put his clothes back on, grimacing as his arm movements set off flares in his lower back. "My name is Gabriel Wolfe."

"I am Alina Kaliyev. My daughter is Nadya. Tell me, Gabriel. Who did this to you?"

He shrugged. "I really don't know. I was going to dinner with my client." *Shit! Who I need to contact.* "Then they appeared. They didn't take my phone or my wallet, so not robbers."

Alina shook her head. "There are many violent men, even gangs, in Astana. They like to kidnap foreigners for ransom. It is a big problem here. The police do nothing. They are not well paid, so bribes work well."

But they didn't seem to want that either. Just to give us a good kicking. And my attacker left me, but not for dead. This thought prompted Gabriel's aching muscles to send up another distress flare.

"Please, do you have any painkillers? Aspirin? Paracetamol?"

Alina got up from the sofa, smiling. "Yes. Also ibuprofen, codeine, even morphine if you want it?"

Gabriel blinked in surprise.

"Morphine? No, thank you. Just paracetamol please. Maybe some ibuprofen, too. I can take them at the same time."

After swallowing five tablets with a glass of water Alina had brought from the kitchen, Gabriel leant back against the sofa cushions.

"You speak English very well. And you have morphine. Are you a doctor? A nurse?"

"Thank you. And, yes. I am a general practitioner. A family doctor, you call it this?"

Gabriel nodded. "Or GP. Like you said, a general practitioner."

He looked around the room, at the old but serviceable furniture. He saw plenty of books and a small, flat screen TV, a couple of pictures on the wall. But it looked temporary, somehow. Not like a family home, still less that of a doctor, who he imagined even in Kazakhstan would be able to live better than this kind woman appeared to.

She followed his gaze and shook her head with a sad smile.

"You are thinking is poor place for a professional to live."

He shrugged and reddened, embarrassed at being caught revealing his thoughts so obviously.

"It's nice. I suppose salaries here are low for everybody compared to the west."

She laughed, a joyful sound in the small room. "No! Actually, pay for doctors in Kazakhstan is good. But I am," she hesitated for a second and glanced at her daughter, "divorcing my husband. He abused me and Nadya. With his fists, you know? He liked to hit me there, too," she said, pointing at Gabriel's back.

"I'm sorry. I wish I could help. I hate men who do that."

"Maybe you can." She spoke to her daughter. The implication was clear. *Go to your room.*

Nadya rolled her eyes and clutched Gabriel's hand tighter. She replied. *I want to stay. He needs me.*

Once more Alina spoke, and this time her tone of voice carried an extra note of command. Gabriel knew how to use his voice to bend men to his will and nodded appreciatively at the way this second instruction shifted Nadya off her bottom. Reluctant, pouting, she dropped his hand and stomped away through the door. Her footsteps were audible all the way down the narrow hall. The adults looked at each other, waiting.

One.

Two.

Three.

Bang!

The bedroom door slam: standard practice for disaffected children everywhere.

Gabriel smiled at Alina and was rewarded with another of hers, lighting up her face and crinkling the soft pale skin at the outer corners of her eyes.

"So. What can I do to help you?" he asked.

"Artyom comes by every single night. He bangs on the door. He frightens Nadya. Calls out her name. Calls me *qanşıq*. Is the Kazakh word for the female dog. You know?" Gabriel nodded, grimly, a plan forming in his mind, whatever Alina might ask. "He is rich. Says he will have lawyers take Nadya away from me."

"Do you want me to speak to him?"

"No. What I want is for him never to come back."

"I can't—"

"Kill him? Do not be silly. But you can threaten him, yes? You can make him frightened to come back. If he thinks you will be here to watch for us."

"Does he speak English?"

"Some. He is a businessman. He works for KazPetroGas, it is an oil company."

16

A DEBT REPAID

After answering more of Gabriel's questions, Alina stood.

"Would you like something to eat?" she asked.

"Yes, please. If it's not too much trouble. Anything would be good. A sandwich. Bread and cheese."

"Nadya and I had spaghetti with meat sauce earlier. I will heat some up for you."

With Alina gone, Gabriel checked his phone. No message from Carl. He called up his contact details and tapped the number. Five or six seconds of silence passed, then a click as the call connected. Gabriel inhaled, ready to ask how Carl was doing, how he'd managed to get away. The call didn't connect at all. Instead, a high-pitched continuous tone whined from the phone's earpiece. Then it cut off and a pre-recorded message in an American accent announced that the number called was out of service.

That doesn't make any sense, Gabriel thought. Even if Carl had dropped his phone in the chase, or the attackers had relieved him of it and smashed it under a boot sole, that wouldn't affect the number itself.

He reached round to the back of his head. Under his probing fingertips, he found the smooth, rounded blobs of congealed blood that sealed the cut. Then he leaned forward and rubbed the site of the kidney punch. That would be the one to cause more problems. Blood in the piss would mean a trip to his doctor when he returned to the UK.

His speculations about his own health, and that of Carl, were interrupted by Alina's returning with a white china bowl heaped with spaghetti and a rich-smelling ragù of shredded meat, tomatoes, red peppers, mushrooms and garlic. He breathed in deeply through his nose and sighed.

"That smells wonderful. Thank you."

Alina smiled and handed him a thick, green-tinged, stemmed glass brimming with a deep-red wine that smelled of blackcurrants and ripe plums.

Gabriel forked the herby, spicy food down, twisting the spaghetti around and around into great, glistening mouthfuls, and washing it down with gulps of the wine. The wounding and subsequent spell out cold – literally – on her doorstep had made him ravenous, and the food was gone in just a few minutes. He checked his watch.

"It's nine thirty. What time does your husband normally arrive?"

She put her hands out and shrugged, making a *who knows?* expression.

"Ten, eleven, midnight. Late, like I said. So he can wake up Nadya. Make sure she hears the names he calls me."

"I need some things. Can you get them for me?"

Gabriel gave Alina instructions to assemble a few household items in the kitchen. That done, they waited.

Half an hour later, a loud knocking on the flimsy front door startled them both. Gabriel had been half-asleep, under the combined influence of shock, alcohol, the painkillers and the huge portion of pasta Alina had served him. He looked at Alina. Her green eyes were wide with fear and apprehension, and her face was pale, her cheeks drained of their earlier pink tinge.

"Don't be frightened. I won't let anything happen to you. Or Nadya. Go to her and keep her company. I'll call for you when I'm ready."

With Alina and Nadya safe in the girl's bedroom, and the

knocking increasing in ferocity, Gabriel stood and made his way into the hall. The husband – what had Alina called him? Artyom? – was shouting now. Angry oaths, including multiple references to *qanşıq*.

Gabriel readied himself. Inhaled once, deeply, then let it out again in a sigh. Tensed his muscles, ignoring the pain. Reached out and placed his left hand on the door handle.

Adopting a fighting stance, with his left foot in front of his right, knees flexed, Gabriel pushed down on the door handle and then, in one explosive movement, pulled it back so that it banged against the wall.

In front of him, fist raised, eyes wide, stubbled cheeks suffused with blood, stood Artyom Kaliyev.

Taking advantage of Kaliyev's surprise, Gabriel leaned forward and grabbed his tie, then yanked him across the threshold, pulling down so that the man stumbled. His ungainly progress was stopped dead by Gabriel's right knee, pistoning upwards as Kaliyev's chin jerked down.

With a satisfying *clack* as his jaws snapped shut, Kaliyev fell full-length onto the hall floor, and lay inert.

Kaliyev was not a big man, maybe a couple of inches shorter than Gabriel – five foot six or seven – and no more than ten stone. Gabriel hooked his arms under Kaliyev's armpits and dragged him down the hall, thankful that the landlord had fitted linoleum instead of carpet, and into the kitchen, where he hefted him onto a pine kitchen chair. Using the pairs of tights Alina had provided, Gabriel lashed Kaliyev's arms behind him, winding the stretched nylon ropes in and out of the slats of the chair back before tying them off. He repeated the process at Kaliyev's ankles.

"Alina! You can come in now," he called out.

She appeared in the kitchen, a look of fear in her eyes, which disappeared as she took in her husband's trussed limbs, lolling head and closed eyes. She placed her thumbs against his eyes and lifted the lids. The eyeballs were rolled back in their sockets so that only the lower edge of the dark-brown irises were visible.

"What now?" she asked.

"We wait. Does he speak Russian?"

Alina nodded. "He does. Most Kazakhs do, but people like Artyom speak it fluently."

Fifteen minutes passed, during which Gabriel asked Alina to teach him a few rudimentary phrases in Kazakh. Somewhere in his genetic makeup, a random mutation had bestowed on him a facility with languages that had surprised and then amazed his parents. His mother being half-Chinese, his ability to pick up first Cantonese and then Mandarin was pleasing, but not especially noteworthy. But then, as he heard visiting diplomats speaking amongst themselves at embassy cocktail parties, he seemed to absorb their languages through his skin. By the time he entered the SAS, the 25-year-old Wolfe was fluent in six languages, Russian among them, with a working knowledge of another half dozen.

He was just repeating back to her a key phrase he wanted when the husband moaned, opened his eyes, then lurched forward and vomited over his own lap.

Gabriel ignored the acrid stench and went to work. He tapped the man on the forehead twice. As his eyes snapped open, struggling to focus on Gabriel's face, Gabriel spoke to him, in a mixture of Russian and English. As he spoke these disjointed phrases, he synchronised them with a sequence of eye movements he'd learned many, many years ago, as he studied with Zhao Xi.

"You know why you are here, but not for how long."

"*Koshka sidel na kovrike.*"

"Count to ten then *skazhite tsveta radugi.*"

"Think of your earliest childhood memory."

"*Kto prezident Kazakhstana?*"

"Now tell me how many sides a hexagon has."

His traumatised brain struggling to process these random and conflicting instructions, Artyom Kaliyev experienced a phase change in his consciousness. The faster beta waves associated with wakefulness were replaced by slow-cycling theta waves that distorted his perceptions of reality and made him receptive to hypnosis. As his grasp of where and even *when* he was deserted him, so did his ability to think rationally.

Gabriel was monitoring the other man's skin tone, breathing and eye coordination like a hawk watching a rabbit way down below its fluttering wings. As Kaliyev's eyes moved independently of each other, he pounced. Speaking in phonetically learnt Kazakh, he issued his orders.

"You will leave Alina and Nadya alone."

"You will never come near them again."

"You fear Alina. She has the power to blind you by looking at you."

"Do you understand?"

Kaliyev nodded his head as a drunk might, a floppy gesture of assent with no crispness to it. A string of spittle dribbled from the corner of his mouth. Gabriel took the man's chin between his thumb and forefinger and raised it so that he could look the man in the eye.

"I will be watching you, Artyom. You will know this. And I will kill you if you harm or threaten Alina or Nadya."

Then he slapped him on the forehead with the outstretched fingers of his right hand.

Kaliyev shook his head and stared up at Gabriel, who was looming over him, a nine-inch cook's knife in his right hand. His eyes widened and he stuttered out, in English, "No-no. Do not hurt me."

"I won't. This is to cut you free."

Gabriel slashed at the tights binding Kaliyev to the chair. As his limbs came free of their bonds, Kaliyev stood, uncertainly, like a newborn calf. He turned to Alina, then inhaled sharply and looked away.

"Let me go. I have to leave. I mustn't be here."

He turned and fled the kitchen. His footsteps in the hall were hurried, and moments later, the front door slammed. Then all was quiet.

Alina stood there, just staring at Gabriel. Then she took the knife from him and very slowly, replaced it in the knife block. She turned.

"It worked."

"It usually does. But have you thought about moving? Getting away from here?"

"How can I? Nadya is at school here. My clinic is here. Our friends are all here."

Gabriel looked at her, then. Saw the doubt already creeping into her face.

"Then get yourself a good lawyer."

17

FIRED

Back at the hotel, and with his muscles starting to stiffen and ache despite the painkillers and alcohol, Gabriel stopped at the front desk.

"Has Mr Mortensen returned, please?" he asked the balding and bespectacled young man on night duty.

"Mr Mortensen has checked out, sir," he said, looking down and retrieving something from the shelf hidden beneath the top of the reception desk. "He left this for you." He handed over one of the hotel's white envelopes. On the front, it simply said, "WOLFE."

Frowning, Gabriel thanked the man and went up to his room.

Inside, he stuck the card key in the slot that activated the lights, then sat on the bed to open the envelope. Inside was a folded sheet of paper. He unfolded it and read the message.

I hired you to protect me.

You failed.

·   ·   ·

95

I've returned to the US.

If you want the rest of your fee, get a lawyer.

Gabriel rubbed a hand over his face. *Shit!* The guy had a point. But where had those men come from, and why had there been so many of them? And why hadn't they taken anything? Too tired from the night's adventures to find any coherent answers among the jumble of thoughts fighting for airtime in his overstressed brain, Gabriel undressed and climbed into bed. Sleep wouldn't come, though, and as he lay there, listening to the sound of a distant dog barking and the occasional truck lumbering past the hotel, crashing up through the gears after the road junction, he let his mind go wherever it wanted to.

He wondered what Britta was doing. Hoped she was safe. He realised he'd never had that precise feeling about the redheaded Swede before. On hazardous joint operations with Swedish Special Forces, on arduous training exercises in places either numbingly cold or swelteringly hot, on semi-authorised infiltrations deep into enemy territory, he'd known she was up to the job, and at least as deadly a fighter as he was. Yet now, doubts had begun to creep in and make themselves felt. Not doubts about her competence. Not exactly. More like doubts that she would survive. Having circled each other for years like two wary animals who feel a mutual attraction yet know each is potential trouble, they had found a new way of being together – almost conventionally happy in their engagement, he thought – and now he feared its being taken away. One random shot from a cornered trafficker or slashing blow from a knife-wielding terrorist, and down she'd go, and with her, Gabriel's chances of a normal life.

18

MORTENSEN VANISHES

MANHATTAN

Carl Mortensen AKA Guy Jaager flew first class to New York via Frankfurt. The next day, after clearing immigration and customs at JFK, he slid into the back of a yellow cab smelling of pine air freshener and gave Erin's address on Fifth.

"Very smart address, sir," the Indian driver said. "You are successful businessman?"

"Me? No. But my boss is. And she's a woman, by the way."

"That is America, sir. Land of the equal opportunities. Myself, I have PhD in computer engineering. My plan is to work for top US tech company."

Whatever, Jaager thought. *Just shut the fuck up and drive.* He hated taxi drivers. Hated the surly ones, the talkative ones, the newly arrived immigrants with their shit sense of direction and even worse command of the English language. Hated the experienced ones with their stories of celebrities they'd driven to this party or that opening.

Had his driver been able to read minds, he would have been only slightly mollified to discover that he wasn't alone in being on Jaager's hate-list. The Dutchman hated all kinds of other groups. Politicians. Officers. Feminists. Government employees. Lawyers. Middle class liberals. Jews. Blacks. Hispanics. Asians. Left-wingers. Animals rights freaks. Vegetarians. Vegans, God help us – he reserved a special contempt for them, with their crazy "philosophy," giving up meat and cheese and even leather, then walking about letting the whole fucking world know how goddamned *good* they were.

So just who, exactly, did Jaager *not* hate? It was a short list. His former comrades in the *Légion Étrangère*, the blacks excepted. The Afrikaners, who after black majority rule were really the oppressed minority in South Africa, according to a mercenary he'd fought with in Zambia in the nineties. And, occupying a glistening white palace in his heart, though he would never tell her this, his current boss, Erin Ayers.

She was tough, and he admired her for that. He'd loved the way his instinct to avenge the insult perpetrated on her by the English cyclist had been allowed. He'd seen her negotiating with white-shoe lawyers acting for her business rivals and just take them apart. Not with her hands, or with weapons – she had Guy for that sort of work – but with her command of the details of the financial transactions she was orchestrating.

She was also ruthless.

* * *

He'd flown over to Bulgaria with her to talk to the local managing director of one of her companies; the man was being threatened by a gang of extortionists. Having pressed the man to reveal the name of the gang's leader, threatening him with the sack, and a lawsuit besides, she had driven with Guy out to a mountain village presided over by a looming château surrounded by thick woodland. There, the boss of the thugs lived in apparent splendour. Erin brought the hired BMW X5 to a stop in front of an ornamental fountain in the centre of a circular gravelled drive in front of the house.

"Nice place," was all she said.

Then she opened the tailgate and collected two assault rifles. She handed one to Guy and cocked her own, a swift efficient movement that sent the charging lever clacking back against the stop and Guy's heart banging against his ribs.

She pressed the doorbell. After giving her name to the black-leather-clad man who came to the door and peered through the gap left by the security chain, she shot him through the left eye. Switching to full auto, she blasted the chain into shrapnel and kicked the door open.

Four more men came running, pulling pistols from their waistbands. Erin and Guy didn't even give them time to aim their weapons. All four went down screaming, blood, tissue and brain matter splattering the walls of the hallway as they crumpled, marionettes suddenly dropped by a bored puppeteer.

"Veshkov!" Erin yelled in a thrillingly deep contralto voice that actually gave Guy the beginnings of an erection. "It's Erin Ayers. I've come to get my money back."

Rifles swinging left and right, fingers crooked round the triggers, Erin and Guy walked through the ground floor of the château, kicking at doors and knocking huge Chinese vases from their pedestals to shatter on the tiled floor.

A slam from the upper storey. Somebody had just locked themselves into a bedroom.

Looking at each other and nodding, Erin and Guy raced up the two separate wings of the curving, iron-railed staircase before meeting at the top in a hallway hung with oil paintings of ruffed noblemen and uniformed soldiers. From under the door of the second room along the darkened passageway, light was seeping out, fanning across the dragons woven into the deep-red carpet.

They took up positions each side of the door. Then Guy drew a pistol from his belt and fired three rounds into the lock.

His shots were answered by a fusillade from the other side, the rounds smashing through the oak, leaving thin beams of light

99

spearing across the hall that illuminated the far wall like miniature spotlights.

Guy fired again, and again received an answer. He pointed at the door and mouthed to Erin, "Nine."

A third time he fired, and a third time the wood of the door was splintered with shots from inside the room.

With the air around them thick with the smell of burnt propellant, and the noise from the shots still reverberating in his ears, Guy looked down. Fifteen holes.

He cocked his head. Yes! There it was. The sound of a pistol magazine being ejected.

"Now!" he yelled, and burst into the room.

Veshkov was crouching by a double bed, fumbling with a magazine, trying to jam it home into the butt of a pistol. Guy thought it might be a Glock 19. That would fit with the fifteen shots fired. But at that point he didn't care.

He leapt forward and knocked the pistol from Veshkov's hands.

Erin came in behind him, rifle pointing at Veshkov's head.

"You have five hundred thousand euros of mine. Where is it?"

Veshkov put his hands up. He was white-faced and shaking. He pointed to a pine dressing table.

"In there," he said.

Guy moved to the other side of the room and opened the top drawer of the cabinet. Bundles of high-denomination banknotes were jammed in behind socks and underwear. He turned and nodded at Erin.

Erin stepped back a few paces, then shot Veshkov in the face. He died instantly, leaving most of the contents of his skull on the wall behind him.

Half an hour later, as the burning château lit the horizon, Erin and Guy were sitting in the local town's only restaurant, eating steaks and drinking the local red wine. She was laughing and telling him another story about her father.

* * *

The taxi driver's voice roused him from his daydream.

"Yes, sir? We are here?"

Guy paid the man, careful to calculate the tip to just below what would be considered acceptable in the city, and got out.

The uniformed doorman nodded. Guy nodded back, and went inside. He walked past the receptionist – another curt nod – and down to the bank of elevators.

Inside the vast, white space, he looked around, wrinkling his nose as he did every time he took in Erin's art collection. Brâncuşi, Giacometti, De Kooning, Lichtenstein: she'd told him the names – Jew names, he'd thought at the time – and explained why they were so good; but to him the sculptures looked like tourist tat from some African market. And the paintings – Jesus! Crappy daubs that looked like they'd been done by a mental patient or a kid with a comic book fixation.

The cleaning crew had obviously been in that morning. The place smelled of lemon, and every surface, from the stainless-steel kitchen surfaces to the white marble floor, sparkled under halogen downlighters. What Guy really wanted to do was sink his frame into one of the squashy, white, leather sofas, or maybe the luxurious-looking swivelling recliner chair in matching white hide. Then he saw his boss through the plate glass windows overlooking Central Park.

Erin beckoned him to the terrace. Even though it was still only March, it was warm outside, and Guy inhaled deeply, catching the scent of spring: pollen, he supposed, or sap rising.

"Have you eaten?" she asked him, greeting him with kisses on both cheeks. To her, this was merely a social greeting. To him, it was both unimaginably pleasurable, and a reminder of her unattainability.

"I'm not hungry, boss."

"Thirsty, then?"

"A beer would be good. Please."

When she returned from the kitchen with two beers – some

fancy Japanese brand – and had taken a long pull on her own bottle, she gestured for him to take one of the two transparent Perspex chairs facing each other across a matching table.

"You get what I asked you to?"

"Everything. He couldn't stop blabbing about his pals in the SAS, all his friends, his childhood teacher, his woman. I got it all, boss. Your briefing gave me exactly the right questions to ask. It was too easy."

"Good. I'll email Sasha. Your eye all right? That's a proper shiner you've got there."

He touched the purplish-green bruise that encircled his right eye, as bright and colourful as stage makeup. He winced.

"I went down early, like you said. But that fuck still used a cosh on me. I gave him a good kick before I ran, brought that peasant to his knees."

"Sorry, Guy. But it had to look realistic. I don't want to tip Wolfe off. Or," she smiled, "not yet, anyway. What about him?"

"Oh, I think he got a solid beating. I counted at least ten of them."

Her brow furrowed.

"He's alive, though?"

Jaager nodded.

"I called the hotel from Frankfurt. Wolfe got back in one piece."

She smiled.

Inside, Guy boiled with rage at Wolfe. It was clear to him that Erin admired the man. Maybe more than she cared for Guy. Well, no battle plan survives contact with the enemy. That's what that old Prussian, von Moltke, said, wasn't it? Maybe Erin's plan could be adjusted.

19

NO REGRETS

LONDON

Three days after his trip with Carl to Kazakhstan was aborted, Gabriel was sitting opposite his psychiatrist. Today, she was wearing a lime-green hijab above a well-cut, black, silk suit. He looked around the office, at the abstract painting on the wall, at the row of medical and psychiatric diplomas on the wall, at the bookshelf, stuffed with textbooks on psychiatry, psychology and philosophy. Then back at her. He crossed his arms, then remembered reading somewhere that this was a defensive body posture, and uncrossed them.

Her brown eyes were smiling as Gabriel adjusted his position in the chair, his eyes tightening as one of the bruised muscles in his back cramped momentarily.

"Still not completely relaxed about visiting a trick-cyclist, Gabriel?" she asked. She was referring to a slip of the tongue he'd made on his first visit.

"It's not that," he said, smiling back. "I just ran into a bit of trouble on a trip to Astana. Gangsters after my client."

"Astana. That's Kazakhstan's new capital, isn't it?"

He nodded, marvelling, once again, at her ability to remain unflappable whatever he told her. Mind you, he thought, a shrink who had the vapours every time you swore or told her a hair-raising story wouldn't exactly be fit for purpose, would she?

"Since 1998. It used to be Almaty."

"What took you to Astana? And this 'trouble'?"

"A client. He said he wanted protection. From bandits."

Gabriel paused, frowning.

"But you're not sure?" she prompted.

He rubbed a palm across his face and shrugged.

"I don't know. He got hit, too, then he managed to get away. I ended up playing the Good Samaritan for a woman who took me in."

"Then what is it? What's troubling you?"

"Honestly? I'm not sure. He was pleasant enough, then, when we got attacked, he just took off. Literally. Left me probably the tersest note I've ever received that basically told me to sue him for the balance of my fee."

"And will you?"

"Sue him? No. What would be the point? He's a tycoon. Probably has lawyers check his Starbucks bills for him. No, I'll chalk it up to experience."

"Tell me about being a Good Samaritan."

Gabriel related the story of his helping Alina. Throughout, Fariyah remained very still, occasionally writing in the black-covered notebook perched on her knee.

When he finished, she looked at him. No smile this time.

"You took her word for it? That he was abusive?"

"Well, yes, of course. Why would she lie?"

"I don't know. But I know people do tell lies. All the time. Did he hit her, this man?"

"She said he did."

"Did you see him hit her?"

He paused before answering. Not to recall the scene as Kaliyev buckled before him. But because he was beginning to doubt he had acted as he should have done.

"No, I didn't. I got my retaliation in first."

"Then you tied him to a chair and hypnotised him, and planted a posthypnotic suggestion in his subconscious. A very frightening suggestion at that. How do you feel about the way you acted?"

"It was justified. He was a violent, powerful man who was terrorising his wife and daughter."

"According to her."

"What are you trying to say? That she was lying so I'd beat up her husband? He was banging on the door late at night. Threatening her."

"In English?"

"No. No, of course not. In Kazakh."

"Do you speak Kazakh?"

Gabriel clamped his lips together, which had the effect of forcing him to breathe, noisily, through his nose. He could feel his pulse speeding up, and he didn't like the sensation.

"No. I don't. But he called her a bitch. She told me that word."

"And on the strength of a single shouted word, you knocked a man unconscious, bound him and messed around in his head. Was that the action of a Good Samaritan, do you think?"

"Look. I thought you were supposed to be my friend. To be helping me. Why the cross-examination?"

Fariyah closed her notebook, and put it on the desk beside her. She leaned forward and reached for his hands, which he reluctantly gave her.

"Gabriel," she said, softly. "I am your psychiatrist. My job is to help you recover from your PTSD. Not to be your friend. Friends might buoy you up, whatever you've done. My job, as you know, is to understand the stories you tell about yourself and add a story of my own that helps you to relocate yourself inside yourself, rather than outside yourself."

"I don't know what that means. 'Inside' myself. Isn't that where I am?"

"Let me try to explain. When we are psychically integrated, that is to say, when our emotions do not trouble us, when we feel in control of our own minds and behaviours, able to function without the help of stimulants, or depressants, or psychoactive substances of any kind, whether prescribed by our doctors or not, we exist inside ourselves. We understand that we are in control. That also means we are responsible. For our actions, our thoughts, feelings and beliefs.

"But when we have experienced some form of trauma, we can become detached from ourselves. To a greater or lesser degree we are psychically disintegrated. You see how the word has both meanings? To disintegrate is to come apart. Go to pieces. It isn't just buildings or enemy tanks that can disintegrate. We, ourselves, can, too. And when that happens, when we feel out of control, ruled by emotions like fear or anger, we can be said to be living outside ourselves."

"So what are you saying? That I'm psychically disintegrated? Mad?"

She smiled and shook her head.

"You are very, very far from mad, Gabriel, as I think you know. But my questioning made you defensive, angry even, did it not?"

Gabriel wanted her to let go of his hands, but felt that she'd take it as a sign of rejection. Not of her, but of her role. He stayed still, though he could feel his palms sweating inside her grip.

"Honestly, yes it did. He was pushing her around. Frightening her. And Nadya. I just redressed the balance."

Now, finally, Fariyah released his hands. She leaned back in her chair, turning to retrieve her notebook.

"Let's say you did. Let's say you performed a good act. If he'd gone to the police, which, frankly, he would have been well within his rights to do, you might have been arrested. Thrown into jail. Charged with assault. Unlawful imprisonment. Who knows what the Kazakh penal code allows for situations of forced hypnosis? Was it worth the risk? To help Alina and Nadya?"

"Yes." Gabriel answered without hesitating, even for a second. "Yes, it was. And I'd do it again."

"Our time is almost up," she said then. "I want you to come and see me next month. I want to talk about your sense of justice in a little more detail. Perhaps we can unravel its beginnings."

20

ITEM ONE

SALISBURY

While Gabriel was settling into a comfortable armchair in a consulting room at the Ravenswood hospital in Mayfair, Sasha Beck was out walking. Not for fun. She never walked for fun. For physical exercise she preferred lengthy martial arts sessions with one of her teachers around the world. Or sex. An onlooker might conclude that Sasha liked rough sex, and in a way, they'd be right. Although the person who felt the roughness was usually the man, or occasionally woman, she'd chosen as her partner. A gondolier in Venice still nursed a black eye and a set of eight long, deep scratches in the skin of his back and shoulders from his own recent encounter with the assassin. Ask him whether he'd go back for a second bout, though, and he would nod vigorously before begging for her current whereabouts.

No, not for fun. Sasha was walking to a job. Nevertheless, she still had time to look around and take in the view. Before her, rolling hills, cross-hatched with fields of pale-green, brown and the startling, acid-yellow of oilseed rape. She shook her head and spoke aloud.

"It may be pretty, but rape? Really? Time for a rebrand, darling."

She thought back to her conversation the previous night in a pub outside the village from which she was now walking away.

"You asthmatic, are you, dear?" the landlady had asked, as she dropped a slice of lime into Sasha's gin and tonic. Sasha had just sneezed.

"No. Though I am allergic to dogs," she said, pointing at a large, fat and smelly yellow Labrador that lay by the fire, its flank heaving up and down in its sleep.

"Lot of folks are, though. Allergic," the woman continued. "I blame the rape. Down here, leastways."

"You get a lot of rape, do you?" Sasha asked, pointedly looking around at the collection of mostly male drinkers.

The woman laughed, a liquid, throaty sound that spoke of nicotine addiction.

"Not that kind of rape! Oilseed. In the fields. It's in full flower now. Causes all kind of breathing problems. Hey, Phil!" she called across to a middle-aged man in a ratty brown jumper and jeans, who was nursing a pint of beer and studying a tabloid newspaper. "Which paper did that story about rape giving folks asthma?"

"*Mail*, weren't it?" he said in a thick rural accent that made his words sound like *Mow-wernert* to Sasha's ears.

The landlady nodded, resting her large breasts on the bar top. "That's right. The *Mail*. Don't know why they call it rape, mind. Nasty name for such a pretty plant."

"It's Latin," Sasha said, then took a sip of her gin and tonic. "For turnip. *Rapum*. In Italy, they serve a lovely green vegetable called *cima di rappa* – turnip tops."

"Well," the landlady said. "You live and learn, don't you?"

. . .

The thick, oily fumes emitted by the plants clogged the back of Sasha's throat, but as she wasn't allergic to them, they caused her no more problems than a gluey sensation on her tongue. The sun was out, in any case, and she was enjoying the sensation of its rays warming her back through her Sasta Kauris camouflage stalking jacket. Slung across her back was a matching nylon gun bag containing a Remington Modular Sniper Rifle. For urban contracts, Sasha favoured a McMillan CS5 that she could disassemble and carry in a backpack. Out here in the country, long guns were a part of life, and, in any case, she had a way of looking at people that tended to make them veer off or pass by quickly with a muttered, "good morning."

She consulted her map, then turned left along a hawthorn hedge, its pale-green-and-white buds waiting for some temperature or chemical signal to open. The field climbed up the side of a hill and ahead, its topmost branches shrouded in a few remaining wisps of mist, was a fat-trunked oak tree. Her nest. She'd picked it out on her reconnaissance, during which she'd observed the target walking a regular route around the fields. The tree gave an excellent field of fire; cover, should she need it; and some protection from the rain.

Julia Angell pulled on her Dubarry knee-length boots, a fiftieth-birthday present from her husband. She knew the Irish firm's boots weren't the sensible option, and at almost three hundred and thirty pounds a pair, they certainly weren't the cheap option. Wellingtons were better for repelling rain, and wouldn't melt the corners of your credit card. But she'd coveted a pair of Dubarry boots ever since she'd seen them in a window of the local gunsmith. The tan-and-tobacco colour scheme, the laces that encircled the tops, the sheer romance of them made her desperate to own a pair. She anointed the leather parts with dubbin after every walk as an article of faith, and she kept them straight with the cedar boot trees that ever-thoughtful Mike had also given her.

While she dressed for the walk, Scout bustled around her feet, erect tail wagging from side to side like a hyperactive metronome. The ginger-coloured dog could barely contain himself, and encouraged his mistress by skipping in increasingly impatient circles around her.

"Right, mischief," she said, straightening, and clipping lead onto collar. "Let's go. See if you can flush out a rabbit."

Twenty minutes later, humming a tune that had become stuck in her brain after hearing it on the radio first thing that morning, Julia unclipped Scout to tear off through the crops. She stood and looked around, smiling as she breathed in the warm pollen scent that for her always said, winter's over.

* * *

"Hello, darling," Sasha whispered, as her quarry appeared through a gap in the hedge that marked the division between two fields. "Pretty dog. I suppose he'll be good company for your husband after you're gone."

She put the Zeiss Victory RF binoculars down onto the camouflage ripstop nylon groundsheet. She bent to retrieve the gun bag and unzipped it. The weapon that emerged bore very little resemblance to the wooden-stocked shotguns and hunting rifles favoured by the farmers and aristocrats in this part of southern England.

The Remington was fitted with an AAC Blackout flash hider, a Schmidt & Bender Polar T96 telescopic sight and a bipod. Timur Kamenko had, on her instructions, supplied the gun painted in a woodland camouflage pattern of browns, blacks and greens. On one memorable contract, while scrunched down in some bracken on the Isle of Arran, where a Syrian businessman liked to hunt red deer, a robin had fluttered down from an overhanging tree and perched on the barrel. Only when Sasha hissed at it did the bold little bird return to the safety of the tree.

She settled onto her belly and began preparing for the shot. Right hand around the pistol grip, index finger held straight against the outside of the trigger guard. Left under the slotted fore-end. Right cheek pressed against the pad on the left side of the stock.

The first few times she had killed for money, she had vomited immediately afterwards. But it was more from the excess adrenaline washing through her veins than any heightened emotional state. That brush with the reaper in the snuff-movie apartment in LA had changed something inside her. Perhaps it had never been fully present in her to begin with, but whatever empathy she might have had for her targets had ebbed away along with the blood of the two men who'd planned to rape and kill her on camera.

In one, fluid, lift-pull-push-lock movement, she worked the bolt to chamber one of the .308 rounds. The bolt was so well machined that its progress back and forth was almost silent. The barest metallic *snick* reached Sasha's ears as its front end pushed the round home. She checked the target's progress with the binoculars, then switched to the scope.

The woman stood five nine or ten in her boots. A full figure, and black hair loose around her cheeks. She was laughing as she threw a stick for the dog, calling to it as it raced away into the crops.

Sasha stilled herself. The woman was on the move again, but she was maintaining a steady pace, and Sasha barely needed to worry about leading her with the cross hairs.

Sasha uncurled her finger and reseated it around the trigger, squinting as the sun emerged from behind a cloud, then breathed all the way in.

* * *

Four hundred yards away, Julia looked up. She'd caught a flash of light on the next hillside, almost as if someone were signalling to her. She shrugged, then looked around for Scout. He was nowhere to be seen. She inhaled, and pursed her lips, ready to whistle for him.

She did not exhale.

The woman, the fight arranger, the wife, the mother, died instantly, while her skeletal muscles still held her upright. The .308

copper-jacketed soft-point round that stole her life from her entered her forehead one inch above the bridge of her nose. It punched through the bone, destroyed her brain, and burst from the rear of her skull, spattering the hedge behind her with blood and tissue.

* * *

Sasha worked the bolt to eject the brass, catching it in mid-air as it turned end over end. She pulled out a small penknife from a jacket pocket and prised out a narrow spike with her thumbnail.

A few minutes later she packed away her equipment, unzipped her jacket and walked away. She wasn't worried about the bullet. Assuming it was ever found, it would reveal little. She always loaded her weapons wearing nitrile gloves, and if the police had the budget to analyse the striations on the copper casing, all they'd discover was that it had been fired by no gun on their database. Dead end.

"You're a dangerous man to know, Gabriel Wolfe," she said, smiling, as she descended from the hill to pack her equipment into her car.

* * *

Gabriel reached his village a little after six that evening. As he drove up the narrow road that led to his cottage, he had to pull in as a dark-grey Audi A4 came thrashing around a corner towards him, blue lights flashing their staccato warning at him from the radiator grille and the dashboard. He parked on the gravel at the side of his cottage, not bothering to put the car away, and went inside.

He checked his answering machine. The red light was on and the digital display showed a 3. He took his jacket off and slung it over the back of a kitchen chair. Then he pulled a bottle of white Burgundy, a Marsanne, from the fridge and poured himself a generous glass, took a mouthful, topped it up, then ambled over to the machine and hit the play button.

21

"I KNOW WHO DID IT"

The voice was Mike Angell's. He sounded as if someone had just punched him in the face. Numb, flattened somehow.

"Gabriel, it's Mike. Mike Angell. I, er, it's Julia. She was walking Scout. And then she was, she's been shot. The police are here. They say she was murdered. Oh, God. Sorry to be the bearer of bad news, but you're a friend. A good friend. And I—"

He heard broken sobs, and then the continuous high tone as the message ended. Gabriel stood completely still. He looked down at the black box as if willing it to chirp up that it was a joke. He felt a weight in his gut as his stomach churned. The next message played.

"Hi, Gabriel. It's Steph at the pub. Don't know if you heard, love, but it's terrible. Julia Angell's been killed. The pub's full of coppers. It's just so awful. Come in when you can. Most of the village is in here. The police are talking to everyone."

. . .

He dragged a chair out from under the table and sat heavily. With his hands dangling between his knees, he waited for the next message.

"Mr Wolfe? This is Detective Superintendent Anita Woods. Please call me as soon as you receive this message." A mobile number followed, repeated twice in a clear voice with no trace of an accent.

Gabriel sat and let his head drop forward. *Oh, Julia. What happened? People don't get murdered around here. It's why so many Londoners move down.* His throat thickened but no tears came. Perhaps he was too wrapped up in the latest discussion with Fariyah Crace. He sighed deeply and stood. Suddenly he wanted company very, very badly. Maybe the pub was the answer. He'd probably find the detective there.

He was at the back door, pushing the handle down when the landline phone rang again. He lunged across the kitchen and grabbed the handset from the cradle, fumbling and almost dropping it. He jabbed at the answer button and brought the phone to his ear.

"Hello?"

The caller was a woman. Her tone was light, mocking.

"Hello, darling. I know you haven't been in long. Have you heard the news?"

For a second he couldn't place the voice.

"Who is this?" he hissed.

"My, my," the woman answered, in a tone suddenly dripping with antebellum southern charm, "have you forgotten me already, dear boy? I would have thought our recent … encounter … in Hong Kong would be fresher in your mind. It took a great deal of ingenuity to effect my escape from your Triad friend. Though I'm sorry to say his two female companions have gone to visit with their ancestors."

Gabriel saw a face as if lit by a flash of lightning. Dark, bruised-cherry lips; finely curved black eyebrows; straight, black hair tied back in a ponytail. His jaw clenched. Sasha Beck. An assassin who had been hired to kill him. And failed.

"It was you, wasn't it?"

"What was?"

"Don't fuck with me."

She reverted to her normal voice, a playful London accent that dipped and swooped through the social registers, from lady of the manor to East End tough. She sighed.

"Oh, darling, there's nothing I'd like better. But, since you're being so direct, yes. It was me. Well, I pulled the trigger. But as you know, I'm a hired gun. Literally. The question you should be asking is who paid me to pull it."

"Tell me, then. Who hired you?"

"Can't. Client confidentiality."

Breathing steadily through his nose and struggling to contain an urge to scream at her down the phone, Gabriel uttered two final sentences.

"I'm going to find you. And then I'm going to kill you."

"Not if I find you first, darling."

Then she hung up.

In the pub, the atmosphere was feverish. Those villagers not being interviewed by uniformed officers or detectives were standing round in groups, foreheads creased with anxiety, leaning towards each other as they talked. Many of the women – and a few men – appeared to have been crying. Their faces were red and blotchy, the women's streaked with black where their mascara had run.

Nodding greetings to the few people he knew, Gabriel shouldered his way through to the bar.

Steph, the landlady, was serving, alongside her husband. She hurried over as Gabriel laid his elbows on the wooden bar, its surface dented and scarred by countless thousands of pint pots and pewter tankards. Her plucked eyebrows drew together and her mouth turned down as she spoke.

"Oh, Gabriel, love. Here you are at last. What can I get you?"

He rubbed a hand over his face. Shock had made it hard for him to think clearly. Even to choose a drink.

"Gin and tonic, please, Steph. Large one."

Drink in hand, he took a long pull then turned around, looking for a friendly face.

A woman he didn't recognise came over to him. She was short, maybe five five, and on the plump side. Bleached blonde hair cut into a shaggy bob. Red slash of lipstick in a face lined by years, and by laughter, but not cigarettes to judge by its clear, smooth skin. Grey suit jacket over jeans, and flat, black pumps. She was carrying a spiral-bound notebook in one hand and in the other, either the world's biggest gin and tonic, or a pint of mineral water with ice and lemon.

"Excuse me, sir," she said, pocketing her notebook then extending her hand. "Are you Gabriel Wolfe?"

You must be Anita Woods. You guys are the only people to call anyone sir *these days.*

"I am," he said, shaking the offered hand. "You are?"

"Detective Superintendent Woods. Wiltshire CID. I am the SIO, sorry, the senior investigating officer on this tragic case."

And you talk like a press release.

"You mean Julia's murder. Why don't you just say so?"

Her face remained impassive.

"Look, I know this is a terrible time to be asking questions, and I know all this," she waved her hand around at the saloon bar's milling crowd, "is a bit chaotic, but if we're to stand any chance of finding the person who did it, we need to start now. And I'm sorry for the euphemism. It's just not everyone is comfortable with the unvarnished version."

"Well, I'm fine with it. You don't talk much like a cop by the way. More long words than usual."

"Usual? You spend a lot of time talking to police officers, do you?"

Gabriel thought back to two Metropolitan Police detectives he'd worked with tracking a cult leader to the rainforests of Brazil.

"No. Not lots." He sighed again. "Look, I'm sorry, OK? We got off on the wrong foot. Julia was my dear friend. I met her the day we moved down here."

"We?" Anita asked, pulling out her notebook and placing her drink on a table nearby so she could make a note. "Are you married?" She looked him up and down. "With a partner?"

"No. And no. Though I am engaged. I meant me and Seamus. He was my dog. Can we go somewhere quieter to talk, please? There's something I have to tell you. You won't like it, but it will help, I promise."

"This place is a bear pit. Where do you suggest?"

"I live down the road. Can you come to my house?"

"Fine. Lead on."

She turned and called out to a male detective who was in the middle of an interview with a fortyish man in a pinstriped suit who looked as though he might have known Julia to judge from his red-rimmed eyes.

"Matt! Give me a call if you get anything, OK? I'm popping out for a while."

He nodded and returned to his interview.

At Gabriel's house, he offered a coffee.

"I'd rather have something stronger if you've got it."

"I thought you guys didn't drink on duty."

"Yeah, well, I thought dog walkers didn't get murdered by snipers in rural Wiltshire. You live and learn."

Gabriel poured them both a whisky and then turned to face her.

"I know who did it."

22

SUSPENSION OF DISBELIEF

The detective's eyes popped open, bright white, framed by dark, steeply arched eyebrows.

"What? How? No, scratch that. Who?"

Gabriel pulled out a chair and sat down, motioning his guest to do the same.

He swigged some more of the whisky, feeling its warmth hit his stomach and combine with the gin to make his head swim for a second. He shook his head.

"Her name is Sasha Beck. Well, that's what she calls herself. But it could be an alias. I mean, these people like to stay under the radar, so you never know."

Anita was scribbling notes in her notebook in an oversized scrawl.

"Wait. Hold on," she said, looking up. "What do you mean, 'these people'?"

Sasha's an assassin. A hit woman."

"I know what assassins are, thanks. Fictional. They don't exist in real life. Or not in bloody Wiltshire, anyway."

You're drinking whisky with one right now.

"I'm afraid they do exist. I've … run into Sasha before. She's the real deal."

The detective frowned. "Look, Gabriel. I know a little about your background from Mr Angell. He gave me your name when we were asking him about Mrs Angell's friends here. You were in the army, right? He thinks you … might have been Special Forces."

Gabriel nodded. "That's right. Why?"

"I want to try and phrase this right because, believe me, I don't want to give any offence, but are you sure this isn't some sort of fantasy you're living out to compensate for civilian life being so boring?"

Gabriel laughed then, a genuine sound startled out of him by the detective's well-meaning question.

"What makes you think my life is boring?"

"Compared to what you did before, I meant."

"It's not, OK? But that's beside the point."

"So tell me, what *is* the point?"

"Like I said. Sasha Beck did it. She's a professional killer. Which means you will never catch her."

"All right. Let's say, just for the sake of argument, that I believe you. How do you know it was her?"

"She called me. About half an hour ago. To tell me."

"That's great! We can get your phone records and trace the number."

He shook his head and pressed his lips together as he began to realise Sasha was playing him.

"She called my landline."

"Doesn't matter. We can still find the call."

"Why waste your energy? She'll have used a burner phone or a call diverter or some clever piece of technology she bought on the dark web."

"You seem to know a lot about her MO. Anything you want to share with me?"

He spread his hands wide. "It's very simple. She is a professional. In a field where a single slip gets you killed. I'm telling you, you won't find her. Not unless she wants you to. And if she does, I'd be really, really worried."

"So, what? We just walk away from investigating your friend's murder? Is that what you're saying?"

"No," he said, feeling his temper rising, despite the fact Anita was simply doing her job. "I'm saying go on with your investigation. But while you're doing that, I'm going to find her myself."

Anita put her notebook and pen down on the table. She leaned forward and looked at him, hard, eyes unblinking, lips set into a straight line.

"I must advise you against that. You are a civilian. You have no powers of arrest. And if she's as dangerous as you say she is, trying to contact her would be a very dangerous course of action."

"Now you sound like a police officer again."

"Which is what I am. A very senior police officer. A very senior police officer in charge of investigating every murder in this glorious county of ours, not to mention those of serving armed forces personnel across the whole world. And I am advising you, sir, not to take the law into your own hands."

"I wouldn't dream of it."

"Why don't I believe you?"

"I don't know. I'm not a mind reader."

Something in the detective seemed to snap. She scowled at him.

"I don't know if you're trying to be funny, or taking the piss, or whatever the fuck you're doing, but your friend, Julia Angell, just took a bullet from some fuck-off, high-calibre, sniper rifle not a mile from your front door, and I am personally heading up the investigation into her murder. So let's have a little bit less of the macho posturing and a little bit more cooperation, all right?"

Gabriel shrugged. He hadn't meant to enrage the cop, but now he had he found he didn't really care.

"I want to see where she was shot."

"Impossible. We've got CSIs crawling all over it. They haven't found the bullet yet. It could be vital."

"It won't tell you anything. She'll have worn gloves when loading her rifle. It'll be a .338, a .308 or a .300, maybe a 7.62. A soft point, or maybe a ballistic tip. Nothing custom or hand loaded, just a regular brand like Federal, Remington or Winchester. Lapua maybe, or Black Hills. Probably a boat tail round – they fly straighter."

"All of which is very impressive, or maybe not, given your service record. But we're still looking for it."

"What about the sniper nest?"

"Yes, we're on that."

He shrugged. "I could help you. I've worked with snipers. I know what to look for. Please. I'm sorry for being off with you. It's been a long day and I'm still in shock that she's gone."

Anita appeared to relent. Her shoulders dropped and her eyes lost the tightness in the surrounding muscles that had pulled them into slits.

"Tomorrow morning. Nine a.m. Come up to the white tents on the field. I'll be there. Maybe you can help us pinpoint where the shooter was hiding."

23

KILLER

The woman's face was pin-sharp in the scope's reticule. Dark, bruised-red lips curving into an ironic smile. Long, straight hair drawn back into a ponytail with some sort of clasp. The dog was being a pest, though. Every time Gabriel had her lined up for a head shot, the terrier would bark and its mistress would fling the ball for it to retrieve. He kept his finger curled round the rifle's trigger, concentrating on his breathing.

His chest felt wet, despite the sun on his back and the dry earth beneath his ground sheet. He looked down. The dent his torso had made in the ripstop nylon was full of blood. It was seeping through his clothing. The smell was an intense coppery hit that made his eyes water. He could taste it in the back of his throat.

The wind whispering through the branches of the tree above him was actually human voices. Dozens of them. Talking to him. *You killed us*, they said. *You did. Gabriel Wolfe, killer.* He shook his head and settled down more firmly into the pool of blood, which squelched as his weight forced it out between his rib cage and the edges of his combat jacket.

Then he saw his moment had arrived.

The dog was nosing around for the ball in a hedgerow. The

woman was standing perfectly still, shading her eyes against the sun with a hand pulled into an approximation of a salute.

He moved the cross hairs up a fraction until their meeting point was centred on her forehead.

Breathed in.

Tightened his finger on the trigger.

Breathed out.

Squeezed until the trigger released the spring that sent the firing pin into the primer pocket in the centre of the cartridge case.

The woman looked at him. Her smile was gone. She looked terrified.

It wasn't Sasha Beck any more. It was Julia Angell.

"Gabriel!" she screamed across the field at him. "What have you done?"

He tried to answer, but his throat had filled with blood. He coughed a gout of it onto the grass in front of him.

He was riding the boat tail round as it cruised towards Julia's face, straddling it, wind ruffling his hair as he sped on towards his friend's death.

Then he was with her, holding her upright despite her buckled knees. She was weeping, and the dog was yapping around their ankles.

At the moment of impact, he thrust her forwards to meet the bullet and dived to one side.

As her face disappeared, he hit the ground and rolled away. The thump of the rifle report caught up with the bullet as it exited her skull and buried itself in the ground under the hedge.

Up on the hill, a figure waved at him, then blew a kiss.

Julia was lying beside him, arms and legs spread at unnatural angles, a runner in mid-sprint, but horizontal. Her voice sounded inside his head.

"You did this, Gabriel. Now you have to stop her doing it again."

He turned to speak to her, but the world had turned dark. Three luminous green numbers floated in space.

3.08

Gabriel groaned and sat up in bed. His chest was slick with greasy sweat, and the sheet beneath him was soaked.

He put his face in his hands and wept. Loud sobs wracked him, and he hammered his fists against his forehead.

When he was done, and all that was left was an ache in the muscles between his ribs and over his kidney, he climbed out of bed and sank to his knees. With his arms above his head, he bent forwards until his palms were touching the rug in front of him, in a pose of submission.

Gabriel had never prayed before. Never really thought about God before. Had seen too much cruelty and death to believe in an all-powerful, all-knowing, and all-good being. But something in him told him now was a good time to ask for help.

With his eyes closed, he began to speak.

"Please, God. I have always tried to be a good man. But people get hurt around me. People I love. Help me keep them safe. Please. Help me protect Britta. I love her, God. Please don't let Sasha Beck take her from me. I know that's what she wants. I can tell. Help me. Amen."

He stayed in that position, prostrate before a God he wasn't even sure he believed in, until the sun came up. At some point he fell asleep. When he awoke, the numerals on his bedside clock showed 7.15. He tried to move and yelped as his frozen muscles creaked into action and blood flooded them. The numbed nerves woke up, too, with a surge of pain as the screaming muscles demanded relief.

He staggered into the bathroom, showered and shaved, then returned to his bedroom to dress for the search for the sniper's nest.

.   .   .

At 8.55, he was striding across a meadow towards the white tent erected around the scene of Julia's murder. His dark-brown moleskins were tucked into high, leather boots. A hiking jacket in bright red kept the wind off. A tight knot of plain clothes officers stood to one side. As he approached the perimeter formed from plastic stakes strung with blue-and-white police incident tape, a uniformed constable stepped forward, right hand extended, palm up.

"Sorry, sir, you'll have to move back. This is a crime scene."

"I know. Detective Superintendent Woods asked me to meet her here. I'm not one of the ghouls hoping to see something bad."

This seemed to take the young PC by surprise. He blinked, once. Then regained his composure.

"Wait here, please, sir."

But Gabriel had no need to wait for the young officer to find Anita Woods.

She detached herself from her colleagues and walked across the rough ground to where Gabriel was standing.

"It's OK, Lee," she said. "He's offered to help me find the shooter's vantage point. Friend of the victim and ex-army, too. Knows a bit about snipers, does our Mr Wolfe. Come with me, Gabriel."

Thanking the constable, Gabriel dipped under the incident tape, catching his hood on it with a snapping sound. Leaving the clearly disgruntled PC to knot the fluttering ends of the tape back together, he entered the tent behind Anita.

He drew in a sharp breath. Dead bodies held no worries for him. He'd created many and seen many more. In fact, there was no body. What remained was somehow even worse. More shocking. In front of him was a roughly human-shaped depression in the long grass by the hedge. The narrow path where countless walkers' boots had rubbed and flattened the turf to a hard, mud track was only a couple of feet wide. Each side of it was long, unmown grass. The shape Julia's body had made ran east-west, across the north-south path. Beneath the round indent her head had made was a huge, sticky mess of blood and the mottled, porridgey mess of grey and red tissue that he knew to be parts of her brain. The hedge to the side of the body was spattered with blood and more tissue on its glossy, pale-green leaves.

"Oh, Jesus, Julia, I'm sorry she came for you, not me."

"You all right?" Anita asked, touching his elbow.

"Yeah, I'm fine. I dreamt I killed her. Pulled the trigger."

"Look, it's traumatic, OK? Takes people in different ways. Some people get survivor guilt, you know?"

"Yes. 'It should have been me,' that sort of thing?"

"Exactly. But you didn't pull the trigger. This Sasha Beck character did. According to you. Now look." She stepped round the indent, which was still being processed by a couple of crime scene investigators in white Tyvek overalls. "Our blood spatter expert was here yesterday. From the direction and shape of some of the blood droplets, she can pin down the origin of the shot to a pretty tight angle. Combining her assessment with the direction of travel, footprints before Julia fell, the entry wound and other factors, we've narrowed it down to a fifteen-degree segment."

She turned her back on the edge and extended her arms in front of her in a narrow V.

"I've got guys out there searching already, but why don't we go outside and you can do your Special Forces voodoo and maybe save us some time?"

Outside the tent, Gabriel turned in the direction Anita had just indicated. Between them and the horizon, he could see a dozen or more uniformed officers combing the field, poking through tussocks of grass with long, thin poles.

He shaded his eyes against the sun, which was streaming down from a cloudless sky, and scanned left to right along the horizon.

"The world record for a confirmed sniper kill is 2,707 yards. With an Accuracy International L115A3. But they're strictly controlled, and while she could have got one, there are easier rifles to get hold of on the grey market. I'd bet she did it from no more than a thousand yards, probably less. Julia was a civilian target. No weapons, no armour, no cover, no support, and no awareness she was a target. I'd find somewhere no more than five hundred yards out. Just enough to stay out of sight and avoid compromising the kill by being spotted."

As he spoke these words, he was simultaneously aware that he'd slipped into that damned ingrained habit of seeing everything as a logistics or strategic puzzle. *Your friend is dead, you idiot and you sound like you were impressed with Sasha's planning!* He ground his teeth together and squeezed his eyes shut. Opened them again.

24

BRASS

Anita had one eyebrow raised as she scrutinised his face.

"Seems I'm not the only one who speaks in service lingo." Then it was her turn to frown. "I'm sorry. That was unnecessary. Let's leave the sensitivities about our language till we catch this woman."

Gabriel shrugged. "Whatever you say. Like I told you last night, you won't."

He pointed to a stand of trees on the brow of a low hill about four hundred yards away from where they were standing.

"You see those trees?"

"Mm-hmm."

"There's an oak on the extreme right. Uninterrupted field of fire from there down to here. It would give cover, some rain protection. I'd say we go take a look."

"Lead on, Macduff."

They trudged up the incline in silence until they were within twenty yards of the tree. Anita stopped Gabriel with a hand on his right bicep.

"Stop. OK, if that is where she was shooting from, there could be physical evidence. Hairs. Fibres. Skin cells. Sweet wrappers, even. I've seen it all. Even the so-called professionals get careless from time to time. We get a break, we could find her. I'm going to get a couple of the CSIs up here, and one of my colleagues."

She made a call, and five minutes later, they were joined by two of the crime scene investigators and two more detectives, a man and a woman.

"Lindsey, Ben, this is Gabriel Wolfe. Gabriel, this is Detective Sergeant Lindsey Robinson and Detective Constable Ben Whicherley. Gabriel lives near here and was a friend of the victim. He's ex-military and reckons that oak tree over there could be the place where the shooter was positioned. Get a couple of uniforms to put a cordon round it, please."

She turned to the CSIs, who were holding their kit boxes and waiting to be given the go-ahead to start ferreting around for evidence.

"We believe it was a professional hit. So whatever we're going to find, it's going to be small. Shiniest tweezers, please."

They smiled and went to work, walking towards the tree with slow, controlled steps before dropping to their knees and crawling the last few yards.

The female detective spoke. She had white-blonde hair cropped and gelled into short spikes.

"Gabriel?" He nodded. "What makes you think it's a pro job? More likely to be a local shooter with a bad case of the crazies, don't you think? Or some village dispute gone to shit?"

He shook his head.

"Like I told your boss, I know her. She called me last night. Told me she did it."

She turned to Anita, a frown of disbelief creasing her otherwise smooth forehead. "That right, boss?"

"Apparently so. We're checking with the phone company. But at the moment, that's the theory I'm working on."

The detective shrugged. "Sounds a bit too Mafia for this neck of the woods, but OK."

Her male colleague wandered away to watch the CSIs at work. She continued with her questions aimed at Gabriel

"Do you know who'd want Mrs Angell killed?"

"I honestly don't. She used to be a fight arranger in the movies. Did that action film about zombies that won all those awards a few years back. She could have made enemies in that business. Lots of firearms guys hang around the scene, she told me. But I can't see it. Someone losing out on a payday and then coming after her with a rifle. Really?"

"I don't know. You'd be surprised what turns people into killers." She squinted at him. "Or would you?"

He shrugged. "I don't know what turns people into killers. If you mean soldiers, they're not killers." Her eyes widened. "That's not the point of their job. It's part of the job, sometimes, but it's never the point. I've met killers. They have this look in their eyes. Dead, cold, scary. Torturers too, and executioners. *They're* killers. They enjoy it. You can tell. But whether they were born to like it, got changed somehow or just learned to like it, I couldn't tell you."

"Let's leave the philosophy for another day, then. Because—"

She didn't get to finish her thought because one of the CSIs shouted across.

"Ma'am? We've got something."

Gabriel and the three detectives ran towards the spot where the CSI was kneeling under the oak tree.

"Whoa!" she shouted, both palms out. "Stop there. I'll come to you."

She stood and, as if walking on coals, placed her feet delicately, one in front of the other, as she stepped her way from the trunk to where the small party of investigators was standing.

She held her right hand out.

On the palm of her turquoise nitrile glove lay a brass cartridge case.

With the index finger of her other hand, she pushed it so that it rolled over.

A collective gasp.

Someone murmured, "Fuck me!"

The yellow metal of the cartridge was not completely smooth. It was engraved in a tiny, but completely legible, copperplate hand. Anita read it out.

"Fury is coming for you. SB." She looked up at Gabriel. "Kiss, kiss."

"Who's SB?" Lindsey asked.

"Sasha Beck," Anita said, cutting across Gabriel, who closed his mouth so that his back teeth came together with a *click*. "She's the assassin, the pro he's been telling us about." She turned to Gabriel. "Right, it looks like you had it down from the beginning. I'd like you to go down to the station with Lindsey and Ben. Tell them everything you know about this Beck woman."

"I can't. I need to get after her. She won't be hanging around. She'll be on a plane to Tokyo or Berlin or Marrakesh. You have to let me go. There's nothing to tell, anyway. She's a hit woman. If she left the brass it's because she felt like it. You won't get fingerprints."

Anita's voice hardened. She took a half-step closer to Gabriel and poked a stiff index finger into his chest.

"You'll go to the station."

A beat.

"You'll be interviewed."

A beat.

"If, as you claim, you know the murderer, then that puts you in an interesting position."

A beat.

"And if you think I'm going to let our only decent lead go swanning off to Morocco on a one-man vigilante mission, you've got another think coming. Understand?"

Gabriel nodded, sensing that her next move would be to arrest him.

"Can we make it quick, please?" he asked.

25

SUSPICIONS

At the police station, the detectives took Gabriel to a room furnished with two bright-green sofas at right angles to each other. A wooden coffee table sat between them. The walls were blank, and painted in a complementary shade of green to the sofas: darker but not oppressively so.

"Can I get you a coffee, Gabriel?" Lindsey asked. "Ben, want one?"

"Magic! And a biccie, if there are any left."

She snorted. "Fat chance! That tin'll be empty bar a few crumbs. So, coffee?"

Gabriel answered. "Yes, please. Milk, no sugar."

While she was gone, Gabriel turned to her colleague. He was young. Younger than Gabriel, at any rate. Maybe late twenties. Smooth cheeks, not much stubble. Curly brown hair cut short so he didn't look like a hippie.

"What line of work are you in, Gabriel?" he asked now. Conversational tone of voice. No notebook or tape recorder.

"Security contracting." Catching a fleeting frown on the detective's face, and realising he'd been abrupt, Gabriel immediately tried again. "Which sounds very gung ho and paramilitary, I know. But it just means I help people who need advice."

"On what?"

"On, uh, well, on security." He didn't want to reveal that his work had involved killing foreign politicians, going undercover, fighting his way into – and out of – the territory of hostile gangs of terrorists, infiltrating cults and all manner of extremely *gung ho* activities. "You know, corporate stuff, mostly. Foreign executives who feel a bit jittery in a country where only the bad guys are allowed to carry guns."

"Pays well, does it?"

Gabriel shrugged. "Better than the army did, that's for sure." He aimed for a rueful tone of voice that might distract the detective, but was beginning to think he might have underestimated him.

"Probably better than what we get, I'd imagine."

"I don't know. I get fallow periods when I'm not making anything. No pension, either."

Ben frowned. "No, I suppose not. But you make enough to afford a Maserati, don't you? The boss told us about your motor."

"I bought it when my parents died. From my inheritance."

At last he seemed to have gained the upper hand, at least for the moment. The detective looked down, blushing. When he raised his eyes, he looked directly at Gabriel.

"Sorry. For your loss. Which is what they teach us to say, by the way, but I mean it. My parents are both still alive, thank God. I didn't mean to get in your face. Truth is, this is my first murder. I mean, we get the odd wounding or scrap that gets out of hand in one of the garrison towns around here, but nothing like this."

Gabriel was about to comment when Lindsey reappeared with a tray bearing three blue-and-white striped mugs of steaming coffee that clinked together as she put the tray down. All three took cautious sips. The coffee was revolting. Gabriel blew across the surface and drank again before setting his mug down on the coffee table.

"What do you want me to tell you?"

Lindsey spoke first.

"Can we start with the victim? I mean, Mrs Angell. How did you know each other?"

"We met each other walking our dogs. You know how it is. You strike up a conversation about your dogs, or the weather or something, and then you meet again, and a friendship starts up. That's how it was with me and Julia. I found out she was a fight arranger and we had some things in common because of that, so——"

"In common like what?" Ben asked.

"Unarmed combat. Martial arts. Weapons training."

"Because you were a soldier, right?"

"Right. And because I was brought up in Hong Kong by a man who taught me karate."

"You're good with weapons, I'd imagine," Ben said. "Being in the SAS and that."

Gabriel frowned. "Have you been checking my background?"

Ben shook his head. "No. Must've been someone in the pub yesterday."

Gabriel knew that was a lie. He'd never told anyone about his service in the Regiment. Even Julia. He wasn't ashamed of it. The reverse was true. But there were enough people bragging about being ex-Special Forces who'd never been anywhere near a regular army base, let alone one housing the SAS. A small group of SAS veterans had even formed an unofficial team to visit men claiming they'd served in the Regiment. Gabriel had been invited to join it but had declined. "The Walter Mitty Unit" they called themselves. If someone was posting on social media about their time in the SAS, a couple of the lads would find him, and turn up on his doorstep. Suggest they come in for a brew and a chinwag about the old days. They'd ask the guy a few simple questions, "Who was your boss at the time?" "Where did you operate?" "Did you know X or Y?" "Wasn't it a blast when we hit that terrorist cell in Somalia in '97?" If he couldn't answer correctly, or tried to bluster, they'd put the hard word on him. Maybe give him the impression that continuing with his fantasising could prove injurious to his health. It always did the trick.

"Yes," Gabriel said, bringing himself back to the present. "I am good with weapons. Most soldiers are. It goes with the territory."

"Ever do any marksmanship training? Competitive shooting for the army? Stuff like that?"

"What the fuck is this?" Gabriel said, turning around and leaning towards the young detective, taking pleasure in seeing him flinch and draw back involuntarily.

"What the fuck is what, Gabriel?" Lindsey said calmly, smiling.

"Asking me about sniper training. Surely you don't think I had anything to do with Julia's murder, do you? I was driving down from London when it happened. I couldn't have done it. I mean, anyway, why would I? We were friends, I just told you." He could feel himself heating up inside his shirt and jumper and a smell of sweat gusted up from his chest.

"How do you know when it happened?" she asked. "We don't have a time of death, yet, and we certainly haven't released any details to the media, though God knows they want us to."

"I was driving through the village yesterday afternoon. I saw the tent on the field and the cars with the blue lights. It must have happened before I arrived."

Suddenly he saw the situation from their perspective. *He* knew he was streaking along the old Roman road between London and Salisbury at well over a hundred miles an hour when Sasha was gunning down Julia. But he couldn't prove it. Julia had been killed by a high-calibre rifle round. He'd claimed he knew the killer and then suggested to their boss it was an international assassin, like something out of a James Bond movie. He'd also just admitted he was good with firearms.

Lindsey spoke next.

"Let me ask you something, Gabriel. Do you know the first thing they teach us about solving murders?"

Gabriel shrugged. Bit back a suggestion that it might involve going after clearly identified suspects. "Surprise me."

"Ninety-nine times out of a hundred it's either a spouse or a lover. I know on the telly it's drug gangs and turf wars and all that shit, but out here? In the real world? It's people fucking people they shouldn't. The loyal wife gets wind of hubby's affair and bam! Or little miss bit-on-the-side runs out of patience and offs the missus to give herself a clear run." She sat up straighter in the chair and asked her next question with a soft, inviting tone of voice. "Were you and Mrs Angell having an affair, Gabriel?"

He reared back.

"What? No! Of course we weren't."

Lindsey persisted, asking more questions in that calm, quiet, unsettling voice.

"Why 'of course'? She was an attractive woman by all accounts. Husband sounds a bit boring. You're a man of action. I'm not judging you. It's just human nature. Maybe those dog walks turned into something else?"

Gabriel laughed. The suggestion was so ridiculous. He'd barely had enough time to sleep with Britta, let alone conduct an affair.

"OK, you know what? I'd be within my rights to walk out of here right now, or get a solicitor. I'm sure your boss didn't authorise this line of questioning and frankly, you're wasting time you should be spending chasing the only solid lead you've got. The one *I* gave you. And before you say anything, it wasn't to throw suspicion off me, it's the truth. You're looking for, but you won't find, an assassin named Sasha Beck."

26

MEANS, MOTIVE AND OPPORTUNITY

Lindsey placed a calming hand on his shoulder.

"Look, let's not get ahead of ourselves. We're just looking at all the angles. You can see that, can't you, Gabriel? You're not under caution; this is just a chat about your friend and what you know. I accept what you said about Mrs Angell. How about we move on to this Sasha Beck woman? Who is she and how do you know her?"

Gabriel paused for a moment. He knew that the police regarded witnesses who didn't answer straight away as possibly preparing a lie, but he also knew he had to be extremely careful. His work for The Department placed him under obligations of discretion that made signing the Official Secrets Act – which he had also done – look like writing an IOU for a five-quid poker debt.

"Sasha Beck is a hit woman. An assassin. I met her in Hong Kong when I was visiting a friend."

Ben smiled, shaking his head. "Sorry, Gabriel, if I can just back up a bit. How did you know she was a hit woman? I mean, it's not exactly the sort of thing someone admits to in casual conversation, is it? 'Hi, I'm Gabriel, I'm in security contracting, what do you do?' 'Hi, I'm Sasha, I'm an assassin.' Or is that how things are done in your world?"

"I know what she does because she had a contract on me."

"So, what, she's an assassin but not a very good one, is that what you're telling us? A trainee? Given that she obviously failed." Ben looked at Lindsey, presumably hoping for a laugh at his wit. But she was stone-faced, scrutinising Gabriel as he negotiated the line of questioning.

"No," Gabriel said, trying to hold in his mounting anger and disbelief that they were treating him as the prime suspect. "She is very accomplished at what she does. But so am I. I managed to throw her off."

By hitting her with a date-rape drug given to me by a Triad boss, and then hypnotising her.

"Can you think of anyone who would want Mrs Angell dead?" Lindsey asked him then.

At last! They were starting to act like proper detectives.

"No, is the short answer. Like I said to Anita," he hoped using their boss's Christian name might give him some sort of advantage, "she may have had professional rivals, but I can't see that being a motive for murder, can you?"

"You'd be surprised," Lindsey said, straight faced. "I'll be discussing every possibility with Detective Superintendent Woods later today."

Gabriel made a mental note to stop name-dropping.

"She was happily married. Tons of friends in the village. She had a good income, a bit unpredictable, like mine, but she was doing OK."

"How about Mr Angell? Anything you know about him that would ring an alarm bell? Even a tiny one?" she asked.

"Mike? Hardly. He's a teacher. History. Active in the local church. Volunteers for a local charity driving old people into town to do their shopping."

"A pillar of the community, is that what you're saying?" Ben asked.

Resisting the urge to shout, Gabriel contented himself with clasping his hands together between his knees and breathing in, then out, slowly before answering, using the pause to slow his heart rate a little. He was developing a strong urge to hit the young detective somewhere it would hurt.

"I'm saying that Mike's one of the good guys. You should be looking elsewhere."

"Fine," Lindsey said. "Let's look at the casing. What did it say, Ben?"

Ben pulled out a notebook and made a show of flipping the pages over until he came to the one he wanted. He cleared his throat and recited the message as if he were a schoolboy competing for a public speaking prize.

"Fury is coming for you. SB." He paused and looked at Gabriel. "Kiss, kiss."

Lindsey looked up at the grey ceiling, then frowned back at Gabriel, her lips pulled to one side in a sceptical expression.

"You said Mrs Angell had no enemies. Nor does her husband. And, to be honest, even if she did have people who wanted to get to her somehow, round here the usual approach is to feed poisoned meat to the dog, or torch somebody's car, not hire an assassin. I mean, that's a bit over the top, isn't it, Ben?"

"Last year, this bloke got caught sleeping with his best mate's wife. By the best mate. He went down to town – the best mate, I mean – bought a baseball bat from that sports shop on Catherine Street, drove to the other bloke's house and did a number on his motor. Beautiful BMW M3 in Dakar Yellow. The insurance company wrote it off. He'd done every single body panel, every window, all the lights, and finished it off by slashing the tyres, levering the filler cap off with a screwdriver, and pouring a bag of sugar into the petrol tank."

"Classic," Lindsey said. "So, Gabriel, if she had nobody who'd want to kill her, the question is, why is she dead? You see," she said, holding up a hand as Gabriel opened his mouth to speak, "that shell casing bothers me."

"Bothers you how? I told you what it means."

"No. You told me who it's from. The question is, who's it *to*?"

"Isn't that obvious?"

"*Is* it obvious? Not to me."

"Sasha was talking to me. It can't have been Julia, can it? She means Fury is coming for me."

"Hold on," Lindsey said. "It's not got your name on it, has it? It could have been meant for her husband. Or her film company, or the leader of the parish council for all we know."

Gabriel sighed, and rubbed his fingertips hard against his scalp. He started counting points off on his fingers.

"One, I'm the only person in this village, probably in this whole county, who knows her. Sasha, I mean. Two, the kisses. I think, I don't know how to put this, but she's—"

Ben interrupted, "Wait. Are you telling us she fancies you? This international assassin has a crush on you?"

Gabriel frowned. "I know it sounds off, but yes. Basically, that is what I think."

"And three?" Lindsey asked.

"What do you mean, 'three'?"

"You were counting off points. Nobody does just two. There's always three."

"Oh, I don't know. It's just, I can tell. Trouble like this has a habit of following me around."

Like when I got tricked into murdering a Zimbabwean politician in the not-too-distant past.

Lindsey got out her notebook. "I want a list of your friends in the village. Apart from the Angells. Work colleagues, too. Family. Anyone who might be at risk from this Sasha character." Her hand hovered above the blank page. Gabriel said nothing. She looked up at him. "Well?"

"There isn't anyone."

"No one at all? Football mates? Ex-army buddies. Parents? Siblings? Come on, Gabriel, there must be someone you kick back with?"

Gabriel suddenly became very still. Cold inside, as if he'd woken after a night sleeping rough.

"Britta! Oh, shit!"

"Who's Britta?" Lindsey asked, making a note.

"She's my girlfr—, she's my fiancée." A frown flitted across

Lindsey's face, a blade of cloud across the sun: blink and you'd miss it. Gabriel didn't miss it. "It's recent. I wasn't thinking clearly."

"Surname?"

"Falskog. She's Swedish," he added.

Lindsey looked up at Gabriel from her notebook. He couldn't read her expression. A half-smile cut with, what? Cynicism?

"Congratulations. Place of work?" An urgent note had crept into Lindsey voice and her manner had become all business.

"She moves around. It's government stuff. There isn't really an office. Not as such."

Lindsey put her pen down and looked at Gabriel. She turned to Ben.

"Do us a favour, Ben. Get another round of coffees in."

He drew in a sharp breath but obviously decided not to say anything.

With Ben gone, Lindsey faced Gabriel head on. She made a show of closing her notebook and putting it beside her on the sofa.

"Listen, Gabriel. Here's a picture I'm getting in my mind. You're ex-SAS. Now you work as a private *security consultant*. You're on first-name terms with a woman who you claim, and the evidence seems to back you up, is an assassin of some kind. Clearly a woman with a pretty sick sense of humour, and a shitload of self-confidence, if she can spare the time after killing an innocent civilian to engrave a little message to you on a shell casing, then leave it behind. You forget you just got engaged, and when you do remember, all you'll tell me is your fiancée does *government work*. Let me ask you something. Do I look like an idiot?"

"No. You look like an intelligent woman doing a difficult job under very trying circumstances."

"Thanks for the compliment, which I choose to take at face value. In which case, let me ask you another question. One to which I hope you will respect me enough to give a straight answer. Does she work for—"

Gabriel made a decision.

"MI5."

"Pardon?"

"Britta works for MI5. She was on secondment from Swedish Special Forces, but they made the arrangement permanent. I don't exactly know where she is at the moment. London is all I know. I can't say what she's doing, but she's tough and she's trained."

"I want to get a message to her. We need to let her know that her life may be in danger. If Beck is sending you a message by killing your only friend down here, then she might go after Britta next."

"But why not go after her first? What would be the point of killing Julia when she knows about Britta?"

Lindsey spread her hands wide.

"Maybe she doesn't know about Britta."

Released from his interview with the detectives, Gabriel was driven home by a WPC in a marked car. It was impossible not to feel that he had committed a crime. He stared out through the side window seeing the city as a prisoner, rather than a concerned citizen trying to "help the police with their enquiries." God, how different that sounded when you were the one being prodded and probed with innocent-sounding questions that suddenly turned into an interrogation about your military training.

As soon as he reached the sanctuary of his cottage, he called Britta. He sat on one of the kitchen chairs while he waited for Britta to answer.

"Come on, come on," he said, willing her to pick up.

He stood again, and paced round the small room. Finally the ringing tone stopped and Britta's voice came on the line.

"Hi, how are you?"

"Hi, darling, it's me I—"

"Got you! This is Britta's voicemail. Leave a message."

"Sasha Beck's in the UK. She killed Julia. I don't know why. You have to be careful. Call me, OK? Call me."

He ended the call, then repeated it as a text.

27

SASHA BECK, BRITTA FALSKOG

LONDON

"Beautiful hair, darling," Sasha muttered. It was eleven in the morning, and she was slumped in the driver's seat of a dirty, dark-grey VW Passat estate, holding the viewfinder of a digital SLR to her eye. Like all her equipment, the camera was the best out there: a very expensive Canon. Through the long lens, the plait at the back of the woman's head glinted in the sun like stripped copper wire. The woman was dressed in tight, faded jeans, a white shirt and a brown leather jacket, loose enough to conceal a pistol in a shoulder or belt holster.

The car was parked between two panel vans, each vying with the Passat for the amount of grime a single vehicle could carry. One advertised the wares of a fruit and vegetable wholesaler – "Harris's Market-Fresh Fruit and Veg" – the other was plain white under the dirt, although the slanting sun revealed the ghost of a Royal Mail logo, presumably from the vehicle's previous life.

The light-industrial estate was sandwiched between the King's

Road and the river in a huge swathe of land untouched by public transport routes, tube stations, or anything that might tempt the casual shopper or tourist away from the boutiques and restaurants of Chelsea's main thoroughfare.

Diagonally across from Sasha, the MI5 agent was sitting at an easel. The paper clipped to the top of the easel fluttered every few seconds as the breeze caught its lower edge. The image taking shape was of the warehouses disappearing to the vanishing point at the end of the long cobbled street that led to the Thames. Every now and then, for show, she'd dip and scribble a brush on one of the circles of watercolour pigment by her right knee then dab it onto the paper. But the painting in front of her didn't change. It had been prepared in an office inside the MI5 headquarters building on Millbank the day before by an intelligence analyst with a sideline in watercolours.

Roughly three hundred yards down from the easel towards the river was a set of black-painted double doors with an inset wicket for pedestrians. The doors exhibited rather more elaborate security than the other premises along the strip, which, for the most part, housed small, light-industrial businesses, or the stock of market traders. These neighbours would have been surprised to learn that the nondescript frontage currently being watched by Britta Falskog concealed the UK headquarters of a people trafficking gang, presided over by an Armenian gangster named Dmitri Torossian.

Sasha put the camera into the passenger footwell, picked up a black ostrich-skin handbag from the seat beside her and opened it. The pistol inside came from her UK armoury. She maintained three separate caches of weapons, in three separate houses: one each in Connecticut, a forest in Bavaria and the north coast of Cornwall. That way, she could complete contracts without the bothersome business of shipping weapons by air.

The pistol was new. A SIG Sauer P938 Extreme Micro-Compact, chambered for 9mm rounds. She'd had it customised, as she did all her pistols, this time switching the black-and-grey, snakeskin pattern Piranha grips for the real thing, in python. A lot of her male counterparts went in for the bigger calibres, .45s and .50s being favourites among the Russians. Although she owned a couple of these hand cannons, for the most part, she tended to prefer weapons that didn't dislocate your wrist every time you fired them. In any case, pistols were only good for close work, in which case a 9mm was perfect, and even a .22, such as the Smith & Wesson 2213 strapped to her right ankle, would get the job done if you stuck it in a person's mouth, or ear, or shoved it tight against their chest. She racked the SIG's slide, then replaced the pistol in the bag.

Sasha got out of the car. She pulled her trouser leg down over her boot, and the ankle holster just above it. Then, tilting her face up to catch the sun, she sauntered down the street towards Britta. Not feeling the need for camouflage, she'd dressed that morning in a canary-yellow trench coat over a silk blouse the colour of blued steel.

At the sound of Sasha's heels clicking on the cobbles, Britta looked round. Sasha watched as the agent's face composed itself into an open, friendly expression. *Very good, darling. Almost perfect, in fact. But I caught that frown. Where's your gun, then? In the art box?*

"You're very talented," Sasha said, looking over Britta's shoulder at the painting.

"Thank you. I like to find these forgotten parts of London. Trees and wildlife are so boring."

"Hobby?"

"Yes, that's right."

A ringtone jangled loudly. A loud bell sound like an old-fashioned desk phone.

Sasha saw the woman's eyes flick down to her art materials box and followed her gaze. Noticed the butt of a Beretta 92FS pistol poking out from the mess of half-squeezed tubes of paint, cleaning cloths and brushes.

"Answer it, please, I'm just a nosy tourist taking up your time."

The woman shook her head. "It's fine. If it's urgent they can call again, can't they?"

Sasha adjusted the bag on her shoulder and leaned closer, breathing in deeply through her nose as she did so.

"I love your perfume. What is it?"

"Excuse me?"

"Your perfume, darling. It's exquisite."

"It's Rossy de Palma. Etat Libre d'Orange."

"Well, I must look out for it next time I'm flying."

She reached into her handbag, enjoying the taut-muscled expression on the other woman's face. Closed her hand round the rectangular object and pulled it clear.

28

CAUSES OF DEATH

Sasha squeezed hard on the side of the gold case, popping it open with a snap. Inside, twenty cigarettes were held in the highly polished interior by two scarlet elastic ribbons. She took one, then offered the case to Britta.

"Want one?" she asked.

"No thank you. They will kill you, you know."

"I very much doubt it," Sasha said, then laughed, and flicked her pony tail back behind her head. She withdrew a vintage, gold Dunhill lighter from her bag and thumbed the knurled wheel set into the long edge to produce a flame. Once she'd lit her cigarette, she blew out a cloud of smoke, away from Britta.

"I don't want to be rude, but I came here to paint," Britta said. "So, if you don't mind …"

"Oh, God, I'm sorry. Here you are, indulging your," she paused, "hobby, and I'm rabbiting away, distracting you." She made to move away, then turned, as she heard a buzz from the phone in the art box. "Oh, one thing though, darling."

"What's that?"

"You'll do much better if you use a brush that actually matches the strokes on the paper. That one's three times too wide."

Then she turned away and strolled back to her car.

She turned on the radio, found a channel playing classical and pulled away.

"There, now," she said to herself, as the orchestra belted out Beethoven's Fifth, "that'll give your poor little boyfriend something to worry about."

* * *

Britta pulled her phone from the art box the moment Sasha walked back to the scruffy grey car. She swiped the screen to call up the alerts: one missed call, one voicemail message, one text, from Gabriel. She tapped the text icon first.

Sasha Beck in UK. She killed Julia. Be careful. Call me.

She played the voicemail next, and heard Gabriel giving her the same information, only with a panicky tone in his voice she'd never heard before. She was about to call him back, when a loud slam from further up the street made her stop. She dropped the phone back into the box and resumed her act, dabbing away at the paper and noticing for herself the mismatch between the brush she was holding and the narrower strokes the intelligence analyst had already made. She switched brushes, not that she thought Torossian would be much of an art critic.

The double doors of Torossian's unit swung back on themselves. A well-built man wearing a black, leather, bomber jacket secured them back against the wall with cabin hooks then beckoned to somebody inside. A white transit van reversed out of the unit and swung round so it was facing Britta. She bent her head to the easel, peering over the top of the frame. Bomber Jacket closed and locked the doors, climbed into the passenger seat of the van and slammed the door shut. The van roared up the street towards Britta, moving out just enough to avoid sending her into the wall of the unit beside her, though the slipstream almost pulled the painting free of its clips.

"Sorry, Gabriel. I'll be as careful as I can, but I have work to do, too," she said, before making a call on another phone and then strolling down towards the unit with the black doors.

* * *

Back at her hotel, Sasha called her client. Noon, UK time.

"It's Sasha, darling," she drawled as soon as Erin Ayers picked up.

"With good news, I hope. It's a bit bloody early for chit chat."

"Yes, thanks, I'm well. You?"

A sigh at the other end of the line, which crackled with transatlantic static.

"Fine, thank you, Sasha."

"Good. Me, too. And yes, I have good news. You can put a line through item one."

"And my message?"

Sasha smiled as she thought of the clever way she'd chosen to deliver it.

"Signed, sealed, delivered, as Stevie Wonder said."

"Thank you. Keep me posted."

"I will darling. Ciao, ciao."

* * *

Gabriel hadn't even put his phone down when it rang. The sound, loud in the quiet kitchen, made him jump, which was odd. Jumping at loud noises was not something Gabriel Wolfe normally did.

He'd squatted behind dusty mud-brick walls in Afghan villages while insurgents sent RPGs in from the surrounding hills. Didn't jump.

He'd been woken at three forty-five in the morning at Sandhurst by a regimental sergeant major banging two saucepans together six inches above his head. Didn't jump.

153

Wearing a traditional goatherd's outfit in a market in Kosovo, he'd been chatting to a couple of local militiamen when a car bomb had gone off in the corner of the square. Didn't jump.

There'd been a special screening of *The Exorcist* at a camp in the middle of the jungle in Borneo. While the rest of his troop were twitching, jumping, and in one case – which earned its owner months of pisstaking and a new nickname – screaming, Captain Wolfe had remained calm. He'd been too busy analysing the images on the gently undulating screen and trying to figure out the exact movements of the young actress that were causing all the trouble.

But he was jumpy now.

"Who is this?" he said, breathing shallowly.

"It's me, Old Sport," Don Webster said. "Would have thought you'd have the old puss winking at you from the screen, no?"

"Oh, sorry, Don. I do, but I'm a bit distracted right now."

"Yes. And I know why."

"What? How?"

"Well, you didn't think this black-ops stuff was just about dressing up in combat gear and rushing around shooting bad guys, did you? I'll let you in on a little secret. There's a standing order, been in place for donkeys' years. Anything iffy happens within a ten-mile radius of one of our operatives' homes or places of business and the Director – that's yours truly for now, as you know – gets a call."

"You heard about Julia, then?"

"Yes, I did. And first of all, I'm genuinely sorry for your loss, Old Sport. It can be a lonely life, notwithstanding your newfound relationship with Milady Falskog, and one needs all the friends one can get."

"It was Sasha Beck. The assassin I told you about in my debrief after the business in Mozambique. Last time I saw her was when I left her hogtied on the floor of a gambling club in HK."

"Yes," Don drawled. "Obviously managed to effect an escape. What can you tell me? I only have the bare bones from our police liaison."

Gabriel filled his boss in on the details of the shooting. The shell casing, the sniper nest, the content and direction of the police interview. When he finished, Don paused before he spoke.

"Mm-hmm." The characteristic sound of the older man's breathing through his nose. "Look, you're a grown up. I know you can take care of yourself. But I'm going to send someone down to give you a bit of support on this one, OK? Just until we can figure out what's going on. And, by the way, if you see Beck you're authorised to use deadly force."

"Chance would be a fine thing. She'll be long gone by now. Probably drinking champagne with some oligarch on a yacht in the Med."

Wishing Gabriel well, Don ended the call.

29

A CAT MAY LOOK AT A QUEEN

MANHATTAN

Erin and Guy were talking. While his boss strutted up and down in front of the picture window, Guy contented himself with the view from his chair on the far side of the table. Trying to time his glances, he looked up from under his lowered brows, taking in the swell of her breasts beneath the white silk blouse. Every time she turned her back to stare down at Central Park, he relaxed, and allowed himself to gaze at her bottom, then slide down her thighs, her calves, her ankles to those beautiful feet, shod in the high heels he fantasised were digging into the flesh of his back

"Why don't you let me help, boss?" he asked her. "It would be twice as quick with two of us working on it."

"Like I said before, Guy, I'm not in a hurry. And I need you here. You're my bodyguard, aren't you? How are you going to guard my body if you're in England?" She smiled at him then and came to sit opposite him, her back to the window

Was she taunting him? She'd positioned herself so the sun

streaming in through the vast expanse of glass silhouetted her figure inside her blouse. He didn't know. He didn't care.

"I just thought, we could get through the early stages quicker so you could have more time with him."

"Yes, well that's very sweet of you, but I don't pay you to think, do I? Now, go and get the car, would you? I fancy a drive upstate."

* * *

In her room in a B&B in England's New Forest, not ten miles from Gabriel's cottage, Sasha Beck was preparing for the next item on her list. With loving care, she unwrapped the explosive .40 rounds from their tissue paper and loaded them into the magazine of her M&P Shield. The rounds were based on an American design: an aluminium tip sealed with lacquer, with a lead azide centre that would explode on impact. Although the originals had been heavily restricted since John Hinckley's failed assassination attempt on Ronald Reagan in 1981, these particular rounds were still in production at the factory owned by Sasha's sometime client, Timur Kamenko.

30

HOT PURSUIT

SALISBURY

The house felt too small, all of a sudden. Gabriel could feel a hard knot of tension balled up in his stomach. Normally he'd go for a run and blow it off that way, or meditate, slowing his breathing and his pulse as he systematically relaxed his mind and his muscles. But he was too on edge even for this.

He grabbed his car keys from a red lacquer dish on the hall table and headed round to the garage. While the plastic roller door creaked and twanged its way upwards, he reflected on the event that had led to his acquisition of the Maserati. Dad, lying in a coma on the deck of his boat. Mum out cold in the cabin, her brain so befuddled with gin that when she woke and discovered her husband's body, she either fell or jumped overboard to drown. Life could be snatched away from you while you weren't looking. He didn't want that to happen to him.

With a decisive *clack*, the door settled into its mount bolted to the ceiling of the brick garage. He was lucky to have a place to keep his car. Most of the houses he could afford when he bought the cottage had nothing but a bit of the road outside the front door. He'd kept looking until the agent had called him about Pear Tree Cottage. Now, the Maserati glowered at him from the dark, the huge radiator grille like the mouth of a shark, ready to scoop him into its maw if he came too close.

He skirted its predatory front end and lowered himself into the driver's seat. This was his favourite moment of any drive. His pulse ticked up a notch further as he inserted the key into the ignition. The red engine-start button seemed to glow under his thumb. With the smell of leather percolating into his brain, he pressed the button. The V8 fired up with an angry growl, then settled down to a smooth if snarly idle. He pulled on the right-hand gear-shift paddle mounted behind the steering wheel to select first and eased the big sports car out onto the drive. Blipping the garage door closer button on the keyring, he signalled right, a habit even though the road was quiet, and pulled away down the narrow lane that led to the edge of the village.

This was a familiar ritual for Gabriel, and he enjoyed trundling along past the post office and village stores at a stately twenty-nine miles per hour. He buzzed the windows down, the better to enjoy the engine note. Ahead, past a row of neat brick and flint cottages, he picked out a small steel circle mounted on a pole. To most people, the diagonal black bar on the white disc indicated that it was permissible to take their speed up to sixty. To Gabriel, it was a challenge. It said, how fast can you go before you have to brake for the traffic lights on the main road away from Salisbury? Today, engine howling, exhausts bellowing, he managed 110. Not his fastest, but his head felt a little blurry after the events of the day. Around the oncoming bend, a set of traffic lights waited. He'd never found them on green, so he took his foot off the throttle and braked hard into the bend, dropping down through the gears and bringing the Maserati to a smooth standstill a couple of feet behind the white line.

Stage one completed.

Stage two, a fast hill-climb.

The lights turned to amber. He kept his foot on the brake.
Green.

He slipped his foot off the brake pedal and floored the throttle. With a protesting squeal from the rear tyres, he slewed the car round in a hard left turn for the hill, controlling the slide and powering out of it with just enough opposite lock on the steering wheel to keep the Maserati's nose pointing roughly dead ahead.

Something flickered in the corner of his eye.

He checked his mirror.

Something low, black and fast was keeping pace with him, fifty or sixty yards behind the Maserati's rear end. The car had the distinctive, wide-mouthed grille of an Aston Martin. He jammed his right foot down on the throttle, revelling in the howling engine note as the engine breathed freer, sucking huge gusts of fuel-air mixture into its eight cylinders.

With a bellow from its twin exhausts, the Aston Martin pulled level.

Gabriel looked out of his window for a second. What he saw almost made him lose control of the car.

Behind the Aston's wheel, turning to grin at him, was Sasha Beck.

She gave him a short wave, then he heard the downshift. With a scream from its exhausts, the black DB9 leapt forward so fast that for a moment, Gabriel had the eerie sensation that his own car had stalled.

"No!" he shouted.

Ahead, she pulled in just in time to avoid a head-on collision with a car transporter, earning a prolonged blast from the driver's air horn, a blast so long that the Doppler shift as it shot past on the other carriageway was audible to Gabriel.

He glanced at the speedometer. One twenty.

Then the white numbers and needle blurred.

His heart rate spiked and a flicker of anxiety ran through his gut.

He shook his head. Looked ahead. Then glanced back.

Pin sharp.

But it was too late. In that split second, the Aston had pulled further ahead of him.

Now the Maserati was barrelling down a hill towards a lane-merge sign. Traffic had backed up.

Ahead, the Aston was braking hard. The red lights seemed unnaturally bright to Gabriel and left trails behind them as he shook his head again.

Gabriel switched his right foot from throttle to brake and dug down hard, pulling back on the left-hand paddle to step the Maserati down through the gears. The transmission protested as he forced each lower gear to accept higher revs than the designers had thought prudent. The car squirmed and wriggled, like a horse resisting a restraining pull on the reins. The rear end of the Aston Martin filled his vision and he began to brace for the impact, buzzing both side windows down in case the doors jammed shut.

31

JUST NOT CRICKET

Gabriel's vision had telescoped down to a sharp circle of focus with the Aston at its centre. Everything else became first a blur, then vanished altogether. Tunnel vision, they called it in training. The disorientating phenomenon where your awareness of anything beyond the aggressor facing you diminished until it was useless to you. The instructors had all manner of clever techniques to widen that circle back out again, so that you had other options besides a head-to-head engagement with the enemy.

But that was just what he wanted right now.

Anti-lock braking system juddering, the Maserati came to a stop a few inches from the back of the Aston. He reached for the door handle, intending to jump out and wrestle Sasha from her car.

Then the traffic cleared the pinch-point in the road, and Sasha squealed away, pulling round a caravan and flooring the throttle. The Aston's six-litre engine roared, and she was gone.

Not caring who, or what, might be coming, Gabriel wrenched the wheel over and overtook the caravan, earning a bleat from the towing car's horn. Sasha was a couple of hundred yards ahead, but his desire to catch her was overwhelming and he gritted his teeth, and ground his foot down to hustle the big GT forwards, down the long, straight road that led to the New Forest.

At the next slip road, a slow, banked, left turn that would take them west, towards the huge empty expanse of moorland and woods, she indicated, dabbed the brakes, and peeled off the main carriageway, scrubbing thirty miles an hour off her speed.

He followed, wrestling with the Maserati's wheel as the big sports car fought against him in its desire to pursue a straight path as dictated by physics, rather than the curving one dictated by his muscles.

Eight tyres screeching, twenty cylinders thrashing, the Aston and the Maserati heeled over, despite their race-bred suspensions, as they flew round the quarter-turn slip road before emerging onto a local road that snaked up towards a series of S-bends and into the forest itself.

Together, the two cars streaked along the sand-coloured road, their engine notes combining in a hellish shriek. In a couple of miles, Gabriel knew, the road would emerge into a flat, empty, largely featureless area of gorse-studded moorland. The threat wouldn't be vehicular traffic, but rather the four-legged kind. Donkeys, horses, cows, pigs, sheep – all manner of semi-domesticated livestock grazed and roamed across the more than two hundred square miles of the forest. Hitting a pheasant at these sorts of speeds would be alarming. The same collision upgraded to an impact with a stationary quadruped weighing perhaps a quarter of a ton would be spectacularly, bloodily, explosively fatal.

Gabriel jammed his right foot down all the way through the soft carpeting under the accelerator pedal to the steel beneath. The engine screamed as the auto box sensed the change in fuel/air flow and dropped two gears. He came up hard behind the rear end of the Aston then pulled out to overtake. He had a vague idea of running Sasha Beck off the road but nothing beyond that.

The cars' engines set up a weird beat in the air between them, a pulsing sound that was almost palpable. Gabriel's ears throbbed uncomfortably under the onslaught.

He edged up on the Aston's front and turned to look over at Sasha.

She lowered her own window. She was still smiling.

The muzzle of the pistol that appeared above the lower edge of the frame was black, but a satin finish where the car's bodywork was glossy. Decent calibre, Gabriel thought, as time started to slow down. A .40 or .45, maybe. He could see the individual lands and grooves of the barrel's rifling. They would put the twist on the bullet she was about to fire at him.

She pointed it straight across the gap between them, then lowered her arm and aimed down towards the front of Gabriel's car.

And fired.

This close, Gabriel could see the flames that spurted like an orange tongue from the pistol's muzzle.

This close, he could smell the burnt propellant ejected across the two-foot gap between the cars.

This close, he could feel the burning particles of smokeless powder that burst into the Maserati's cabin and stung the skin of his face.

His nearside front tyre exploded with a bang almost as deafening as the report of the pistol. As the big coupe shimmied and bucked, time slowed down still further.

The steering wheel shook itself free of his grasp and spun wildly back and forth as the remaining earthbound front tyre bounced and struggled against the competing forces tearing at it from left and right.

Then the rear end lost traction, and as its momentum caused the car to begin a clockwise rotation, the front tyres hit a raised ridge of earth and grass at the side of the road. The nose dug in and the rear lost contact with the ground. Slowly, oh so slowly, the two tonnes of Italian steel, leather, aluminium and plastic climbed skywards, spinning and twisting like a big game fish trying to avoid the gaff.

Inside the cabin, as the cocoon of airbags inflated around him, Gabriel had time to observe the objects floating around him. A pair of Ray-Ban Aviators that had come unclipped from the sun visor. A notebook tucked into the door pocket, and the pen that he'd slipped under the elastic around its cover. A road atlas of the United Kingdom, whose pages flapped lazily as it flew above his head. His pulse was loud in his ears and he could feel the sharp tug of the seatbelt around his stomach. Then he was buffeted into unconsciousness, travelling down, down into a spiralling kaleidoscope of reds, yellows, blues, browns, greys, and black.

But every journey, however colourful, has its end.

The Maserati landed on its nose, seesawed two or three times, then flailed sideways through the bumpy scrub, bursting the driver's and passenger's doors open until it skidded and rolled to a halt, on its roof, in the middle of a cricket pitch someone had created in the centre of a couple of acres of flat grass. Having protected the driver from the worst of the impact, the airbags deflated with loud hisses.

Conscious again, his ears ringing, Gabriel was dimly aware of a black figure approaching the car. She seemed to be floating. Then he realised she was upside down. *No. Wrong. Not her. Me. I'm stuck. I'm fucked. She has a knife.* The figure came closer.

He watched as the silvery blade of the knife entered the cabin and headed for his heart. He closed his eyes. Felt the point searching beneath the seatbelt. Sighed deeply. *Goodbye, Britta. Sorry it had to end this way.*

32

ITEM TWO

Gabriel heard the knife go in over his heart, a rough-edged sound, halfway between a snap and a tear. Then a second, swift slash over his groin. The roof leapt towards his face and dealt him a hard blow to the temple. He landed in a compressed tangle of limbs, his head thrust hard against his chest, almost cutting off his air supply.

Strong hands grabbed him under armpits and dragged him clear.

"Come on, darling," the black figure said. It smelled lovely. Like an angel. "Help a girl out, can't you?"

Somehow, he found the energy to dig his heels into the ground and backpedal, pushing himself from the wrecked sports car as the figure pulled back on his armpits and moved him away, inch by painful inch.

He felt sick. The ringing in his ears changed to a roar. The lights dimmed, then went out altogether.

He opened his eyes. His shins and knees were agony. Groaning, he rolled over and vomited onto the grass. The acidic smell woke him up. His back was pressed against something hard. He twisted, wincing at the pain the movement ignited in his neck. The surface was a shiny black mirror. He could see himself distorted in its complex curves.

A metallic scrape made him look up.

The figure was standing above him. It was pulling a large, stubby cylinder apart. As he watched, the figure's blurry outline sharpened, and its hazy details resolved themselves into a woman's face. Sasha Beck's face. He remembered. The chase. The gun. The impact of the round.

"You," he croaked. "You—"

"Well," she drawled. "I suppose that's better than 'Where am I?' But I had expected a little more imagination from you, darling. Now, I'm sorry about this, but orders is orders."

She turned away from him and placed the fat tube to her shoulder. Widening her stance, she turned side-on to his car.

"What are you doing?" he said, looking up and trying to place the olive-green … *thing* she was pointing at the Maserati.

She cocked her head to one side and laid her cheek against the side of the tube.

Raised it a fraction.

Then did something with her right hand.

A jet of flame whooshed out of the rear of the tube: he felt its heat singeing the top of his head and half fell, half rolled sideways to protect himself.

With a hissing wail, like a large creature bellowing in pain, the projectile left the muzzle, trailing a white plume of smoke.

Two milliseconds later its high-explosive, squash-head payload hit the rear wing of the Maserati, just below the petrol filler cap.

The world turned white.

The *boom* was deafening.

Pieces of red-hot metal and melted plastic rained down over the neatly clipped grass, and a few pattered to earth just yards from Gabriel's outstretched feet.

When he opened his eyes, the Maserati had vanished. All that remained was a blackened, twisted skeleton with four warped brake disc rotors hanging from the axles.

The Aston's engine fired up with a low growl, and he had to roll away to avoid being hit by the rear wheels as Sasha executed a wide, sliding circle around the burning wreck, gouging deep, brown ruts into the pristine turf of the cricket pitch, before pulling away, back onto the road.

A hand slid out from the driver's side window and waved.

Just before putting down her copy of Wuthering Heights, and turning out her bedside light, Sasha sent a text to her client.

Item two completed. Such a shame. SB xx

* * *

Beep. One thousand. *Beep*. One thousand. *Beep*. One thousand.
Pull the ripcord.
Look up to check the canopy.
No, wait.
This isn't a jump.

He opened his eyes. Tried lifting his head. Big mistake. He'd experienced worse, but it wasn't worth comparing different levels of pain this intense. *I guess I'm alive.*

He settled his head back onto the pillows and slept.

"Gabriel?"

He opened his eyes again.

A doctor, deep-brown skin, crinkly hair scraped back and tied at the nape of her neck, stethoscope dangling over the outside of her unbuttoned white coat, was looking down at him.

"Gabriel? I'm Doctor Sendrathan. Do you know where you are?"

"Hospital. Salisbury District, at a guess. That or Southampton."

"Good guess. Southampton, actually. The ICU. That's—"

"Intensive care unit, I know."

She smiled. "You were in bad shape when you arrived here, you know. Concussion, severe bruising to your lower legs and arms, lacerations. But I wonder if you can help me out with something that's been puzzling me."

"Ask away, doc."

"Your car is a burned-out wreck. According to the fire fighters, it looked as though someone had not just torched it but blown it up. And yet you have what I must call, though I am sure they are very painful right now, superficial injuries. You should be dead by rights, may God forgive me."

"Airbags are wonderful things," he said, closing his eyes again. The room smelled of antiseptic and bleach. The bleeping of the heart monitor was getting on his nerves. He wanted to be out of this place, back at home where he could surround himself with his own things, his music, pour a glass of wine, and try to forget what had just happened.

A voice came whispering to him on the wind, floating somewhere high above the electronic bleeps and the distant murmur of conversations from the general ward beyond the screens surrounding his bed.

"A bad thing happened, Gable. A bad lady did it."

He groaned. The doctor bent over him.

"Are you all right, Gabriel?"

Don't worry, it's just my dead brother talking to me. The one I killed.

"I'm fine. But some painkillers would hit the spot about now, if you have any going spare."

"Oh, I'm afraid we can't give you anything right now. You're, what shall we say, maxed out? The nurse will be round in one hour with your medication. Until then. I'm afraid you will just have to grin and bear it."

. . .

They moved Gabriel from the ICU to the men's general ward the following day. Gabriel joined eleven other men, all ages, though mostly older men with grey or white hair, and liver spots on the bony hands resting on the outside of the bedclothes.

That night, sleep took a long time to come. Partly it was the symphony of electronic bleeps and the asthmatic wheezing of the man in the next bed. Partly it was Gabriel's own thoughts that raced each other round the inside of his skull like greyhounds after rabbits.

In the dark, staring up at the ceiling, with a soft glow from the desk at the nurses' station at the far end of the long room, he tried to sort through what he knew.

Sasha Beck was in England. She'd been hired to kill Julia Angell. Apparently to send a message to him.

The message said, "Fury is coming for you."

Then Sasha had lured him – there was no other word – into a high-speed car chase, shot his tyre out, rescued him from the wreck, and finally, blown the Maser into pieces with an RPG.

But why not simply kill him? Why not use the rifle? Or the pistol?

OK, Wolfe, think hard. Who have you pissed off so badly that they'd come for you?

Trouble was, the people who he'd gone up against were all dead. That was the deal with working for The Department. Don's favourite phrase was that they brought the bad guys, "to justice, not into custody." The only person who hadn't met that fate had just saved him from burning to death in his own car.

He rolled his head from side to side, easing the tension. The last set of painkillers were kicking in and he felt the blissful easing of the pain from his legs.

Two days later, he was discharged. He took home with him a white paper bag full of boxes of pills. Antibiotics for an infection that had set in from one of the cuts on his face, and two different types of painkillers: a generic codeine-paracetamol mix – "six a day, don't go over the dosage," Doctor Sendrathan had said – and ibuprofen, "for when the pain dies down a bit."

The front door scuffed over a disordered pile of post, including the usual junk mail and flyers from local business. One envelope caught Gabriel's eye. It was brown, long, slim, and carried only his first name, written in a strong, flowing hand in blue ink. The final curve of the "l" was smudged slightly. *A fountain pen user, then. Old school.*

He made a cup of tea and while the leaves were steeping in the brown china pot, he sat at the kitchen table and opened the letter, slitting it with a paring knife he pulled from a slotted beech block on the work surface. He extracted a single sheet of pale-blue writing paper. More handwriting.

Dear Gabriel.

Don assigned me to keep you company for a few days, just until we can get a handle on what's going on.

I'm staying at the Angel Inn.

Call me when you get this. 07700 900713.

Best wishes,

Eli Schochat

The signature was a bold flourish, and smeared lightly along the top edge of the capital *E*. Maybe he's a lefty, Gabriel thought. But then why make life difficult and use a fountain pen? He shrugged. He had bigger problems than puzzling out Department operatives' penmanship.

He checked his phone. They'd taken it away from him in the hospital, explaining that patients wouldn't take enough rest when they had their phones with them. Miraculously, neither the screen nor the case were damaged.

He opened a text from Britta.

Think I met Ms Beck. Very odd woman. I'm fine. How are you? X

Yes, how *am* I? He took a while to compose a message that would keep Britta on high alert without worrying her unduly.

Good. Had a run in with her. I'm fine, too. Can you talk?

Britta must have been holding her phone. The reply was instantaneous.

Run in? Don't hide stuff from me, Wolfe. Can't talk.

OK, he tapped out. She blew up my car, but pulled me clear. Cuts and bruises but I really am OK. Just be safe, yes?

Another buzz.

Sorry about your car. You can get another one. Something sensible. JOKE!! You be safe too, ja? Love you, gotta go. xx

. . .

Gabriel had read in a Sunday paper that the text most commonly sent by men was a single letter. He used it now.

K

He called Eli's number. It was answered on the first ring.
"Hello?" A woman's voice.
"Oh. Uh, is Eli there? Please?"

33

ALLIES

Whatever Gabriel had been expecting, it wasn't laughter.

"It's pronounced *Ellie*, not *E-lie*. Don wrong-footed you, I'm afraid. He has that annoying playful streak, doesn't he?"

"Sorry. Yes, you could say that. I'm home now if you want to come round."

"Give me fifteen minutes. I need to pack and check out. Pear Tree Cottage, right?"

Gabriel emptied the teapot and made a fresh brew, with twice the amount of tea.

Fourteen minutes and thirty seconds later, he heard the *scrunch* of feet on the gravel outside the kitchen door. He looked up from the screen of his MacBook.

Beyond the glass was a young woman wearing a dark-green waxed jacket over jeans and hiking boots. Dark, reddish-brown, wavy hair loose around her jawline. Large, grey-green eyes, rimmed with kohl. Tanned skin. Wide, smiling mouth. She waved.

Gabriel stood, went to the door, and admitted his visitor.

"You must be Eli," he said. "Sorry about the mix-up before."

She shook his hand, then held him by shoulders and kissed him twice on the cheeks. She smelled of sandalwood and lemons. Shampoo, he thought. Or shower gel.

"Don't worry about it. I get it a lot. I think Don enjoys it. He sent me to Russia with a minister last month. The poor guy couldn't keep his eyes off me."

She was standing with her hands on her hips. Gabriel's gaze slipped involuntarily to her chest and, hurriedly, back up to her eyes.

"Come in," he said, noticing the smile playing at the corners of her mouth, "I've made some tea."

"Excellent," she said, taking off the jacket and arranging it on the back of one of Gabriel's pine kitchen chairs. "I haven't had a brew since breakfast."

"A brew?"

Her eyes widened. "What? That's what you call it, isn't it?"

"Yes. I mean, in the army, we did. But I didn't know the Israelis did, too."

She nodded and switched the smile back to full power, miming applause. "Very good! Was it my looks or my name?"

He shrugged. "Both, I suppose. Your name, how do you say it?"

"Shock-at," she said.

"So, Eli Schochat. A Jewish name. Hebraized. From Reznick, or Schechter?"

"Reznick. The Hebrew word for changing your name to a Hebrew name is *l'avret*. My family came from Poland originally. My grandfather escaped the Holocaust by three months. Took our family to Spain first, then the US, and finally, Palestine. Your scholarship is very impressive, by the way."

"Thank you. I spent some time fighting alongside an IDF unit in the nineties. My partner there, Amit Meron, spent some time teaching me a few words. She was a linguist like me."

She took a sip of the tea. "Mm. Good. How come you ended up working for The Department?"

"I was going to ask you the same question."

She grinned. "But I asked you first."

"I served under Don in the SAS. Then he recruited me a couple of years ago. It seemed natural to go back to taking his orders. Plus I was working in advertising, which was doing my head in."

Eli laughed. "Oh, yeah. They're all, like, 'Buy this cream and have eternal youth.' Such bullshit."

Gabriel felt an instant liking for this woman. No nonsense. No small talk.

"So come on then," he said. "What's your story?"

She leaned back in her chair and laced her fingers together behind her head.

"Started my military service on my eighteenth birthday. Volunteered for combat missions and did three years. Then I applied to the *Mista'arvim*. Your buddy Amit tell you about them?" He shook his head. "Special Forces. Counterterrorism. Finding and killing those bastards knifing Jewish kids on their way to school, or rocketing hospitals. Three years there, then I got a call from a quietly spoken man called Yehudi Na'vretz. He was a deputy chief at Mossad. He asked me if I would like to serve my country at the highest level a soldier could without going into politics. I said yes. He recruited me for *Kidon*."

"Tip of the spear," Gabriel said.

"Exactly. The sharp end. We were dealing with the most-wanted terrorists. I went all over. Iran, Syria, Lebanon, Germany, the Netherlands, Norway, even the US once. Then, after completing my ninth mission for Director Na'vretz, he called me to his office. This was January last year. There was another man with him. That man was Don Webster. He was recruiting for The Department. Which is funny. You know why?"

"Why?"

"Because Mossad translates literally as *The Institute*. So I went from The Institute to The Department. Sounds exciting, doesn't it?"

Gabriel smiled. Smart, dangerous, attractive and with a sense of irony.

"You took the job. Obviously."

"Obviously. And here I am."

"So you're what, twenty-six? Twenty-seven?"

"Twenty-six. You?"

"Born in 1980. So a bit older than you."

She laughed. "Fuck! You're an old man. No wonder Don thought you needed somebody to look after you! On that subject, I brought some stuff with me. It's in the boot of my car. I'm parked up the street. OK to bring it in?"

Gabriel nodded, then watched as she spun round and left at a quick march, her boots loud on the shingle outside the door.

Five minutes later, he heard her car pull in off the road and park next to his garage. His garage that he wouldn't be needing anytime soon except for storing garden tools. Well, he could always find some time to try out a few new cars. This, *situation*, was more important.

Eli knocked twice on the window and beckoned him outside. He joined her at the back of her car, a metallic charcoal Audi RS6 estate.

"Nice," he said.

"He is, isn't he? Four-point-two V8, twin turbo. Goes like stink."

"He?" Gabriel asked, smiling. In his mind, cars were always female. Sexist, he supposed.

"Naturally. He's called Moshe."

"After Moshe Dayan, right? Defence Minister in the Six-Day War."

"Yes, very good. He's a hero of mine. So what do you call your car?" she asked, pointing at the garage.

"I did call her Kali, after the Indian goddess. Very fierce. But she's history now, I'm afraid. What's left is in an evidence garage somewhere, being inspected by explosives experts from the police."

"What happened?" Eli said, her hand resting on the tailgate but not opening it.

"The woman who shot my friend, her name is Sasha Beck. She shot the tyre out with some sort of explosive pistol round. The car flipped. She pulled me free then blew her to fuck with a man-portable anti-tank weapon."

Eli frowned, creasing thin lines in that smooth, tanned forehead. "Or in this case, woman-portable. OK, so it's good I'm here. Let's see what I've brought you."

She pulled the tailgate open. As it reached the top of its travel, Gabriel peered inside the cavernous load space. The rear seats were folded forwards and the floor was taken up with several olive-green canvas bundles.

"If those are what I think they are, let's get them inside first. The police have been showing a lot of interest in me since Julia's death, and I'd hate for them to get wind of who I really am."

She smiled. "Ooh, Gabriel Wolfe, the big, bad, black-ops guy living right under their noses. That would make for some interesting canteen gossip, wouldn't it?"

He grinned. "Something like that."

They each grabbed a bundle and took them into the house. A second trip saw all the lumpy packages safely inside and laid on the floor of the kitchen. With the Audi locked, they went back inside.

"Just like Christmas," Gabriel said, squatting to unwrap the canvas from one of the longer bundles.

She cleared her throat loudly. "Christmas? Wrong time of year. Plus I'm a good Jewish girl."

She was smiling as she said this, and her eyes creased at their outer corners.

"Sorry. Hanukkah. Better?"

"Much. Though as it's April, Pesach would be more appropriate. There!" she said, pulling back the flap of canvas on her own bundle just as Gabriel did the same to his.

Lying before them were two Heckler & Koch G36 assault rifles. Each was equipped with a compact torch mounted under the barrel, and a ZF 3 × 4 degree dual optical sight on the ridged Picatinny rail screwed to the top of the receiver. Khaki slings completed the accessories.

They unwrapped the smaller bundles. Gabriel whistled his appreciation. In front of him were two spare 30-round magazines for the G36s, and eight fibreboard cartons of 5.56mm NATO ammunition, fifty rounds to a carton. Altogether, they had over 400 rounds. Eli pointed down at the hoard in front of her. Two semi-automatic pistols and more ammunition, this time 9 x 19mm

Parabellum hollow point rounds. She handed one of the pistols to Gabriel.

"SIG Sauer P226. Your favourite, right? Don was most specific on this point when he sent me down to see the armourer."

"That's right. Don always wanted me to use a Glock, but he never pushed it. We could pretty much choose our own loadouts. Yours is nice, too. What is it?" He knew exactly what it was. Had identified it from his mental database of infantry weapons as soon as it came free of its wrappings, but he felt he'd done enough showing off for one day."

She picked it up and turned it this way and that in her hand before aiming at the ceiling light.

"Jericho 941. AKA Baby Eagle. Israel Weapon Industries. Based on the Czech CZ 75. Very reliable. A real man-stopper."

"Or woman." He couldn't resist the jibe.

"Or woman."

"What's it chambered for?"

"Forty-five ACP. I've got suppressors too, look."

Two stubby black cylinders nestled alongside the boxes of ammunition.

Gabriel pointed at the remaining bundle.

"What's in that one?"

She smiled. "You'll love it."

34

TIPPING OFF THE TRAFFICKER

While Gabriel and Eli were examining their weapons, Sasha Beck was en route to her next destination. Sitting behind the wheel of her Aston Martin as she powered northwest from Salisbury, she made a call.

The voice on the other end was rough, male, with an accent part eastern Mediterranean, part Russian. "Who is this?"

"It doesn't matter, darling. But I'm a friend. There's a woman painting pictures up the road from your little lockup there on Bagleys Lane. She's an MI5 agent, gathering intelligence on your operation. Her name is Britta Falskog. Pick her up for me and keep her safe and there's a quarter of a million pounds in it for you."

"What the fuck is this? Who are you?"

"OK, look. I don't have time for all this. You are Dmitri Torossian. Born in Yerevan in 1971 to Tigran and Milena Torossian. You are currently, and I stress currently, a high-ranking member of *Sev Artsivnery* – the Black Eagles – Armenia's most dangerous criminal organisation. Gor Baghdasar, your boss, is a personal friend of mine and he gave me your details. Now, you have an artist to catch, yes?"

She hung up. Smiled. *Well, Gabriel, darling. That should put the cat among the pigeons.*

* * *

Eli opened the package, spreading the flaps of canvas left and right. Two bayonets lay side by side. Their edges caught the light and glinted wickedly. "Just in case we need to be completely silent."

Gabriel surveyed the materiel Eli had brought with her. He approved. Now at least the odds were evened up in terms of weaponry. Sasha had a long and a short. So did he. Plus, he had a partner, whereas he was certain Sasha would be working alone. He began to imagine a scenario where they'd draw on each other like old-time cowboys in the centre of a western town. Eli interrupted his train of thought.

"I've got more ammunition in the car. Beneath the boot floor. Oh, and these."

She reached up to her jacket and fished out two pieces of plastic from an inside pocket, handing one to Gabriel. They were virtually featureless white rectangles. Just a coat of arms and a phone number. A landline phone number with a +44 for the UK.

Any curious, or startled, police officer apprehending a tooled-up Department operative anywhere in the world would be asked to call the number. On doing so, they would be greeted by a polite receptionist – the phone was staffed around the clock every day of the year – and asked for the name of the operative and their own warrant or ID number. They would be instructed to end the call and wait for a call back. Within five minutes, a member of staff from their own headquarters would call them and, again politely, request that they allow Mr X or Miss Y to continue about their lawful business. They would further be informed that to talk to anyone about what they had seen would be to invite instant dismissal, without pension, and with criminal proceedings. It worked every time.

After they'd stashed the weapons in a locked cupboard under his staircase, Eli announced she was going out for a run. He'd given her his spare room, and she emerged in running gear. Service in the IDF, then Israeli Special Forces and Mossad, not to mention her work for The Department, had honed what was obviously an athletic physique to begin with into a compact, tightly muscled fighting machine. Gabriel had seen all shapes and sizes of soldiers, from giant infanteers who could probably bend an AK-47 into a pretzel, to diminutive commandos who'd cheerfully take enemy fighters apart with their bare hands. Eli fell somewhere between the two. Five seven. Probably no more than nine stone, virtually all of it muscle. She had hips, yes, small, high breasts, and a cute rear end, but woe betide the man – or woman – who made an unauthorised move on her. He had a strong intuition that they'd end up drinking their food through a straw for a few months if they did.

That evening, after Gabriel had cooked lamb chops, slightly pink, French beans dressed in a mustard and caper sauce, and new potatoes, he poured them both another glass of the Barolo they'd been drinking with the food. They took the wine into the sitting room. He put some music on from the hard drive connected to his hi-fi: Oscar Petersen, playing "Night Train." As the lazy, precise playing of the Canadian piano genius filled the room, Gabriel spoke.

"She left me a message. Engraved on the brass she used. 'Fury is coming for you, Wolfe.' And two kisses. I've been trying to figure it out. What do you think it means?"

Eli paused, and took a sip of her wine. He liked that. Too many people were ready with an instant opinion on any subject, an answer to any question, regardless of its complexity. Almost as if they'd just been waiting to be asked. He preferred people who thought first.

"Start at the back. Two kisses. Someone likes you. Who? The client?"

He shook his head. "I don't think so. They've had my best friend killed, and they've destroyed my car. I don't think they're massive fans, to be honest."

"Probably you're right. So the assassin, then. Sasha Beck."

"I think so. I've met her a couple of times before. She's—" He stopped mid-sentence. What *was* she? A psychopath? But they didn't have feelings, did they? Isn't that what all the books said? Or was that some garbage he'd picked up off Wikipedia? "She's weird. She seems to find what she does amusing. Or maybe it's life she finds amusing. I think she, I mean, I don't know why, but she seems to—"

"Fuck me, Gabriel, you are beating around the bush, aren't you? She fancies you, yes?"

"Yes. But that's weird, isn't it?"

"Why? You're a very handsome man. Very sophisticated. You speak languages. You can cook. You know about different cultures." She pressed her open hand to her chest as she said this. "Any woman, even a hit woman, would find you attractive. I know I do."

Her gaze was frank, appraising. He blushed. He supposed if you'd grown up in a country besieged by enemies, and you'd served in one of the world's toughest militaries, coyness probably wasn't high on your list of attributes.

"I'm engaged, Eli. I can't, you know. I mean, you're very attractive, too. Gorgeous, actually. I may have had a tad too much to drink to be as articulate as I'd like, by the way."

She leaned her head back and laughed. It was a full-throated sound of genuine good humour.

"Oh, you poor English boys and your good manners. Don't worry, I'm not going to jump your bones. I was just telling the truth. So Sasha Beck fancies you. Maybe that could work in our favour. Now, the rest of the message. What was it again?"

"'Fury is coming for you, Wolfe,' with a comma after 'you,' by the way."

"Your assassin is a precise woman. Goes with the territory, doesn't it? I noticed all your books are organised alphabetically, fiction on the left, non-fiction on the right. And your kitchen cupboard would have a sergeant major in tears of joy. But it says, *Wolfe*. Not, *Gabriel*. Whoever told her to write that hates you, in my judgement. Sasha Beck herself would use your first name."

"What about the main part? What does it mean? Obviously the client is mad at me, but it's such an odd phrase."

She pulled her phone out. "Let's Google it. Hold on." Her thumbs danced over the screen and moments later she frowned. "Well, that's not much help."

"What does it say?"

"Did you know there's a boxer called Fury?"

Gabriel hitched his shoulders and let them drop. "Vaguely. I don't really follow it."

"All the hits are a threat some other boxer made to him. 'I'm coming for you.' Could this be some boxing fan who's after you?"

"Honestly? I have no idea. But it sounds about as plausible as any of the scenarios I've been able to imagine."

"OK. So I'll search each word in turn, starting at the front."

After a few more seconds, she grimaced. "Fury. It's a war film. And a word that means very angry. I think we could have worked that one out for ourselves. Nope. Bad idea. We need to think laterally. More wine, please."

Gabriel poured two more glasses.

"It could be some kind of literary reference. You know, Shakespeare, or something," he said.

"Yes. Or a code of some kind. Some crazy wants to tie you in knots figuring out their game. You know, a control freak. Someone who likes having power over people. Who do you know who's good at that stuff?"

"What, control-freakery?"

"No, idiot!" she laughed again. "Literary stuff. Cultural symbols, all that shit."

Gabriel thought for a moment. Took a sip of the Barolo. He could feel the beginnings of a headache building behind his eyes. The wine was powerful. Combined with the weak opioids Doctor Sendrathan had prescribed him, it was making his brain feel two sizes too big for his skull.

A memory swam into view.

35

TEMPTATION

A bunch of the lads sitting around under a desert camo net strung across some poles driven home into the sand. Rifles – M16s, because back then, The Regiment preferred them to the British Army's SA80s – leaning against the side of a stripped-out pickup truck. Gabriel had been sitting in a yoga pose, eyes closed, focused on his breathing. Ben "Dusty" Rhodes was playing blues on a harmonica, the soulful, yearning sound of Sonny Terry and Brownie McGhee's "Stranger Blues" floating out over the desert. Damon "Daisy" Cheaney was writing in his journal, an obsessive habit he pursued at every available opportunity. And, because Mickey "Smudge" Smith – God rest his soul – was out of action with a fever, the fourth member of their patrol was a twenty-five-year-old import from The Royal Green Jackets.

Johnny "Sparrow" Hawke was originally from Durham. He'd moved around a lot as a child, as had Gabriel, because his dad was in the Army himself. Sparrow's way of passing the time was to solve crossword puzzles. Not the simple, five-letter-word-meaning-snow-leopard kind either. The full-fat cryptic variety. He'd sit for hours, scratching at his cropped blonde hair, tapping a pencil against his

ANDY MASLEN

front teeth, occasionally snorting with amusement before filling in a
solution.

Gabriel quietened his mind as he inhabited the memory more fully.
What had Sparrow been talking about? How you couldn't hope to
solve the really hard Times crosswords unless you knew your
Shakespeare, your Jacobean dramas, your world religions and their
stories, your classics.

"Take this clue," he'd said, that baking hot morning, fifty Celsius at
least and climbing, despite its only being nine in the morning. "Nine
across. Falstaff's ancient weapon is spoilt, unhappily. Six letters."

Gabriel considered this, his eyes drifting open, as the distant
booms of heavy artillery reminded them that this particular puzzle
had a deadline coming. He slapped at a sand fly buzzing round his
face, scratched his beard and tried hard to imagine what this
nonsense meant.

"Falstaff's from Shakespeare. I get that. And an ancient weapon
could be a blunderbuss or a trebuchet. A javelin."

"Yes," Sparrow said, with a patient smile like a teacher spending
one-to-one time with a particularly stupid child, his blue eyes
dappled with blotches of sunlight coming through the camo netting.
"But it's six letters. You're not approaching it right. It's not a
general knowledge quiz. Look, it's in two parts. Falstaff's ancient is
the first part. Weapon is spoilt unhappily is the second. Do you see
it yet?"

"For fuck's sake, Sparrow just tell him the answer!" This was
Daisy, looking up from his journal.

"Patience, grasshopper," Sparrow said, his Geordie accent
lending a comic angle to the line from the *Kung Fu* TV show.
"Falstaff's 'ancient' was a Shakespearean character called Pistol.
See? Pistol is the weapon."

"So what's the rest all about?" Gabriel asked.

"Come on, boss, surely you can see it? Spoilt unhappily? It's the word spoilt but an anagram. That's what 'unhappily' signifies — it's the setter's code word."

Gabriel nodded, and smiled. "OK. Spoilt is an anagram of pistol. Very good." He checked his watch. "Time to go, boys," he said, standing and reaching for his rifle."

* * *

Gabriel looked at Eli, who has leaning back against the sofa cushions, eyes closed, almost asleep to judge from her breathing. He watched her chest rising and falling for a few seconds, then went to the kitchen and called Don.

"What is it, Old Sport?"

"You remember Johnny Hawke?"

"Sparrow? Yes, of course. I remember you all. What about him?"

"Is he still serving? In the Regiment? Or did he RTU?"

"I don't think he returned to unit. Let me make a call. Might be the morning before I get back to you. That all right?"

"Fine, yes."

"Want to tell me what this is about?"

"I want to talk to him about the message Sasha left for me on the shell casing. See if he can help me figure out what it means."

"Good idea. Always was a clever chap. Speak soon. Goodnight, Gabriel."

"Goodnight, boss."

He returned to the sitting room, went over to Eli and shook her shoulder lightly.

"Huh? Oh, hi. Is it time to go to bed?"

"Yes. But how do you fancy a trip tomorrow?"

"Where to?"

"I'm not sure. It's to meet an old friend."

"Sure. Why not?"

Eli stood and stretched, reaching up towards the ceiling until her shoulder joints cracked. Two little pistol shots. Gabriel looked at her as she held the pose. She was staring directly at him. It was an invitation. Unmistakable. He'd once gone out with an anthropologist. Robyn had specialised in chimpanzees. She told him over dinner once that humans still betrayed their baser instincts by subconsciously adopting primitive behaviours. "Say a woman fancies you," she said. "She lifts her arms up. She's displaying her breasts for you. She can pretend she's just yawning, or stretching and she may even believe that's all she's doing. But inside there's a horny little chimp waiting to jump out."

Eli put her arms down, hooking her thumbs in the waistband of her trousers.

"So, Gabriel Wolfe. Where am I sleeping tonight?"

Not so long ago he would have suggested that, perhaps, she might find his bed more comfortable than the spare. But things had changed. Britta was a part of his life now. The beautiful Israeli was smiling, her grey-green eyes half-closed. Waiting. She closed the gap between them and reached her arms around Gabriel's neck to draw him closer.

He could feel her breasts pressing against him through her thin T-shirt. She stretched up and placed her lips, soft, plump, inviting, against his. He could taste the wine on her. The kiss was long, her breath whispered across his cheek. Then she drew away.

"Well?" she said.

Gabriel thought of Britta. Her pale, freckled skin compared to this woman's tanned, olive complexion. Her coppery hair, bright where Eli's was deep, reddish-brown. He opened his mouth to speak.

36

UNARMED RESISTANCE

Gabriel surprised himself with his answer. "I think that the spare bedroom would be best. You're a beautiful girl, Eli, believe me. But I'm engaged. To a woman I love. I'm sorry."

She pouted, but only for a moment. She put her hand on his cheek.

"She's a lucky girl."

Don called at eight the following morning. Gabriel had been out for a run. Eli was still asleep.

"Got you some good news, Old Sport. Sparrow's still in the Regiment. Better yet, he's leading a war-fighting course at Credenhill. I spoke to the CO to clear it. They're expecting you sometime today."

Gabriel smiled, and felt the band of tension that had been intermittently squeezing his chest over the previous week loosen a fraction.

"Thanks, boss. I'll get going as soon as Eli's ready."

"What's with the 'boss', Old Sport. Don not working for you?"

"It's not that. I don't know, I just feel this is serious. More like battle than a mission."

"Well, whatever works for you. And how is Ms Schochat? Still in bed, you say?"

Gabriel hesitated. "Yes. Eli's fine. Fantastic asset. I think we had a little too much red wine last night, though."

"Asset. Yes, well, I suppose that's one way of describing her. I wouldn't call her that to her face, though."

The call ended. Gabriel made coffee and toast and took it up to Eli's room. He knocked on the door. The voice that answered was breathy.

"Yes. Come in."

He balanced the tray on one upraised knee and twisted the knob with his free hand. He went in.

Eli was doing press-ups. She was wearing pale-grey briefs and a matching vest. She didn't stop while he placed the tray on the top of the chest of drawers beside the window.

"Thanks, Gabriel. You OK?"

"Yes, fine, thanks. How are you?"

"Head's a bit thick. But OK. Look, about last night."

He shook his head. "It's fine, really. There's no need to apologise. I – we – had a bit too much to drink. It's been a fuck of a stressful week for me and—"

She jumped forward and stood to face him. Her nipples were erect beneath the fabric of the T-shirt. Her face was covered in a sheen of sweat. She smelled good.

"What are you talking about? I wasn't going to apologise. I was going to say my timing was off. But it's not just Sasha Beck who fancies you. So, keep that in mind. Now, pour me some coffee, would you? I'm going to have a quick shower."

Gabriel complied. Then, as she turned her back on him and began to pull the vest up and over her head, he left, hurriedly, knocking into a lamp as he went.

. . .

At five past nine, they were on the road, Eli behind the wheel. As soon as they were out of his drive, she floored the throttle. Gabriel was slammed back against the padding of his seat. Eli was an expert driver. She positioned the car on a racing line through each bend, keeping the power on and picking up speed as she entered, then left, the village.

He smiled. "It's a thirty limit here, you know."

"Listen," she said, dropping down into second, and provoking the engine into a roar of climbing revs, "we've got a bootful of firearms and enough ammunition to take out a terrorist base, plus ID cards that put the police back in their box. Do you really think a traffic cop's going to trouble us?"

She turned to look at him as she said this and for the first time in his life, he wanted to be in a car going slower.

"Could you keep your eyes on the road, please?"

"Not nervous, are you? What is it, having a girl drive you? Are you a sexist pig after all, Mr Wolfe?" she asked, reaching across to squeeze his knee.

They reached the end of the village as she asked this, and the Audi surged forward under her right foot's urging, the sound from the gaping twin exhausts a deep bellowing shout, pierced by the whistle of the turbochargers.

"Not at all. But it's bad enough having one woman trying to kill me without doubling it."

It was a limp joke, but she took it in the spirit he'd intended it.

"Fine. Eyes front and centre, *Segen Rishon* Schochat," she barked. "That was my rank, by the way. First Lieutenant. How about you?"

"Captain."

"Never made it higher, then?"

"I wasn't great at strategy. I guess you could say I was more of a tactician than a politician."

The line sounded rehearsed – because it was. The truth was more complicated. After leaving Smudge Smith's mutilated body behind in a bullet-shredded clearing in the Mozambican forest, Captain Gabriel Wolfe MC had resigned his commission. Gabriel had, finally, recovered Smudge's remains and laid him to rest in a cemetery in southeast London, but the past was still the past.

"Me? I liked action. If they'd've let me, I would have stayed a *Samal Rishon*."

"Which was?"

"Staff sergeant. A squad leader."

"That's the trouble with the brass, isn't it? Always promoting people to jobs they don't want to do."

37

REUNION

HEREFORD

According to the signs on the gates at the Special Air Service base outside Hereford, the visitor is approaching RAF Credenhill. In fact, the Royal Air Force maintains no such base. While they waited for the heavily armed guard to check their credentials, Gabriel and Eli sat in silence. He returned five minutes later, still unsmiling. Gabriel recognised the look. It was the standard, "don't fuck with me" expression. Eyelids lowered a fraction, jaw tight, mouth a grim, straight line, muscles in the chest, neck and shoulders taut to increase the wearer's bulk.

"In you go, sir, miss," he said, in a baritone voice that would grace any nearby choir that would have him. As long as they didn't mind frightening small children listening in the front row.

Eli drove smoothly and slowly around the perimeter road and parked outside a low, brick building. As they left the car, a tight squad of eight men, each carrying a fully loaded Bergen that cleared the top of his head by a good foot, ran by, their boots clumping in unison on the tarmac.

Johnny Hawke had called Gabriel en route and told him to come into the main training complex and find him in Room G16. He pressed the entry phone call button to the left of the heavy reinforced steel door and waited.

"Yes, sir?" A brisk, clipped, Yorkshire voice was asking the question.

"Gabriel Wolfe and Eli Schochat to see Captain Johnny Hawke."

"Hold on, please, sir." A ten-second pause. "OK. Push the door, please."

The solenoid rattled in its housing as it held the bolt back, and Gabriel shoved the door hard, disengaging the latch with a *clack*.

Inside, they looked left and right down a corridor. Marching towards them was a short, compact man of maybe thirty. Clean-shaven, black hair cropped very short, bright blue eyes fringed with dark lashes. He was smiling, and Gabriel noticed he had a gold tooth on the right side of his jaw. A flicker of anxiety squirrelled its way into his mind. He was remembering a man called Davis Meeks. A Hells Angels chapter president, Meeks had been an early opponent in Gabriel's new career as a government enforcer. He, too, had favoured dental bling.

The man arrived, smiling broadly now, hand outstretched. Gabriel shook hands.

"Sergeant Major Sam Arkley at your service." Then, "Oh my good Christ! It's Wolfie, isn't it? How are you, sir?"

Gabriel smiled. "I wasn't sure you'd recognise me, Sam. Can I introduce my partner? Sam, this is Eli Schochat, late of Mossad and now working with me in government service."

Gabriel watched as the Yorkshireman performed a lightning-fast body scan on Eli with his eyes before shaking her hand, too.

"Pleased to meet you, Eli."

"You too, Sam."

"Government service, eh?" he said, turning back to Gabriel. "Still sending the Queen's message then, Wolfie?"

Gabriel shrugged. "Something like that."

"Oh, I get it. Top secret, very hush-hush. 'If I told you I'd have to kill you,' eh? I'd like to see you try. I had you on your arse in the mud on more than one occasion, did I not?"

Gabriel laughed. "Only because I let you. Didn't want to embarrass you in front of the other lads, did I?"

Still bantering with Gabriel, and making the odd comment to keep Eli included, Sam led them down the green-carpeted corridor to an office, sparsely furnished with a single, cheap wooden desk and a couple of hard chairs. The only picture on the wall depicted Queen Elizabeth II, aged about forty, Gabriel judged from her youthful appearance and lustrous dark, wavy hair.

"Wait here, please," Sam said. "I'll go and extract Sparrow. That is to say, Johnny. I believe we're teaching them how to kill people with kitchen implements this afternoon."

He winked, then about-turned and left at the double.

Eli turned to Gabriel. "I once killed a Hamas terrorist with a skillet. I was undercover, working in a cafe. Short-order cook. They were using the place as part of an escape route. He came through the kitchen and I beat his brains out with it. What's the most unorthodox weapon you've ever used?"

Gabriel thought back. His had been a thirteen-year period of service, first in the Parachute Regiment and then the SAS. Everyone ran out of ammunition at some point, in some firefight, in some theatre. Everyone found themselves up close and personal at some point in their war-fighting career. It went with the territory. The weekend warriors and the Soldier of Fortune-reading fantasists thought it was all laser-equipped AR-15s and Glocks with high-capacity magazines. But he, and every other soldier since the Tommies squelched their muddy, bloody way through the trenches, had known that sometimes the bullets just ran out and you still had to fight. In the trenches they'd used nail-studded clubs, entrenching tools, lengths of four-by-four timber intended for shoring up the corpse-studded walls. He'd never been a fan of sharing kill stories, never used the easy slang of "slotting" enemy fighters. But faced with Eli's openness and candour, he felt the need to give her something in return.

"I was chasing the enemy down a corridor. Urban environment, loads of civilians about. I didn't have my gun with me, but I'd grabbed the nearest weapon off a wall. It was a Zulu lion spear. Somebody had sawn the shaft down to about four feet, but the blade was about eight inches long, double sided and very sharp. It was pitted with rust, or it may've been old blood. I'm not really sure."

Eli was leaning forward, eyes wide, lips parted slightly. "Then what?"

"I was yelling as I ran after him. He was only a kid, really, probably only twelve or thirteen."

"Doesn't matter. They can still be killers. Look at Vietnam. Look at the Palestinians."

"I know. I'm not sure this kid was, though. He may just have been in the wrong place at the wrong time. He ran into a room off the corridor and went to slam the door just as I drew level. The spear was horizontal, pointing at the door, and as he slammed it, the butt was jammed against the opposite wall. The force drove the tip of the spear, the *kidon*," Eli grinned, "through the door. I heard a scream from the other side. I pulled the spear out and opened the door. He was standing there clutching his stomach. He took his hands away and I thought his guts were going to spill onto the floor, but it turned out all I'd done was carve a crescent-moon gash into the fleshy part of his palm." Gabriel paused, wanting to get his timing right. "Luckily the school nurse was a good seamstress and she put a few stitches into his hand and that was that."

Eli's mouth dropped all the way open. "The what?" Then she punched him on the chest. "Shit! You were at school yourself?"

"Yup. I was thirteen. David Harries was always taunting me, so one day I decided to teach him a lesson."

"But you said you didn't have your gun with you."

"That's right, I didn't. It was at home. A BSA .177 air pistol. I did take it in a few weeks later, though. Pigeons used to roost on the roof of the chapel block and I decided to help the chaplain out by shooting a few. All that happened was I got expelled. After that, I—"

Gabriel's explanation of his tutelage under Master Zhao would have to wait. The door to the office swung open and in walked "Sparrow" Hawke, dressed in black Levis, trainers, black T-shirt and grey marl hoodie.

"Boss! You don't look a day over forty!"

The two men hugged, clapped each other on the back, then stood back from each other. But only for a second. Sparrow turned to Eli. "Captain Johnny Hawke, at your service ma'am." He executed a graceful bow, then took her right hand in his and pressed her knuckles, briefly, to his lips.

"Eli Schochat, at yours," she replied, smiling. Then she turned to Gabriel. "Are they all as good looking as Sparrow here?"

Gabriel smiled, then wondered at the instant pang of jealousy he felt as she praised Sparrow's looks. In truth, he was a very handsome man. The extra years since they'd last met had been good to him. The scruffy blond hair was still all there – no shaved head to disguise a receding hairline for him. The blue eyes still had their piercing stare, though softened by fans of crow's-feet spreading from the outer corners. His gaze had a wariness that hadn't been there when he and Gabriel had served alongside each other. Yes, you had your second sight that allowed you to anticipate ambushes and booby traps before you blundered into them. But Sparrow had acquired that set of the jaw, that permanently watchful look that marks a man of action after a few years. A look those who pushed pens or flew desks never needed.

"Oh, much better," Gabriel said, mustering as much insouciance as he could manage. "We used to call him Quasimodo behind his back."

"Hey, boss," Sparrow said. "There's someone else I brought with me."

Clearly waiting for his cue, a second man rounded the edge of the door and stepped into the room. He was smiling broadly, showing large, even teeth. His face and hands were heavily tanned, and his sandy hair was tipped with almost-white peaks where the sun had bleached it.

"Hello, boss," he said, quietly.

Gabriel looked, just for a second, then smiled. "Hello, Dusty. It's good to see you again."

They embraced, and Gabriel felt a weight lifting from his shoulders. The last time they'd met had been at Smudge's funeral. This time, at least, there was a chance they could avert any more deaths.

The four drove into Hay-on-Wye and found a table in The Old Black Lion, a low-ceilinged pub with a flagstone floor, scrubbed wooden tables, and hunting scenes hanging from the walls between swags of dried hops. Their drinks ordered, and the small talk out of the way, the conversation turned to the reason for Eli and Gabriel's visit.

Their words were masked by the ping and clatter of a nearby fruit machine, and the soft rock music issuing from a ceiling-mounted speaker. Gabriel spoke.

"A friend of mine was murdered five days ago. Killed by a sniper."

"Where?" Dusty asked.

"Salisbury. Our village."

"Shit!" Dusty and Sparrow said in unison. Then Sparrow continued. "A sniper? How do you know? I mean, why call it that when it was probably some farmer or hunter?"

"Because," Gabriel sighed, "I know the shooter. She's an assassin. Freelance. She left her brass behind with a message on it for me."

"Bloody hell. Must have been a short message," Dusty said.

"It was. It said, 'Fury is coming for you, Wolfe.'"

Eli put her pint down. "Don't forget the two kisses," she said.

"The what?" Sparrow asked.

"She put two x's at the end," Gabriel said. "We're working on the theory that she fancies me."

"Fuck off!" This was Dusty. "Only you, boss – and no offence – but only you would think a hired shooter had the hots for you."

Gabriel could feel his cheeks heating up. Nothing like having the piss ripped out of you by your comrades, past or present, to cut you down to size.

"Either way," he said, "that's what she wrote. Carved it in with some sort of pointed tool."

"And that's why we're here," Eli said. "If someone's out to get Gabriel, we need to figure out who. And that message is all we have to go on. Gabriel said you're the top man for solving puzzles, Sparrow. So what do you think?"

Sparrow took a pull on his beer then wiped the froth away with the back of his hand.

"So it said, 'Fury is coming for you, Wolfe.' And," he winked at Eli, "two kisses."

"We looked up *fury* in the dictionary, but it didn't tell us anything beyond the obvious," Gabriel said. "Clearly, someone is pissed off at something I've done, but, I don't know, why go to the trouble of writing it? It's not as if I wouldn't have worked it out for myself."

Sparrow scratched his chin. "It might not be fury as in anger. Or not directly. It might be *a* fury."

"What do you mean *a* fury? Is a fury a thing, then? Not just an emotion?"

38

FALSKOG, OUT

LONDON

The sun was low in the sky, casting a dusty golden light over the cobbled street where Britta sat, still observing the men, vans and, occasionally, young women, arriving and leaving from Torossian's lockup. Out of boredom as much as any genuine desire to be creative, she'd started paying closer attention to the painting in front of her. Each morning, she was given a new, half-finished artwork by an assistant at the MI5 headquarters building before heading over to Chelsea. The doors to the lockup had been closed for twenty minutes, and she was squinting over the top of the easel while simultaneously dabbing a few dots of burnt umber paint onto a sun-kissed wall in her painting.

She leaned back to admire her latest brushstrokes – *Not bad, Falskog, not exactly Jenny Nyström, but not bad.* – when she heard breathing close behind her. She was just about to enter her well-rehearsed routine about being an amateur and wanting peace and quiet when a cold, hard, metal object was pushed, gently but firmly, into the nape of her neck. Freezing, she glanced down at her bag, where the Beretta lay, tantalisingly out of reach.

"Don't even think about it," a deep, phlegmy voice said. "Stand up."

The pistol muzzle was removed from her neck, and she heard the man step back. She stood, keeping her breathing slow and steady, readying herself.

In her peripheral vision, she caught the blur of an arm reaching down towards her art box. One more second, she thought.

As the arm withdrew, carrying with it the black shape of her pistol, she pivoted at the hips, leaning over forwards and at the same time kicking out backwards with the sole of her boot. She connected somewhere in the man's midsection and heard an *ooph* as her foot knocked the wind out of him. Whirling to deal a disabling blow with the edge of her hand, she stopped mid-strike.

Beyond the doubled-over assailant, a second man stood, pistol in hand, aimed at her head. Short, slim, dressed in a beautiful deep-blue silk suit and open-necked white shirt. Designer stubble cloaking a square jaw, brown eyes so dark she couldn't discern the pupils. He smiled, revealing even, white teeth.

"You are Britta Falskog, and I claim my five pounds," he said. Then he gestured down the road towards his unit with the pistol. "Over there. Get going."

She turned and walked away from her easel, wondering how her cover had been blown. *Shit! Sasha Beck.* She noticed a loose cobble in front of her and made a minute adjustment to her path so that she was walking straight towards it. Letting her leading toe catch against the raised lip of stone she stumbled and waited for the second gunman to close the gap between them. It was an instinctive reaction and ninety-nine people out of a hundred would act according to their instincts. Her captor was no exception: she heard his steps change rhythm. Judging her timing perfectly, she spun round, intending to close with him and disarm him. Surprise was always a powerful advantage and most shooters were no good with the pistols they carried.

But Blue Suit had moved back, not forward. He stood there, laughing at her. Then he closed the gap between them and spoke.

"Nice try."

He stepped in again and swung the gun towards her left temple.

39

GODDESS OF THE UNDERWORLD

HEREFORD

"Technically, it's *Furies*, plural," Sparrow said. "Alecto, Tisiphone and Megaera. They were chthonic deities who—"

"Wait," Dusty said. "Kerthonick whats?"

Sparrow smiled. Ever the patient teacher. "*Chthonic* means *beneath*. They were goddesses of the underworld. The Greek name for them is *Erinyes*." He pronounced it *e-rin-iz*. "Picture a hag with bat's wings and snakes for hair."

"Huh. Sounds like my mother-in-law."

Sparrow ignored the second interruption. "Mortals could call on them to avenge crimes committed by children against parents, or the young against the old. The worst punishment they inflicted was tormenting madness. It was reserved for people who had killed a parent. Perhaps whoever hired the shooter sees themselves as a Fury. Out to avenge a crime against authority of some kind."

"But I've always *been* authority," Gabriel said. "At least, I've been the one *acting* on authority. Like you guys. Not committing crimes, going after the ones doing it."

"*We* know that. But this Fury character, he doesn't see it like that. From where he's sitting, he's the innocent victim and, I don't know why, but he sees you as the perpetrator. Is there anyone you can think of who might have that view of you, however warped?" Sparrow added.

Gabriel frowned. "I've been through this. Not to put too fine a point on it, but anyone who I might've pissed off to that degree is dead."

"Maybe it doesn't mean that at all, Sparrow," Dusty said. "Maybe it's just some sick bastard who likes to wind people up."

Gabriel shook his head. "I don't think so, Dusty. I have a feeling this is personal. They also had the assassin do a number on my car."

"Oh fuck! Not the Maserati? Please tell me they didn't fuck up that beautiful motor?"

Gabriel finished his pint. "They did. Royally. Blew it to shit with an RPG."

Dusty put his palm to his eyes. "Jesus!" Then, as if realising the loss of his car might figure lower in Gabriel's mind than that of his friend, he pulled it away again. "Sorry, mate. I mean, your friend was the real crime. It's just—"

Gabriel shook his head and smiled ruefully. "Forget it. It's a fucking nightmare whichever way you look at it. Julia dead. The car. Someone's out to send me the mother of all messages. If I could figure out who, I could start to do something about it."

"Can you tell us who you've been going up against recently?" Sparrow asked. "That might give us some sort of a clue."

"I wish I could. But I can't. Simple as. Sorry. But the Fury thing, that he thinks he's some kind of avenging spirit, that's a start."

Eli spoke. "Hey! Hang on. You keep saying *he*. What if it's a woman?"

"It's not a sexist thing, Eli," Sparrow said. "But you play the percentages, don't you?"

"Maybe you do. But consider what we know already. Fury isn't doing their own dirty work. They're hiring somebody else. Percentages say that makes it more likely to be a woman."

"Not necessarily," Sparrow said. "Could be a white-collar type. Some alpha-male, corporate guy. They'd go down the subcontracting route."

"OK, I'll concede that. But also, the shooter's a woman. Would a corporate silverback hire a woman over a man? But anyway, that's not my point. My point is, you said the Furies were female deities. Despite the snakes and weird animal body parts. I think it's very unlikely that a man, especially a crazy one, would identify with a female character. Much more likely he'd call himself, I don't know, Samson or Beowulf or Spartacus. You know, some righteous dude with a sword and leather underpants."

"Blimey, Sparrow," Dusty said. "Looks like you got yourself a rival for Squadron brainiac."

Eli tucked a loose strand of hair behind her ear. "My mum's a professor of psychology at the University of Tel Aviv. She read the classics to me for my bedtime stories. She'd be pissed off with me for not spotting the Fury link."

"I think you're both right," Gabriel said. "I think Fury is a woman. And I think she sees herself as punishing me for some imagined transgression against the established order of things."

* * *

While Gabriel, Eli, Dusty and Sparrow debated the possible identity of Fury, Sasha Beck lay back in a deep bubble bath at a nearby hotel. The water smelled of rose petals, courtesy of a few drops from a bottle labelled Attar of Roses that stood on the corner of the claw-foot tub. Her phone lay on a cork-topped bench seat by the side of the bath. Next to it was a cut-glass tumbler of gin and tonic, garnished with five, blue-black juniper berries, two slices of lime, and a single kaffir lime leaf.

The phone was set to speaker and as she sipped her drink, she cocked her head towards it, the better to hear the conversation in The Old Black Lion.

Through the bathroom door she could, if she so chose, see her weapon for the contract. It was leaning against the wardrobe, an antique tallboy in dark, smoke-stained wood with a mirror inside the door. The rest of her kit was laid out on the desk between the desk phone and the wooden stand of complimentary stationery emblazoned with the hotel's logo.

The drinkers in the pub were getting up to leave. She heard Gabriel say he was going to think about who might fit the crude profile of Fury they'd concocted.

"Good luck with that, darling," she said to the phone; then she laughed. "You could try for a million years and you wouldn't even come close."

She was probably right to feel superior. After all, she was working for a dead woman.

She drained her drink, straining out the ice and the various bits and pieces of vegetation with her small, neat, front teeth. Her skin was pink from the hot water, and slippery with rose-scented foam.

Over the years, she had assumed a variety of identities for her contracts, but the outfit she'd laid out on the bed for this one had very little to do with the camouflage or the all-black, ninja-style rigs she usually favoured. But given the target, she thought it would work perfectly. She dressed carefully, as always, then checked her weapons.

* * *

At the base, after the thirty-minute stroll back, Gabriel and Eli shook hands with the two SAS men.

"What are you up to now?" Sparrow asked Dusty. "Want to hit the gym?"

"Nah, mate. Going to my room to chill out. I'm working on a new tune."

* * *

Sasha Beck smiled as she listened in to the quartet saying their goodbyes, then switched off the app monitoring Gabriel's phone.

The boiler suit she was wearing was breathable, but still felt hot over her costume. It was a readily available item more often purchased by painters and decorators. She was crouching in a patch of scrub on the northwestern tip of the base, looking up at the ten-foot chain-link fence and its spiral topping of razor wire. As she wasn't planning on going over, but through, the wire was merely interesting rather than challenging.

First, though, she needed to meet her first date of the evening. A man she had not been commissioned to remove, but who stood, literally, between her and her intended target.

He was attached to the military police who patrolled the base. His name was Matt Reynolds, though he was known on base as Baskerville. On meeting him on his rounds, or at the kennels, it wasn't hard to see the origins of his nickname.

In a nondescript blockhouse backing onto the guard house, with a concrete floor and play breeze-block walls, lived his dogs: Molly, Kika, Hengist, and Horsa, who were brothers, Bondi, Sheba, Tiny (who wasn't), and Duke. Apart from Duke, a Doberman pinscher, and Kika, a Rottweiler, the dogs were all German shepherds. They would be unlikely to win prizes at the local dog show, having none of the charm or striking black-and-tan colour schemes of their more domesticated cousins. These were war dogs, pure and simple. They'd all done stints on the battlefield, but had found a permanent home at Credenhill, protecting and serving the men and women who worked there.

Sasha had monitored the dog handler for the previous three nights. She knew which areas of the base he patrolled, and when and where he approached the wire. Tonight, she'd positioned herself where he would come within forty yards of her position.

40

ITEM THREE

Crouching in the shelter of the shrubs and low trees, she slid the long gun from its black nylon case. It was a DanInject IM dart rifle. First things first: she screwed a new 45-gramme CO_2 cartridge into the end of the forestock. Next, she extracted a 1.5 millilitre dart. At the hotel, she'd loaded it with a mixture of one part medetomidine and two parts ketamine. The cocktail of anaesthetic chemicals was tuned to put a big animal out of action in thirty to forty seconds, and keep it unconscious for at least an hour. Unlike surgical anaesthetics, which need to be injected into a vein, Sasha's 'signature mix,' as she thought of it, was more flexible, and would act equally quickly if injected into a muscle. She removed the silicon plug from the tip of the needle, pocketed it, then loaded the dart into the rear of the breech.

She dragged some dead bracken over to the fence, crawled underneath it and waited. The light was fading, but it was still bright enough to see by, and certainly to shoot by.

After fifteen minutes, she heard the dog handler's footsteps crunching over the roadway beyond the wire. She raised the rifle and settled her cheek against its American walnut stock. The manufacturer had thoughtfully positioned the manometer so that it faced the shooter, to the left of the Swift 1.5 – 4.5 x 32mm telescopic sight. She adjusted the pressure to 12 bars, which was perfect for a 40-yard shot according to the manufacturer's pressure tables.

The dog, perhaps sensing the intruder, began barking. A deep, raw-edged sound that erected the hairs on the back of Sasha's neck. It was a primal response that no amount of training could neutralise. And she liked it. Animal responses were often what kept you alive where training might cause you to be overconfident.

"What is it, Kika? Some idiot fancies a trip to A&E, d'you think? Come on, let's check it out."

Sasha sighted on the handler's chest. And waited.

Sixty yards.

Breathe in.

Fifty-five.

Breathe out.

Fifty.

In.

Forty-five.

Out.

Hold.

Fire.

The rifle was, as its makers claimed, virtually silent. The dart left the barrel with a whispery *snap* and travelled the short distance to the handler's chest in less than half a second.

On impact, the dart delivered its payload so swiftly the dog handler had no chance to pull it out before the chemicals were in his pectoral muscle, right over the heart.

"Fuck, what the fucking hell?" he said.

He looked down, and stood completely still, as if the shock of seeing the slim plastic cylinder with its crimson tuft dangling from his jacket was too much to process. The dog was barking furiously and straining at the lead in its efforts to get to the fence.

Sasha calmly reloaded, aimed, and put a second dart into the animal's left flank.

She could tell the handler was trying to call for help. His jaw was working and incoherent groans were issuing from his lips. But it was too late. The knees buckled, sending him sideways and down. The dog was in the way, and he fell over its back, thumping to the ground with the lead tangled around his ankles.

Whining now, the dog staggered a couple of times, pulled off balance by her master's collapse. She licked his face a couple of times and then flopped to the ground, chest heaving.

"No time to waste, darling," Sasha whispered. She pulled a pair of wire cutters from her rucksack and in under a minute had cut an inverted V in the wire. She pushed the triangle of infill flat with her boot and was through seconds after that.

She knew from her research that although a great many support staff worked on the base, few were SAS members, most of whom were on operations or training around the world. She consulted her hand-drawn map and ten minutes later was at the rear of the living quarters where the target had his room. She stood up and unzipped the boiler suit. She left it with her rucksack under a bush, and straightened her jacket. Then she marched around to the front of the building and went in. Nobody saw her. But then, why would they? She'd planned her infiltration for mess hall and had observed that this corner of the base was deserted every evening between 18.00 and 18.45. All except for those soldiers who'd rather practise the harmonica than go to the gym or get some food down them.

She knocked on Sergeant Ben "Dusty" Rhodes's room and entered.

The man was lying on his cot, a silver harmonica to his lips. She'd listened to him earlier, and observed him through high-powered, night-vision-equipped binoculars, ever since Erin had passed on the intel gathered by her trusty lapdog Guy. Rhodes started up, eyes wide. "What the fuck?"

"Ben Rhodes, I am arresting you on suspicion of being the worst fucking harmonica player in the Western Hemisphere, and certainly in the Regiment," she barked, drawing an inflatable truncheon from a plastic holster at her waist.

He was on his feet now. But the sight of a uniformed police

sergeant with a weapons-grade scowl on her face and stocking tops visible under the hem of her mini skirt had temporarily disabled the situational awareness for which members of this particular Special Forces outfit were famed.

"Who the fuck, I mean, why? I'm not, you can't—"

"Oh, but I can. We received a tipoff from Sparrow and Tigger that your playing was criminal, and now you have to take your punishment. Now, hold your hands out, and then I'll show you how we treat repeat offenders."

She pulled a pair of pink, fluffy handcuffs from her belt and held them out in front of her, allowing her deep, black-cherry lips to curve upwards into something halfway between a smile and a pout.

He was shaking his head now, and smiling, even as he held out his hands towards her. "I don't fucking believe this. Did those bastards smuggle you in or something?"

"Amazing what you can fit in a laundry basket, sir," she replied closing the fluff-covered, Metropolitan Police standard-issue handcuffs around his wrists. "Now lie back, please, while I read you your rights."

She pushed him then, lightly, in the centre of his chest, and he willingly subsided back onto his bed.

Switching her phone to speaker, and playing a slinky blues number she'd thought was appropriate, Sasha began unbuttoning her navy uniform jacket. Beneath it she wore a white cotton blouse, which she also removed, revealing a black lace push-up bra. The soldier gasped his admiration. "Very nice. I must play more bad harmonica."

* * *

Sasha feels the usual calm descending on her. It's been like this ever since those two sleazebags in the LA apartment tried to turn her into the star of a snuff movie. Her heart is just idling, really. No adrenaline, despite the presence beyond the four walls of the barracks room of a few dozen support staff.

"Quiet, sir. You'll have your chance to say your piece later. Now," she says, grasping the tab of the silver zip closing her skirt at the side. "You have the right to remain silent. Anything you do not mention," down goes the zip, "which you later rely on in court," she shimmies out of it and kicks it to one side, "may be given in evidence."

She stands before him wearing black lace panties, stockings, suspenders and, incongruously, high, black combat boots. She sees he has an erection swelling the front of his trousers.

Oh, well. At least you'll die happy, she thinks.

She turns away and bends over.

She reaches into the inside breast pocket of her jacket.

She turns back to face him, flicking out the short, lethally sharp blade of her Benchmade Infidel automatic knife. She takes two paces over to him, and plunges the blade up to the hilt in the side of his neck.

His eyes widen in horror. *Is it horror at being caught out?* she wonders. Or just the knowledge that the claret hosing out of his carotid artery means death is just seconds away?

He opens his mouth to scream, and although she knows the most he'll be able to manage is a gurgle, she clamps her palm over his lips and *shushes* him until the thrashing ceases and the corneas lose their shine.

Dressed again, she peers round the door. The corridor is empty, still. A stroke of luck, although with the knife she's pulled from the dead man's neck and the Mini Uzi 9mm machine pistol she's concealed in the back of the jacket, she's not overly concerned about meeting resistance.

She's round the back of the barracks twenty seconds later, pulling the boiler suit into place, sprinting on silent feet back to the fence, stepping around the unconscious forms of the dog handler and his faithful mutt, easing through the chain-link and away.

The klaxons and the alarm bells will be sounding soon, but Sasha doesn't care. She is a non-person in this country. She exists on no databases. She has no fingerprints. She has no documentation any branch of officialdom would recognise or be able to search for. She picks her way back through the woods to her car, pulls the camo netting free, blips the fob to unlock it, stashes her kit, and pulls away onto the long, straight road towards England.

From another hotel, in another part of the country, she sends a text.

Item three, part one, completed. SB xx

41

BANK JOB

SALISBURY

Gabriel received the news about Dusty the next day. It was Don who broke it to him. Gabriel was sitting at the kitchen table drinking coffee and reading the paper. Eli was out running.

"Hello, Old Sport, got a minute?"

"Hi boss, yes, what's up?"

"Things have escalated. She took out Ben Rhodes yesterday evening."

Gabriel put the mug down, slopping half the remaining coffee onto the table.

"What? How? He was on base."

"I know. Troubling doesn't even start to cover it."

"How? I mean, Dusty, was he——"

Knife wound to the neck. He'd have bled out in under a minute. He was in handcuffs, too. Pink fluffy ones."

"Oh, Jesus! This is all on me. And I still have no fucking idea what's going on."

Don's tone hardened. "Right. Thing the first, this is not on you. This is on Sasha Beck and her client. Thing the second, she's now upped the ante to stratospheric levels. I've just got off the phone with Harry Torrance, he's Director, Special Forces. He's, hmm, how can I put this? Incandescent might, just, cover it. Wants this woman terminated with extreme prejudice. He was all for sending the lads undercover. I had to remind him of a few salient points of domestic law before he'd even think of calming down."

"So is The Department going to take it on?"

"Yes. It is. We are. I've spoken to the PM and the Privy Council. They green-lighted the operation at 0745 this morning. I'm putting an intel team on it, see what they can come up with. You're in play, obviously, along with Eli, but I'm putting a second team on it, too. If you, or the Int team, find out Beck's location, or her client's, then we're going in mob-handed. No single-handed heroics, understood? This is nine-to-one or nothing. Harry practically offered to put up a bounty himself."

Gabriel swigged the last of the coffee.

"OK, that's good. That's good. But Dusty. Shit, boss, he didn't need to die. Not for me."

"No, he didn't. Nobody *needs* to die, Gabriel. But sometimes we do. The police are there now, interviewing, looking for evidence. It was an outside job, so the MPs aren't involved. Media are being kept well away, and the lads aren't talking, so we can keep a lid on it for a while yet, I hope. Listen, I think it might be a good idea for you to go away for a few days, or maybe a little longer. No sense making yourself an easy target for Beck. I don't know what her filthy little game is, but it doesn't take a genius to work out that someone's out to fuck your life up, pardon my French."

"OK, I can think of an errand I need to run. It'll keep me busy for a few days, and out of the way, too."

Eli arrived back ten minutes later. After showering and changing into jeans and a white T-shirt, she joined him at the kitchen table.

"I have to go away for a few days," he said. "Switzerland."

"What's there?"

"I need to find a bank. One of those discreet ones."

Eli sucked her lower lip in.

"Do you know how many banks like that there are in Switzerland?"

Gabriel shrugged. "More than five?"

She laughed. "Yes. More than five … hundred. Look, I've seen the expression on your face whenever you have to research anything online. Why don't you at least let me identify a good one for you?"

Over the next twenty minutes, Gabriel outlined what he wanted, and Eli took notes, pausing occasionally to check something on the web.

"Give me an hour or so. You can cook me one of your lovely dinners as payment."

42

DISCRETION IS THE BETTER PART

ZURICH

The city was sweltering in an early spring heat wave. As Gabriel checked into his hotel, the desk clerk informed him, in perfect, unaccented English, that the temperature outside was thirty degrees Celsius. Her name was Gaby, according to the gold badge pinned on her jacket. Tiny enamelled badges pinned below it indicated she spoke Serbian, English, Italian and German.

"You are staying with us for three days, Mr Wolfe?"

She knew this from the monitor in front of her, but this was just part of the standard hotel dialogue. He nodded.

"Yes. I have some business to do, then I plan on some sightseeing."

She handed him his keycard enclosed in a cardboard folder that had the Wi-Fi password written on in biro, smiled a professional smile, then turned to the next guest waiting to check in.

Once inside his room, he unpacked. After arranging his spare clothes, running kit and wash bag, he turned to his briefcase, a battered Hartmann constructed from brass, plywood and the same leather used to make industrial belting. It wasn't particularly pretty to look at, bearing the scuffs and scrapes of many journeys, but it was virtually bombproof and carried a lifetime guarantee.

The catch slid silently to the right, and he pushed the lid back on its brass hinges so that it rested upright. The case contained thirty sheets of paper. These were US bearer bonds, each one to the value of one hundred thousand dollars. In all, three million. They were to have been payment from a corrupt American businessman to Sasha Beck for a contract on Gabriel's life. Things hadn't worked out so well for Beck on that occasion, and even less well for her client. Gabriel had held onto the paper, figuring that it might come in useful to have some untraceable, ultra-portable wealth. He was glad of it now. The bonds were 30 centimetres by 18 centimetres, printed on thick, creamy paper, engraved with a variety of stamps, signatures, presidential portraits and official insignia along with copperplate text promising the bearer that the paper in their hands was all it said it was.

While still in England, he'd made an appointment to see the managing director of a small private bank deep in the heart of Zurich's financial district, which, as far as Gabriel could see, meant Zurich itself. Eli had given him the details, and it seemed completely on brief. Although he hadn't been specific as to the exact nature of the items he wished to deposit, he had alluded to the need for secrecy, and given the total sum involved. The quiet, precise voice at the other end of the line had assured him that he would be delighted to welcome Herr Wolfe personally and discuss what arrangements would be suitable.

Outside the hotel, sweating in his lightweight Prince of Wales check, wool suit, Gabriel flagged down one of the city's cream Mercedes E-class taxis and gave the driver the address.

It took fifteen minutes to reach the street where Händler und Ziegelhaus SA had its offices. The architecture along the route was a strange mixture of classical buildings with ornate decoration, and modern blocks painted in sky-blue and a deep, brick red. Gabriel paid the driver, including a generous tip, and walked up to the front door, which was closed and bore no obvious corporate insignia or branding. It was a solid rectangle of forbidding timber, painted a deep, glossy burgundy. To the left was a polished brass plaque that told the reader it was the bank's headquarters. Standing to the right as he looked at it was a tall, blond-haired man with prominent cheekbones and a gaze that seemed more threatening than welcoming. His cold, grey eyes were shadowed by a top hat in black silk, and his massive frame was clad in a bottle-green frock coat decorated with gold epaulettes and matching triple rings at both wrists. His feet were big, shod in mirror-polished, black shoes, what Gabriel would call Oxfords, though he didn't know the German equivalent.

He looked up at the giant and spoke in English.

"I'm here to see Herr Krieger."

"Name, please?"

"Wolfe."

"Wait, please." The doorman pulled out a phone, turned away from Gabriel and muttered a few words in German. Gabriel caught his own name but that was all. Wordlessly, the giant opened the front door for Gabriel and waved him inside with a white-gloved hand the size of a dinner plate.

Beyond the front door, the building was silent, apart from the ticking of a grandfather clock standing between two doors polished until they resembled toffee. The floor was decorated with black and white tiles set in a chequerboard pattern. The lighting was provided by three gold chandeliers set centrally in the high ceilings of the hallway, which stretched back from the door for at least forty feet.

Gabriel walked down the corridor and had not gone more than a few steps when a slim, blonde woman, appraising eyes in a pale shade of blue, stepped out from a side door and spoke to him in English.

"Mr Wolfe? Welcome to Händler und Ziegelhaus. I am Trudi. Herr Krieger will be with you shortly. Come with me, please."

Gabriel followed the blonde's long legs down the hall. They were clad in sheer tights that whispered as her legs brushed together. She stood at a door and motioned for him to go in. The room was furnished like some sort of nineteenth-century salon. The furniture was dark and polished to the same high gloss as the doors, and upholstered in dark-blue velvet. A low table, inlaid with different-coloured woods to represent swirling leaves, was positioned to the left of the one of the chairs, its shining surface bearing that day's *Financial Times*, *Frankfurter Allgemeiner Zeitung*, *International Herald Tribune*, and *Washington Post*.

"May I offer you a tea or coffee? Or a bottle of water?" she asked, smiling and revealing perfect white teeth.

"Coffee, please. Milk, no sugar. Thank you."

"You're welcome," she said with another smile, then turned and left him alone to wait.

He took a chair and flicked through the first few pages of the *FT*, more for something to do than out of a genuine interest in whatever big companies and their shareholders were doing.

Trudi reappeared at his side after a few minutes, placing a plain white bone china cup and saucer on the table. She was close enough for Gabriel to smell her perfume, a deep, spicy scent, before she straightened and withdrew with, "Herr Krieger won't be long."

She was right. Gabriel was still blowing on the surface of the fine-smelling coffee when he heard footsteps outside the door. He put the cup onto its saucer with a *clink*, stood, and turned to face the door. The elderly man who appeared might as well have had "Swiss Banker" tattooed on his forehead, so closely did he match the stereotype. Krieger was Gabriel's height, but soft where Gabriel was hard, his midriff swelling outwards, his chin pushing lazily over the starched white collar of this shirt. His white hair was brushed back from a high, shining forehead and gold-rimmed, half-moon glasses perched on his nose. Gabriel detected only a single jangling note in the major chord of respectability he emitted. Beginning on the right side of his forehead, just below the hairline, a thin scar cut down across the creases in the tanned skin, bisected the eyebrow, paused over the eye, then restarted on the right cheekbone and continued for a couple of inches. It looked old, and to judge from the smoothness of the skin to each side, had evidently been a clean wound.

"Mr Wolfe," Krieger said with a broad smile. "Welcome, welcome. It is my great pleasure to greet you on behalf of our humble firm. Has Trudi been looking after you?"

"Yes, Herr Krieger, thank you."

The older man smiled again. His voice was warm and low, as a favourite uncle might speak to a nephew.

"Please, you must call me Walti. It is short for Walter."

"Then you must call me Gabriel."

Krieger laughed. "Just so, just so! Gabriel, bring your coffee and your case, and let's go to my office. It is upstairs, and I am afraid we have no elevator here or, how do you say in England, lift?"

"Yes, lift. The Americans say elevator."

"This building has a preservation order on file with the city council. Very old. Very important." He chuckled. "Which means we keep fit, no?"

Gabriel had sat in many offices since leaving the army. He had become something of a connoisseur of the differing styles in which their occupants decorated, furnished and adorned them. From Russian Mafia bosses with acres of white leather and chrome, to corporate tycoons and their shrines to good taste and expensive modern art, he'd seen it all.

Krieger's eyrie, which they had reached after five minutes of steady climbing up a succession of narrow staircases, was different again. The walls were lined with leather-bound books in burgundy, navy, bottle-green and black. All had gold tooling on their spines in a gothic script Gabriel couldn't decipher. Freestanding silver frames in alcoves between the books held photos of Krieger smiling at the camera and shaking hands or simply standing beside similarly bourgeois-looking men with white hair, tailored suits and looks of well-fed self-satisfaction.

When they were sitting facing each other across a mahogany desk inlaid with a wide rectangle of gold-tooled, black leather, Krieger interlaced his soft, white fingers in front of him and spoke.

"So, Gabriel. You said on the phone you wanted to open an account with us, yes? If I may ask, how did you settle on our firm?"

Gabriel nodded. "I researched all the private banks in Zurich. You seemed to offer the sort of discretion I'm looking for."

"You won't find another bank with a finer pedigree, or a lower profile. Our competitors enjoy spending money on corporate branding consultants, and expensive modern headquarters. We prefer to let our reputation speak for us. And you? What line of business do you follow?"

"I'm in defence contracting. Security work."

Krieger nodded once more. He smiled at Gabriel. "One or two of our other clients are in a similar line of work. It is a borderless business, is it not? South Africans, Americans, Chileans, Russians, everyone needs help with," he paused, "security."

"Yes, they do. I wonder whether we could—"

Krieger's eyes widened and he spread his hands as if to say 'What was I thinking of, gossiping when you have money to deposit?'

"Forgive me. I am an old man, and sometimes I underestimate the value of other people's time. We are both men of business. So, let us *get* to business. You have, perhaps, some assets you wish to deposit with us?"

"I do. And I am correct in assuming that your bank is used to handling non-standard financial instruments? Securely?"

Krieger leaned back in his chair and bestowed a complacent smile on Gabriel.

"Gabriel. May I share a little of our history with you? It will not take long, I promise you." He continued without waiting for Gabriel's assent. "Franz Händler and Hans-Rudolf Ziegelhaus established our firm as a finance house for spice merchants in 1685. Our founders had the good fortune to be born with names that reflected their future careers. *Händler* means trader, or dealer. *Ziegelhaus* means brick house. You see? Our field of expertise and the safety of our premises. Since that time, we have supported international, and then global, trade. Over the intervening three centuries, we have developed expertise in each new way of trading, each new way of representing money. From stocks and shares to bonds, derivatives, exchange-traded funds and, what shall we call them," he paused, "unorthodox asset classes."

Gabriel opened his case on his knee and removed a large, brown envelope. He placed the briefcase back on the floor by his left ankle and slid the bearer bonds out from the envelope. He laid them on the desk, just over the centre line. Krieger's territory.

43

DAS HAUS DER TOCHTER

He watched as the Swiss banker reached forward and gathered the stiff sheets of paper into his hands and turned them around to face him. Something caught Gabriel's eye as the banker collected the bonds. As his hairless left wrist extended from the pristine white shirt cuff, the tip of a tattoo, etched in a smudge of dark indigo, flashed briefly at him from its inner surface. Krieger's lips, thin and a pale purplish-pink, moved as he scrutinised the printing. He lifted one of the bonds between his fingertips and brought it to his nose, inhaling deeply, with his eyes shut. Next in Krieger's display of showmanship, he switched on the desk lamp, an art deco construction in chrome and green glass, angled the shade towards him, then held the bond in front of the light.

Finally, he ran a manicured nail over the rear surface of the document while listening to the *scritch* the ridges made.

He laid the bond back on top of its fellows and peered over his half-moon spectacles at Gabriel.

"We will need to have them formally assessed by our technical department, of course, but my banker's intuition tells me you have the genuine article there, Gabriel. If I may ask, how did you come by these? They are a somewhat exotic instrument to be playing nowadays."

Gabriel smiled.

I took them from the corrupt CEO of an American defence contracting company in payment for a failed attempt on my life by an assassin he hired. Then I blew his brains out.

"An inheritance," he said. "My father was a trader, just like Franz Händler."

Krieger nodded, as if this catch-all job description explained everything.

"Just so, just so. Well, we can discuss the details of your facilities with us as soon as we have verified the authenticity of your bonds. Though, as I said, my senses tell me we shall have no problems on that score. Would you be able to return tomorrow? I can have one of our experts available then to assay your bonds."

"Yes, of course. What time?"

"Oh, ten in the morning? We like to keep gentlemen's hours here."

"Fine. Ten it is."

Krieger frowned then, though to Gabriel the expression looked theatrical. "Gabriel, I wonder, are you here in Zurich alone?"

"Yes. It was just a flying visit, literally. Purely business," Gabriel said, replacing the bearer bonds in his briefcase.

"Then, you would be doing me a great honour if you would join me for dinner at my club this evening. It is behind 157 Storchengasse. Meet me there at seven. I think I can guarantee you an entertaining evening."

The club was called Das Haus der Tochter. The name, and the street number, were engraved on the small brass plaque screwed to the stonework to the right of the door. The door itself was open, and Gabriel, as he approached, saw no sign of any security. Or not the physical kind; a CCTV camera monitored the comings and goings of the club's patrons from its mount above the fanlight.

Gabriel still wore the same suit he'd arrived in. But between his meeting at the bank and now, he returned to his hotel to change into his running gear. An hour's run had taken him out of the centre of Zurich and into a large public park where he'd burned off some energy completing laps. Then he'd returned to the hotel for a shower and changed into a fresh shirt.

The lobby was brightly lit by a huge crystal chandelier hanging from a length of chain. Around him, men in evening dress were wandering between what was obviously a bar, and other rooms, chatting in that quiet, amiable way wealthy people often do when they feel most at ease. A few women walked past arm in arm, wearing long gowns and dripping with expensive-looking jewellery. All appeared to be well past sixty, if not seventy. All were white. All glanced at Gabriel as he made his way to the reception desk, then looked away. One man in particular gave him a hard stare as he passed Gabriel's chair. He was fiddling with something pinned to his jacket as he walked away.

Gabriel felt a vague sense of unease. To be wearing a lounge suit instead of a dinner jacket was part of it, and the failure of his host to advise him the club had a dress code irritated him. But something else was bothering him.

All good soldiers had it, to a degree. The indefinable ability to just *know* when something was off. Training was a part of it. Situational awareness was the technical name given to it by the instructors. But in Gabriel, the attribute was honed to a far sharper edge. He didn't know if he'd been born with it, or whether he'd developed it later, maybe under the guidance of his mentor, Master Zhao. But it had kept him, and his men, out of trouble on more than one occasion.

Before he could pin it down, the receptionist behind the tall black granite desk spoke to him, breaking his concentration. She wore a white blouse under a charcoal grey suit, cut to flatter her figure.

"Good evening, sir," she said, in English. "You are Mr Wolfe?"

"Yes. You're clearly expecting me."

She smiled, revealing large, uneven teeth, the canines crossing slightly in front of the incisors. Her hair was a rich, dark brown, and shining in the light from the chandelier.

"Herr Krieger let us know he was entertaining a guest from England this evening."

Gabriel fingered the lapel of his suit.

"I didn't realise the club had a dress code. I'm sorry if that——"

The receptionist smiled at him again. "Oh, no, sir. We do not have a dress code. There is a private party in one of our function rooms, that is all. Please take a seat and I will let Herr Krieger know you have arrived."

Gabriel's irritation was smoothed out by the receptionist's assurances that he wasn't committing a social gaffe, and he took a seat on a deep-red Chesterfield sofa. The leather was worn, but smooth and soft to the touch. The brass nail heads around the edge of the padding were as highly polished as the club's nameplate outside. He plucked the knees of his trousers up a fraction to avoid bagging the fabric, crossed his legs, ankle to knee, and sat back to wait for Krieger.

He didn't have to wait long.

"Gabriel!" a man's voice called from across the lobby. It was Krieger. The old man was walking towards him, hand outstretched. He wore the same suit he'd been wearing at their meeting.

Gabriel stood and shook Krieger's hand, which was warm and dry, the bones and sinews visible beneath the papery skin. He gestured at another couple dressed to the nines and chatting as they moved through the lobby.

"For a horrible moment, I thought I'd have to go back to my hotel and change."

Krieger put his hand to his chest. "My dear Gabriel. You must forgive me. I hope I did not cause you any embarrassment. An old man's foible, to assume everyone knows what he himself does."

"It's fine. The receptionist told me. A private function."

"Ah, well, they hold them all the time. I only come a few times a year, with guests." He held out his left arm. "Come. Let's get a drink."

· · ·

The bar was of a kind Gabriel loved. Dark; lit by table lamps, not overheads; leather club chairs that accepted you like old friends; booths around the edge and a long, curved zinc bar top behind which dozens of bottles and glasses glinted with rich promise. Above the bar itself was a huge gilt-framed mirror, its upper edge an art deco sunrise in alternating bands of paler and darker gold. In a corner, a jazz trio – piano, double bass and guitar – were playing "Fly Me to the Moon." They appeared to be the only black people in the entire club, although Gabriel supposed there might be guests already sequestered in one of the private rooms.

Krieger motioned him towards one of the booths, and he slid in with his back to the wall so he could command a view of the bar. Tall, narrow drink menus stood waiting in the centre of the table, and Gabriel pulled one towards him. Krieger smiled at him and did the same. The menus were printed on glossy black card, decorated with the club's logo – a stylised version of the building's exterior in white line artwork.

A waitress appeared by Gabriel's side a couple of minutes later. She was mid-thirties, plump where the receptionist had been slim, blond where she had been brunette. She wore black-framed glasses that magnified her eyes, which were a shade of brown that was almost amber.

"Sir, may I bring you something from the bar?"

"A martini, please. Made with Tanqueray Number Ten."

"Olive or a twist, sir?"

"Olives, please. Three. And please tell the bartender not to make it too dry."

"Very good, sir. And for you, Herr Krieger?"

"Well remembered, Marta," Krieger said with a smile, which she reciprocated. "I think tonight I shall have a Manhattan. Made with Canadian Club. Thank you."

With their drinks before them, Krieger raised his cocktail glass. "My father taught me that banking is built on relationships, not money. To relationships, Gabriel."

"To relationships."

They clinked and drank.

Gabriel felt the final shreds of apprehension dissolving as the alcohol hit his stomach. The martini was ice-cold and very good. The bartender had followed Gabriel's instructions to the letter and allowed just enough of the vermouth to remain in the glass to add some herby off-dryness to the gin. He let out his breath in a sigh.

"Is everything all right?" Krieger asked.

Gabriel took another pull on his drink and then set the glass down on the cocktail napkin the waitress had provided.

"I had some bad news before I left England. Well, two lots of bad news."

"Would you like to tell me? I am old, and have heard much bad news in my time. I may not be able to help, but sometimes speaking these matters aloud takes away some of their sting."

Gabriel made a split-second decision. Why not? He was far from home and as a Swiss banker, Krieger was probably as watertight as a doctor – or a shrink – when it came to secrets.

"Six days ago, a close friend of mine was killed. Murdered. Then, yesterday, a former comrade was killed. I am certain it was the same person."

Krieger's eyebrows, already on their way up at Gabriel's first sentence, arched higher at his second.

"My dear boy, that is terrible. Most terrible. And you said 'comrade' – this was a soldier who died? You were a soldier yourself?"

"Yes. I was in the army. Thirteen years."

"Aha. And you served in…?"

"The Parachute Regiment."

This seemed to please Krieger.

"An elite force, no? Only the SAS is better. Here in Switzerland, we have national service, as you may know. It is every young man's duty to perform his military service." Gabriel sipped his drink as Krieger spoke. Judging his feelings, wondering whether he would be safe to continue speaking. Krieger continued. "And you know who it was? The killer?"

236

Gabriel nodded, thinking that the number of killings he'd caused, witnessed or actually performed since leaving military service was now approaching his total while in uniform. "Pretty sure, yes."

"And you have informed the authorities? The police?"

"I have, but they won't find her. She's a professional. The question is, who hired her?"

Krieger downed the remainder of his drink. "Drink up, Gabriel. I sense we shall need more of these." He signalled to the waitress for two more. As the jazz trio moved into "Summertime," Krieger leaned forwards across the table.

"You know what they say about murder, Gabriel?"

"What?"

"That it is only ever for one of two reasons. Love or money."

"I don't think someone hired a hit woman because they love me, if that's what you're saying. And I haven't got any money. Or not enough to have someone able to afford an assassin's services to come after me."

Krueger shook his head and smiled. "No money? You came to my office this afternoon with three million dollars' worth of US bearer bonds."

"I know this woman, Walti. The killer, I mean. I've met her. Three million is her standard fee. Her client wouldn't come out ahead by killing me over the bonds."

If Krieger was surprised at Gabriel's admission, he disguised it perfectly. Perhaps he'd simply seen too many things to be shockable any more.

"No," he said. "That is not what I am saying. Because the old adage has it wrong. There is a third motive for murder. Love, money … or power."

He paused as the waitress returned with fresh drinks, removed the empty cocktail glasses and replaced the napkins. He nodded his thanks to her, then resumed talking.

"Does a serial killer murder for love? Does a dictator? No! Or money? No, again. But power? Yes. For that he will kill again and again. Perhaps it is a question of power that caused this person to commission the killings of your friend and comrade."

Gabriel frowned, and sipped his drink. Then he shrugged. "I honestly don't know. It could be. But again, I don't really have power. I work for people who do, but then why come after me?"

"And you're sure they are coming after you? That your friends weren't the real targets?"

Gabriel put his drink down and scratched at his scalp through his hair, ruffling it into spikes.

"Yes. I mean, I think so. There are details that make me believe that."

"Hmm. Well, I do not say that they want power *from* you. Simply that if neither love nor money seem to offer a motive, the third member of that trinity might."

"You have a point, Walti. But offhand I'm struggling to think who it must be." The coffee he'd consumed in his hotel room, coupled with the martinis, prompted a new question. "I'm sorry, could you point me to the restrooms?"

"Of course, dear boy. Out of the door and then across the lobby to the corridor. They are down on the right at the end."

Gabriel stood and made his way out of the bar, following Krieger's directions to a dark-wood-panelled restroom. When he came out, he was about to return to the bar when he heard a woman's whimpering cry, a shout and then a snatch of a song in a deep, male voice. It appeared to be coming from behind a door at the end of a second corridor that doglegged off the first.

He walked down the thickly carpeted corridor and placed his ear against the door. From inside he could hear more shouting, though it appeared to be encouragement rather than anger. He heard humour in the voices. But something else too. A sound he'd heard on active duty and in his work for The Department. The sound was cruelty.

He placed his hand on the brass doorknob, twisted it and eased the door open just enough to peer round. What he saw made him stop breathing for a second.

44

DINNER AND A SHOW

The room contained perhaps a dozen small, circular tables, the same sort as those scattered through the bar he had just left. Each hosted two or three of the dinner-jacketed men and their expensively dressed companions he had seen milling about in the lobby when he arrived. The room was lit by dozens of tall, white candles and shaded red lamps in the centres of the tables. Heavy, red velvet curtains shrouded the tall windows. Wine glasses and place settings crowded each table top. Nobody was looking at the door, which was behind the tables; instead, all eyes were fixed on a tableau on a small, low stage at the far end of the room.

The stage was hung with a backdrop painted to resemble some sort of military barracks surrounded by barbed wire. And in front of the backdrop, a scene was being played out that almost made Gabriel retch. Two tall, blond men dressed in the unmistakable black uniforms of the SS had hold of a cowering, dark-haired woman by the wrists. She was naked from the waist up, her lower limbs barely concealed in a torn scrap of greyish brown fabric. They were grinning down at her as they dragged her across the stage to a hard wooden chair. The woman was struggling, and Gabriel thought he detected real fear in her dark eyes.

At one of the front row tables, he saw a man he'd noticed earlier, crossing the lobby in front of him. And then he saw the object that had triggered his spider sense. Pinned to the left breast of the man's dinner jacket was a military decoration. The ribbon was black, white and red; the medal itself was a black-and-white cross. The Iron Cross, a Nazi-era military medal.

Another whimper from the captive woman dragged Gabriel's attention back to the stage. The two blond men had forced her to sit astride the chair with her chest against its back and were lashing her wrists together. Now Gabriel noticed that one had a coiled, black leather whip hanging from his belt.

He didn't decide to act. He didn't pause to reflect. He moved.

"No!" he shouted as loudly as he could.

He threw the door wide open so that it banged against the wall and sprinted between the tables towards the stage.

Over a chorus of shouts and cries of indignation in German, he barged his way past the last two tables standing between him and the stage.

The two men dressed as SS guards had turned to face him. They were no longer grinning. But they weren't running either. They were squaring up for a fight. Which was a mistake.

As the nearer of the two men raised his fists and swung, Gabriel ducked under the incoming blow, pivoted on his left hip and kicked upwards towards the man's jaw. The force was all he could muster, and he heard the crunch as the sole of his shoe connected, breaking the mandible and toppling the man to the floor with a scream of agony. The second man leapt forwards and grabbed Gabriel from behind, struggling to get his meaty forearms secured against his throat.

Instead of trying to loosen the man's grip, Gabriel let himself fall. As gravity pulled him down, the man instinctively went to compensate, adjusting his grip. He shouldn't have. In that moment, Gabriel's right elbow stabbed backwards into his groin, bringing forth a wheezing cry and freeing Gabriel from the stranglehold. He whirled round, drew his foot back and stamped onto the man's left knee. It was an ugly, but brutally effective move, and as the man's cruciate ligaments audibly sheared and snapped, Gabriel closed in and chopped him across the throat with the blade of his right hand.

Both assailants down on the ground and no longer a problem, Gabriel bent to the woman and untied her hands.

"Run!" he shouted at her and pointed to the door.

Covering her exposed breasts, she took one look at her erstwhile captors, spat at the closer of the two, then ran for the door and disappeared through it.

He turned.

The audience for the perverted spectacle he'd interrupted were on their feet, eyes wide in shock. Nobody was moving though, either towards him or for the door. They were looking at each other. Then something happened that surprised Gabriel.

First a single, white-haired man at the front, then others and, finally, the whole room, began to clap. Their faces, so recent paralysed with shock, now broke into smiles. They whistled, they called, "Bravo!" They came towards him.

"What?" he shouted. "Are you applauding me? You fucks! This isn't part of the show. They were going to torture her and you were going to watch."

The man who'd started the applause came towards him, arms wide. In English, he said, "Was this Peppi's idea? Did he send you?"

Breathing heavily, Gabriel turned to check on the two men he put down. The one with the broken jaw was unconscious, blood leaking from his mouth. The one he'd crippled was moaning softly to himself, holding his ruined knee with both hands. He turned back. Grabbed the man's satin lapels. And thrust his face close.

"The show's over."

Then he stepped back and punched him in the throat. The man went down. Now there were screams. Two or three other men sprang at Gabriel, but they were amateurs. Or perhaps, they had once been professionals, but the passage of time had rendered them shadows of their former selves. Hands were scratching at his face, and feet were going in. One lucky punch caught him across the bridge of his nose and for a second, stars flickered in his vision. Then all went dark. Just for a second.

The lights came back on a split second later, but this was not a candlelit dining room in a Zurich dining club.

This was the hot, hard light of the African sun.

45

CLOSE TO CONTACT

Rounds were coming in fast, like a swarm of hornets in 7.62mm calibre. White-hot, and very, very angry. The machetes wouldn't be far behind. Gabriel could feel the adrenaline swamping his system, but he maintained discipline. *Fight our way back to the extract point. Stay tight.* He dealt with the militia fighters systematically as they arrived in front of him. Putting them down with expert blows to the soft, vulnerable spots his instructors had shown him. Throat, groin, solar plexus, kidney.

The second member of his patrol was right there; they were back-to-back. She stopped the last of them and then dragged him away.

"Come on, Gabriel," she said in an urgent whisper. "Let's get you out of here before the police arrive."

"OK, OK. Let's go," he said.

Gabriel looked up from the bed. Eli was coming towards him with a glass of water. He realised he was in his hotel room. He pushed himself up onto his elbows.

"Eli! What are you doing here? How did I get back here? I was at a club. With Walti. I mean Krieger, the bank manager."

She sat beside him and held the glass out. "Drink this."

He took a sip and then placed the glass on the bedside table. "What time is it?"

"Eleven. You've been out for a few hours. I gave you a sedative."

The memory of the tableau at the club flashed across his brain.

"That room. I think I hurt a lot of people. The police'll be looking for me."

She wrinkled her nose. "I'm not so sure they will. And yes, for the record, you did hurt a lot of people. So did I. But they're not going to be calling the authorities. Not with their little Nazi amateur dramatics club in the spotlight."

"What about the woman they were using? Where is she?"

"I met her coming out. She's in a safe place now, with some people I know here."

Gabriel sat up and swung his legs off the bed.

"Do you want to tell me what's going on?"

"I'm your minder. I'm minding you." She smiled her disarming smile.

"You were following me."

"Not exactly. Well, yes, I mean in a technical sense I was following you. But wasn't it better that I had your back?"

"Walti? I left him in the bar. He would have heard the racket."

"Don't worry about Walti. You can see him tomorrow."

Gabriel called in at Händler und Ziegelhaus at ten the following morning on the way to the airport. While Eli waited in the cab – an immaculate cream E-Class – he went inside, after following the same routine with the gorilla on the door. The receptionist, Trudi, was on duty and she smiled when she saw him.

"Good Morning, Mr Wolfe. Are you here to see Herr Krieger again?"

"Yes, I am. But no appointment this time, so if he's busy, I can leave a message."

"No, no, he has the morning free and said to show you straight into his office if you came in."

Sitting opposite Krieger in his office, Gabriel didn't waste any time.

"I'm sorry for deserting you last night, Walti. I had an episode related to a health condition. A colleague took me back to my hotel."

The old man smiled and placed his liver-spotted hands palm down on the desk.

"Yes. I heard a commotion outside the bar. Lots of shouting. Are you all right now? Some people were calling for the police to be summoned."

"I'm fine. Listen, did you know what that private function was?"

Krieger's eyes flicked away from Gabriel's own, then back again. "Tell me."

"It was some kind of Neo-Nazi event. A dinner. They were re-enacting—"

He found he couldn't go on. The memory was jolting his pulse and he fought to restore some sort of internal balance, falling silent.

"You know, Gabriel, yesterday I said I was an old man. And that I had heard much bad news in my lifetime. I have also experienced much bad news at first hand."

He stopped speaking and unclipped the gold cufflink on his left wrist. He folded the cuff back on itself and then plucked at the sleeve until it slid up his forearm.

Gabriel inhaled sharply. He was looking at the remains of the tattoo he had glimpsed the previous day. It was the letter B followed by five crude digits. He looked up at Krieger.

"You were in the camps?"

Krieger nodded. "Herzogenbusch. It was in the Netherlands. In Vught. I was six when I was taken there with my parents. They died, but I was adopted by the other prisoners. They shared their food with me, tried to shield me. Somehow, I survived until the Canadian Army liberated the camp in 1944."

Gabriel pointed at Krieger's forehead.

"I thought maybe that was a duelling scar. Did they do that to you?" Krieger nodded. "But then how are you, I mean, Swiss banks were notorious for their connections to the Nazis. And you're running one?"

Krieger smiled. "After the war, Gabriel, I didn't go back home. There was nothing there for me, and nobody. I left for Palestine, as it was then called. I spent the next twenty years living in Israel. I went to work for Mossad as a young man, tracking down Nazis. We developed a plan to track them through gold and looted art treasures in the European banking system. And, to cut a long story short, as you say, here I am. A respectable Swiss banker with a good, solid Swiss-German name. The bank is real, by the way. The profits fund our operations here. Every month, I send a report to my handler in Israel, and he takes such action as he feels is necessary. But time is running out. For me. For my fellow survivors. And for the Nazis themselves. Nobody is getting any younger."

"What will you do about Das Haus der Tochter?" Gabriel asked, realising he'd leaned right forward in his chair and was staring intently as the old man told his story.

"I shall email my handler. The Swiss police will no doubt prefer to stay away."

A suspicion that had been swirling far out to sea in Gabriel's brain made landfall.

"You know Eli, don't you?"

Krieger smiled.

"Smart boy. Yes, I know Eli very well. We first met when she began working for Mossad. We keep in touch. She let me know you'd be coming."

Still trying to process Krieger's story, Gabriel reached down and pulled the bearer bonds from his briefcase.

"I actually came in to give you these," he said, handing them to Krieger across the desk. "If your documents specialist says they're genuine, please open my account. If they're not, burn them or put them in a museum. I leave it to you."

Krieger smiled. "Very well, Gabriel. Thank you for placing your trust in me. And for your actions last night."

Then Gabriel's phone buzzed. He knew it would be Eli hurrying him along.

"I have to go. Thank you, Walti. For sharing your story with me. I am sorry."

The old man smiled. "No need. I am alive. I am doing important work. Thanks be to Him. And one last thing. As we are to be friends, I think you should call me by my Hebrew name. I am Amos Peled. *Amos* means bearer of burden and *Peled* means steel. I chose it very carefully."

Gabriel stood and offered his hand.

"Goodbye Amos. Shalom."

"Shalom, Gabriel."

Outside, Eli was staring out through the taxi's wide window. When Gabriel appeared she mouthed something at him and tapped her watch. He was inside the car a few moments later.

"I was about to come and haul you out of there. How did you get on with Walti?"

Gabriel smiled. "Amos is a charming man, as it would appear you already know."

She smiled back. "He could be helpful in finding Sasha Beck. And her client. People who can drop three million on a contract generally don't bank on the High Street."

"Maybe. And he's got contacts at Mossad, too."

"So have I," she said, a little indignantly.

"What do you suggest then?"

"OK. This somebody, let's call them Fury. No. Better idea. We'll call them Ebrah." She pronounced it *eb-raw*. "It's the Hebrew word. What do they want?

"At this point, I'm not exactly sure. They're sending a message to me."

"Obviously. But what else?"

Gabriel furrowed his brow. "They killed my friend. My best friend. Then Dusty. My comrade. Then they destroyed my car."

"And what does that say to you?"

247

"It says, they want to take away things, people, who I care about. It's why I'm worried about Britta."

"But why not simply go after you? You said Sasha Beck shot your friend with a rifle. Anyone that good could just as easily have killed you."

"So they don't want me dead. They want me alive. To witness everything."

Eli shook her head. "It's so systematic. And so high risk. Who breaks into the fucking SAS? You must have *really* pissed somebody off."

"Then let's make me bait. I'll put myself right out there in harm's way. If they don't want me dead, maybe that'll draw them out. Maybe Sasha will confront me. I reckon I could take her in a one-on-one."

"Oh, sure, macho SAS man. Aren't you forgetting she just took down a serving member of the Regiment? Inside their base? You're fit, as I think you know, but you're not serving anymore."

"It doesn't matter. She doesn't have the element of surprise with me."

46

ITEM THREE, PART TWO

OXFORDSHIRE COUNTRYSIDE

After leaving the SAS with a full military pension, a chest full of medals, and a prosthetic arm, Damon Cheaney found himself a job as an estate manager for a landowner in Oxfordshire. He had his own cottage in the magnificent grounds of Chesterley House and a job as varied as the seasons. One day, he might be feeding the pheasants reared in the field to the north of the main house for the shoots organised by the owners, filling the blue plastic drums with a special mix of his own devising. Another, planting hornbeam saplings to create a new woodland avenue from the formal gardens to a nineteenth-century folly beside a small trout lake.

On this particular day, he'd worked solidly from seven until six, setting posts for a new fence line to enclose a field intended for sheep. He heated some soup in the microwave, ate it with wholemeal bread he'd baked the previous weekend, and then slumped in front of the TV with a can of beer. Waking at nine to discover he had no idea what had been happening in the game show he'd been watching, he stumbled up the stairs, unfastened his arm and laid it on a chair beside the bed, and was asleep within minutes of his head settling onto the pillow.

So deep was his sleep that he didn't even stir when, five hours later, the intruder squeezed through the narrow gap she'd opened between the door and the jamb. She looked over at the bed, face impassive, then scanned the room looking for the prosthesis.

Breathing slowly and shallowly, she slid her feet across the carpet until she reached the chair. There, she crouched and withdrew a small cling-wrapped package from her jacket pocket. She freed the small piece of grey, puttyish material from the wrapper and squeezed it between her thumbs and fingers until she'd moulded it into a thin, roughly circular sheet perhaps four inches in diameter. Then she pushed it into the socket at the elbow of the prosthetic arm. Holding a pen torch in her mouth she hooked out one of the wires running between the battery and the actuator of the forearm, connected it to a length of detonator wire and pushed the naked copper end of the wire into the layer of plastic explosive she'd just moulded inside the arm.

As silently as she'd arrived, she left, closing the door behind her.

At seven that same morning, the intruder was sitting in her car, which was parked in a layby on a narrow country road running just seventy-five yards from the edge of the cottage's neat front garden. She was sipping coffee from a brushed aluminium cup.

The explosion was loud, but not deafeningly so, the amount of plastique needed to kill a man being insignificant in terms of demolition work. A handful of pigeons burst from a nearby tree and clattered away across the fields, but apart from the birds, there was no reaction to the blast, which was only marginally louder than a car backfiring.

Emptying the cup and screwing it back onto the flask, she crossed the road at a trot, re-entered the cottage and mounted the stairs two at a time. The bedroom was a mess. Blackened and charred walls, spattered with blood, and the remains of the man's torso splashed across the bed. The prosthetic arm was mangled and blackened, but the forearm and hand were recognisable. She pulled a folded sheet of notepaper from her hip pocket and inserted it between the thumb and index finger, left the arm on the dresser and, for the second and final time, pulled the door to behind her.

When Damon's employers raised the alarm at noon that same day, after he had failed to show up for a meeting, the police found the note. It read, in its entirety:

Who's next in the Daisy-chain, Wolfe?

Owing to the fragmented nature of policing in Britain, the force in whose jurisdiction this part of Oxfordshire fell was a completely different organisation to the one in Wiltshire where Detective Superintendent Anita Woods was investigating Julia Angell's death. The same went for Hereford, and the murder of Ben "Dusty" Rhodes. It meant three separate murder investigations, each one of which missed the vital links between the deaths.

At a sprawling ranch-style property set in fifteen acres of land in upstate New York near Ithaca, Erin Ayers glanced down at her buzzing phone.

Item three, part two, completed. SB xx

* * *

Halfway round his run, Gabriel stopped by a fence to answer his phone. He leaned on the top rail and looked across the valley towards the spire of Salisbury Cathedral. A light mist hung over the low-lying land, so that the spire appeared to hang in mid-air. The incoming call was from Don Webster.

"Hello, boss. Everything all right?" he said.

"Far from it, Old Sport. Very far from it. I'm afraid it's more bad news. Damon Cheaney was murdered this morning."

Gabriel stared towards the hanging spire. "Oh, God. Beck?"

"Looks like it. From what you've told me about her, there's no question."

"How?"

"Early indications from the police pathologist are blast trauma. I sent one of our chaps over to have a look. Seems she put C-4 into his prosthesis. Blew him to pieces. She left another message, too. 'Who's next in the Daisy-chain, Wolfe?'"

"Shit! I'm sorry, boss, I—"

"Right! That's the last apology I'm going to hear from you, Old Sport. I told you this isn't on you. Here's what I want instead. I want to know how she, this Sasha Beck, knew Damon's nickname from the Regiment. Any thoughts?"

Shivering despite the spring warmth on his back and the sweat he'd built up running, Gabriel tried to focus on Don's question. "I can't think of anything now. Give me thirty minutes. I'll call you back."

* * *

At the house, Eli was reading something on her phone. She looked up as Gabriel came through the back door into the kitchen.

"Hey. Everything OK? You look pale."

"No, not all right. She just killed another one of my friends."

"I'm really sorry, Gabriel," she said, getting to her feet and coming towards him. "Who?"

"A guy I served with. Damon Cheaney. Him, me, Dusty and Smudge: we were a patrol. There's just me left from it now."

Eli embraced him for a second, but Gabriel pulled away and went to the sink. He filled a glass from the tap and swigged it down then sat at the table.

"What do we do now?"

Gabriel swiped his hand across his eyes and down over his nose and mouth.

"The first thing I have to do is figure out who knew Damon's nickname was Daisy. She left a reference to it in a note for me."

"So who would have done?"

"Nobody outside the Regiment. And none of us would share something like that. Or only with people who could be totally trusted, like wives or parents. No, she got it some other way. There must be a leak somewhere."

"Could you have told someone? Outside the SAS, I mean?"

"That's what I've been racking my brains trying to think of. I'm going for a shower. Maybe something will shake loose in my brain."

Ten minutes later, Gabriel was back downstairs again, running gear replaced by jeans and a white shirt. He found Eli in the sitting room listening to an early Nils Lofgren album. She looked up from the leather armchair in which she was curled like a cat.

"Any joy?"

He shook his head. "Nothing."

"OK. I have an idea. Didn't you tell me you could do hypnosis?"

"Yes. But I'm not sure I'm steady enough to do it on myself right now."

"Maybe not, but I could try. I did some training in hypnosis on an interrogation course."

Gabriel shrugged. "Sure. I need to do something. I'm starting to feel powerless."

"You didn't look powerless when you were taking out a roomful of neo-Nazis in Zurich," she said with an encouraging smile.

"That's not what I mean. We need a breakthrough. A single piece of intel that will give us a starting point for a counter operation."

"Right. Come and sit down." Eli led Gabriel by the hand to the sofa and pushed him, gently, down into its saggy embrace. "Put your hands by your sides and close your eyes."

Gabriel did as he was told. As he closed his eyes, he wondered whether she'd try and repeat her earlier advances. Then dismissed the thought as unworthy. She was trying to help and by God, he needed some help right now.

"Now what?"

Eli looked at Gabriel and began speaking in a soft, low voice. "I want you to picture a photograph album. A big white photograph album with lots of pages stuffed with pictures."

"OK, I'm doing that."

"Just focus on your breathing for a little while and look at the cover. Give the album a name." As she talked in a soothing tone of voice, Eli mixed her instructions with random phrases designed to disorientate the subject. "Open the cover. Start turning the pages. Each photo is you with someone you've spent time with over the last month. Can you see them?"

"Mm-hmm. Yes, I can see them."

"Good. Is there a picture of you with a stranger?"

She watched his eyelids, noticing the way they rippled and bulged as the eyes beneath scanned left to right.

"Yes, there is."

"Who's is the stranger, Gabriel?"

"It's Carl Mortensen."

"Who is Carl Mortensen?"

"A client."

"Where are you? In the photo, Gabriel. What's the location?"

"Kazakhstan. We're in an SUV. Middle of nowhere."

"What are you talking about?"

"Just stuff. Small talk. He's asking me questions."

Matching her breathing to Gabriel's, Eli felt ready to press a little harder.

"I want you to picture his words as captions under the photos. OK?"

Gabriel mumbled assent. "OK."

"Good. Now, read the captions. What's he asking you about?"

"My friends. From home. From the Regiment."

"Who, Gabriel. Who is he asking about?"

"Dusty. And Daisy. And Julia. And Zhao Xi. And Britta. I told him. I told him everything."

Gabriel's breathing had become ragged and his eyes were flicking beneath the lids, left and right, up and down. Eli could tell it was time to end the session.

"Gabriel, I want you to listen to me very carefully. I am going to bring you back now. I will count to ten and once I say ten you will be awake. You won't be in any distress, but you will remember everything you've seen and read in the photo album."

She began counting and as she uttered the word 'ten,' Gabriel's eyes opened. He stared straight at her.

"I've been played," he said. "Mortensen didn't need protection at all. It looks like we found the leak. It was me."

"Yes, but now we have something concrete to go on. We find Mortensen, we find the client. Maybe he even works for him."

Gabriel nodded. He was thinking about the two other people he'd given up to Mortensen. And he had to ring Don and explain it was he, Gabriel, who'd supplied Sasha Beck's client with the details of his friends and comrades in arms.

After speaking to Don, who had batted away Gabriel's apology with a brusque, "Enough!", Gabriel rang Zhao Xi.

"Hello. You have reached Zhao Xi. Please leave your message." The message, first in Mandarin, then in English, was anything but reassuring. Gabriel hurriedly tried to compose a suitable warning.

"Master Zhao, it's Gabriel. I think you're in danger. It's a woman, long, dark hair, dark-red lips, very fit, athletic physique. She might be coming to kill you. She was the one I left tied up at the Golden Dragon. Please be careful. Call me when you get this message."

Eli watched him as he ended the call and put his phone down.

"You know, we could really do with a break. Because this

woman, I get the feeling she's zeroing in on you. If you're calling Zhao Xi, then who's left? Just Britta? Then you?"

"I know. I just, it's impossible to know how to stop her. And I'm worried about Master Zhao. He's an old man now."

"You said he was a martial arts expert."

"Yes, I did. But she's a trained killer and in peak condition. She can't be more than mid-forties."

Gabriel was pacing around in the kitchen like a tiger behind glass at a zoo. He made a decision.

"I'm going."

"What? Where?"

"To Hong Kong. I need to get to Zhao Xi before she does. At least then we'll be two against one."

"Three," Eli said, getting to her feet.

Gabriel shook his head. "No. I'm going alone. You should stay here in case the police come up with something, or Don does. Plus if I'm wrong then she's still here and after Britta. This way we can cover more of the bases."

Eli frowned. "I don't think that's such a good idea. It's not what Don told me to—"

"I don't care what Don told you!" Gabriel shouted. "It's not your life that's being dismantled by a fucking assassin."

She put her hands up, palms towards Gabriel, placating. "OK, OK, look, you're a grown-up, I get that, but you could be making yourself an easier target."

Gabriel turned to face her. He was finding it hard to think straight. He had a tight band of tension around his chest that was squeezing tighter by the hour. He wanted to do something, anything, but there was nothing *to* do. Not in England, anyway.

"No. I'm going. You stay here and guard the fort. I'll have my phone, so let me know if anything happens."

47

ITEM FOUR

HONG KONG

Thirty-six hours later, Gabriel's plane touched down at Hong Kong International Airport.

At the same time as the huge rubber tyres shrieked against the runway, Sasha Beck was standing at the front door of Zhao Xi's house in the mountains. She had booked her kendo lesson in the name Tamsin Cho, and had spent the morning with a movie makeup artist perfecting her new look. Gone was the long, straight, dark-brown hair; she'd tucked it away under a pageboy wig in a harsh shade of red. The trademark bruised-cherry lipstick was also absent, in favour of a pale, frosted pink. But the key to her disguise was the work she had asked the makeup girl to perform on and around her eyes. Using slivers of latex, specialised adhesive, and foundation, she'd added subtle epicanthal folds to the inner corners of Sasha's eyes to create the illusion of Chinese ancestry. The addition of full eye makeup had pushed Sasha's true identity far into the background.

She was wearing a pale-grey-and-pink tracksuit and all-white trainers, and carrying a pink-and-white gym bag with a Hello Kitty motif on the side. The bag contained a towel, a bottle of water and a black kendo outfit, including armour and helmet. The kendo sword itself, the *shinai* – narrow slats of bamboo, bound with narrow strips of white leather, with a white leather hand grip – was slung over her back, holstered in a wide tube made of black plastic on a strap of woven cotton.

She pressed the doorbell and stood back, shy smile applied to her mouth with as much skill as the makeup artist had applied the lipstick.

The old man who answered a few moments later was much as she had expected. Late seventies, trim, clear-eyed expression. And, best of all, not a trace of suspicion on his face.

"You are Tamsin?" he asked.

"Yes, sir, I am," she said in a transatlantic accent she'd chosen to suggest someone who'd spent half her life in Hong Kong and half in Manhattan.

"Then, please come in. And you do not need to call me sir. Though, if you wish, you may address me as Master Zhao."

The queue for Immigration snaked around red nylon barriers clipped into chromed, waist-high poles so that the passengers on Gabriel's flight were facing each other as they inched their way towards the glass cubicles housing the immigration officers. Gabriel saw the tired faces of mid-ranking executives, the excited faces of families soon to be reunited with loved ones and the unreadable faces of travellers whose purposes weren't clear. He doubted any of them were in Hong Kong to try to prevent the murder of their childhood mentor.

At the mountainside house, Zhao Xi and Sasha Beck AKA Tamsin Cho were preparing for their training bout. She unlaced her trainers and removed them, along with short, white socks prevented from disappearing under her heels by fluffy, pink pom-poms.

Zhao Xi was waiting for her in the centre of the quartet of unbleached cotton crash pads laid out in his dojo. To his right was the floor-to-ceiling window that gave onto the thickly forested hillside and the harbour far below.

"You are a six-dan, yes, Tamsin?" he asked now.

"Yes, Master Zhao. My work at the bank is so stressful, but I have been training for seven years. It's my one release. I am so grateful to you for offering to teach me while I am here."

He inclined his head. "A master must have pupils, no?"

She joined him on the mats, wearing her metal-grilled helmet and protective armour. Both fighters wore the same black outfits. Both were roughly the same height, though Zhao Xi was a little heavier and broader across the shoulders. And both held the traditional kendo *shinai*.

They squatted and touched the tips of their *shinai* together, then stood and began circling each other.

Finally though Immigration, Gabriel headed out to the front of the arrivals lounge and on towards the ferry.

He checked his watch and realised he'd left it on UK time. He thought of changing it, but then just shrugged and left it alone. His phone had automatically updated to Hong Kong time so he decided to use that. As the ferry chugged across the green water of the harbour, he called Zhao Xi again. It went straight to voicemail.

As it would, because Zhao Xi never brought his phone into the dojo. The first few sallies came from Sasha as she probed the teacher's defences. She was careful not to reveal the full extent of her skill and made sure her attacks and feints were well telegraphed and occasionally clumsy. He parried them all easily and landed a few admonitory smacks on the top of her helmet as if to say, "You need to try much harder than that."

With a yell, she launched herself at him in a furious combination of blows that he parried or deflected. Then the blow she had planned all along: a slashing overhead move that missed Zhao Xi's helmet. Rather than pull up, she increased the force behind the blow, bringing the *shinai* down with such force onto the hard wooden floor outside the four mats that the bamboo shattered into razor-edged pieces.

She took her helmet off.

"Forgive me, that was so clumsy."

He shook his head, without removing his own helmet.

"No matter. Would you like to borrow a shinai?" he asked, gesturing at a rack of identical bamboo weapons behind him.

"No thank you, Master Zhao. I have a spare."

Turning, she walked the short distance to the bench on which she'd left her gear and unscrewed the lid from the black plastic tube.

Gabriel climbed into a taxi, having endured an agonising fifteen-minute wait in another long queue, and gave the driver Zhao Xi's address. He buzzed the window down, inhaling that characteristic aroma of the city: traffic fumes mixed with incense from the many roadside shrines, and the wild, swirling blend of cooking smells from cuisines stretching from Ethiopia to Italy. People were everywhere, crowded onto the narrow pavements that themselves were interrupted every dozen yards or so by building works or an inspection tent over an open manhole. And above them all, the glass-and-steel skyscrapers loomed, bouncing the sunlight around like a hall of mirrors.

As the car dodged and veered in and out of the traffic, the driver keeping the heel of his right hand over the horn button, Gabriel tried to remain calm. He'd alerted Zhao Xi, and the man was no pushover. He might even be able to capture Beck if she were to approach him.

* * *

Sasha Beck pulled the *shinai* from the tube. Another long, slatted bamboo construction identical to the ten or so ranged behind Zhao Xi. She stood and turned to face Zhao Xi, who was standing still, watching her. Then she pulled a second weapon from inside the *shinai*. This was very different. It was the weapon the *shinai* had replaced in the transition from war to sport: a *katana*, or Samurai sword.

Through the horizontal metal bars guarding the old man's face, she saw his eyes widen in surprise.

"It is you," he said. "The one Wolfe Cub warned me about."

"Oh, that's so sweet," Sasha said, abandoning her New York-inflected accent for her own, a voice that swung between country-house drawing room and London council estate as whim dictated. "You gave him a pet name. And, yes, I am she. Though I had no idea he'd warned you."

She raised the *katana* in front of her and swished it from side to side a couple of times, finding the balance of the blade.

In a flash, Zhao Xi attacked, catching her unawares, and clattering the bamboo *shinai* against the side of her head hard enough to disorientate her for a second.

She staggered backwards and counter-attacked, dancing forward and cutting at his right arm with the viciously sharp edge of the *katana*.

* * *

Gabriel's taxi driver had escaped the hurly-burly of the city and was making good progress up Stubbs Road towards Zhao Xi's house. Gabriel leaned forward.

"Can you go any faster? I'll double the fee on the meter."

"Sure thing," the driver said.

The engine protested as the driver slammed his foot down on the accelerator, but the raging motor under the bonnet had clearly been worked like a farm horse. Despite the influx of extra fuel, it only managed to make extra noise and put on maybe ten miles an hour extra.

* * *

With a deft inside-out manoeuvre, Sasha Beck brought her blade inside Zhao Xi's guard and cut deeply into his right bicep. He staggered back, dropping his *shinai* and grabbing for the spurting wound with his left hand. His right heel caught on the edge of the mat and he tumbled onto his back.

She leapt forward, both feet off the ground, *katana* held in front of her and then, as she landed, drove the point of the sword forward and down towards his heart.

With a noise like thin twigs snapping, the blade penetrated his lacquer armoured breastplate and plunged on between two ribs into his chest.

His eyes popped wide and his mouth spasmed open. No sound emerged beyond a hissing outbreath.

Sasha withdrew the sword, wiped it on his trouser leg and turned to sheath it in the protective bamboo outer. When she walked back to the body it was perfectly still. A trickle of bright-red blood had escaped his lips and was pooling beneath his left cheek on the polished wooden floor. She pushed the tips of her index and middle fingers – not roughly – into the space beneath his jaw where the carotid artery is found. She left them there for a count of five and discerned no pulse. Blood had soaked his clothing and was spreading out beneath his torso.

She straightened and went to the bench against the back wall to retrieve her gym bag.

A noise made her stop. A car engine, out of tune, by the sound of it, was thrumming at the front of the house. She took one final look at the body, regretting that she wouldn't have time to leave her message, and then spoke one final time to the man who had invited her to call him Master Zhao.

"I'm sorry, darling. But your Wolfe Cub royally pissed off my client. And when Erin Ayers is pissed off, people get hurt."

Then she slid the plate glass door to one side and sprinted through the lovingly tended garden and disappeared into the thick foliage beyond.

* * *

"Hello? Master Zhao?" Gabriel called from the kitchen. After paying the taxi driver, he'd rung the bell, but after Zhao Xi had failed to materialise, he'd kicked the back door down.

He ran through the house, throwing doors open and glancing inside each room before going on to the next. He knew he was being irrational, that Zhao Xi might simply be out, shopping perhaps, or walking, but he was held by a terrible fear that he was too late. That he was about to lose someone else precious to him.

Finally, he reached the dojo. Seeing the prostrate form of his mentor, he ran to him and knelt by his side. The blood had spread into a wide irregular shape beneath the old man's body. He checked for a pulse. Nothing. Then he placed his ear against Zhao Xi's lips, hoping, praying for a breath.

He was rewarded.

48

CLIENT CONFIDENTIALITY REMOVED

"Wolfe Cub, is that you?"

"Yes, Master. But you're hurt. Badly. We have to get you to a hospital."

Zhao Xi's voice was riven with pain. "No, Wolfe Cub … My time on Earth is at an end."

"No! You're alive. You're breathing. They'll fix you up."

"Remember how I taught you … to slow your heartbeat?" Zhao Xi's voice was barely audible and Gabriel had to lean right over him to make out his words. "You were good but … our training ended before I could take you to the limit." He paused to take another slight breath. "After she killed me … I slowed my heartbeat down far enough that she … that she detected no pulse. I prayed you might find me."

Gabriel's face was wet with tears and he crouched over his mentor, willing him not to be dying.

"No, Master. She didn't kill you."

"Listen to me. I must give you … one last piece of advice. You know the assassin. You told me that before." He drew in a shuddering breath, then continued. "Look for … for Erin Ayers. She is the person behind this."

"Erin Ayers? I've never even heard of her. Who is she, Master? Where should I look?"

But Zhao Xi didn't answer. Couldn't answer. That last, shuddering breath he'd drawn in now escaped his parted lips in a whisper like a faraway wind through the bamboo growing on the hillside.

Gabriel didn't try to revive his old master. The man who had raised him, changed him from a surly, rebellious teenager into a man, was dead. Instead he sat with his back to the wall and stared at the body, letting the tears flow down over his cheeks and into the collar of his shirt. He hammered his fist into the floor.

"I failed you, Master!" he shouted, and he slammed his fist back down again. "I let her reach you and kill you. Why didn't I see it?"

Finally, after half an hour had passed, Gabriel got to his feet and called the police and an ambulance. While he waited, he went through to Zhao Xi's study, hoping to find some sort of guidance on what to do.

The room was sparsely furnished. It contained just a plain wooden desk and a simple chair, made of bamboo with a rattan seat. The top of the desk was pale, sanded wood in which the grain was visible, the wavy pale and dark bands like the intricate patterning on a damascened sword blade. At the rear of the desk top were three small, green figures carved in what Gabriel knew to be jade: a monk in a robe, walking with a long pole; a man fishing, wearing a wide-brimmed hat to keep the sun off; and a dragon, its sinuous body undulating behind a snarling head.

In a daze, Gabriel pulled open the drawer beneath the desk top. It contained several large brown envelopes. He spent the next ten minutes opening them and sorting through the documents each contained. In the last envelope was a smaller envelope headed:

In the event of my death.

. . .

He was about to open it when he heard sirens outside and went to let the police and paramedics in.

* * *

Gabriel showed the two detectives, a man and a woman, where Zhao Xi's body lay. They introduced themselves as Detective Inspector Danny Lu and Detective Sergeant Rachel Tan. The dojo smelled of incense and, he realised for the first time, blood. Then he stood back, while they circled the body, taking photographs on their phones. The male detective turned to him.

"You know this man?"

"He is, was, my mentor."

"You see who did this?"

"No. I arrived by taxi and he was dying when I found him."

"Anyone come the other way?"

Gabriel watched the way the detective was studying him, eyes narrowed, looking for a tell of some kind.

"No. But look," he said, pointing at the sliding glass doors that led onto the garden. "There are foot prints in the moss."

Zhao Xi's lawn was composed entirely of moss. In the Surrey town that was Gabriel's home before he came to Hong Kong with his parents, the suburbanites would have raked it out to encourage the grass. Xi had done the opposite, plucking out individual blades of grass to ensure an even, springy carpet of the bright-green moss. Now, though, the carpet was dented by widely spaced footprints, showing as darker, shadowed ovals on the otherwise smooth surface.

"OK, we'll have those photographed and checked."

The female detective, petite and wearing rectangular tortoiseshell glasses, spoke next.

"Any idea who'd want the old man dead?"

What do I say? Yes, it's an assassin, and go through the whole rigmarole I did with the detective in the UK? Or plead ignorance and chase her down myself?

"Sorry, no."

She paused for a second, as if expecting him to say more. When he didn't, she resumed her questions.

"Are you here on business, Mr—?"

"Wolfe. Gabriel. No, I came out to see Master Zhao on a whim."

As soon as he said it, he realised it was a misstep. The detective pounced.

"A whim? You flew to Hong Kong from the UK?"

"Yes, but like I said, he brought me up. I lived here as a teenager."

"You didn't say that. You said he was your mentor. And it's a long way to come on a whim, isn't it? Supposing he was out when you called. What were you going to do, fly home again on another whim?"

Gabriel could feel his pulse banging in his temples and at the base of his throat. He was fighting to stay calm when all he felt like doing was screaming at the detective.

"Look. I have money, OK? I can fly where I want, see who I want. Why are you asking me all these questions? I called you, didn't I? You don't think it was me, do you?"

The male detective had returned from the garden, where he had been kneeling beside the footprints.

"Keep cool, Mr Wolfe. At the moment, we don't think anything. Detective Tan and I are just following basic procedures. And you'd be surprised how many killers think calling it in is the best way to throw us off the scent. Would you come to the police station with us, please? I'd like to ask you a few more questions, maybe get your fingerprints and a DNA sample, just to rule you out."

Gabriel felt trapped. This wasn't a steaming jungle or an arid mountain pass where he could fight his way out against insurgents or terrorists. This was a city. With a police force. Two of whose finest were standing in front of him, with pistols on their hips and suspicious expressions on their faces. He could refuse and risk being arrested or comply and get snarled in the Hong Kong justice system while they interviewed him.

He had an idea. A high-risk idea to be sure, but when had playing it safe been a part of his makeup?

"Yes, fine. Let's go in."

. . .

Twenty-five minutes later, having been spirited through the traffic in a police car with blue lights flashing and sirens wailing, Gabriel sat opposite the two detectives in a small interview room. The walls were bare, painted a flat, battleship-grey. The furniture consisted of a rectangular metal table and three chairs. No mirror, no obvious cameras or recording equipment.

It was the woman's turn to speak.

"This is just a standard witness interview Mr Wolfe. Or may I call you Gabriel?"

"Gabriel's fine," he said with a smile, feeling jumpy as he contemplated the risk he was about to take.

"OK, so, Gabriel," she smiled, and he noticed she had very small teeth, "to recap, you came to Hong Kong, as you say, on a whim, and travelled straight from the airport to your mentor's house, where you found him dying on the floor of his dojo. Is that about right?"

Gabriel nodded. "Yes, it is."

"And you say you have no idea who did it."

He paused. "Actually, I do have an idea who did it. In fact, I know who did it."

Both detectives leaned forwards, placing their elbows on the scratched surface of the table. Lu asked the obvious next question.

"Who?"

"An assassin named Sasha Beck."

Gabriel leaned back and waited.

"OK, first, why did you say you had no idea who killed him when we asked you the first time?" Lu asked.

"Because I thought you wouldn't believe me."

"What changed your mind?" Tan asked, her pen poised over her notepad.

"I know someone who can corroborate it."

"And that person would be——?" she asked, eyes widening.

Gabriel inhaled deeply; spoke on the outbreath.

"Fang Jian."

Detective Tan put her pen down on the table and closed her notebook. She looked at Gabriel and he could sense those dark-brown eyes trying to drill into his brain.

"You know Fang?"

Gabriel thought back to his meeting with the Triad leader. How long ago was it? A few weeks? More? "We met last year."

"On a whim?"

"It was a social call. Zhao Xi knew him, and he introduced me. In the course of our meeting, Sasha Beck turned up. Mr Fang ..." he scratched the back of his neck, searching for the right words, words that would earn him a Get-Out-of-Jail-Free card without sending "Ricky" Fang in the other direction. " ... met Sasha Beck and extended her his hospitality."

Lu spoke.

"Funny. People to whom Ricky Fang offers *hospitality*," he laid heavy, ironic emphasis on the last word, "tend not to reappear."

"She's a professional. She escaped. Ask Mr Fang."

Tan opened her mouth to speak when a double knock at the door stopped her. A man wearing a white lab coat poked his head through the gap.

"Detective Lu, I've got the preliminary findings for you."

He handed Lu a typewritten sheet and disappeared.

Lu looked down at the sheet, pursing his plump lips as he read.

"The footprints on the lawn. They were running away from the house. Shoe size, thirty-eight. That's a UK size five. What size are you, Gabriel?"

"Ten."

"No fingerprints or body fluids, but one long, red hair recovered from the dojo."

Gabriel ran his fingertips through his short, black hair.

"Wrong colour, wrong length."

Lu stood. "I'm stepping out to make a couple of calls. Gabriel, do you want a coffee or tea? Water?"

"Tea would be good, please. Milk no sugar."

Lu turned to Tan. "Rachel, would you make Gabriel some tea while I check out his story?"

Gabriel noticed the way the female detective's lips tightened and a frown flickered like lightning across her otherwise smooth forehead. Maybe she resented being the tea girl every time they had a witness to interview.

"Of course. You want one, Danny?"

He shook his head. "I'm good."

She looked at Gabriel. "Don't go anywhere," she said with a smile.

Ten minutes later, both detectives were back. Tan handed a white china mug of tea to Gabriel, which he sipped gratefully.

"I just spoke to Ricky Fang," Lu said. "He confirms your story, more or less."

Gabriel wondered whether the young detective inspector enjoyed calling a Triad leader by his old nickname. Perhaps he was just asserting his authority.

"Then I'm free to go?"

"Yes, but please stay in Hong Kong for the next few days. We may have further questions for you."

"I plan to. Someone needs to sort out Zhao Xi's affairs. He doesn't have any family. Can I get back into the house?"

Lu nodded. "I'll call ahead."

At the house on the hill, the crime scene officers were still in the dojo, pottering about in their white Tyvek suits and pale-blue nylon booties, but nobody tried to stop Gabriel as he made his way to the office. Sitting at the chair behind the desk again, he picked up the envelope marked with Zhao Xi's handwritten note on the outside and opened it. Inside was a single sheet of paper on which, in elegant handwriting, Zhao Xi had listed the name, telephone number, email address and street address of a firm of Hong Kong-based solicitors – Ophelia Tsang & Partners LLP – as well as a name and a mobile number. For a partner at the firm, Gabriel assumed.

He called the mobile number. It went straight to voicemail:

"Hello. This is Kenneth Lao. I'm sorry I can't take your call right now. Please leave your name and number and a brief message, and I will call you back."

"Hello, Mr Lao. My name is Gabriel Wolfe. I am calling to let you know of the death of one of your clients. His name was Zhao Xi. Please call me back as soon as you can."

He left his own mobile number, then hung up.

Suddenly overwhelmed by fatigue, he sighed heavily and closed his eyes, letting his head hang back and his arms flop slackly by his sides.

He had no urge to cry anymore. Just a slow-burning rage banking up inside him, a surge of lava just below the crust of his sanity, waiting for the narrowest fissure to open, through which it could explode, immolating anyone in its path. He pushed himself back until he was balancing the chair on its two back legs, his own dangling like pendulums, the back of his head bumping gently against the wall behind him.

This was a frustration unlike anything he had ever experienced, in his military career or since. An identified enemy, but one operating not only outside the rules of war, but also the plain old criminal law. A shadow, unseen by any law enforcement agency except as the unknown perpetrator of hits from Macao to Mexico City. He'd met her, but seemingly only because she'd wanted him to. Now she was flying round the world killing the people dear to him, and he could do nothing about it. Or not precisely nothing. He rocked forward suddenly, eyes wide. How could he have forgotten? He had the client's name: Erin Ayers.

Forget Sasha Beck for now. He could track down Ayers, and through her, get to Beck. Then he would kill the assassin and save Ayers for last.

While he waited for the lawyer to call back, he Googled "Erin Ayers." He found plenty of women with the right name, from nurses to lawyers, horse trainers to scuba instructors, but they all seemed far too respectable to be hiring top-end assassins. His profile, such as it was, ran:

. . .

Extremely wealthy

    Criminal connections

    Psychopathic/obsessive personality?

    Sees themselves as an avenger of a crime against authority.

    Calls themselves "Fury" – knows the classics – private education/Oxbridge/comes from rich family?

    Personal grudge against me (met me?)

None of the apparently ordinary women with social media profiles or websites for their home-based businesses fit that particular bill.

He tapped a number in his contacts. It belonged to Fang Jian's personal hacker, a young guy who called himself Wūshī – the wizard. Wūshī had helped Gabriel track down a US defence contractor, a piece of research that had ended well for Gabriel, but less so for the defence contractor.

Wūshī answered on the first ring.

"My man! Speak to me!"

Gabriel couldn't help smiling at the try-hard American accent the young man affected. Given Wūshī's prowess behind a computer keyboard, Gabriel would have forgiven him for speaking like John Wayne.

"Hey, Wūshī. How are you?"

"I'm good man, I'm good. Still doing my thing for our mutual friend, you know?"

"Yeah, I know. I need a favour."

"Sure, man, anything. Hope it's something more challenging than calling up some half-assed *secure* corporate website like last time."

"Try this. I'm looking for someone called Erin Ayers. And before you ask, yes, there are hundreds of women called that according to Google, but I have a strong suspicion the one I'm looking for isn't on Facebook."

"OK. You got my interest. Give me a little time and I'll call you back."

Just then, Gabriel's phone vibrated in his hand. Call waiting. He said a quick goodbye to Wūshī and accepted the incoming call.

"This is Gabriel Wolfe."

"Mr Wolfe, ah, this is Kenneth Lao, of Ophelia Tsang and Partners."

"Thanks for calling back, Mr Lao. You heard my message?"

"Yes, I did. And I am terribly sorry for your loss."

Gabriel frowned. "How do you know it was my loss? I could have been anyone reporting Zhao Xi's death to you."

"No, Mr Wolfe. You could not. I have known all about you since you were a boy. Can you come to my office? We need to talk face to face."

49

GHOSTS

Kenneth Lao's office was on the nineteenth floor of a glass-and-steel office block on Chater Road, sandwiched between two huge retail outlets: Louis Vuitton and Giorgio Armani. The building was directly above a five-way junction heaving with cars, motorbikes, bicycles, taxis and Hong Kong's blue-red-and-yellow double-decker buses. Having passed through the layers of uniformed building security, main reception, and Ophelia Tsang & Partners' own receptionist, Gabriel was ushered in to the office of Kenneth Lao.

It was, he thought, elegant. The only word to describe it. The walls to the left and right of the large mahogany desk were finished with matching built-in bookcases, in which ranks of legal books stood shoulder to shoulder, as if defending the law through their own, leather-bound stolidity. Behind the desk a floor-to-ceiling window gave out onto the International Finance Centre, the harbour beyond that, and, across the water, the skyscrapers of Kowloon. But it was the man behind the desk, rising now to greet him, hand outstretched in welcome, who interested Gabriel.

As they shook hands, Gabriel appraised the lawyer. Mid-sixties, athletic build, smooth skin blemished with acne scars, and a sharpness about the eyes that the crinkles at their outer corners did nothing to disguise. His suit was well cut in the style Gabriel thought of as "high Hong Kong style" – narrow lapels, a sheen to the soft brown fabric and a narrow profile that accentuated the older man's physique. In his leather jacket, T-shirt and jeans, Gabriel felt underdressed.

"Please, Gabriel, sit. Tea? Coffee? Something stronger? I have some very fine Japanese whisky. I confess, since receiving your call, I have had recourse to it more than once."

Gabriel checked his watch; it was seven thirty. "A whisky would be good."

"How do you take it?" Lao said, crossing the thick, dark-blue carpet to a red-and-gold lacquered cabinet that opened to reveal glass shelves full of bottles, cut-glass tumblers, and a chrome ice bucket and tongs.

"Straight please, Mr Lao."

Lao turned, smiling. "Please, call me Kenneth. Here. Let us toast our dear friend."

Gabriel took the tumbler in which an inch of dark amber liquid swirled smokily and clicked it against Lao's.

The whisky's aroma was heady, and once the volatile alcohol molecules had dissipated, he could savour the whisky's perfume: he could smell the dried fruits and spice of a Christmas pudding, chocolate below that, and just a hint of cloves. He took a sip, rolling the spirit round his mouth before swallowing. No fiery hit, just an instant, all-pervading warmth that made him sigh with satisfaction, or was it relief to have found a friend in Hong Kong?

"Good?" Lao asked, placing his own tumbler on the blotter in front of him.

"Extremely. What is it?"

"That is Suntory Yamasaki Sherry Cask 2013. It was a gift from a grateful client." Lao dropped his voice to a conspiratorial whisper. "Thirty-two thousand Hong Kong dollars for a single bottle. The Japanese win all the international whisky competitions nowadays."

"Have they stopped mixing it with Coke, too?"

Lao laughed. "Oh, there are still plenty of Philistines out there, I assure you, though most prefer hot or cold water, depending on the season."

He paused and Gabriel sensed this was his cue to begin talking. Then his phone vibrated in his pocket.

"I'm sorry, do you mind if I check this? It could be important."

"Please, go ahead."

Gabriel pulled out his phone. It was a depressingly short text from Wūshī.

Erin Ayers = ghost. Not on dark web. Not anywhere. If she = real, she = super powerful. Be careful.

He replaced the phone in his pocket, his face impassive. Holding his tumbler lightly, and tilting it this way and that so that the whisky caught reflections from the downlighters in the ceiling, he asked his first question.

"Did Master Zhao talk about me to you?"

"Often. He and I were great friends as well as client and lawyer. We sparred at his dojo whenever I could get away from," he swept his arm around the office, taking in the books with their gold-tooled spines, "all this. When you were growing up, he shared your achievements and," a pause, a smile, a nod, "occasional setbacks. He was very proud of you, you know."

Gabriel nodded, felt a lump solidifying in his throat, then tried to melt it with another slug of the whisky.

"I know. And now he is dead. Because of me."

Lao steepled his fingers and rested his chin on their tips.

"How so?"

Gabriel explained, once again, the events that had brought him to Hong Kong, too late to save Zhao Xi.

"You must not blame yourself for Xi's death," Lao said, once Gabriel had concluded his narrative. "The person to blame is his killer, and her client. This Erin Ayers person. Do you have any idea who she is?"

"No. But I'm working on that. My employers also have intelligence resources, so I hope I'll be able to find her soon."

"And then?" Lao said, frowning.

"And then I will take care of things."

Lao touched his fingertips to his lips. Then spoke.

"Good."

"Good? I thought you'd tell me to go to the police."

"I have been a lawyer for many years now. The law is a wonderful mistress. She has provided for me and for my family. And I do believe I have played my part in serving justice. But from what you tell me, this woman is beyond the reach of the legal system. So I say to you, do what you believe to be just. And if you need any help from me or my firm, you must only ask."

Gabriel let out a breath he hadn't realised he'd been holding in.

"Thank you, Kenneth. Can we talk about Master Zhao's things now, please?" He reached into the inside pocket of his jacket and withdrew the slim envelope from Zhao Xi's desk drawer. "I found this, which led me to you. Do you have his instructions for a funeral?"

Lao nodded. "Do not worry. I have all Xi's papers. I will take care of the funeral arrangements. There is something else you should know while you are here."

"What?"

"As I think you know, Xi had no living relatives. His parents died some time ago, and he was an only child, unmarried to the end. We will need to complete probate on his will, but I can tell you informally that you are his sole beneficiary."

Gabriel blinked. He hadn't given the idea of a will a moment's thought. It made sense, though. He'd been like a son to his master.

"What does that mean?"

"Well," Lao said in a more formal tone, straightening in his chair and unsteepling his fingers, "his assets were substantial. And now they are yours. The house, of course. Some investments. And then there is his collection."

Gabriel felt he was being played a little. He knew the lawyer was enjoying this part of the process, even in the midst of his own grief at losing a friend.

"Collection?"

Lao nodded, smiled again. "Xi collected jade. His collection is one of the best in Hong Kong, if not the mainland. You must have seen it during your time with him?"

"I can't remember. To be honest, I was always more interested in the practical side of his life. The figurines on his desk. Were they part of it?"

"The monk, the fisherman and the dragon? Yes. Not the most valuable pieces, but probably worth around nine hundred thousand Hong Kong dollars each at today's prices. The mainland Chinese are very keen."

Gabriel's eyes popped wide as he thought of the little carved figures standing in plain view on Zhao Xi's desk. "That's—" was all he could manage to croak out.

"About three hundred thousand pounds at today's exchange rate," Lao said, with what appeared to Gabriel to be a lawyerly satisfaction.

"How, I mean, are there more than that? You said a collection."

"Altogether, I believe Xi had amassed somewhere in the region of thirty pieces. You are a rich man, Gabriel."

In his hotel room that night, Gabriel lay on his back on the wide double bed, trying to make sense of the day's events. At a stroke, literally, since the police had called him to confirm that his old master had been killed by a single thrust from a *katana*, he had lost one of the few people he had ever truly loved and become the possessor of property, artworks and investments in Hong Kong worth upwards of four million pounds. Add the US bearer bonds now sitting in a vault in Zurich and he was a very rich man indeed. A very rich man around whom people were dying. Good people. Blameless people. People whose only besetting sin was to have been friends with Gabriel Wolfe. He was a plague. A virus. Come into contact with him, and death was a certainty. His best friend in

England, gone. Two former comrades, gone. And now his mentor, the man who had saved him from himself and turned him into a man, gone. Gabriel felt hollow inside. No tears came, though. In their place, a darkness intensified behind his eyes, like an oncoming storm, bruised charcoal-and-purple thunderheads swelling and boiling, with sickly yellow forks of lightning spearing down and killing everything in their path. Erin Ayers and her paid hitter Sasha Beck were about to discover the true meaning of fury.

50

DOUBLE-BOOKED

While Gabriel tossed and turned in his hotel room, searching for sleep, Sasha Beck was leaving hers. She was due back in England, but had accepted, on the spur of the moment, another hit. Normally she didn't double up on assignments, but the client was one of her oldest, and the target was a soft one: a businessman with some unsavoury connections was blocking her client from acquiring a formerly state-owned oil pipeline in Siberia. Plus, and this had been the clincher, the target was in Hong Kong too, booked to fly to Paris that night.

"And they say there are no such things as coincidences," she said to herself with a smile as she zipped her soft, black leather bag closed and moved to the bathroom.

In her travels, Sasha had met – and learned from – a great many professional people. Not exclusively killers, either. Just people with skills she thought she might find useful one day. Or, simply, that intrigued her. On a trip to Los Angeles a few years earlier, she'd found herself in the San Fernando Valley, home to the city's porn industry. In a bar after her day's work, she'd got talking to an attractive, if dull-eyed, blonde who told her about her work in "the life" as she called it: basically, sex work, from movie-making to prostitution, nude-modelling to trading sex for favours, and occasionally drugs.

The blonde gave her name as Sherry, "you know, like how the French say, 'sweetheart'?" Sasha bought her another martini or three and quizzed her about her work. The conversation turned to the tricks of the trade and a day later, Sasha found herself in Sherry's apartment, learning to suppress her gag reflex by practising blow jobs on a banana. "You learn how to deep throat, baby, and you can get a better fee for the scene, know what I'm sayin'?" Sherry had said in a lazy, floaty voice Sasha ascribed to pills or the half-smoked joint held loosely between her first and second fingers.

Now, in the harsh, white light of her hotel bathroom, Sasha looked in the mirror and held up a slim, white, plastic cylinder from which a length of nylon thread dangled. The cylinder was the approximate size and shape of a tampon. On the marble sink-surround in front of her was a tiny bottle labelled *methylone*. The drug, which she'd bought from a pleasing young woman earlier that day in a club, was a little chemical backup for Sherry's teaching. Sasha unscrewed the lid and took a sip. Instantly she felt the hit as the drug crossed the blood-brain barrier and streaked along her brain's serotonin pathways. She retched once, dryly, then smiled as the sensation of nausea passed, and with it, her gag reflex, as the responsible vagus nerve became desensitised and shut down.

She smiled at herself in the mirror.

"Here goes nothing," she said, then poured the remains of the methylone onto the plastic cylinder, placed it in her mouth and swallowed.

She felt a little discomfort as it went down, but that was all. And down it stayed. Sasha trimmed the nylon thread so that she could conceal the end in her cheek.

The target was a South African named Krit Pender. Finding him would be child's play. First, security.

Finding no weapons, fireworks, matches, bottles of liquid, or blades of any kind in her luggage, or about her person, the attentive security officer waved Sasha through.

She immediately went to the information desk in the departure lounge and asked them to page Pender, explaining that she was his secretary. The smiling young woman at the counter was only too happy to oblige, especially as Sasha had spoken to her in flawless Mandarin, explaining that her phone had no signal inside the airport. The woman bent to the stand-microphone on her desk, flipped the button in its base and spoke.

"This is a message for Mr Krit Pender. Please come to the departure lounge information desk on level one. Mr Krit Pender, to the departure lounge information desk on level one."

Sasha bestowed her best smile on the young woman.

"*Xièxiè*," she said – it sounded like *she she*.

"You're welcome," the woman said, beaming.

Sasha strolled away from the desk, her smart, navy-blue suit complemented by a red, white and blue scarf knotted at her neck. While she waited for Pender to arrive, she opened her carry-on and extracted a neat navy, red-and-white forage cap, which she settled at a jaunty angle over her hair, which today she wore in a French pleat against the back of her head. The methylone was still active in her brain's chemistry, bringing with it the careless high of a mild antidepressant. Her vision had also sharpened, and she used its heightened acuity now to scan the milling crowds as the woman at the desk repeated her message.

"Mr Krit Pender. Message for Mr Krit Pender. Please come—"

Stupid name, Sasha thought, as she swivelled her head left and right, a predator on high alert. There! The target was striding across the concourse towards the information desk. An immensely fat man, well over six feet tall, in a shiny, silver-grey suit that screamed "designer" with every flap of its scarlet-lined jacket. His countenance was florid, beneath a thatch of wiry reddish-blond hair cut *en brosse*. The frown and the set of the thick lips communicated his displeasure at being summoned away from his seat in the Air France First Class Lounge.

Sasha moved to intercept him. No need for the young woman

on the desk to have to deal with him. Falling in step with Pender, she touched him lightly on the left forearm, causing him to stop mid-stride and turn to stare at her.

"Mr Pender?" she said, adopting a French accent.

"Yah. Who the fuck are you?"

I am death. "I am Melinda Schwartz. Air France Executive Privilege Club."

"Schwartz, eh? Another troublemaking black, yah?" Then he bellowed with laughter at his own joke, reddened jowls shaking.

Sasha smiled demurely, bowing her head, staring at a point six inches to the left of the man's second shirt button.

"Captain Marais has asked me to invite you, on his behalf, to sit with him for takeoff. Would you like to follow me, please?"

"What? Up front with the flyboys? Hah! I knew I made the right decision flying frog airlines. Lead on, Blackie!"

High heels clicking on the polished stone floor, Sasha led Pender out of the concourse and through a set of double doors.

"Secret passageway, yah?"

"Something like that, sir, yes. Stay close, please. It is the next door on the right."

Sasha arrived at a plain grey door and stood aside to let Pender in front of her. She pulled the door open, and, as Pender pushed past her, shoved him hard in the small of the back, followed him in, and shut the door.

Pender stumbled, catching his foot on a cleaner's bucket, and sprawled onto the concrete floor.

Sasha gripped the end of the nylon thread in her cheek and drew it out in a single, flowing movement, coughing as the plastic cylinder emerged from her mouth.

"What the fuck is this? You're fucking with the wrong man," Pender said, struggling to get to his knees and looking balefully at Sasha, his pale-blue eyes slits in his face.

"No, darling," Sasha said, cracking the cylinder in half and withdrawing a shiny steel object. With a snap, she pulled the metal object out at both ends, transforming it into a perfectly cylindrical, needle-pointed stiletto that locked with a *snick*.

"You," she bent down and jabbed it hard into the spot she'd picked a few minutes earlier.

"Are fucking," she withdrew it, leaving Pender gasping as blood welled through the front of his shirt.

"With the wrong," in it went again, an inch to the right of the first blow,

"Woman." A third blow, forming an equilateral triangle of entry wounds over the man's already failing heart.

With blood pooling beneath Pender's body and, worse for him, she knew, inside his chest cavity, Sasha wiped the pencil-thin steel on the man's suit jacket, closed it and packed it away in its little plastic scabbard. Then she left.

Just before boarding, she sent three texts. The first, to the man who'd paid her three million to despatch Pender, read,

Job done. 2nd payment now due.

The second, to Erin Ayers, read,

Item four, completed.

And the third, to Gabriel Wolfe, read,

Sorry about Master Zhao, darling. But you know what they say. Live by the sword … SB xxx

51

WHO IS TIMUR KAMENKO?

SALISBURY

Two days later, Gabriel was sitting at his kitchen table with Eli, devouring a plate of bacon, eggs, and toast with hot sauce shaken over the lot. By no coincidence whatsoever, Sasha Beck was enjoying a continental breakfast not two miles away, in a rural pub where she had booked a room for a couple of nights.

"What day is it?" Gabriel asked Eli, using a triangle of toast to mop up the remains of the yolk, which had turned coral-pink thanks to the sauce.

"You have been busy, haven't you? It's Saturday. Listen, I'm sorry about your old friend. That's terrible, what she did."

Gabriel heaved a sigh. "It is. But to her I think it's all a game. I don't know if she enjoys killing people or finds it amusing. I met her after she'd blown an office building in Harare to shit and she could have just come from a game of bridge. Then in Hong Kong—"

Eli's eyes widened. "You spoke to her?"

"No, I mean the last time I was there, not this one. She dropped a couple of bouncers outside a gambling club and strolled in as if she was there to while away a few hours at the tables."

"What, she's a psychopath? Is that what you're saying?"

He shrugged and took a swig of tea before answering.

"I don't know, maybe. But there's definitely something off about her."

"Other than being a paid killer, you mean," Eli deadpanned.

He smiled. "Other than that, yes. Did the cops try to get in touch while I was gone?"

She shook her head. "Nobody's been round. They would have called you anyway."

"I know, and they didn't. So either they've decided I can't add anything, or they're avoiding me."

"So why don't you call them? I'm going for a walk. See you later."

Anita Woods sounded stressed when she answered her phone. Learning that Gabriel was her caller didn't seem to improve her mood.

"Yes, what can I do for you, Gabriel?"

"I just wondered whether you'd made any progress on the case."

"Well, strange as this may seem, we haven't. Looks like your Mystic Meg act was on the money. No witnesses. No forensics worth shit. And to top it all off, your *friend*," she laid heavy sarcasm on this last word, "Mr Donald Webster swooped down like some fucking secret agent overlord and relieved us of the investigation. I was told in no uncertain terms to spend my time and energies on solving another case."

"Look, I didn't mean to be a smart-arse when I told you that you wouldn't find her. It's her profession. And I'm sorry Don did his act. But that's the way we work."

If he'd been hoping this apology would mollify the detective superintendent, Gabriel had misjudged the situation.

"Oh, well perhaps you'd like to tell *Don*," even heavier sarcasm, "next time you two are sipping dry sherry in Whitehall, how grateful

I am to be treated like some rookie straight out of Hendon Police College in front of my team."

She ended the call before he could think of anything that might repair the damage.

He'd barely had a chance to put his phone away when it rang in his hand. It was Don.

"Jesus, Don, are you psychic or something?"

"What's the matter, Old Sport?"

"Nothing. Well, nothing really. I just got off the phone to Detective Superintendent Woods. She was, how shall I put this?"

"Royally pissed off and spitting feathers?"

"Something like that."

"Couldn't be helped. I needed the brass from the shooter, and she was stamping her size sixes and getting all territorial with me."

"So you gave her the queen and country speech?"

"More or less. It never goes down well, but this was, I think, a record-breaking performance. I'd avoid any entanglements with the Wiltshire CID for a while if you can possibly help it."

"I'll do my best."

"I'm sorry about Zhao Xi, Gabriel. I really am. After I got your text, I put in a call to Britta's boss over at MI5. But she's undercover and their SOPs call for a total comms blackout except for a weekly debrief."

"I know. I've been trying to reach her myself."

"You worried?"

"No. Britta can take care of herself. I warned her Sasha was around and causing mischief, so she'll be on her guard."

"Let's hope so. Now, I may have something that will help you track down the mischievous Ms Beck, and possibly her employer."

"What is it? I told you I have a name but nothing else."

"I had our technical bods run some analysis on the bullet casing. Turns out it has a very unusual metallurgical composition. The exact chemistry went over my head, something of a goose at school, I'm afraid. But we know who manufactured it."

Gabriel sat down and pulled a pencil and notebook from a

drawer beneath the kitchen table. "Who? I thought it would be a standard brand like Federal."

"The lab boys ran it against our database. Over seventy manufacturers on it: everything from shotgun shells to tracer rounds. They matched it to a factory in Kazakhstan."

Gabriel's heart stuttered. *Back to Astana, then.*

"I didn't know there were any ammunition manufacturers there. I thought they all got their stuff from the old Soviet producers."

"You're right. Or at least partially right. There aren't any official ammunition manufacturers in Kazakhstan, or not yet. They're building one as we speak. But there is one unofficial supplier. They specialise in what you'd call the grey market. People who have trouble getting ammunition from Federal, say. Or, to be honest, any of the approved NATO or former Soviet suppliers."

"Warlords, you mean? Criminals?"

"Yes to both of those. Plus militias, terrorists, hitters like our friend Ms Beck, and good old-fashioned gangsters. If they don't fancy knocking over an official shipment or breaking into a factory, they just turn up at the gates of TK Industries with a suitcase full of dollars and hey, ho, away they go with as much ammunition as they can carry."

Gabriel scribbled down the name.

"TK Industries?"

"Yes. Owned by a chap goes by the name of Timur Kamenko. Interesting CV. Started off as a low-grade thug in a street gang, worked his way up through the ranks till he took it over, then invested his ill-gotten gains in this manufacturing plant. Saw a gap in the market, like the best entrepreneurs do, and bingo! Supplies ammunition to half the bad guys around the world. Now he harbours political ambitions, too. Heads up this ultra-nationalist party called Kazakh Purity."

"So how come he hasn't been shut down?"

"Protection, in a word. Man's extremely well connected to the current establishment, not to mention extremely rich. We talk occasionally about mounting an operation, but it's never risen high enough up the old to-do list."

"But now?"

"But now, I think we could envisage sending a small team in. You could gather some intel, maybe discover who Erin Ayers really is. Take things from there."

"Me and Eli?"

Don chuckled. "In one, Old Sport. I've made the usual arrangements. Why don't you pop up to town to see me? I might even stand you lunch."

52

NEIGHBOURHOOD WATCHING

MANHATTAN

Erin put the phone down, smiling. She was alone in the penthouse. Guy was at an empty house on her land in Ithaca, getting things ready.

"So, Miss Falskog," she said out loud. "Now you're mine. Poor old Gabriel will be beside himself with worry. Only just got engaged and now his fiancée is in the hands of his mortal enemy. Well, boohoo to both of you."

She poured herself a generous measure of Grey Goose vodka, added a handful of chunky ice cubes, and took it out onto the roof terrace. The night was clear and cold, but the fur coat she wore over her nakedness kept the chill out. She stood, leaning against the reinforced glass wall, and looked down and to her left. The traffic streaming up Fifth Avenue past Trump Tower and alongside the park was beautiful to her eyes. They were guzzling gas, streaming music and wearing out tyres from companies she either owned directly or held significant stakes in, and they were making her rich.

She raised the heavy tumbler and toasted them before sinking half the vodka in a single gulp. Her phone rang.

"Erin, it's Ava. Are you in Manhattan?"

"Yes, I am. At the penthouse. Are you looking for some company?"

"Mm-hmm. We just finished our executive council meeting. I'm on West Fifty-Seventh."

Erin felt her nipples tightening beneath the fur coat. "Come over. Now."

Sitting opposite Erin in the sunken bath was a slim, auburn-haired woman with large, heavily made-up eyes of smoky grey. Both women were drinking from tumblers of vodka on the rocks. Ava Blankefeld's small breasts were just covered by the water. She was trailing her fingertips across them as she spoke.

"Things are looking good for us at the moment, you know."

"You and me 'us' or you and the Free America movement 'us'?"

Ava smiled, and deep dimples appeared on each side of her mouth. "Both, actually. Now the political situation is more favourable to Free America, I'll be in New York a lot more often."

"Yes, well Free America sounds a lot more respectable than 'white supremacists,' doesn't it?"

Ava grinned. "It does. But it isn't just about rebranding. Look around you. Look at your own country. Look at Europe. Ordinary people are waking up to the lies the liberal elite having been feeding them since the end of the Second World War. And they're turning to people who offer something different. People like your father, God rest his soul."

"Oh, I doubt God is very interested in resting Daddy's soul. Probably sees it as somewhat tarnished. But as to your main point, yes, I agree. People are starting to ask what globalisation has done for them, apart from giving them shitty jobs that don't pay the bills, and taking away their pride."

Ava sat up and Erin watched the water streaming over her

breasts. She leaned forward and kissed Ava on the lips, then drew back a little.

"Poor fools," Ava said. "When we're making so much money out of globalisation, it almost seems unfair to be winning them over to our side."

Erin shrugged, finishing her drink. "You'd still be better for them than the alternative. Well, better for the whites, anyway."

She stood, enjoying the way Ava's gaze trailed up her body, and stepped out of the bath. Wrapping herself in a white towel, she headed for the bedroom.

"Come on," she said, looking over her shoulder. "It's been ages."

On the banks of the boating lake, far below in Central Park, Guy stood as still as a sentry, looking up at the penthouse through binoculars. He watched as the two naked women strolled from bathroom to bedroom. A voice to his left made him turn.

"Hey, buddy," a tall, thickset man called over. He was striding towards Guy, hands hanging loose by his sides, accompanied by a shorter, fatter man wearing gold-rimmed glasses. "What're you doing?"

Guy faced the two men, adjusting his balance as he did. "What's it to you?"

"Neighbourhood Watch, and we don't like Peeping Toms."

The two men had arrived in front of him now. Neither looked like a fighter, although something was making them confident. Maybe they had concealed carry permits. He scanned their waists, then the spaces under their arms. No telltale bulges, but their clothes were loose enough to make spotting a pistol a game of chance.

"Me neither, but I'm working security for my employer. She likes me to check on her from time to time."

"Oh, yeah," the fat man said, in a sarcastic tone of voice. "Check in with binoculars. What, were you training them on her bedroom?"

Uncomfortable with the man's pinpoint accurate observation, Guy decided attack was the best form of defence.

"Listen, boys, I'm not doing anything wrong, so why don't you just patrol somewhere else before I decide to exercise my rights to protect myself?"

Now he did see something. The taller man had placed his right hand on his hip and the blocky shape of a pistol appeared as his wind breaker was pushed back.

"I have a better idea. Why don't *you*," he pointed with his left hand, "find somewhere else to take your evening constitutional, and we'll head in the opposite direction?"

"Fair enough," Guy said, preparing to move.

The two men nodded and the wind breaker dropped back to cover the pistol.

Guy moved.

He leapt forwards, closing the gap between him and the two men to less than an arm's length. He spread his own arms wide, grabbed them by the sides of the head and clattered their skulls together with a noise like a fairground coconut shy.

They dropped, beasts stunned by an expert slaughterman, into an untidy pile of limbs at his feet.

"*Hoerenjong*! Next time don't fuck with the big boys," he said, before strolling away, to a bar he liked that served Bavaria Hollandia, the beer he'd learned to love as a teenager in Rotterdam.

53

LIES WE TELL OURSELVES

LONDON

Gabriel had two hours before his meeting with Don. He was spending the first in the private consulting room of Fariyah Crace at The Ravenswood Hospital in Mayfair.

"How have you been," she asked, sitting opposite him and smiling.

Gabriel scratched at his scalp.

"Up and down. Things are rough at the moment."

"Tell me about the downs."

"OK. Since I last saw you, my best friend, two of my former comrades from the Regiment, and my childhood mentor have all been murdered by a female assassin called Sasha Beck. She's been sending me messages as well. Taunting me. She also destroyed my car, not that I care about that. I have been interviewed by the police in Wiltshire and Hong Kong, and I'm not entirely sure they've ruled me out as a suspect."

Fariyah's expression didn't change. Or not in any melodramatic way, eyes widening, mouth dropping open, hands flying to cheeks. Gabriel supposed she had either heard worse or been trained to mask her own emotions no matter what. But he did notice the way her pupils contracted for a split second, and that the fingers holding the pen above her notepad tightened so that the brown skin of her knuckles paled.

"I am very sorry for your loss. I know how much Zhao Xi meant to you, and I'm sure your other friends were equally important to you. How are you coping?"

"I'm working. I have a solid lead on who's behind it all. The client, I mean."

"In yourself, I meant. How are you sleeping?"

He paused before answering, then decided lying to one's psychiatrist was a somewhat pointless exercise. It would be just as easy simply not to go to an appointment as to go and then avoid the truth.

"Very badly," he said. "Drink helps, but I'm awake for a couple of hours in the night worrying about who's next. And the nightmares are back, worse than ever."

"Who do you think might be next?"

"Britta. My fiancée?" Fariyah nodded. "She's working undercover, and I can't reach her. I'm frightened she's already been taken."

"Have you heard anything from her?"

"No. She's not returning my calls and—"

"No, I meant the assassin."

Gabriel sat back, recalibrating his answer. "No. No, I haven't."

"But you said she's been sending you messages. So if you haven't heard from her she can't have done anything to Britta, can she?"

Gabriel inhaled deeply and let the breath out in a sigh.

"I suppose not. And she's tough. Britta, I mean. I wouldn't bet against her in a face-off with Sasha Beck. It's just I spent my whole life avoiding being tied down and then the moment I decide to go for it, this ... this *shit* happens."

Fariyah frowned. "It's funny, isn't it? How we use that phrase – 'tied down' – to mean entering an enduring loving relationship. Is that really how you feel about marriage, Gabriel?"

"Of course not!" he said, then realised he'd answered too quickly. "Of course not," he repeated. "I want this. She does, too. We're right for each other. We love each other."

"Love is a strange thing, Gabriel, believe me. Tell me, what do you think marriage will be like?"

"What?" he asked. "What do you mean? It will be like being married, won't it? Like normal people."

Fariyah smiled. "That really isn't much of an answer. Let me put it this way. If you picture a typical day in your marriage to Britta, say five years from now, what will you be doing?"

Gabriel stared at the ceiling. He was trying to follow Fariyah's suggestion and finding it almost impossible. He closed his eyes. Tried to visualise a room with the two of them in it. Or a park. Or a theatre. Nothing. "Well," he began, playing for time, "I suppose we'd be —" *stripping assault rifles, going undercover in a Thai drug smuggling operation, trading shots with stoned militia fighters —*

He opened his eyes and focused on the plump face of his psychiatrist.

"It won't be a typical marriage. But we'll make it work. She wants kids. That's normal, isn't it?"

"Very. Which one of you will do the three a.m. feeds, do you think?"

Gabriel could feel his heart thudding in his chest. He felt unaccountably anxious and rubbed the sweat from his palms onto the thighs of his jeans.

"I don't know. Is this important?" His voice sounded strained, even to his own ears. God only knew how he sounded to a trained shrink.

"I'm sorry," she said. "I was being unnecessarily provocative. You said there were ups as well as downs. Tell me about them."

He shrugged. "It's not meant to balance the scales or anything, but I took out a bunch of Nazis in Switzerland and rescued this girl they were using for some sort of grotesque reenactment. And whether I like it or not, I seem to have become a wealthy man. But only because that bitch murdered Zhao Xi." He shouted this last phrase and clapped his palm across his mouth, eyes wide with shock at the violence of his reaction. Tears started from his eyes and, silently, Fariyah passed him a box of tissues.

"Tell me, Gabriel. Tell me again about Michael. It all stems from that one moment in your life, doesn't it?"

Gabriel let out a pained sound, somewhere between a moan and a deep, shuddering sigh. He rubbed both hands over his face and then let his hands fall to his lap.

"I told you before about what happened. How I kicked a ball into the harbour and told him to go and fetch it. How he drowned."

"Yes, you did. You told me what you did and what Michael did. The things that happened. But I want you to tell me what it *felt* like."

"That's just it. I can't. I don't remember."

"That's all right. Those memories may come back one day, or they may stay buried deeply inside you for ever. So instead, can you tell me how you feel about it now?"

Gabriel steepled his fingers under his chin, leaned back in the armchair and looked at the ceiling.

"I feel, when I think about what I did, to Michael, and to Mum and Dad, I just feel so guilty. One minute we were a happy family and the next, I blew it apart."

"How do you know you were a happy family?"

"Of course we were, what do you mean?" he said, sharply.

She held up her hands, placatingly. "Many families are happy, of course. But in my experience, many are not. Or not as happy as their members believe. Are you familiar with Leo Tolstoy's famous line about happy families from his novel *Anna Karenina*?"

"No. Tell me."

"Tolstoy wrote, 'All happy families are alike; each unhappy family is unhappy in its own way.' I wonder whether there was any unhappiness in your family. Your father was a senior diplomat at a very challenging time in Hong Kong's history. You have told me you were bullied at school because of your mother's, and your, mixed heritage. There may have been stresses and strains in the family of which you were unaware. You were only nine when Michael died, yes?"

"That's right."

"Well, nine is very young to be able to fully grasp all that happens within a family, let alone one's parents' marriage."

Gabriel could feel anger bubbling just below the surface.

"What are you implying?" he said in a low voice.

"I am implying nothing. I am telling you that a nine-year-old boy isn't always the best judge of the state of his family."

"Even if it wasn't always perfect, so what? I still killed him, didn't I?"

"Oh, Gabriel, there you go again. Let's remind ourselves of the facts. You kicked a ball into the water. You told Michael to get it. He chose—" she paused and held her hands up again as Gabriel leaned forward to interrupt, "—yes, he chose to go along with you and then, in a tragic accident, he drowned. Let me ask you. Did you expect him to drown? Did you want him to drown? Did you *hope* he would drown?"

Gabriel heard Fariyah's words as though through ear defenders, blurry and muffled, overlaid with a high-pitched ringing. He felt a cold descend over him and seep into his belly. Sweat broke out on his forehead and he felt nauseous. All of a sudden, he was remembering. A two-year-old boy, raging at his mother as she breastfed the new baby. Beating at her legs with his impotent, balled fists. Standing over the cot, looking down and hating the swaddled infant as he lay, gurgling contentedly to himself. And then, the turbid green water of Victoria Harbour. The floating timbers and snaking, half-submerged ropes at the dockside. And

(No! This wasn't how it happened.)

that sudden, savage impulse as he

(I didn't want him to die.)

kicked the ball high into the air over Michael's head

(It was an accident.)

and into the water, before shouting at the brother who idolised him to—

(No, it wasn't. I said, "Get the ball, you idiot!")

dive in and retrieve it.

("I hope you die. Then Mum will love me again.")

"Oh, God, no!" Gabriel moaned. "I did. I wanted him to go. I wanted Mum and Dad to myself."

54

HEALTH AND SAFETY

Don Webster looked up as Gabriel was shown into his office by a secretary. Seeing his visitor's face, he narrowed his eyes.

"Everything all right, Old Sport? You look like you've seen a ghost."

Gabriel's voice was curiously flat, as though reciting poorly learned lines in a school play.

"I'm fine, thanks. I've just seen Fariyah Crace. We had what she called a breakthrough. But there is more work to do. Her words."

"Well, I'm glad to hear it. She's done some amazing work with some of our people. Now, let's get your stuff sorted."

Don got up and walked to a table positioned under the window of his office. Gabriel joined him. The view wasn't much, just more glass, steel, and concrete office blocks, but if he pressed his face against the bulletproof glass and looked down at a forty-five-degree angle, he could see the tips of some trees growing in a small square below.

On the table were a few pale-green cardboard folders, stacked loosely together. Don opened the top one. He selected a map, opened it out and jabbed an index finger down into a largely green area, devoid of settlements, centring his fingertip on a cluster of grey rectangles joined to a motorway by some sort of access road.

"That little block is TKI's manufacturing plant. Kamenko has an office there. His house is over here," he lifted his finger and stabbed it down again about five miles to the east. "He conducts most of his political business in Astana, but uses the house to meet his cronies in Kazakh Purity."

Next, Don drew out a set of stapled sheets of A4, clipped to the front of which was an eight by ten colour photograph of the man himself: Timur Kamenko. High, flat cheekbones, a heavy ridge of bone above his thick, dark-brown eyebrows, brooding eyes and a slit of a mouth.

"Ugly bugger, isn't he?"

"I've met uglier."

"So you have, so you have. Well, he's ugly on the inside as well as the outside. Suspected of war crimes in the Balkans and elsewhere. Ran a little outfit that specialised in rape as an instrument of terror."

"You want us to bring him in? Or deliver the Queen's message?"

Don shook his head.

"Much as I'd like to, my political masters – and mistresses – would rather we left Kamenko alone. For now. Bigger fish to fry and so on."

"Do we know what sort of security he's got around the factory?"

Don opened a third folder and extracted some grainy but legible aerial photographs. Several were close-ups, with armed figures clearly visible.

"Our friends across the pond supplied these. Kamenko's your typical Eastern Bloc heavy – bunch of hired thugs with AK-47s and cheap leather jackets. Nothing you and Eli can't cope with, I'm sure," he said with a wink.

A fourth folder yielded passports and travel documents for Gabriel and Eli, or Mr and Mrs Craig Esmond, according to the machine-printed details.

"So that's everything?" Gabriel asked. "And the mission? Go in, find Kamenko, identify Erin Ayers or at least get some sort of lead on her, then exfil?"

Don returned to his desk and motioned Gabriel to the chair opposite him.

"Not quite all, Old Sport. You see, although the Privy Council want Kamenko left alone, I did manage to persuade them that it mightn't hurt our broader SASOs if—"

"Sorry, Don, what the hell are SASOs?"

"Sorry. More bloody bureaucrat-speak. They have more acronyms than the Army, and that's saying something. SASOs are security and stability objectives. Broad policy goals for our global presence, both armed and diplomatic."

OK, got it. You were saying?"

"A few top cops, counterterror people and politicians might sleep a little easier in their feather beds if Mr Kamenko's factory were to suffer a, what shall we call it …?"

Gabriel smiled for the first time since leaving Fariyah's office.

"A business-critical health and safety situation?"

Don nodded. "You speak the lingo admirably. Yes, possibly something a little more permanent than a slip-and-trip hazard."

Gabriel started to rise, then sat down again.

"One last question. How are we getting in? And out?"

55

KNEES AND ELBOWS

Britta woke from a dream where she'd been fishing for lake trout with her *farfar* Falskog. Grandfather had just been showing her how to gut a fish when the scraping of the lock in the door jarred her into wakefulness. She sat up on the mattress and ran her fingers through her hair. It hadn't been washed for five days and was greasy to her touch.

The one called Zuko appeared in the open doorway, dressed in that universal gangster style: black, leather bomber jacket and tight, stonewashed jeans. He leered down at her as he placed a plastic plate in front of her. It bore two slices of white bread, spread with strawberry jam. A mug of black coffee followed it. His rubbery features were arranged into an expression she could read only too well: *If I was in charge, I'd have fucked you by now.*

Just try it, she thought. *You'll be eating your own cock.*

After he locked her in again, she devoured the bread and jam, slurping gulps of the bitter coffee down on top of each bite. They'd allowed her at least the semblance of a civilised prison cell. The room had no window, but she had enough space to walk around in, if only repetitive sets of six paces forward, and six back. A tatty bible lay beside the mattress. It was the only reading matter in there with her and she'd begun on page one of Genesis on the first night they'd kept her there.

She didn't believe in God, not after what she'd seen people do to other people. But reading the simple, affirmative verses reminded her of *Farfar* and *Mormor* and their cosy cottage outside Uppsala. Reading the Bible together on winter evenings with the log burner roaring and the smell of *Mormor*'s cinnamon buns baking in the oven. How she'd always beg for just one more of the delicious, warm *Kanelbullar* and how *Mormor* would say no, at first, then relent, her grey eyes crinkling with humour, and offer the tray of buns to her granddaughter.

The lock scraped again, and this time her visitor was the leader. Torossian himself. Every day, he would come in and engage her in conversation. About history, about politics, about science – the man seemed voracious in his appetite for knowledge. Perhaps his men were cut from less inquisitive material than their boss. She hadn't found a way to use his thirst for conversation against him – yet – but talking was still more interesting than sitting reading the bible.

"Good morning, Britta," he said, sitting opposite her on a hard chair he brought in with him. She remained sitting, cross-legged, on the mattress. The chair was the only one in the room. "How did you sleep?"

"Like a baby. I was dreaming about gutting fish," she answered in a pleasant voice, smiling up at him.

On his first visit, she'd leapt up at him when she detected a wavering in his attention, and been rewarded with a pistol-whipping. The man's reflexes were as fast as a cat's, and although he was happy to talk about Aristotle or Nelson Mandela, space travel or European history, he was equally happy to dish out violence. She kept still now. The time to escape would be once she was out of the lockup, which would have to happen soon.

"And I'm sure you were very good at it, too," he said, grinning. "I'm afraid you will be our guest for a little while longer. My contact is on her way back from a business trip. She should be here tomorrow to pay for your release."

"And then what?"

He shrugged. "Then, I don't know. I will be a quarter of a million pounds better off, and you will no longer be my concern."

"Don't bet on it. Once I've dealt with her, I'll be back for you and your gang of thugs. We have what we need to put you away."

"Everything except the power of arrest. And you may be surprised to know that those people who *do* have that power will not be exercising it on me. You'll find that I am not the only one swayed by the promise of large sums of money."

"It doesn't matter who you've bribed. We'll just work with another force to bring you in."

"We'll see. Now, take your clothes off."

Britta's eyes opened wide.

"What?"

Standing, he looked down at her. "You heard me. Undress now." He pointed the pistol at her. "You're going tomorrow and I've been looking forward to this."

"Fuck you!" she said, pushing herself back against the wall then sliding up it so she was facing him.

He thumbed the hammer back.

"You can get out of this alive. And who knows, you might overpower Sasha and escape. Then you can come back for me and try your luck. But right now, you're going to take your clothes off or I'm going to put a bullet into each knee. Then each elbow. A little trick I learned from an Irish friend of mine. You'll find it takes the fight right out of you. Not fatal, but very painful. And I'll still have you."

She stared at him, breathing hard, weighing her options. With the hammer back the trigger pull would be light. And Torossian was no amateur.

She looked down and pulled on the free end of her belt.

"I'll find you," she said.

Torossian nodded, and smiled.

56

QUIET CARRIAGE

Gabriel's phone rang. He was sitting in the quiet carriage on the train down to Salisbury, and a number of elderly people with their noses buried in books or bent over newspaper crosswords looked up, their noses wrinkled with annoyance. He moved to the space between the carriages.

He looked at the screen. And frowned: Private Number.

"Gabriel Wolfe."

"Hello, Gabriel. It's Sasha."

"What the fuck do you want?"

"Oh, darling, now is that any way to speak to an old friend?"

He fought down an impulse to scream abuse at Sasha Beck, or just end the call, but he breathed his way through it.

"I'm coming for you, Sasha."

"I'm looking forward to it. But in the meantime, you might want to pack a bag."

"Why?" Did she know about his trip to Kazakhstan somehow?

"Because I'm afraid you're about to join the ranks of the homeless. It wouldn't have been my choice, Gabriel, but my client is most insistent. And it's such a pretty cottage, too."

With a cold stone weighing heavy in his stomach, Gabriel asked a question to which he already knew the answer.

"What are you talking about?"

"I'm talking about an FGM-148 Javelin anti-tank missile. Tandem warhead, shaped charges. Somewhat more advanced than that crappy old M72 I used on your Maserati. Cost me a bloody fortune, I can tell you, and as heavy as all get-out. I'll give you five minutes to vacate the premises, as they say, then I'm pulling the trigger."

"I'm not in."

"Then who was that turning the lights on this morning?"

Shit! Eli. He ended the call and made another one.

"Hi, this is Eli. Leave a message."

Clutching his phone so tightly his knuckles whitened, Gabriel spoke urgently.

"Eli, get out of the house. Now. I'll come and find you."

He went back to his seat and sat heavily, causing the elderly gentleman next to him to *harrumph* in disapproval.

"Oh, God, please be safe," Gabriel muttered.

"I beg your pardon?" the old man said.

"Sorry. Talking to myself."

No doubt imagining he had chosen a seat next to the train's resident crazy, the man shook out his newspaper with a crackle of pages and buried his head inside it.

Gabriel closed his eyes and tried to visualise Eli safe. Maybe she'd been out on a run. Maybe she'd driven down to the coast to see the English seaside in all its spring glory. He saw her jogging along the beach, laughing as her bare feet pounded the hard-packed sand at the water's edge, sleek limbs catching the sun, hair flying behind her. Then she stepped on a land mine and her lower legs shattered into bloody shreds and shards of bone, and she tumbled to the sand, shrapnel tearing at her innards, slashing her skin into ribbons. He shook his head and opened his eyes, willing the train to take him home faster. Fast enough to save her.

57

ITEM FIVE

SALISBURY

From her vantage point on the hill, seven hundred and fifty yards away from Gabriel's home, Sasha had an uninterrupted view of the cottage. The light was good, high cloud and the sun behind her. The mildest of crosswinds, little more than a soft breeze, was soughing through the trees around her firing position. All around her, the trees were coming into leaf, sprouting vibrant green foliage. Between her and the cottage, she watched a herd of sheep in a field, moving randomly as they grazed on the lush new-growth grass.

The Javelin was definitely overkill. A hundred and twenty-six thousand dollars' worth of high-tech military weapon system – for which she had paid ninety on the black market – and a missile worth as much as a Porsche 911. But Erin's fee was overkill too, as was her attitude. Whatever Gabriel Wolfe had done to her, she was a woman with a mission.

Possessed of normal emotional responses, Sasha might have been struck by the brutal contrast between the American-made anti-tank missile at her shoulder and the pastoral scene before her. As it was, she was oblivious to everything but the job in hand. According to her watch, her deadline was just ninety seconds away. If he'd been lying about not being inside the cottage, Gabriel would have been out of the house seconds after hanging up on her. On foot, obviously, since she'd destroyed that rather nice car of his. Still, when they were together, she'd buy him a new one. And if he hadn't been lying, she could fire with impunity.

She prepared to fire.

Unlike moving armoured vehicles, structures stay still. Or they do until they're blown up. So target acquisition was all done in a matter of seconds. Having locked the control launch unit's infrared targeting system onto the wall of the cottage housing the vent from the central heating boiler, Sasha switched control to the missile's onboard IR system. It beeped once. Locked on.

She took a breath then let it out. It was a sniper's move, completely unnecessary with a guided missile, but old habits die hard, and it was Sasha's way to be consistent in all her hits, whatever weapon she was using. The clock in her head ticked down from twenty seconds.

"Coming, ready or not," she whispered.

She pressed the trigger button.

The missile left the tube with a damped double-click followed by a brief *phut* as the gunpowder launch charge ejected it from the tube. A split second later, the main rocket motor ignited with a roar, and the missile streaked away, over the trees and the heads of the sheep towards the cottage. As the exhaust gases blew back towards her, Sasha turned aside and held her breath, not wishing to inhale a lungful of lead oxide.

The rear end of the missile glowed white-hot as it sped down the hill towards its target, trailing a thin stream of pale-grey smoke.

She watched, smiling, as the missile's twin charges detonated against the central heating vent. The gout of dark-grey smoke that boiled out from the house was followed by the bright orange flash of the fireball. The boom of the explosion reached Sasha's ears four seconds later. Almost immediately, a second, booming explosion tore the air as the gas main supplying the house ignited.

With the rolling echoes of the explosions bouncing off the hillsides around her, Sasha decoupled the launch tube from the CLU and lugged them separately to her car, where she stowed them beneath a coat in the boot. Brushing her hands together, she turned one last time to watch as the pall of smoke climbed above the ruined cottage. She climbed inside and drove off at a sedate thirty miles an hour.

58

ITEM SIX

MANHATTAN

Erin was sitting on her balcony, enjoying a late lunch of smoked salmon on whole wheat toast, and a glass of champagne, when her phone vibrated on the glass tabletop.

Item five, completed.

She smiled to herself. Then she called a young man she'd met on her previous trip to London. Alix Polhemus was nineteen, and somewhere on the autism spectrum. He was also preternaturally good at hacking computer systems.

Erin gave Alix a set of instructions they'd discussed during their previous meeting, then hung up.

Exactly seventeen minutes after that, the website of Wolfe &

Cunningham, independent security consultants, went dark, drawing a sigh of exasperation from a NATO official who had just found it.

Ten seconds after that, it went live again, now with altered username and password for the webmaster. It bore on its all-black home page – the only one remaining – nothing but an eleven-word message in white capitals.

WE HAVE CEASED TRADING OWING TO THE DEATH OF GABRIEL WOLFE.

The NATO official shrugged and went back to Google.

59

HUMAN REMAINS

SALISBURY

The pall of smoke hanging over the village told Gabriel that Sasha had made good on her promise. He paid the taxi driver and got out. He would have had to anyway because the main road was blocked by fire engines and police cars.

He walked towards his home, threading his way between the emergency services vehicles, until he reached the short stretch of straight road that ran past his cottage. Correction: the wreck of his cottage.

It resembled one of the ruined dwellings he'd seen during his service with the Regiment: black and smoking rubble, twisted pipes sticking out of the ground, a stinking mess of charred fabrics, plastic, paper and metal, and overlaying it all, the stench of burnt rocket propellant and high explosive. The Javelin had destroyed the structure from the chimney down to the doorstep. What the high-explosive warhead hadn't achieved directly, the gas explosion had completed. The fire was out, and the remaining firefighters were playing water over the smoking ruins to ensure the blaze didn't reignite.

As he made his way closer, a soot-smeared firefighter approached him with his hand up, palm outwards.

"Sorry, sir, you'll have to stop there. The police are going to cordon this off."

Gabriel stopped and looked into the blue eyes of the firefighter, bright in the grimy face.

"That was my house. I had a friend staying with me. Have a friend. Was there—?"

"Jesus! I'm very sorry." He looked over his shoulder at the smouldering debris. "It's impossible to say if anyone was inside at this point, sir. Anyone who was, well, I'm afraid they're beyond help. We didn't find any evidence, but ..."

Gabriel knew what the tired-looking firefighter was implying. In the superheated centre of a shaped-charge explosion, human flesh and bones would have vaporised, and the airborne particles combusted like so much dust, till nothing remained.

"The senior investigating officer is over there. She'll want to talk to you. Please tell me you were insured."

Gabriel nodded. "I may need to up my cover, don't you think?"

Without waiting for an answer from the blinking firefighter, Gabriel walked over to a knot of plainclothes and uniformed police officers who had gathered thirty yards beyond the smoking shell of his former home. As he expected, Anita Woods was at the centre of the group.

Seeing him coming, she detached herself and came forward to meet him. Her face bore an expression of what seemed to him to be genuine sorrow, mixed with something harder to read. As if he had brought something evil to her quiet backwater of the countryside where murders, when they did occur, were crimes of passion or fallings out among soldiers, rather than international vendettas conducted by assassins and their mystery clients.

"Gabriel," she said. "I don't know what to say. We've got some military bomb disposal people on their way. I'm just so sorry. Have you got somewhere to stay tonight?"

For a surreal moment, Gabriel imagined she was going to offer her spare bedroom to him. Then reality reasserted itself. He shook his head.

"It doesn't matter. I'm going away for a while. Travelling."

"I don't think I can let you do that. We're going to need to talk to you again. In detail."

Wearily, Gabriel drew from his wallet the plastic card Eli had given him.

"I'm sorry, too, but that's not going to happen. Call this number. They'll explain everything. I have to go. There's someone I need to find."

He waited for her to tap in the number on the card, then, as she brought the phone to her ear, signalling him to wait with the other hand, he turned and walked away.

His phone rang.

"Gabriel, it's Eli. Where are you?"

Thank God. "At the house. Where are you?"

"I'm in the New Forest. I decided to do some sightseeing while you were in London. I got your message. What happened?"

"She hit my house with an anti-tank missile. A Javelin, if you're interested."

"Fuck me! So it's gone, then?"

"Potential for development."

"You Brits and your gallows humour. You make us Israelis look like clowns. Are you all right? Really?"

"Me? I'm fine. But I'm just about the only one who is, aren't I? Everyone I care about is dead, except Britta, I mean. And I can't reach her."

"What did Don say?"

"He's given me a dossier on a guy called Timur Kamenko, a Kazakh politician with a nice little sideline supplying ammo to the world's criminal underworld, including Sasha Beck. We're going to find him. And when we do, we're going to get him to tell us about her client. I have the name now. Erin Ayers."

"Good. How are we getting there?"

"Don said NATO and Kazakhstan have a security cooperation

deal – a memorandum of understanding – so we're flying military and landing at Sary-Arka Airport. Their air force has a fast jet base there, and it's not too far from Kamenko's operation. He said we'll get full on-the-ground support. We're a married couple engaged in defence analysis for the British Government. Mr and Mrs Craig Esmond."

"There's just one thing. All our gear was in the house. We need some new weapons."

"Don said he'd sort things with the Kazakhs. It's not a problem."

"OK, good. I need to come back and get you. Meet me at the pub. We can get something to eat and then, wait, where are we flying from?"

"RAF Odiham. It's the HQ for the Joint Special Forces Aviation Wing. Don's lined up a Raytheon Sentinel R1. Long-range. It'll take us there in one hop."

"I'll see you shortly. And Gabriel?"

"What?"

"Try not to worry about Britta, OK?"

60

MEMORANDUM OF
UNDERSTANDING

KAZAKHSTAN

Sary-Arka Airport was another name for the airport Gabriel had flown into with Mortensen. It seemed the Kazakh government couldn't make its mind up about what to call it, although Gabriel felt the "International" tag was a little overblown. It sat in a huge, featureless plain extending for hundreds of miles in every direction. A white-and-red, two-storey structure, framed by a control tower, a pair of red-and-white floodlight masts and a couple of air bridges, it was never going to win any architecture prizes. The most interesting feature was its name, rendered in stylised capitals of the official Cyrillic alphabet, which made it look as though the airport's name was CAPY-APKA.

Gabriel and Eli were met off the Sentinel by their Kazakh Ground Forces liaison. He was a tall, imposing man with a craggy jaw and deep-set eyes of a piercing blue, maybe early sixties, and with the easy bearing of a soldier used to command.

"Mr and Mrs Esmond, welcome," he said, his mouth widening

into a smile of what appeared to Gabriel to be genuine good humour. "I am Colonel Ulan Sultanov at your service." They all shook hands, then the Colonel led them into a Portakabin behind the main terminal building.

"Forgive me, but as a formality, may I see your passports?" he said, once they were seated in a small, functional office decorated with framed prints of what Gabriel supposed were Kazakh politicians.

After the documents were checked and returned, the Colonel spread his hands expansively.

"Your commander, Colonel Webster," Gabriel and Eli glanced at each other, "was somewhat vague on the precise details of your work here but you have the highest NATO security clearance, so I am here to help you in any way I can. We have a memorandum of understanding, as you probably know."

Gabriel nodded and smiled, and borrowed a little diplomatic language from memories of his father. "Thank you, Colonel. We are honoured to be working so closely with the Kazakh Ground Forces. Without your support, our work here would be impossible. May I ask, where did you learn your English? It's extremely good. And is that a hint of an American accent?"

The Colonel laughed, filling the room with the smell of garlic and cigarette smoke.

"Just what I would expect from an intelligence analyst. I trained at West Point, you know? New York State. I am still a Yankees fan."

"Who do you rate as their best-ever player?"

"Oh, Joltin' Joe DiMaggio. Every time. You follow sports?"

"When I can. Work keeps me very busy."

"Oh, but all work and no play makes Jack a dull boy. Isn't that what you Brits say? Now," he clapped his hands together, "I expect you want to be on your way. I have prepared transport for you according to Colonel Webster's instructions. I think you will find it satisfactory." Gabriel watched the man's expression closely. Was that a hint of a smile playing around his lips? "Follow me, please."

Round the back of the building sat a four-wheel drive in sand and olive-green camouflage. The vehicle was the same shape, roughly, as a big, commercial SUV like a Range Rover or a Cadillac Escalade, but bulked up like a body builder with a steroid habit. Clearly cut out for military work, it was slab-sided with heavy-duty bars over the side windows. The ride height was jacked up far enough to drive straight over boulders without scraping the underside. A winch was bolted to the front, to the left of which sat a thick steel towing eye.

"What do you think, darling?" Gabriel asked Eli.

"It's very nice. Darling." She turned to the colonel. "A SandCat, yes?"

"Very good, Mrs Esmond. Yes, supplied to us by Oshkosh two years ago. I can personally vouch for its capabilities. Come, look inside. I have assembled some materiel for you."

Sultanov swung open the rear door. Gabriel peered inside then stood back to let Eli get a closer look. He'd seen two assault rifles, a pair of semi-automatic pistols and several olive-green, steel boxes.

"Would you like to run through what you've provided, Colonel?" Eli asked, bestowing a smile on Sultanov that had the man almost purring.

"Certainly, my dear Mrs Esmond. You have two AK-74M assault rifles. Russian-made like virtually all our equipment, and very reliable. Two GSh-18 pistols, also from our large neighbour to the north. And plenty of ammunition. You may be interested to know that the pistols fire both 9 x 19mm Parabellum rounds and overpressure Russian 9 x 19mm 7N21 armour-piercing rounds. You have plenty of each in the ammunition boxes." He spread his big hands wide and grinned at them. "Just in case you have any troubles during your," a pause, "analysis." Then he winked.

Gabriel and Eli swung their bags into the back of the SandCat, noting the boxes of field rations and water containers thoughtfully provided by Sultanov, and then, with Gabriel behind the wheel, they waved to the colonel and roared away across the concrete apron towards the gate in the perimeter fence he'd pointed out. Next stop: TK Industries.

61

AWKWARD LUGGAGE

The SandCat performed surprisingly well on the road for a military vehicle. The ride was hard, but not harsh, and conversation was possible above the growl of its engine, thrumming away under the reinforced steel armour of the bonnet.

"You know the origins of the SandCat?" Eli asked as Gabriel headed northwest towards the city of Karaganda.

"It's Oshkosh. That US outfit."

"Yeah, but before that?"

"No. But I have a feeling I'm about to learn something new."

"Yes you are," she said, looking out through the windscreen. "It's based on the Caracal, which was designed by Plasan of Israel. Since Oshkosh took it on, they've been using the Ford F550 chassis, plus it has the 6.4-litre Ford V8 diesel under the hood."

"Goodness me. First your Jericho, and now our little dune buggy here. Please tell me there are some nice salt beef sandwiches in the food boxes back there."

Eli laughed. "You wish. I've a feeling it'll be field rations like every army on the planet provides."

"Yeah, well, we can at least get a decent meal tonight."

"Why? Where are we staying?"

Gabriel cleared his throat and adopted a formal "tour-guide" voice.

"Tonight, we shall be staying at the Cosmonaut. Voted the best hotel in Karaganda in 2015. The hotel benefits from a pool and fitness centre, and Wi-Fi in all rooms."

Eli put her boots up on the dashboard. "Great. I fancy a steak and some French fries."

"I'm sure as a discerning gourmet, madam will be able to find what she is looking for in the excellent *Zhuldyz* restaurant."

The SandCat looked grotesquely out of place in the hotel's car park. Gabriel parked at the end of a row, cruising past dozens of glossy black, silver, and gunmetal Mercedes, BMWs and Audis. It towered over them, even dwarfing a Porsche Cayenne SUV parked haphazardly across two spaces.

"What shall we do with the kit?" Eli asked, stretching by the SandCat's steel-armoured flank.

Gabriel shrugged. "Two choices. We lock it inside or take it up to our room. I'd be inclined to leave it here. It's a military-spec vehicle and anyone looking to nick a car would pick one of those," he said, waving his hand at the ranks of gleaming German automobiles.

"On the other hand, if anyone did break in or take it, we're basically fucked."

"So what are you saying, sling a couple of assault rifles over our shoulders and check in as normal with two boxes of ammo apiece?"

"No, of course not! Why are you always so sarcastic?"

"It's not sarcasm. It's British humour."

"Oh, yes, the famous British sense of humour. Monty Python, Benny Hill. I get it. Ha, ha."

Gabriel frowned. "What's up?"

Eli sighed. "Oh, nothing. Sorry. I'm just tired. But I still think we shouldn't leave the weapons in the truck."

"Give me ten minutes. I'll do a quick recce round the back of the hotel. Maybe I can find something to camouflage them with."

Eli continued stretching, bending from side to side and alternately pulling her feet up behind her, leaning on the massive door of the SandCat.

"Don't be too long. I need a shower."

Gabriel trotted off towards the hotel. Avoiding the smart frontage, he headed for the rear of the building. Wherever there's a hotel, there are kitchens, laundries, goods inwards loading bays – all kinds of interesting places. To the rear of the kitchen, easily identifiable by the steaming vents high on the walls that were emitting a delicious aroma of frying meat, Gabriel saw a square-based, wheeled wire trolley about six feet tall and three on each side. In it were squashed dozens of cardboard boxes. Presumably, they'd once held catering supplies. He wandered over, checking left and right for hotel staff, but they were all inside working. None of the boxes were the right size for the rifles. He carried on mooching around, hands in pockets, hoping, if he did meet anyone, they'd take him for a guest off the beaten track.

Rounding a corner, he saw another of the big metal recycling trolleys. Like the first, this one was crammed with squashed cardboard. But then, *result!* Behind it were several big boxes, as tall as a man, stacked one on top of the other. Coming closer, he saw exactly what they had contained. Printed on the tops in black were images of rowing machines and Concept 2 logos. *Aha! The gym manager is refreshing the equipment!*

Gabriel looked around once more. Nobody about. He selected the topmost carton and carried it back to the car, holding on tight as an early evening breeze threatened to tug the unwieldy box from his grasp. Back with Eli, he laid the carton at her feet like a cat with a particularly large tribute for its mistress.

"This ought to do it," he said. You load the stuff in. I'm going to find a trolley."

He returned five minutes later with a showier item than the recycling trolleys he had already seen. This one had a carpet base and fake gold plating on an arching pole that served both as a handle and framework to stop guests' suitcases from tumbling off.

Together, they lifted the rowing machine box onto the carpeted platform. The hotel had even thoughtfully provided a bungee cord, which Gabriel stretched round the waist of the carton before interlocking the two hooks.

With their two holdalls packed around the base, they made their way round to the front door of the hotel.

"You wait here," Gabriel said. "I'll get us checked in, then I'll give you a wave. Just bring it in smartly and we'll take it up in the lift. If anyone asks you what you're doing just speak to them in Hebrew."

He was back within a few minutes, smiling. "Everything good?" Eli asked.

He nodded. "Let's go."

Timing their entrance to coincide with the arrival of a coach party of Russian tourists, they marched around the edge of the reception area and were in a lift heading for the fifth floor a few moments after that.

The hotel's restaurant was huge. On this weekday evening, it was deserted apart from the waiters and one or two guests. Gabriel and Eli had been seated at a corner table large enough for six, covered with a custard-yellow tablecloth and featuring a chunky glass candlestick with a single, fat, red candle burning merrily. They sat adjacent to each other and, once the food had been consumed – two excellent steaks and a mountain of French fries – the conversation turned to the mission. Normally, Gabriel would have waited until they had the privacy of their room, but the nearest diner was twenty feet away.

"Don supplied the GPS references for Kamenko's factory and his house. It's about four hours' driving from here to the factory. I think we need to identify him, hopefully there, snatch him, and then find somewhere quiet to interrogate him."

"Yeah, or we could take him at the house."

"Let's scope them both out, see where he has the most security. He's aiming to be a national politician, so he's bound to have a squad of goons in tow."

Eli nodded. "It's all a bit thin, though, isn't it? Two names."

"Yes. But think of it. We have the name of one of his customers. Admittedly she's retail, not wholesale, but we've breached the first line of defence. These outfits always trade on total secrecy, so that's a problem for him. And we have the name of one his customers' clients."

"He could clam up. Wait it out."

"He could. But come on, Eli, we both know that your CV isn't just running about shooting at insurgents and terrorists."

"I'm not going to torture him, if that's what you mean. The IDF has always been a highly moral fighting force. When virtually the whole region wants Israel destroyed, we have to hold ourselves to the highest standards."

Gabriel shook his head and murmured. "I'm not saying we have to torture him. But we can apply a fair degree of psychological pressure, can't we? Plus, remember, he's a businessman. You and I have had training, but even we'd crack after 24 hours. He's not had that training, so I reckon we can break him. If he knows anything at all about Erin Ayers, we're going to get it out of him."

Eli set her mouth in a line, compressing her lips together. Then she spoke.

"Yes. We are."

62

CRACK SHOT

Timur Kamenko was not aware he was being watched. Nor were his two bodyguards, chosen for their brawn, more than their brains. This lack of strategy in recruiting his security personnel would come back on Kamenko. At six foot two, he was as tall as his protection, but what he matched in the vertical dimension he lacked in all the others. Where he was a trim figure in his two-piece, brown suit and English brogues, the two men flanking him were hewn from altogether tougher material. Both men weighed well over sixteen stone, the greater proportion of it muscle, bone and sinew. Their shaved heads revealed a variety of white scars, mementoes of gang fights, military engagements and their work for Kamenko himself.

They'd arrived ten minutes earlier in a beaten-up Toyota Hilux pickup, and were now waiting to escort their boss to work.

Kamenko was not conventionally handsome. In fact, quite the reverse. His features were asymmetrical and distributed across his face as if purely for function. His nose, broken when he was a young man, was pushed off to the left, whereas his mouth had a definite rightwards slant, as if he'd suffered a stroke at some point. The effect was to give his face a permanent sneer. Yet, despite the effect of his features' trying to escape each other's company, something about his eyes – hard, blue and shaded by thick, brown eyebrows – mesmerised people: customers, employees, suppliers, the few people he called friends, and the politicians with whom he socialised.

He was standing outside the massive double front door of his house. Incongruously, it was built in the style of a Spanish hacienda, with white stucco walls and terracotta barrel tiles on the roof, and would have looked more at home in Miami than the outskirts of Karaganda.

"Nurslan, bring the car round," he said.

The larger of the two bodyguards nodded once, and walked away to a separate garage with two doors.

As the motorised door clattered upwards and recessed into the roof of the garage, Kamenko turned to his other bodyguard, a seventeen-stone giant with arms so heavily muscled, they strained the leather of his jacket.

"I'm meeting the Russian today. He has some plans that I'm interested in acquiring. Try and get friendly with his men. See what you can learn, OK?"

"OK, boss," the man said. His name was Ortekhan, but he was known in the company as *tişqan* – mouse.

* * *

To surveil their quarry, Eli had first driven the SandCat directly into a patch of tall thorn bushes and scraggy undergrowth half a mile from the house.

Now she sat cross-legged on the roof, Swarovski EL 50 binoculars held to her eyes.

"He's got two heavies with him. Real golems."

"Real whats?"

Eli began speaking in what Gabriel had come to think of as her 'teacher voice.'

"The golem was a huge giant made out of clay that a rabbi created to protect the Prague ghetto in the sixteenth century. Very strong, very dumb. You know the type."

"What are they doing?"

"Leaving in a four-by-four. Looks like a Merc G-Wagen."

"Anyone seeing him off?"

She shook her head. "Nope. No little woman handing him a packet of sandwiches and a briefcase."

"OK. Let's leave him to get to work, then check out the house."

They left the SandCat buried in the thorn bushes and made their way to the house on foot. The AK-74s were locked in the back, but they were carrying the pistols, loaded with Parabellum rounds.

The sun was warm on Gabriel's back, and if he hadn't been about to break into the house of an ultra-nationalist politician and illicit ammunition tycoon, he almost could have enjoyed the exercise.

"We'll start at the back, away from the road," Gabriel said.

"Hey, who put you in charge?" Eli asked, with a smile.

"I deferred to you over sleeping with our guns. Now it's my turn. Plus it's my life Erin Ayers is fucking around with, remember?"

The back of the house looked out over the countryside. Nothing to match the rolling pastoral landscape Gabriel was used to. More of a featureless plain dotted with stands of birch trees and thorn bushes. But best of all, it was entirely free of other properties that could overlook either its rightful owner or the two people about to break in. They passed a stone-built well on their way up to the house, capped with a sturdy wooden lid strapped with iron bands.

Gabriel fished out a leather roll of lock picks from the thigh pocket of his trousers. The lock was a simple Yale-type, and he was through in ten seconds.

"Perhaps he relies on his reputation to keep him safe," Eli said.

"Or his golems," Gabriel answered, opening the back door and stepping into some sort of storage room.

Boots were arranged in neatly paired rows, for walking, horse-riding and motorcycling. Coat racks were hung with leather jackets, waxed riding coats, fleeces and hoodies. And arranged on wooden racks, all facing the same way, and gleaming with polish and gun oil, half a dozen long guns: hunting rifles by Sako, a pair of Beretta under-and-over shotguns and, at the very top, what appeared to be a box-fresh AK-47, the precursor of the AK-74s locked in the back of the SandCat, and the granddaddy of all the post-Soviet assault rifles.

"Impressive," Eli said.

"I guess he likes to test-fire his own product," Gabriel replied.

"Hold on. I want to even up the odds."

Eli took down the lowest of the long guns – a Sako – and, working swiftly and efficiently, removed the bolt. Gabriel took the hint and did the same with a second rifle. With all the bolts and firing pins removed and stowed in Eli's backpack, they replaced the guns on the rack.

"Let's split up," Gabriel said. "I'll take the upstairs, you stay down here."

She nodded in agreement. "Stay safe."

Gabriel searched the upper floor systematically, moving from room to room, checking for more weapons. In what was clearly the master bedroom, a large room furnished luxuriously with a huge Chinese rug in jade green and rose pink, red-and-gold brocade curtains, and heavy antique furniture as well as an enormous sleigh-bed made from cherrywood, he found a Russian-made Makarov pistol in a side table. Loaded and one in the chamber. He dropped out the magazine, emptied the rounds into a pocket, then racked the slide twice to eject the round in the chamber. Coming back downstairs, he heard Eli call from the front of the house.

"I've found something!"

He joined Eli in Kamenko's home office, a stark contrast to the opulence of the master bedroom. Just plain white walls, a functional desk made from a thick slab of oak, and grey, steel filing cabinets. Eli was kneeling in front of a scratched, grey-green safe. It was about eighteen inches tall and a foot square at its base, and had no combination wheel, just a keyhole closed with a brass flap, and a polished steel handle.

"Doesn't look like much, does it?" he asked. "You any good at safe cracking?"

She shook her head. "I know people who are, but that's not much help right now." Then she grinned. "On the other hand …"

She reached into a jacket pocket, pulled out a magazine for her pistol, and swapped it for the one currently snug in the grip of the GSh-18.

"Remember Colonel Sultanov said they could fire overpressure Russian rounds? He said they were armour-piercing. Wanna find out?"

"Be my guest."

She stood, and together they backed off to the other side of the office.

She levelled her pistol and aimed at the lock. Then lowered her gun arm.

"Wait," she said. "I don't fancy getting hit by a ricochet."

Gabriel went to the desk and upended it, then dragged it across the room to form a rudimentary firing position.

They crouched behind it and Eli once again aimed at the safe.

The report in the small room was deafening.

The uprated load of propellant exploded with a shattering bang and filled the office with the smell of burnt gunpowder.

They peered through the drift of smoke towards the safe.

The keyhole was now more of a key cave, widened from its original quarter-inch to a ragged edged, inch-wide cavity.

Gabriel skirted the desk and knelt in front of the safe. "Great shooting," he said with a grin. Then he pulled down on the handle and yanked it towards him. Its lock destroyed by the steel penetrator at the core of the bullet, the door opened silently.

Inside, charred at their edges and smouldering with crawling orange trails of sparks, were a handful of buff cardboard folders. Gabriel grabbed them and batted out the burning edges with his palm. He took them out of the room, following Eli, and together they began opening the folders on the kitchen table.

Eli looked across at Gabriel as she turned over documents in her folder.

"You're the linguistics expert. Do you read Kazakh?"

"If it was Russian, we'd be good, but I can't read this. They both use Cyrillic letters and some of the words are kind of close, but there's nothing I can get a handle on."

"What do you think they are?"

"At a guess? Political files. He probably keeps all his business stuff at the factory."

"Hmm. Could be useful. We should take it back with us. Give it to Don. If he doesn't want it, I bet he knows people who do," she said, still flicking through the documents. Then she drew in a quick, short breath.

"What is it? Find something?"

She looked down, then up at Gabriel. "Nope." A small smile. "Just a paper cut." She sucked her finger and handed the files to him with her free hand. "Here, take them. Then I think we should wait for Mr Kamenko. Plus I'm hungry and there's cheese in his fridge."

63

LE DÉMON BLANC

MID-ATLANTIC

Britta woke up with a metallic taste in her mouth and a fierce headache. Around her, their eyes either closed in sleep or wide open in terror, were half a dozen young women and girls. Some seemed barely out of childhood. Some were dark-skinned, some fair, all were slim and, she supposed, attractive one way or another, though their faces, pale and strained, bore the signs of long hours in captivity. They were lying on filthy mattresses and shackled by chains that looped through ring-bolts set into the floor. The air was rank with the smell of urine, sweat and naked fear.

Her ears buzzed with the after-effects of whatever drug Torossian had administered at the cargo terminal at Heathrow. Above that sound was the deep thrum of jet engines and wind noise. She shivered violently; the cabin was unheated.

"Hey," she said to the nearest woman, slender, black-skinned, dark-brown eyes rimmed in red. "Are you OK?"

The woman started, and jerked her head round to look at Britta.

"No, I am not OK. I have a lot of pain," she looked at her groin, "down there. Do you know where we are going?"

Her accent suggested to Britta that she had only been passing through Britain, and had originally come from somewhere in West Africa.

"I'm sorry, no. My name is Britta, what's yours?"

"I am Marguerite. I come from Mali, but *Le Démon Blanc*, he took me in London."

Britta tried for an encouraging smile. She wasn't sure she'd succeeded.

"I am Swedish. Listen to me. When we get to wherever we are going, I will try to help you. But do what they say, OK?"

The woman nodded, and smiled, but it was a pitiful expression, and Britta knew that she didn't believe this redheaded stranger could actually help her. *Well, maybe not*, she thought. *But I'm going to stop him hurting anyone else.*

64

ELI ADMITS EVERYTHING

KAZAKHSTAN

Snapping closed the gold-plated catches on his Louis Vuitton briefcase, Kamenko climbed out of the back of the G-Wagen. He leaned in at the driver's window.

"Put it in the garage, then you can leave. I'll see you tomorrow."

"OK, boss," the giant known as "mouse" said. "Have a good evening."

Kamenko grunted noncommittally and walked away.

Inside, he placed his briefcase on the floor, hung up his coat, and wandered through to the lounge to fix himself a drink.

He opened the polished doors of the antique cocktail cabinet and smiled as his eyes took in the array of expensive imported spirits. French cognac, Mexican tequila, American whisky, Icelandic vodka. He smiled as he trailed his finger along the bottles before stopping on the black-and-white label of a bottle of Jack Daniels.

"Ah, yes, Mr Daniels. Tonight we'll spend some time together dreaming of Kentucky, yes?"

He poured a generous measure of the spirit into a heavy-bottomed tumbler decorated with gold tracery on its outside, took a pull, grimaced as it hit his empty stomach, then smiled as the bourbon's heat entered him.

"I'm more of a gin and tonic woman myself," came a voice from behind him – a voice speaking English.

* * *

The tall Kazakh whirled round, slopping whisky onto the carpet. His eyes widened in shock and his mouth dropped open. Eli enjoyed watching people caught unawares. That look as you disarmed a terrorist, or shot a suicide bomber outside their own home was priceless. She added the shocked expression on Kamenko's face to her stock of memorable moments.

A semi-automatic pistol aimed at the face tended to focus the mind, Eli had found in her career. That this particular pistol was held by a smiling young woman at least doubled the effect. And that she was sitting in an armchair in what she supposed its owner regarded as a safe space armour-plated it.

"Who the fuck are you?" Kamenko growled, in heavily accented but perfectly understandable English.

She noticed that after his initial mishap with his drink, his hand was steady. Not so much as a ripple troubled the surface of the remaining bourbon.

"Me? I'm Eli Schochat. Late of Mossad, now working for the British Government in a security capacity for a deniable black-ops outfit called The Department. My boss is the ex-Commanding Officer of the SAS. Name of Don Webster."

Before Kamenko could formulate a response, his eyes flicked over Eli's right shoulder to the door. She heard the footsteps too, and, when the door opened, spoke without taking her eyes off Kamenko.

"Timur Kamenko, meet Gabriel Wolfe. Gabriel and I work together."

She knew Gabriel would also be pointing a pistol at Kamenko, and relaxed, just a little.

"The goons are gone," Gabriel said.

"Excellent. Then it's just the three of us."

"I said, what do you want?" Kamenko said, glowering at Eli, then at Gabriel.

"No, you said, 'Who the fuck are you?'" she said. "But I'll tell you what we want. We want to know about Erin Ayers."

Kamenko's heavily browed forehead furrowed and he drew his head back.

"Never heard of her."

"Good. That means we get to do this properly. Gabriel, would you mind?"

With Kamenko bound to his office chair with thick black plastic cable ties, Eli resumed her interrogation.

"Let's start at the beginning. Tell me about Sasha Beck."

"Who?"

"Sasha Beck."

"Who's she, your girlfriend?"

"Oh, Mr Kamenko. That's not very original. Look, I know what you're thinking. I'm just some silly little girl playing at soldiers and making up stories about being a spy, and you can just wait it out until your bodyguards come back in the morning to save you. So let's begin again, with me showing you just what a mess you're in."

She picked a black-and-yellow pencil off the floor where it had rolled when Gabriel tipped the desk over. Holding it between her thumb and middle finger she tested the point with the tip of her index finger. Lightning fast, she spun the pencil round, and jammed it, point-down, into the flesh just above Kamenko's left knee.

Gabriel's hiss of indrawn breath was almost drowned out by Kamenko's howl of pain, but not quite. Eli still heard it. Deep-red blood welled up around the shaft of the pencil, glistening darkly in the light from the table lamp.

"You bitch!" Kamenko said through clamped teeth, his lips

drawn back like a threatened dog as he strained against the cable ties.

"Oh, that's nothing. When I want to be a bitch, believe me, speech will be one thing you're not capable of. Now, let's try again. I'll make it easy for you. A simple yes/no question. Is Sasha Beck a customer of yours? Think hard, Mr Kamenko. I can see lots more pencils on the floor."

Kamenko's gaze dropped to the floor, then his eyes met hers again.

"Yes."

"Good. Because we already knew that. So now I feel we are building a nice trusting relationship. Keep going like this, and you'll come away from this with only a little hole in your leg, and sore wrists."

* * *

"Timur," Gabriel said from his position behind Kamenko, causing Kamenko to jerk round to try to see his second interrogator. "I'm sorry. I had no idea Eli was going to do that. I specifically said to avoid physical violence. But you must understand, it's vital we identify Erin Ayers. We already know she hired Sasha Beck, who, as you've just admitted, buys her ammunition from you. Is there anything, anything at all, you can tell us?"

Kamenko nodded. "Yes."

"What?" Gabriel prompted.

Kamenko smiled. "Go fuck your cock-sucking whore of a mother!"

65

BETRAYAL

The ringing in his ears wasn't noticeable at first. Gabriel thought it was simply an after effect of Eli's armour-piercing shot at the safe. But it grew in volume, making him shake his head. His vision darkened, leaving a tunnel of light through which he could see Kamenko's grinning face.

He saw his mother's face, streaked with tears, then bloated from her time in the water after she'd drowned.

The jolt in his right wrist barely registered.

Nor did Kamenko's scream.

As the smoke reached his nostrils and the smell of burnt propellant reach the olfactory bulbs deep in his brain, he blinked, and observed the black-walled tunnel expand until his vision, then his other senses, returned to normal.

The Parabellum round had passed through Kamenko's left foot and into the floor. Blood was pooling beneath the sole of the brogue; the perforations in the tan leather were filling with it.

Kamenko was thrashing in the chair, and Gabriel watched as the edges of the cable ties bit into the skin of his wrists.

"You can put a lot of rounds into a man before killing him," Gabriel said, bending to hold Kamenko's head still and speaking close to his ear. I know exactly where to place them. So, I'm going to ask you one more time. "Who is Erin Ayers?"

"I don't know, all right?" Kamenko said, panic clear in his voice. "She never talks about her clients. Sasha, I mean."

"Well that's bad news for you, then, isn't it?" Eli said, selecting another pencil.

"No! Please, wait," Kamenko said, pleading now. "She said one thing. I said her client must have been rich if she could afford Sasha just to play some twisted game. And she said the woman owned a penthouse in Manhattan. On Fifth Avenue, overlooking the big reservoir in Central Park. So she could easily afford to hire Sasha."

"Anything else, Kamenko?" Eli asked, twirling the new pencil between thumb and forefinger while keeping the muzzle of her pistol aimed at his head. "That's not much to go on after we've made all this effort to find you."

He shook his head. "That's it. Please, let me go. I'm bleeding. You blew my fucking foot off."

Eli stood. "No. You'll have to wait for your men to find you in the morning." She looked down. "That's not fatal. It's already starting to clot. But you know what? It helps to elevate the wound above the heart." She walked towards him and kicked him in the chest, toppling him over backwards so that his head hit the thick carpet with a muffled thud.

Gabriel and Eli were thirty yards along the road leading away from Kamenko's house when Eli put out a hand and tapped him on the shoulder.

"I forgot something," she said, then turned and ran back to the house.

He stood and watched as her booted feet kicked up dust in Kamenko's yard before disappearing around the corner of the building.

She'd had her pistol, and her backpack with her when they'd left. They hadn't brought anything else into the house with them, had they? Gabriel turned and began walking towards the house.

The noise of the double-tap echoed off the side of the stone-built, two-car garage next to the house.

Five seconds later, Eli emerged from the front door. Her face was spattered with fine droplets of red. She trotted back to Gabriel.

"Why did you kill him?" was all he said.

"It was in the files I was scanning. I can't read Kazakh but I saw one word I could make out: Hamas."

Gabriel nodded. "You told him who we were didn't you? Before I came in. So you weren't planning to leave him alive."

"He was evil, Gabriel. Not just for supplying hollow-points to Hamas or bomb-making equipment. I checked out his political party. Did you?"

"Didn't have time."

"Well it made charming reading. Explicit racist platform, expulsion of all immigrants, links with plenty of organisations hostile to Israel, and a pledge to rid Kazakhstan of Jews *by any means necessary* – their words."

"We should get rid of him. At least make it harder for the authorities to investigate."

Gabriel left the SandCat in the rear yard while he and Eli dragged Kamenko's sagging corpse out of the house between them, the feet wrapped in plastic bags closed with more cable ties, the wound in the knee tied with a towel from the kitchen. With the body lodged in the loadspace, they returned to the house and spent twenty minutes cleaning up in the office and lounge. Having washed, dried and replaced Kamenko's tumbler, they tugged the carpet across to cover the bullet hole in the floor. Lastly, they slid the now-empty safe out of the house on a rug, then half-walked, half-dragged it to the well.

Gabriel pushed the sturdy wooden cap off the well, then, grunting with the effort, they manoeuvred the safe up and onto the lip of the wall.

"OK, let go," he said, then pushed it over the edge.

They leaned over, watching the safe as it tumbled and bounced down the shaft before hitting the water with a deep, echoing splash.

The cap replaced, they ran back to the SandCat and were roaring away from the house looking for somewhere to dump the body.

After half an hour's driving, Gabriel turned off the road and headed for a thickly wooded area about a mile from the road. The SandCat's suspension and 'floating' seats – designed to minimise the effects of landmine explosions on the occupants – soaked up all but the worst of the gouged and rutted terrain. As Eli had done, he simply powered the vehicle into the forest through a gap in the trees, smashing saplings and undergrowth under the huge tyres, until he found a small clearing.

They dragged Kamenko's body from the loadspace and over to a patch of scrubby brambles five feet high. With a heavy rustle and a crackling of the dry grass beneath, it settled, out of sight in the centre of the weeds.

Gabriel looked up and nudged Eli. "See up there?"

She shaded her eyes with her hand. "The bird?"

"Yeah. It's an eagle, or a vulture or something. That's good. Aerial predators will find him, and so will whatever four-legged ones there are. Wolves, maybe. Bears. Certainly foxes."

"Guess what else they have here?"

"Surprise me, professor."

"Caracals – they're wild cats. Like I told you. The SandCat, remember? Plasan originally called it the Caracal."

"OK, good to know. Now let's go. We have a health and safety incident to arrange."

66

NOISE DOGS

They pulled up in a stand of trees a mile away from the factory. It was 5.30 in the afternoon and, like factory workers the world over, the employees of the late Timur Kamenko were driving out through the gates. Gabriel and Eli watched through binoculars as the last of the stream of cars left the factory and drove home to families, or bars in whatever was the nearest town.

By seven, the sun was dipping below the horizon. Time to move. Gabriel put the SandCat into gear and drove towards the factory, looking for a particular geographical feature. Most of the terrain was flat and largely featureless, just the odd tree or shrub struggling to grow taller than a man in the thin, sandy soil. But about five hundred yards from the perimeter fence, he found what he was looking for. It was a depression in the landscape, invisible until you were almost upon it, like an empty lake. He drove down into the depression for thirty or forty yards until he reached the deepest part. Looking up through the windscreen he estimated that the depression was twice as deep as the height of the SandCat. On the side facing the factory, wind or earth movements had built up a natural, eight-foot rampart.

"We walk from here," he said to Eli.

In their dark clothing, he knew they wouldn't have to worry about being spotted by security guards. The moon was mostly hidden by low clouds, giving just enough light to travel by, but not enough to throw a spotlight onto the two interlopers come to cause a permanent stoppage to the factory's production.

She nodded and, shoulder to shoulder, they set off, AK-74s slung across their shoulders, GSh-18s tucked into waistbands.

As they drew nearer, Gabriel laid a hand on Eli's shoulder.

"Check for security," he said.

She brought the binoculars to her eyes, and he heard the whine from the electronics as she switched on the night vision.

"There's a fence, but it looks pretty flimsy. Just chain-link."

"Any wire?" he asked.

"Nope. Out here it's probably just to prevent petty pilfering, though who'd have the nerve to come all the way out here to try stealing some copper or the petty cash tin from a guy supplying the local Mafia?"

"Good point. What about the gate?"

"It's closed. Can't see if there's a padlock. Judging by the quality of the fence, I'd say it's nothing we can't handle."

"Any guards?"

"Wait, let me look for a bit." She swung the binoculars left and right and waited for a minute. "I can't see anyone. I'm thinking Kamenko was relying on his reputation and his connections plus the isolation to do the job for him, otherwise—"

"What is it?"

"Wait. I see something. Dogs. Two."

"They could be dangerous, but given Kamenko's cut-price security so far, I'm guessing – hoping – they're just noise dogs."

"We'll find out soon enough. Anyway, I've yet to meet a beast that I can't take care of, on four legs or two."

"Me neither," Gabriel said, thinking back to a scrapyard in Estonia defended by two very dangerous dogs he'd had to kill. "But if we can do it by distraction, that would work better for me."

Eli put the binoculars down.

"Let's cross that bridge when we come to it."

. . .

After returning to the SandCat to get a few items necessary for the mission, they made their way back to the factory entrance. Gabriel reached the gates first. They were fastened by a length of chain and a simple domestic padlock. He pushed the padlock into the gap between the gates, inserted a pry bar into the shackle and with a sharp twist, broke it open.

"Split up or stay together?" he asked.

"We always worked in pairs, so I say stick together. Plus, we have the dogs to deal with."

As she spoke, the two animals in questions came tearing around a corner of the nearest building, howling and barking. Gabriel drew his pistol and as the nearer dog got to within thirty feet, fired two rounds into the air. The effect was impressive. The dogs, obviously starved to judge from the prominent ribs sticking through their mangy coats, slid to a stop. Ears back, tails between their legs they growled in a disconcerting unison that raised the hackles on Gabriel's own neck. While he covered them with the pistol, Eli slipped a field ration pack from her backpack, slit the outer casing and squeezed the contents, a sticky brown paste, onto the ground.

"Hey, you scruffy looking things, hungry?" she said, in a soft, sing-song voice. "Chow time, mutts. Come and get it."

She stood back, next to Gabriel.

They watched as the dogs, still growling, looked at the pile of reconstituted meat stew between them and these two strange humans. The animals were clearly torn by an internal battle. Hunger versus fear. The latter emotion, Gabriel guessed, was behind their show of aggression, more than any genuine desire to hurt him and Eli. These were no war dogs, bred specifically for combat. They weren't even proper guard dogs; they were just some local strays that had been rounded up and let loose inside the factory grounds at night.

After thirty seconds or so, hunger won the day, and the two dogs crept forward, heads bowed, occasionally glancing up at Gabriel and Eli, who had their hands resting on their pistol butts. The humans backed off and left the dogs to their meal.

They entered the factory through what appeared to be a rudimentary reception building. Inside the door, they found themselves in a rectangular room with sofas and a simple, low, wooden coffee table on which several magazines were scattered. Behind the desk that ran along one end of the room was a door. The sign was in Cyrillic, and read:

тек уәкілетті қызметкерлер

but Gabriel could guess its meaning:

AUTHORISED PERSONNEL ONLY

67

STOCK TAKING

Beyond the door was a huge, windowless, open space; clearly, the manufacturing facility began here. Gabriel flicked a row of switches set to the left of the door. Overhead pendant lamps flashed into life revealing the main business of TK Industries. Set like obelisks here and there on the smooth concrete floor were lathes, presses, bench drills, and other industrial equipment whose purpose Gabriel could only guess at. Running the length of the vast space was some sort of production line, with stations for workers to sit, or stand, as they worked to assemble the various calibres and types of ammunition.

Blue and red, wheeled plastic bins held empty cartridge cases, sheets and rods of metal stock, and everywhere sealed, heavy-duty cardboard cartons were stacked in towers, pyramids and blocks.

"Any thoughts on how we're going to blow this place?" Eli asked, poking the toe of her boot at a pile of metal waste on the floor.

"They're manufacturing ammunition so the place will be awash with TICs and TIMs. We can use those."

"Sorry, ticks and tims, what are they?"

"Toxic Industrial Chemicals, Toxic Industrial Materials. I'm thinking asbestos, acid, phosphorus, maybe chlorine compounds.

These guys are making brass, so there're probably all kinds of nasty chemicals used to do that."

"Yeah, plus all the propellant, and if they're making grenades or rockets, then there's going to be high explosives, the works."

"So let's find the stock room, shall we?"

They worked their way round the edge of the hall in opposite directions, looking into every door set into the brick wall. Most were open and led to offices or store cupboards housing innocuous materials like overalls or cleaning supplies. At the far-left corner, Gabriel found a door that didn't open when he tried the handle.

"Eli, over here!" he shouted.

Eli joined him. Nodded.

He kicked out at the door, smashing the heel of his boot against the lock. The flimsy mechanism gave way immediately, and Gabriel pushed through into the space beyond. He hit the next set of light switches and, as the neon tubes plinked and flickered into life, let out a low whistle.

"I think we just found the stock room," he said.

The space was two hundred and fifty yards by a hundred at least, and racked out with aisles of steel shelving like a builders' merchant's. Stacked on every flat surface were drums, cartons, gas bottles and pallets groaning with dull metal ingots. One corner was stacked floor to ceiling with beige fibre drums marked *Vihtavuori – 20KG Smokeless Propellant*. Standing idle in the centre of the space was a black-and-yellow forklift truck.

Gabriel thought for a minute while Eli wandered up and down the aisles, for all the world like a shopper looking for tile cement, wallpaper or fence panels.

She returned with a grin on her face.

"I can't read the labels," she said. "But I've seen enough skull-and-crossbones stickers and corroded hands to know this is what we need."

"It's what we need for the explosive. But not the fuse. I don't want us to be anywhere near this place when we blow it, or we'll end up as atoms."

"So what are you thinking?"

"I'm thinking I'm Kamenko. I've got an important client stopping by to pick up some ammunition. I welcome my client like any proud factory manager. Show them the merchandise, give them a bit of lunch and then, guess what?"

Her eyes widened and she pointed at him.

"You invite them to come out the back and do some quality assurance."

"In one," he said. "There must be a weapons room and a range, or just a spare bit of ground out the back somewhere."

Their search for Gabriel's imaginary weapons room took another hour. They found it in a separate brick building behind the main manufacturing facility.

Inside, the armoury was fitted out with steel wall-racks. Arranged in ascending order of size, and potency, were around thirty different weapons. The array started on the left with a pair of Ruger SR22s, dinky .22 rimfire pistols no self-respecting terrorist would carry, but which an assassin might find handy. It continued through a variety of pistols and revolvers increasing in calibre from .38 through .40 to .45 and 9mm Parabellum, and on to the unfeasibly large "hand cannons": chrome-plated .357 Magnum Colt Pythons, .44 Magnum Smith & Wesson Model 29s, and the granddaddy of them all, the .50 Action Express Desert Eagle.

"They love pistols in the Middle East," Eli said, picking up a Colt Python and aiming it at a spot on the wall. "Anyone can get hold of an AK-47. But pistols are status symbols. It's like carrying a sword over there. Point your AK at them and they'll just laugh. Shove a Glock in someone's face, and they really pay attention."

"We need something more like one of those," Gabriel said, pointing at the weapons leaning against the wall on the opposite side of the room.

These were altogether more serious bits of kit. Assault rifles from NATO and former Soviet Bloc countries rubbed shoulders with battle rifles, carbines, submachine guns, heavy machine guns and, at the end of the row, the weapon that Gabriel selected, an RPG-7. The Soviet-designed, anti-tank weapon was in use all over the world, both in official armed forces and terrorist organisations.

Beneath the rocket-propelled grenade launcher were half a dozen warheads. Gabriel reached down for one labelled TBG-7V.

"Know what this is?" he asked Eli.

"Not exactly. I mean, it's a rocket-propelled grenade, but I couldn't tell you the specific warhead type. It's not one I've seen back home."

Gabriel pointed at the Cyrillic characters stencilled beneath the TBG-7V.

"That says *thermobaric warhead*."

"A fuel-air bomb."

"Exactly. When these babies detonate, they suck oxygen out of the surrounding air to create a fucking great fireball. I'm thinking it would make a nice little lighter for the birthday cake candles."

"So either Kamenko was making these, or he was running a sideline as a dealer in ex-Soviet and NATO munitions."

"The second is my guess. Stands to reason. You get a reputation as a supplier of small arms rounds, people are going to start asking you for other stuff. He was probably supplying the weapons themselves."

"Good."

"Good?"

"Yes, dummy! Because we're taking out a bigger part of the supply chain. Not just the ammunition, but the weapons as well."

Back at the storage facility, Gabriel climbed into the forklift. Eli was standing by the door leading to the factory. Both were wearing breathing masks they'd found in a supply cupboard.

The forklift was an electric model. Gabriel thumbed the starter button and as he moved off the engine hummed beneath his seat. He began pushing over barrels of chemicals at random. On some, the lids popped off immediately, releasing their foul-smelling contents in waves that washed back towards the forklift's solid rubber tyres. On others, the lids held firm, so Gabriel applied downward pressure on the sides with the forks until the drums split.

Gradually, a lake of vivid greenish-yellow liquid spread over the floor of the warehouse-like space.

It was taking too long. Gabriel wanted the whole place to be filled with volatile chemical fumes and gas to be a hundred percent certain the place would go up sky-high. Then an idea, risky, but not, he felt, dangerously so, occurred to him.

He drove the truck round in a circle so that a supporting stanchion of a rack of blue plastic drums was right in front of him. He backed up, then lowered the forks and pressed the accelerator pedal to the floor. The truck lumbered forward and rammed the stanchion. With a creak, the structure began to give way as the steel buckled. Gabriel reversed and then drove the truck over to Eli. They watched as the racking collapsed, and dozens of the plastic drums cascaded to the floor and burst.

He slammed the door and together they raced back through the main factory building. Eli was carrying the RPG-7 across her back alongside the assault rifle.

The dogs were still licking at the ground where they'd left them as Gabriel and Eli emerged from the front door of the reception building and ran for the gates. Before they left, they shooed the dogs out then hit the big green plastic button by the main loading bay doors of the factory. Now, they had a twenty-by-four-yard, black rectangle to aim at.

Back at the rampart in front of the hollow concealing the SandCat, they turned to face the factory.

Gabriel loaded the warhead into the RPG-7.

The range was 500 yards. Right on the edge of the rocket's effective range against a moving target. He lifted the RPG to his shoulder.

Then he brought it down again.

68

INDUSTRIAL INCIDENT

Eli turned to him.

"Problem?"

"This isn't going to work," he said. "It's too far to risk it with a one-shot wonder. We have to get closer."

"If we get close enough to guarantee the shot, there's a very good chance we'll be incinerated along with the factory," she said.

"Not if we act like terrorists," he said.

"What do you mean?"

"This thing's armoured, right? So you drive us closer – say, to two hundred yards. I'll fire from the roof. You hit the power as soon as I'm back inside. We'll have to rely on the armour-plating to protect us from the blast wave."

"OK, fine. But with one change to the plan."

"What's that?"

You drive. You told me you were in Mobility Troop with the SAS, right?" he nodded. "So you're the better driver. But I've been fighting people armed with RPG-7s my whole life, and I know the weapon better."

"Fair enough. Come on, then. Let's go."

• • •

Gabriel drove out of the depression, round the natural rampart and powered across the scrubby terrain back towards Kamenko's factory. At what he estimated was one hundred yards, he slewed the big unwieldy vehicle to a stop so that the rear doors faced the factory.

"All yours," he shouted over his shoulder. Then he twisted round in his seat to watch as Eli prepared to fire.

Through the open rear door he could see the factory, and the big, black rectangle in the front wall. The moon had come out from behind the clouds, lighting the landscape with a pure, white light that threw sharp shadow across the ground from every pebble and thorn bush.

Eli climbed onto the roof leaving Gabriel with an unobstructed view of the target.

He heard the clicks and scrapes as she readied the RPG-7, and realised he was holding his breath.

"Fire in the hole!" she yelled.

The blast of the booster charge was drowned out as the main rocket motor ignited a fraction of a second later. Gabriel counted as the grenade streaked towards the factory, trailing an arc of white smoke, eerily lit by the moonlight.

One.

Two.

Thr—

It was a perfect shot.

The grenade, still under full power from its rocket motor, streaked in through the wide-open loading-bay doors.

The blast was huge as the thermobaric warhead detonated. A huge, deep-bellied, blaring *boom* that rolled across the flat land towards them.

Gabriel yelled to Eli, "Get back in!"

She was already swinging down and slamming the rear door behind her.

"Go!" she shouted, slamming her fist against the inside of the rear compartment.

He floored the throttle and mashed his way up through the gears, urging the SandCat up towards its eighty miles per hour top speed. The wheel was alive in his hands, bucking and twisting as the terrain transmitted its shape to him through the steering rack.

He glanced at the wing mirror.

The monstrous fireball was rolling outwards and upwards, a furious orange against the black night sky. Seconds later, two things happened simultaneously.

The leading edge of the initial blast wave overtook the SandCat. And the explosion from the vaporised TICs set off a chain reaction that caused the hundreds of drums of propellant and high explosives stored in the factory to detonate.

The overpressure from the second blast rushed past them, almost upending the SandCat. Gabriel heard the transmission scream as the rear wheels were lifted off the ground. He fought to keep the steering on the straight-ahead. Then the rear wheels thumped down again and after slewing right, left, and then over to the right again, he regained control and they were back, speeding away from the remains of TK Industries.

The blast wave rammed into the air in front of them, banking up the air pressure until its power dwindled. Then the huge volume of compressed air drove the blast wave back towards the factory, spackling the windscreen with a hailstorm of sand, mud, plant material and grit. Gabriel flinched instinctively, but kept the steering wheel straight.

Moments later, he reached the safety of the dried-up lake bed and skidded down into its comforting embrace.

Killing the engine, he jumped out, ran round to the rear of the SandCat and dragged open the door, which was pitted and scorched.

Eli jumped down, came to him, and stretched up to kiss him.

"That was fun," she said.

They climbed to the top of the rampart and watched, no binoculars needed, as the factory continued its rapid, fiery descent into rubble. A series of blasts sent jets of pale-yellow flames hundreds of yards into the air. The bangs reached them seconds later.

Underlying the bassy explosions was the continuous rattle and chatter of small arms fire. But this was not the soundtrack of a firefight; this was hundreds of thousands of neatly packaged rounds detonating inside their cartons.

They stayed watching until it was clear that whatever was left would be no more than a foot or two tall. To the music of sporadic explosions in registers from tenor to baritone, they climbed aboard the SandCat and drove off, back to Karaganda, and their extraction.

69

ORDERS IS ORDERS

LONDON

Don sat back in his leather chair and regarded his two operatives. Eli looked her usual calm, unruffled self. He liked the way she'd take on any mission as if being asked to run errands in Soho for him. She'd travel halfway round the world, deal with person or persons deemed detrimental to the UK's security with extreme prejudice, and return with that lazy smile still plastered on her olive-skinned face. Gabriel, on the other hand, looked as if he had done battle with more than physical challenges. His face was drawn, tight round the eyes and mouth. The stubble on his cheeks gave him a haggard look, and his eyes flicked restlessly around the anonymous Whitehall office Don used when he was working in London.

"Let's start with my thanking you both for excellent work in Kazakhstan," he began. "Our analysts are working through the files you gave us. You'd think Christmas had come early, along with birthdays, the Easter Bunny and the Tooth Fairy."

Eli laughed. "I hope you can use it to build a case for further action."

"Oh, I'm sure we can. At the very least, our friends in the Secret Intelligence Service will enjoy reviewing the material. And tell me about Mr Kamenko. You followed my instructions and left him alone?" He looked at each of them in turn. Waiting for an answer. An answer he felt sure would cause him some trouble with his political bosses.

"Not as such," Gabriel replied, finally, running his fingers across his scalp.

"Meaning?" Don prompted.

"Meaning he is dead, boss," Eli said. "We fully intended to follow your orders, but Kamenko grabbed a gun. It was self-defence. Him or us. I shot him myself."

Yes, I bet you did. "Your version, Old Sport?"

"What she said. He had a Makarov."

"Hmm," Don said, breathing out through his nose. He looked up at the ornate plasterwork on the ceiling, wondering how to handle this instance of disobedience. "On the plus side, that makes it much less likely he'll regroup and start supplying ammunition to the bad guys. And his nasty little nationalist glee club will almost certainly fold up its tent and walk away. On the minus side, I now have to have a very difficult conversation with the Foreign Secretary, a gentleman not prone to forgiveness of his underlings."

"Sorry, boss," they said in unison.

"Yes, well, can't have my people being shot at without being able to defend themselves. The body?"

"Probably inside the bellies of wolves, bears and buzzards by now," Gabriel said. "We gave him a sky burial."

"Good. The house?"

"Put back as it was, minus the safe."

"I think I can spin this with the FS. You two don't need to worry about that. It's what they pay me for. Now, we need to talk about our next move."

Gabriel leaned forward and placed both hands palms-down on Don's desk.

"I need to find Britta. I think they've taken her. I've left dozens of messages and she hasn't returned them. I don't care about MI5 SOPs. Britta would have found a way to let me know she was safe."

Don drew in a deep breath and let it out in a sigh. He nodded, unsmiling.

"I know, Old Sport. I'm afraid I have some bad news for you. I talked to my oppo in MI5. Britta's missed her last three scheduled contacts – and that *is* a standard operating procedure."

Gabriel leaned back, slowly. "Fuck," he said, quietly.

Don watched as Eli turned in her chair and laid a comforting hand on Gabriel's shoulder.

"We'll get her. You know that."

"Or they'll kill her like they did everyone else I care about. Shit! What did I do and who to for all this to be happening?"

For once, Don felt he had little to say to Gabriel that would reassure him.

"I've reviewed all your operations for the Regiment from the day you joined to the day you left. I've also looked at all The Department's files for your operations. Everyone who might want revenge for what you did to them is prevented from doing so because they're dead. It's generally the way we operate, as you know."

Gabriel pushed up from his chair, and looked first at Eli, then at Don.

"We have a name, we have an address, or the best part of one. I fly to Manhattan, track down Erin Ayers, find out where she's holding Britta, then take her out and go get Britta."

Don knew he had to control Gabriel if he wasn't to cause the kind of trouble that would be definitely not spinnable.

"Sit down, Old Sport." Gabriel remained standing, breathing heavily. "Please, Gabriel," Don said, pointing at the chair.

Gabriel sat.

"I'm not going to just sit here while some vengeful, I don't know, some vengeful … twisted fuck," he shook his head, "tortures or kills my fiancée."

"And I'm not asking you to. But this is my problem. When you lot are running about in Europe, or Central Asia, or Africa, killing the bad guys, well, we can usually smooth things over with the authorities, or just leave minimal traces and extract you. No harm, no foul." He permitted himself a small smile. "Except for the bad guys, obviously. But if you go across the pond and start taking potshots at a US citizen – a very, very rich and therefore, we can assume, connected US citizen – that will unleash the kind of shitstorm, pardon my French, that will have you handed your marching orders, me given a gold watch and a nice sherry party at Number 10, and The Department closed down."

"So what, then?" Gabriel said, his voice rising. "What are you saying? Can I go or can't I?"

Don could feel the desperation pouring out of Gabriel in waves, but he knew he could say nothing that would please him.

"No. You can't. I'll put wheels in motion and," he said hurriedly, as Gabriel opened his mouth to protest, "I mean today, and get our American friends onto it. You, I want in the UK. I have the details of the mission Britta was working on here." He reached into a desk drawer and passed a folder across to Gabriel. "Work the UK angle as much as you like. And if you make a mess, you call me immediately, yes? But you stay in the UK." Don looked at the folder clutched between Gabriel's white-knuckled fingers. Hoped it would be enough. "That's an order, Gabriel. Do you understand?"

"Fine. Yes," Gabriel said, but he sounded like a sullen teenager after being grounded, rather than a disciplined soldier accepting a legitimate order.

"What about me, boss?" Eli said.

"Help Gabriel. He may still be a target over here, so be a second pair of eyes and ears."

She nodded.

Because something tells me Gabriel's lost his bearings over this, Don thought. *I need someone focused to look after him.*

* * *

Outside in the street, Gabriel turned to Eli.

"Where are you staying?"

"At my flat, of course! You should bunk with me for now. Once this is over, I guess you'll need to start house-hunting."

Gabriel squinted against the sun as he looked up and down Whitehall. A sudden gust of wind whirled past him and a woman screamed, and he spun round, heart pounding, hand reaching for an imaginary pistol at his waist.

70

LUCKY CHARM

Chasing a flowery umbrella tumbling and bouncing past him along the pavement was a young woman of about twenty-six or seven.

"Stop it!" she shouted at Gabriel.

He just watched as the umbrella flipped over and over towards the Houses of Parliament like an urban tumbleweed.

She shot him a contemptuous look as she passed.

"Thanks," she shouted.

He sighed. "I would have chased it down for her a month ago."

Eli linked her arm through his and pulled him around and back towards Trafalgar Square.

"Good for you. But Britta needs you to be Sir Lancelot. She," she jerked her chin at the receding form of the young woman, "can manage without you. Come on. Let's get a drink."

The pub was full of tourists, rattling away to each other in a dozen languages, taking selfies and laughing as they sipped Diet Cokes or swigged pints of bitter or lager. The sunlight was tinted rose-pink, emerald-green, and royal-blue by the random squares of coloured glass set in double leaded rows across the tops of the windows.

Gabriel and Eli found a quiet spot in a corner, slipping into two chairs just vacated by a middle-aged couple in matching scarlet-and-charcoal windcheaters.

Eli took a pull on her pint of Guinness, then placed it on the beer mat in front of her.

"We'll go back to mine and get going on the file," she said. "Find out who she was tailing and then work it from there."

Gabriel drank half of the large gin and tonic he'd bought for himself. He shook his head.

"You do that. I'm going to Heathrow."

Eli's eyes opened wide. She took another drink of the Guinness.

"Are you sure that's a good idea? You heard what the boss said."

"No, I'm not sure, am I? But what else am I supposed to do? Piss around in London while some psychopath murders the only woman I've ever loved?" He glared at Eli, feeling, suddenly, that he would like nothing better than to run out of the pub, find someone big, and beat the shit out of them.

His raised voice caused a few of their neighbours to glance round, their frowns and narrowed eyes speaking of anxiety that their holiday was about to turn sour. Gabriel stared back at them until they turned away back to their maps and their phones.

"OK. Go. I'll cover for you. If the boss asks, I'll tell him we've split up to cover more ground. If he calls you, you can still tell him you're in London."

Gabriel shook his head, lips set in a grim line.

"He won't call. He never does."

"Then be careful. I know it doesn't mean much, but I'll be thinking of you. Hey, before you go, I want to give you something."

Eli reached into a pocket and withdrew her fist. She opened her fingers to reveal a silver metal badge. The design was a sword wrapped in an olive branch centred on a Star of David, with a banner containing a Hebrew inscription underneath.

"It's the Israeli Defence Forces insignia," she said. "The sword represents war, the olive branch our yearning for peace."

"What does the inscription say?"

370

"*Tsva ha-Hagana le-Yisra'el*. It means The Army of Defence for Israel. It was a gift from my father when I joined."

"Thanks, Eli."

"Keep it close, yes? For good luck. Promise?"

Gabriel drained his glass, then leaned over and kissed Eli softly on the left cheek, wondering whether he'd see her again. And if they'd both be wearing black if he did.

"I promise."

71

INSUBORDINATION IN THE RANKS

MANHATTAN

Erin Ayers was not used to insubordination from Guy. So his behaviour was puzzling, more than enraging. Ever since Sasha Beck had called to say she had the Swede safely confined at the house outside Ithaca, Guy had been edgy. Now he'd crossed over from edgy to something more like the brooding anger of a caged animal.

"You need to calm down," she said now, pouring herself another martini from a jug chinking with ice cubes. "Wolfe will do what he's told, and we'll have him."

Guy was pacing up and down and she looked down, irritably, as his boots ground away at the white carpet.

"But Erin, look at the facts. You've killed an ex-SAS guy's mates and his old foster father, or whatever the fuck he was, and now you've kidnapped his fiancée. I'm telling you, this game is too dangerous. He'll come for you and it won't be with a fucking peashooter, neither. You heard what Sasha said that first time we talked. He's a stone killer."

"Guy!" she shouted, as his abrupt about-turn gouged the heavy leather heel into the carpet once more. "Sit down. Now! I told you, you do not engage Wolfe unless I say so. You do not speak to him unless I say so. And you do not, I repeat, you do *not*, try to kill him. If you do, I'll pay Sasha another three million to kill you. Or I'll do it myself."

Guy slumped into the corner of the white leather sofa facing Erin. Then he put his huge hands on his knees with a slap and leaned forwards. Clearly he wasn't ready to give up.

"Let it go, boss. I know what he did to you, to your father. But this isn't going to end well. I have the same background as him. Please, I am begging you. Let me take him out for you. He still ends up dead, doesn't he? You can even be with me. Watch as he dies."

"I said no. The whole point of this is so I can look Wolfe in the eye as I kill him and explain why his life is forfeit. Now, if you want to make yourself actually useful, as opposed to a pain in the fucking arse, go and fetch the Testarossa for me. I'm visiting someone in East Hampton, and I feel like driving. You can take the rest of the day off."

She watched Guy's back as he stumped off to collect the Ferrari. Erin sipped her drink, reflecting that Guy would have to go after this little business was out of the way. He'd been useful, but she couldn't have the staff countermanding her orders every time they got a stupid crush on her. She thought back to her recent night with Ava. How civilised her company was. Maybe she'd have a spare foot soldier she could borrow. She'd ask her tonight.

72

A FAIR FIGHT?

ITHACA, NY

In a fair fight, who's to say which of the two women would have prevailed?

Ladies and gentlemen! Fighting out of the blue corner, this woman is a former Swedish Special Forces soldier. She stands five foot five, weighing in at 125 pounds. She has seen action in Africa, the Arctic Circle, Scandinavia and Central Europe, is a skilled knife-fighter and a qualified sniper.

Fighting out of the red corner, her opponent is a full-time assassin. She stands five foot six, weighing in at 128 pounds. She has killed men, and occasionally women, on all seven continents using firearms, blades, bespoke weapons, poisons, and her bare hands.

But this wasn't a fair fight. Britta Falskog's left hand was cuffed to a radiator. She had no weapons. She was underfed, she was thirsty, and she was suffering from the effects of intravenous Valium that her captors – Sasha Beck included – had been administering every day since her capture by Torossian. She had a fading, greenish-yellow bruise on her right temple where one of Torossian's men had pistol-whipped her after she'd struggled against the first injection.

As Sasha walked in, Britta turned to the door, clenching her right fist behind her back and readying herself to strike if her captor came within range.

Sasha put a plate of bread and cheese on the floor and pushed it towards Britta with the toe of her right boot. A bottle of water followed it. Then she stood back.

Britta relaxed her fist and ate greedily, washing the food down with great gulps of water.

Sasha stood over her, watching, a smile playing on those dark-red lips, her fine, black eyebrows arched with amusement.

"Not long to go now, darling," she said, once Britta had pushed the plate away. "Gabriel will be here any day now, galloping in on his white charger, come to rescue his lady-love. Sadly, he'll only have the opportunity to watch her being killed by the wicked fairy. Rescue's simply not on the cards, I'm afraid. And then, who knows? Maybe my employer will kill him. Or maybe he'll somehow triumph and realise the wicked fairy loves him after all."

Britta sneered up at her gaoler, replacing her free hand in her lap, willing Sasha to come closer. *Just for a second. Maybe I need to provoke you.*

"You sick *slyna*. Is that the story you tell yourself while you frig yourself to sleep every night?"

Sasha laughed loudly. "Such bravado!" Then the laughter stopped as suddenly as it had begun. "No. Of course not. I prefer remembering how I let him fuck me in the casino in Hong Kong."

"Liar! He said he drugged you and turned you over to that Triad boss."

Sasha leaned down and pulled Britta's chin up with one sharp, deep-red fingernail. Britta shook her head free, glaring up at her.

"Oh, he drugged me all right. But not before I submitted to his advances. He can be very persuasive. As I'm sure you know."

It was all the opportunity Britta needed.

Her right hand jabbed up from her lap, aiming for the soft part of Sasha's throat. But the target seemed to slip sideways, and her fist sailed harmlessly past, jolting her shoulder as her arm reached the end of its travel.

The retaliation was swift and brutal. Sasha punched down, twice, once to the side of Britta's neck, once to the right breast. Britta cried out at the pain exploding in her chest and lunged again at Sasha. It was too late, and the counterattack failed as dismally as her first strike.

Sasha was on her feet again as Britta slumped back against the radiator, nursing her injured breast.

"Close, darling," she said. Then she swung her right boot back and planted a heavy kick into the centre of Britta's left thigh. "But no cigar."

73

LIVE FREE OR DIE

MANHATTAN

Before he boarded the flight to New York, Gabriel had bought the minimum he required: a change of underwear, a couple of T-shirts, and a washing and shaving kit. But for what he had planned, he needed more gear, more clothes and, if possible, a gun. He realised the latter would prove difficult.

The authorities in Manhattan were even stricter than their counterparts in the rest of New York State, he knew, and without US citizenship or any proof of permanent residence, it would be a struggle. Option one: he still intended to try this route. He felt sure Erin Ayers would have muscle. And the muscle would be carrying, or would be until Gabriel took his weapon. Option two: he could find one of the less salubrious parts of the city and hang around late at night looking simultaneously lost, rich, and stupid, then relieve some gangbanger of his piece. Option three: he could try calling in a favour from Lauren. Option four, but a long shot, he could go old school and use his hands and a knife. For now, he decided to concentrate on the less contentious elements of his equipment. A new outfit was first on the list. Gabriel had left London in a hurry, wearing the clothes he stood up in: Levi's, a white T-shirt, a grey hoodie under a leather jacket, and a pair of heavy-soled tan brogues. He had in mind two different looks now. One, something tactical, in case he needed the advantage of stealth. Two, something altogether smarter, should he need to blend in with more sophisticated types that he assumed would surround a rich, powerful woman living in a Fifth Avenue penthouse.

The hotel he'd picked was positioned about halfway up Central Park West, on the block between West Ninetieth and West Ninety-First Streets. The Rockford Inn bore no outward advertising of any kind, just the polished brass number plate to the left of the door. No marquee announced the hotel's presence, no uniformed doorman stood ready to welcome guests. He'd booked a room on the nineteenth floor. Not the penthouse, but high enough to have an unobstructed view of the park, the Jacqueline Kennedy Onassis Reservoir, and the tall apartment buildings beyond on Fifth Avenue itself.

After breakfast in the hotel dining room, he returned to his room to collect his jacket, ready for his shopping expedition. The day was bright, and sun was streaming through the net curtains that billowed across the window facing the park. He went to the window and slid the curtains aside. A small balcony accessible by a single unlocked door overlooked the park. Unlike many of their more cautious counterparts in New York's hospitality industry, the owners of The Rockford Inn were more than happy to let their guests hang over a hundred foot drop if they so chose. Of course, they were still minded to avoid litigation from a guest's dependants or employers. So they asked each guest on arrival to sign a waiver, absolving the hotel of responsibility should they jump, fall or otherwise leave the safety of their balcony for a one-way trip to the sidewalk.

On the way to the hotel from JFK, he'd broken his journey to buy a pair of Bushnell 10 x 42 Legend Ultra HD compact binoculars. They were good out to a thousand yards and small enough to fit in a pocket – perfect for his needs. He raised them to his eyes now and scanned the rooflines of the apartment buildings across the park from him. Each of the penthouses featured floor-to-ceiling plate glass windows. He worked his way along from left to right. In one or two, he could see people moving about inside, and on one roof terrace he even spotted a woman at the balcony. But the distance was too great to make out any facial features and besides, he didn't know what Erin Ayers looked like.

Squinting against the sun, Gabriel added shades to his mental shopping list. His phone rang. It was Amos Peled.

"Good morning, Gabriel, how are you?"

"Good, thanks, Amos. How are you?"

"Very well, thank you. We old men must be careful not to use that question as an invitation to share every ache and pain."

"What can I do for you?"

"It is more a question of what I can do for you. I thought you might like to know that your bearer bonds were indeed the genuine article. You are now a wealthy man. If you would like me to, I can arrange a cheque book and credit card on your account with us."

"That would be really helpful. Yes, please."

"Do you need funds right now?"

Gabriel thought about the credit cards in his wallet. Was Erin Ayers well connected enough to hack into his accounts? He doubted it. But why risk it?

"Could you wire me some money?"

"But of course? How much do you need?"

"Ten thousand dollars?"

"That won't be a problem. Text me details of your bank in the UK, and I will set up a transfer to a correspondent bank in Manhattan. Now, I have other news for you too. My handler in Tel Aviv was delighted with the intelligence you provided about Das Haus der Tochter. He was also not displeased with the way you handled yourself in there. He asked me to relay this message to you." Gabriel heard Peled clear his throat. "Mossad is grateful. We remember our friends. We are in your debt."

·   ·   ·

Half an hour after texting his bank details to Amos, he received a text back instructing him to call in on a branch of Wells Fargo at 1156 Sixth Avenue. Having called in at the bank and collected his cash, he walked down Sixth, turned left into West Forty-Second Street, and six minutes later arrived at the Oakley store at 560 Fifth Avenue. He emerged five minutes later with a pair of M2 shooting glasses with smoked lenses and a firm grip from the black bows.

He headed back up Fifth to 611, the home of Saks Fifth Avenue, trying to ignore the noise: sirens blaring, drivers hitting their horns at people jay walking. Given more time, Gabriel would have shopped for his clothes at more distinctive outlets, searching out tailors and shirt makers in out-of-the-way streets. But time was against him.

Inside the men's department, he picked out a petrol-blue, two-piece Paul Smith suit in lightweight wool and a plain, knitted, navy silk tie from hook + Albert. Shirts next. Normally, he'd opt for French cuffs, but the business of fastening cufflinks seemed unbelievably pointless given what was happening in his life, so he bought shirts with barrel cuffs instead. The young woman serving him, a plump African American in her twenties with deep-red lipstick and her hair tied back in a sleek pony tail, smiled at his choices.

"I like to see a man who knows what he wants," she said. "You know, a lot of our customers – the men, I mean – they leave it to their wives or girlfriends. But the ones who come in on their own, they're generally the ones I like serving the most."

Gabriel smiled back at her, thinking of the irony that here he was, shopping for clothes while *his* future wife was God knows where.

A pair of Bally black Oxfords, black cotton Falke socks, black Paul Smith cotton briefs, and a stone waterproof coat from Engineered for Motion completed his purchases.

"That's it?" the assistant, whose name was Lily, asked.

"I think so. Have I missed anything?"

"Well, unless you're planning on attending the opera, I'd say you're all set."

At the sales desk, Gabriel proffered his credit card, and found he was holding his breath as Lily took it. The transaction went through without any alarm bells sounding or uniformed security guards grabbing him by the biceps, and he let out the air trapped in his lungs with a quiet sigh.

He had to return to the hotel to dump the new clothes. Outside again, this time heading for a couple of Army surplus outlets and one of the few gun shops he'd been able to locate in Manhattan.

The gun store – Ralph Robins Sporting Goods – was on a narrow, rundown street on the Lower East Side, sandwiched between a computer repair store and a firehouse. Gabriel glanced into the shadows and saw a handful of firefighters cleaning the big red-and-chrome truck. The windscreen strip bore the legend, "We Support U.S. Armed Forces." The air around him was rank with the sour-sweet smell of rotting garbage.

He turned and pushed through the door, setting a brass bell jangling on its spring over the door. The place was poorly lit. Gabriel recognised the smell – a woolly, oily, musty reek that said 'old military gear.' Most of the floor space was taken up with circular chrome racks of camouflage jackets, combat trousers and various hoodies, fleeces and shell jackets. He threaded his way through the clothing to the counter at the back of the store.

The man standing behind the counter was overweight, balding, unshaven and had a sheen of sweat on his hairy shoulders, which were exposed by the dirty white singlet he was wearing. It inspired confidence in Gabriel. Not the "won't rip-me-off" kind of confidence that any nervous tourist would enjoy, but confidence that he would be open to Gabriel's proposal.

"Help you?" the man asked, leaning against the glass display case behind him, which was packed, haphazardly, with knives, torches, leather holsters and a handful of tatty-looking revolvers and pistols.

"I hope so. I need a pistol."

"You live in New York?"

"England."

"A Brit, huh? You know, we got the Second Amendment because of you guys?"

Gabriel smiled. "I do."

"Well, you oughta know that to buy a gun in New York, you're gonna need a whole buncha stuff you ain't got. For example," the man pushed himself away from the display case, clearly beginning to enjoy himself, "your birth certificate, and I mean your *American* birth certificate, and proof of residence – *in New York City*. You got any of that?"

"I think you can work out that I haven't."

"Then I think *you* can work out that you're outta luck, buddy. I can do you a nice combat jacket if you wanna play soldiers."

Gabriel leaned a little closer and lowered his voice.

"Look, I respect your position and believe me, as a former soldier, I also respect your Second Amendment rights. But I really do need a gun. Take that Ruger there. The ticket on it says a hundred and eighty dollars. Supposing I were to offer you eighteen hundred for it with a full mag. Would that alter things at all?"

The man stared at Gabriel.

Gabriel stared back, keeping a pleasant but not overly wide smile plastered onto his face.

Finally, the man looked over at the door then back at Gabriel. He spoke, quietly.

"Listen. I'm originally from New Hampshire. You know our state motto?"

Gabriel shook his head. "Tell me."

"'Live free or die.' The only gun control I believe in is a safety catch and a steady hand. And I'm not even sure about the safety catch. But here's the thing. The law's the law. I don't know if you're really Lord Snooty from England or a Fed trying to entrap me, but either way, unless you got the paperwork I mentioned and about six months to kill, you ain't walking out of here with squat. Am I making myself clear?"

Gabriel shrugged. "Crystal. Thanks for your time."

He left the shop, hailed a cab and gave the driver the address of the first of the army surplus stores he'd identified.

An hour later, he was standing in his room looking down at his latest set of purchases. Two full tactical outfits – one black, one in mossy oak camouflage pattern – multi-pocketed trousers, mesh vest, T-shirts, hoodies and shell jackets. Plus: a two-inch leather belt with D-rings and trigger clips for accessories; a black, vinyl, all-purpose holster; caps; gloves; backpacks; and two pairs of SWAT-branded boots, one in sand, one all black.

The hardware would make most NYPD officers, not to mention survivalists, smile in recognition of a man who knew the importance of high-quality equipment. Whether or not he managed to source a firearm, Gabriel knew he could always rely on a knife. He'd picked out, to the store owner's approval, a BÖKER Magnum Black Spear. The blade had a solid locking mechanism and deep finger grooves. Knife-fighting was second nature to Gabriel, and he'd probably despatched as many adversaries with blades as bullets. His second blade was a twelve-inch machete. In the SAS, they'd called them "gollocks," after the Indonesian *golok*. If he went in under cover of darkness, then the 5.11 Tactical light would be his friend. A Suunto A-10 compass and a TacMed tactical first-aid kit, augmented with a more basic set of antiseptics and sticking plasters, completed his purchases.

In the SAS, he'd been taught the importance of understanding not just how every piece of kit worked, but why it worked the way it did, and what to do if it failed. Soldiers in the regular army might be happy pressing the on button or flicking the safety lever. But what if the on button or the safety failed? You didn't just return to base and collect a new one from the stores. You were a hundred miles behind enemy lines, or sitting waist-deep in a swamp, or halfway up a mountain. No. You took apart every new piece of kit and studied how its designers had put it together. You read the manual. You played with it and tinkered with it until you knew it intimately. *Then* you used it. And if it failed, you found a new way to get it working. Your life, and those of your comrades, depended on it.

So now he was sitting at the desk, the second of two mugs of the hotel's coffee cooling in front of him, unscrewing the lens cover on the tactical light, and pulling the innards out. His phone vibrated next to his left elbow and he swivelled it round to check the screen. It was a text from Eli.

How are things?

Good question. How *are* things? He tapped out a short reply.

Not sure. Ready to go but lots of buildings face reservoir. You?

Been stood down. Bored.

He didn't have time for this anymore. His head was buzzing with adrenaline and caffeine. He tapped a single letter and put his phone aside.

K

He finished reassembling the torch and pushed it away. The knife would be fun to play with, but he realised what was troubling him. His so-called lead might work for a team of NYPD detectives with time, money and resources on hand, but he only had one of those three things at his disposal. He'd counted at least twenty apartment blocks on Fifth with a view across the reservoir. It would take weeks to surveil them all thoroughly, and even then, there was no guarantee he'd see Ayers. He needed to find a way to narrow it down. He turned back to his phone and called Eli.

74

COCKTAILS

"Oh, it's you," she said. "After that last text, I thought I was getting the brush-off."

"Sorry, Eli. I'm just, you know, time's not on my side, and I need someone to bounce ideas off."

"No, I'm sorry. You're the one facing some madwoman and her paid hitter. What do you want to talk about?"

Gabriel sighed and looked up at the ceiling as he spoke.

"I have to narrow the search down. At the moment, I know she lives in a penthouse with a view of the reservoir, but it's a big body of water. There are too many buildings."

Eli paused before answering.

"OK, you dress up like a hobo, or a wino, or whatever they call the homeless over there, and you hang around seeing who comes and goes."

He shook his head, even though he knew she couldn't see him.

"Can't you see? That's the problem. I could dress up like Uncle Sam, but it would still leave me with too many buildings to check out. Plus up here? The cops would move me on in seconds. I've been out today, and everyone is in business suits or out for a day's sightseeing."

"Hide in plain sight, then."

"That's where I've got to. I have a suit, but that doesn't solve the problem."

"What about real estate agents? Go in and say you're looking for a penthouse. You're a British millionaire, and you fancy a pad in Manhattan."

"Go on."

"Hang on, I'm making this up as I go along. Right, you say you want it on one of the blocks facing the reservoir."

"That's between East Eighty-Fifth and East Ninety-Seventh Streets."

"Good. So then you say you know this super-rich woman called Erin Ayers has one, and you want one like hers. They assume you know her and they're bound to know about all the big purchases. Then you do your best Hugh Grant, floppy-fringe English accent and charm her address out of the agent."

"That's not bad. But what if they just clam up or don't know her? I had another thought."

"Uh huh."

"I go into Tiffany's and say I want to buy a gift for a friend. I'm new in town and forgot my address book. Does she have an account with them? I mean, she's bound to, right? Then I just get the address off their computer."

"More holes than a colander. She might buy her bling somewhere else. She might pay cash. They might be as tight with their customer data as the realtor."

"Who is strictly imaginary at this stage, remember?" Gabriel said, turning the knife this way and that so the razor-sharp edge caught the sunlight, sending little flickers into his eyes.

"None of these work. Hey, try this. Do you have any friends in New York? People who read the gossip columns, go to charity balls, things like that?"

Blinking away the blue afterimages dancing on his retinas, Gabriel tried to think. But he could feel the beginnings of a headache squeezing his brain right behind his eyeballs, and his thoughts were as undisciplined as raw recruits fresh off the train.

"Nobody. Not here, anyway."

"What do you mean?"

"I mean I've met a couple of one-percenters, but they don't live in Manhattan."

"Like who?"

Gabriel thought about Tiffany's. About diamonds and precious metals. A face and a name swam into view.

"Tatyana Garin."

"Who's she? Russian? A spook?"

"No. She's a businesswoman. Precious metals and diamonds, among other things. We helped each other out last year."

"Call her. Ask her if she knows anyone in Manhattan. People like that all know each other. Different countries are like different streets to them."

The pain behind his eyes was worsening. Gabriel thanked Eli – it was the best idea either of them had had – and hung up. He looked down at his phone, then groaned, rushed to the bathroom and threw up into the lavatory. When he'd finished retching, he splashed cold water on his face and stumbled to the bed. He set an alarm on his phone for an hour.

Why didn't I think of this earlier? Gabriel smiled at his brother and tossed the rugby ball to him. Central Park was bathed in dusty sunlight, and their patch of grass near the reservoir was the perfect spot for some practice. Michael tossed the ball back to him, spinning it expertly so it arrowed through the twenty yards of air between them in a shallow arc. *The beard suits him*, Gabriel thought, as he lobbed a high pass back to Michael.

Laughing, Michael caught the ball and returned it with interest: an even higher throw.

"Drop it, Gable!" he shouted, just as Gabriel crouched under the descending ball.

He glanced sideways, just for a moment, but it was enough. The ball shot through his hands and hit the grass point-down, before rebounding at a sharp angle and bobbling away to a group of people who'd stopped to watch.

Conscious of the audience, Gabriel drop-kicked the ball back to Michael, aiming for the lazy but effective style his games teacher had always praised him for at school. The ball looped over a young tree and straight into Michael's arms, who was trotting backwards, positioning himself directly beneath its flight path.

"Catch this one or the beers are on you," Michael shouted back.

Then he took a couple of steps forward, the ball balanced on his outstretched left palm, dropped it and gave it a mighty kick that sent it high into the air, over Gabriel's head towards the water.

Keeping his eyes fixed on the ball, Gabriel ran backwards, twisting and turning to keep it in sight as it arched over his head. A woman screamed from the crowd of onlookers.

"Look out!"

The ground disappeared from under his feet as he toppled backwards off the bank and the ice-cold water swallowed him.

Looking up, he could see the ball floating on the surface above his head. The bubbles escaping his lips shimmied up through the green water and clung momentarily to the underside of the ball before wobbling around its sides and bursting on the surface.

He kicked out, a strong swimmer, already planning how best to deflect Michael's pisstaking when he got back to shore.

The hand that closed round his right ankle sent a searing pain through his rugby sock and into his skin. He yelled, releasing more bubbles from his wide-open mouth, and looked down.

Kamenko leered up at him through slimed lips and fastened another burning hand around Gabriel's ankle.

Gabriel kicked out with his free leg, but then a second figure swam up from the depths and hooked its talons into his calf.

It was Julia Angell. Half her head was missing, and the exposed brain left filmy trails of blood in the water behind her.

Dusty and Daisy came next, skin peeling away from their skulls, horrific wounds gaping in the bodies as they swam up to him and wrapped their arms around his torso.

"You next, Wolfie," Dusty gurgled, before dragging him down into the darkness. "Erin-iz wants you dead."

Gabriel opened his mouth to scream. The inrushing water flooded his lungs and he felt himself sinking.

He woke up choking, hands clutched around his windpipe, eyes wet with tears.

"Oh, fuck!" he said. Then again. Louder.

He staggered to the bathroom and drank down two glasses of water before sitting heavily on the edge of the bath and regarding himself in the mirror above the vanity unit. His eyes were red, and his black hair stood up in sweat-soaked spikes. Scrubbing his palms across his eyes and then smoothing his hair down, he stood, marched into the bedroom, stripped to his underwear, dropped to the floor and started doing press-ups.

After thirty, he turned over and continued, pushing himself to complete harder sit-ups and crunches than his PT instructors had ever inflicted on him.

Next, he began a yoga routine. No blissed-out meditation this time. He pushed himself to complete the sun salutations faster and faster, building up the pace until sweat was running freely into his eyes and across the skin of his torso, his arms and his legs. They said one hundred and eight was a magical number in yoga. So he completed them.

It was dark by the time he stopped. He was red hot, drenched in sweat and, mercifully, clear-headed. A memory of the nightmare had come back to him as he performed the prescribed sequence of positions and breaths that constituted the sun salutations. "Erin-iz wants you dead," Dusty had said. Suddenly he knew. Erin Ayers had chosen that name herself. She wasn't christened with it. It was an alias. Erin Ayers *was* Erin-iz. She had named herself Fury. But then who was she really?

With this question revolving inside his head, he showered, shaved and dressed, headed out, bought a slice of pizza from a vendor with a cart on Columbus, washed it down with a Coke, then went back to the hotel. He had a plan.

Drinking from a glass of white Burgundy he'd bought at the bar and then taken up to his room, he called Tatyana Garin. The woman had to be at least as rich as Erin Ayers. As CEO of Garin Group, she owned diamond mines, goldfields, land, and other mining resources from Venezuela to South Africa.

"Gabriel! My knight in shining armour. Please tell me you need my help again."

Her Russian-accented English took him flying back to their last encounter. After he had rescued an astronomically expensive handbag she'd just been relieved of by a couple of North London thugs, she'd pledged to repay the favour and had done so, getting him out of Harare on her private jet when a mission had gone spectacularly sideways.

"Yes, I do. And I really hope you can help me this time."

"What is it? Tell me, dear Gabriel, and if I can help you, I will."

"I need to find someone in Manhattan. I know she owns a penthouse on Fifth Avenue overlooking the reservoir. I know her name – Erin Ayers – but beyond that, I'm stuck."

"This woman. I have not heard of her. She is rich, though. Real estate in that part of Manhattan is very expensive. Like Birkin bag, you remember?"

"I remember. So you don't know her?"

"I do not. But that does not mean I can't help you. I have many friends in Manhattan. And one lady in particular, I think, can help you. Her name is Ayesha Solomons. She also has penthouse on Fifth. Near Guggenheim. I text you address. Ayesha is very sociable lady. Very, *lyubeznaya*, you know?"

"Gracious, yes, I know."

"I forget you speak Russian so beautifully. Well, Ayesha likes to know who is coming and who is going. Especially in penthouses. She sees removals trucks and makes point of introducing herself. Invitations for tea, cocktails, you know? Welcome to the neighbourhood. I call her and say you are coming. Then I text you her address, yes? You talk with Ayesha, explain who you are looking for. If she does not know, then this person is ghost."

"Tatyana, you're a star. I can't thank you enough."

"Is not necessary. But I tell you what. We are friends, you and I.

We help each other. Next time I need help with something, I call you and you come to my aid once again, yes?"

"Any time. Thank you again."

"*Do skorovo, Gabriushka.*"

"See you later, Tanya."

Fifteen minutes later, his phone buzzed.

Ayesha Solomons. Penthouse. 1079 Fifth Avenue. She expects you at 6 p.m. xxx

Gabriel looked over at his new clothes hanging in the closet. Something told him a well-cut suit and polished shoes would be more appropriate than an outfit that made him look like a member of a black-ops squad. He reached for one of the shirts.

75

YINSHEN FANGSHI

The direct route to Ayesha Solomons's apartment building would take Gabriel across Central Park. Instead, he turned left out of the hotel and then left again on West Ninety-First Street. He found what he was looking for on Amsterdam Avenue: an upscale florist.

Fifteen minutes later and two hundred dollars lighter in the back pocket, he emerged from Floribus Vitae clutching a bouquet of pale-pink and white peonies, hydrangeas and roses, and blue-green eucalyptus foliage.

The flowers smelled heavily of peach and a slightly musky, smoky aroma he knew from his own garden to be myrrh. *Correction*, he thought, *my former garden*. Despite this unwelcome thought, the scent of the flowers lifted his mood. He was on his way to meet someone who might be able to take him one step closer to Erin Ayers.

Walking through the park, he saw a couple of men joining his path from a converging track coming down a hill. They were dressed in wannabe tactical gear: khaki cargo pants, dark-blue wind breakers and black ball caps pulled down low over their eyes. They appeared to be patrolling, striding side by side and actually in step, though he observed that the shorter and heavier of the two men had to extend his natural stride length to keep pace with his taller companion.

Neither man had any sort of insignia on their clothing. So not park wardens, if such people existed. And not detectives either: no law enforcement officer in plain clothes would so obviously draw attention to themselves. Weekend warriors? "Concerned citizens"? No, he had it. Neighbourhood Watch. Their ostentatious manner, and exaggeratedly vigilant postures said it all. And was that a bulge on the taller guy's waistband? It was hard to be sure with the windbreaker in place, but might he be carrying? There! He patted his hip. Gabriel walked on, adjusting his speed so that all three of them would reach the junction of the two paths at the same time.

Checking his watch as they drew to within a couple of feet of each other, he let himself collide with the taller man, hard enough to make him stumble.

"Oh, my goodness," Gabriel said, playing the flustered Englishman. "I am so sorry. There I was worrying about my appointment and I've crashed right into you."

He straightened the man's wind breaker, taking care to stick the flowers in his face, fussed over the sleeves, and watched the two men relax as his act reassured them he wasn't about to mug them.

"That's OK, sir," said Fat Man. "Here on business?"

"A little, yes," Gabriel answered. "I'm on my way to meet a rather important client and I completely underestimated the time it would take to reach her."

"Where does your client live?" Tall Man asked.

"Oh, er, it's one of those apartment buildings over there, on Fifth, is it? Number 1079. I desperately wanted to be on time and now it appears I'll be late."

"Relax. Look, take that path over there, and it brings you out almost opposite her building."

Gabriel bestowed his brightest smile on the men.

"You, sirs, are both gentlemen and scholars. Many thanks," he said, then hurried away from them in a brisk jog.

"Take care, now!" Tall Man called after him.

You, too, Gabriel thought, enjoying the feel of a chunky pistol tucked into the back of the waistband of his suit trousers. Even though Master Zhao was gone, Gabriel's skill with the Way of Stealth served as a testament to his teaching.

He picked up the pace, ensuring that by the time Tall Man realised he'd been disarmed, Gabriel would be out of sight. The guy would probably be too embarrassed to go to the police anyway. They'd probably regard him as an unwelcome intrusion into their business. As for Courtesy, Professionalism and Respect, which Gabriel had seen stencilled onto the side of a patrol car earlier in the day? He was guessing having your pistol taken off you by a dopey English business-type was neither professional, nor worthy of respect. Though he supposed they might be courteous while explaining Tall Man would be better off leaving law enforcement to the police.

Ensuring his jacket was smoothed down over the pistol, Gabriel entered the softly lit lobby of 1079 Fifth Avenue, nodding to the frock-coated doorman standing beneath the forest-green marquee on the way in. The lobby wouldn't have looked out of place in a bank headquarters. Everywhere he looked, Gabriel saw polished marble, glittering granite, expensive hardwoods and subtle accents of what he assumed was gold leaf. He looked left and right, then headed over to the reception desk, a long, polished block faced with some sort of stripy timber. He decided to maintain the mildly hapless Englishman act. It seemed to work well as a way of putting people at ease who might otherwise be suspicious.

"Hello," he said to the man behind the desk, peering at his name badge as if short-sighted, "Alejandro. I have an appointment to see Ayesha Solomons. My name is Gabriel Wolfe. She's expecting me."

"Very good, sir," the man said, smiling to reveal a row of immaculate white teeth against his honey-brown skin. "Would you like to take a seat while I call up?"

Two minutes later, the receptionist signalled to Gabriel.

"Take the far elevator to the penthouse, sir. You just press *P*. I've unlocked it."

Gabriel smiled and nodded, and walked across the roughly half acre of polished white marble floor to the elevator, clutching the bouquet in what he realised was a sweating palm. Once inside the elevator, he pulled the pistol from his waistband to see what Tall Man had judged appropriate for watching his neighbourhood. He nodded his approval. It was a Heckler & Koch HK45. Putting the bouquet on the floor, he ejected the magazine. It was full: ten rounds of .45 ACP full metal jacket rounds. He sniffed the muzzle. Gun oil, only. Clearly, the guy didn't spend time at the range practising.

The door slid open to reveal a long, wide hallway. Paintings hung on both walls revealed the penthouse's owner to be a woman of extraordinary wealth. He had counted three cubist Picassos, a Hockney swimming pool painting and a Warhol portrait of Marilyn Monroe before a door opened at the far end of the hall and the lady of the penthouse came towards him, her hand extended.

Ayesha Solomons looked to be in her late seventies, with clear, virtually unlined skin and lustrous, silver-white hair cut in a stylish bob that grazed her collar. Though Gabriel had met enough wealthy people to know that money could achieve wonders in stalling the ageing process, her looks seemed to be the result of a good life and a clear conscience, rather than visits to a plastic surgeon. She wore a simply cut suit, the skirt and jacket tailored to fit her slender figure. The fabric was in a pale shade of salmon, with ruffled black ribbons edging the collar, pockets and jacket hem. Her brown eyes were magnified by oversized black-framed glasses. But what mesmerised Gabriel as he shook her hand were the diamonds dangling from her ear-lobes and arrayed at her throat, glittering in the light from the chandelier. They were huge, the size of almonds, and mounted in yellow gold.

"Gabriel, how delightful to meet you," Ayesha said, releasing his hand and leading him by the elbow to the door at the far end of the hall.

"Thank you so much for agreeing to meet me, Mrs Solomons," he said. He'd noticed a plain gold band on her wedding ring finger.

"Oh, I think you should call me Ayesha. Mrs Solomons makes me sound so old, don't you think?"

"Then, thank you, Ayesha."

The drawing room she had led him to was at least fifty feet by thirty, a vast airy space with an entire wall of glass facing Central Park. She took the flowers from him, "Thank you, they're beautiful, and my favourite colours," and took them through a door that, he saw, led to a vast, white kitchen.

Gabriel took the opportunity to take in the view from the penthouse. Somehow, he felt sure it would be a long time before he'd ever be in such a position again. The darkening sky had changed from a sapphire blue to the colour of coral, and the mounded clouds were charcoal above and gold below. On the far side of the water, almost directly across from Ayesha's penthouse, Gabriel could see the Dakota building, its gothic sandstone burnished to a rich yellow by the setting sun.

When Ayesha returned from the kitchen, she was carrying the flowers in a tall, glass vase, which she placed in the centre of a grand wooden dining table with ornately carved legs.

"May I offer you a cup of tea? Or something stronger?" She checked her watch, something very high-end Gabriel concluded from the dozens of tiny diamonds studding the bezel, though he wasn't close enough to discern the make. "It is the cocktail hour, after all. I usually have an old-fashioned about this time."

"That sounds lovely. I'll join you, if I may."

"Good boy."

Ayesha mixed two drinks, taking her time muddling the sugar cubes and water before adding a generous shot of Woodford Reserve bourbon and a dash of Angostura bitters. She garnished the drinks with orange slices and maraschino cherries and handed one of the heavy glass tumblers to Gabriel.

"Bottoms up!" she said, clinking glasses.

"Chin chin!" Gabriel replied, feeling something equally archaic was required.

The drink was perfect, the warm, almost treacly flavour of the bourbon contrasting with the hit of citrus aroma from the orange.

"So," Ayesha said, swirling her drink around and eyeing Gabriel through her spectacles like a particularly inquisitive owl. "You are a friend of Tanya's."

It sounded like a statement, but Gabriel could recognise an intelligence-gathering question when he heard one.

"Yes. We met in London. I rescued her Birkin from a mugger, and we went for a coffee. Then we met again in Africa where I was working, and she helped me get back to England. If I may ask, how do you and Tanya know each other?"

Ayesha smiled, and Gabriel noticed her twisting her wedding ring round on her finger.

"Jack and I met her through Jack's business. He was a jeweller. Started out with a single shop and built the business up to five. Very high-class establishments. We met Tanya in Amsterdam on a buying trip. The friendship grew from there. She stays with me whenever she's in New York."

"Is your husband retired now?" Gabriel asked, guessing he was providing an opening.

"From this world altogether, I'm afraid. He died ten years ago. A heart attack. It was quick, but he was still so young. So handsome. We had plans to travel. It's such a shame."

"I'm sorry."

She leaned across and patted his knee.

"Thank you. Tell me, what is your work that takes you from London to Zimbabwe to Manhattan all in the space of a few months?"

He hadn't mentioned which African country he'd been stuck in. That was obviously from Tanya. He decided, on the spur of the moment, to tell Ayesha as much as he could without breaking his oath to The Department.

"I work in national security. I'm forbidden to say how or who for, but it's a dangerous job, and I go to places and deal with people our government can't deal with through other channels."

Ayesha took another sip of her drink and put it down beside her on a side table.

"How exciting! And now you need my help?"

"Yes, I do. I am looking for someone here in Manhattan. She calls herself Erin Ayers. She owns a penthouse here on Fifth Avenue. It overlooks the reservoir. But that's all I know."

"Why do you say, 'calls herself'?"

"I suspect it's not her real name. I think she called herself that because it sounds like the Greek word for a Fury."

"A vengeful goddess. That is very interesting."

"Why? Do you know her?"

"I do. Now, why don't you make us two more old-fashioneds, and I'll tell you all I can about her."

76

HAVEN'T WE MET?

Their drinks refreshed, Ayesha sat back in her chair and folded her hands in her lap.

"I have lived here for almost thirty years," she said. "Twenty with Jack and ten on my own. I always liked to get on with people. So I've made it my business to know my neighbours, especially the ones on the top floors. If I see the moving men coming, I go round a day or so later and introduce myself. Maybe invite the new people round for drinks. I met Erin last year when she bought her place. And do you know what?"

"What?"

"I threw a little party for her, and she didn't show up. I wouldn't say we were scandalised – we're all too worldly wise for that – but such rudeness."

Gabriel leant forward. "You know which block she lives in, then?" He could feel his pulse racing.

"Of course I do! It's 1083. She's practically next door."

Gabriel felt his heart lifting. This was the best news he'd had for weeks. With a single building to watch, he felt sure he could identify Erin Ayers one way or another.

"Thank you so much," he said. "You have no idea what this means to me."

"Oh, maybe I have an inkling. You don't love her, or why would you forget her address? But she clearly means a lot to you, if you came all this way and asked Tanya for help finding her. So I am guessing, if she's not a friend, then given your job, she must be an enemy."

She was watching him again. He wondered whether while her husband had been building his retail business up, Ayesha had been content to play the supportive wife, or whether she'd had a career of her own. As a detective.

"She is. Not of my employer's. Just of mine."

Ayesha took a sip of her old-fashioned.

"Then forgive an old woman offering a trained fighting man advice, but be careful. I heard she owns the entire building, not just the penthouse. People with that kind of money have power to go with it. Whatever you have planned, whatever wrong she's done you, proceed with extreme caution. Now," she checked her watch again. "It's been ages since I had a handsome young man's company. So I insist you take me to dinner."

* * *

By 6.30 the following morning, Gabriel was stationed on the sidewalk opposite 1083 Fifth Avenue, wandering up and down and checking his watch as if waiting for a colleague or an Uber. He'd dressed in the suit again, figuring that on the Upper East Side, hiding in plain sight called for business attire. He carried his phone and stopped pacing every now and again, pretending to check the screen. Around him, early-rising corporate types were moving past, mainly heading downtown, the women noticeable for the pristine white sneakers on their feet, at odds with the crisp tailoring of their suits.

At no stage did he take his eye off the doorway beneath the bottle-green marquee shading the entrance to 1083. At one point near the start of his surveillance, the door opened, and his pulse jerked upwards as a woman emerged. But she was older than Ayesha Solomons and unlikely to be his target. *Anything's possible, Old Sport*, a voice whispered inside his head, but he dismissed it.

Compared to some of the lurks he'd participated in – waist-deep in leech-infested South American rivers, or posing as a filth-encrusted tramp in Northern Ireland – hanging about one of the wealthiest neighbourhoods in the world dressed in expensive tailoring and handmade shoes was no hardship at all. He bought a hot dog and a coffee from a cart vendor and carried on ambling up and down the fifty or so yards of sidewalk. He was careful to keep one eye out for the two neighbourhood watchers, though he suspected they'd be at work. A girl in a white, spaghetti-strap dress came towards him, checked him out, and smiled. A slim blue tube clamped between her electric-blue lips emitted clouds of coconut-scented vapour that made him sneeze.

"Gesundheit!" she said, then laughed and walked on.

Gabriel spotted a bench just opposite the corner of Fifth Avenue and East Ninetieth Street, and he sat down for a while, crossing his right ankle over his left knee and pretending to study his phone. A beech tree cast dappled shade over his observation post and, as an added benefit, over his face.

Just after 11.00, when the tourist traffic was in full flow between him and the apartment building, he noticed the door opening. He moved to the edge of the sidewalk, facing downtown but looking out of the corner of his eye at the marquee. There! A man and a woman coming out of the door. From the glimpse he managed, the man was tall, with a muscular build, but it was the woman who was sending his spider sense into overdrive. What was it about her that was so familiar? Her face? The shape was regular, the features attractive in a generic way. No, it wasn't her face. Something about her body language made him feel he'd seen her before. The way she placed her feet on the sidewalk, almost like a ballet dancer. *Damn! Think, Wolfe. Where do you know her from?* As he cursed his memory, the man turned and looked straight across the street. Gabriel turned

with him, circling round a group of Japanese teenagers in the bright
plumage he always associated with youngsters from East Asia. He
emerged from the knot of selfie-snapping teens ten yards further
down the street. Now he had an uninterrupted view of the man.
And he recognised him.

77

DIFFERENCE OF OPINION

Staring just long enough to be sure before turning away for a second, Gabriel ground his teeth together. The man was Carl Mortensen. Or, as it seemed now, the hired muscle protecting a woman who in all probability was Erin Ayers. He decided to try an old trick. A clinical psychologist he'd once gone out with had been explaining a part of the brain called the reticular activating system.

"The RAS is mainly there to regulate sleep and wakefulness," Petra had explained over dinner in Taormina in Sicily. "But it also plays a role in attention. Say you're at a party—"

"I'm at a party," Gabriel said, happily drunk on the local organic red wine and smiling sweetly.

"Funny. Someone calls out 'Dave.' Do you look round?"

"No, of course not."

"Exactly. What if someone calls out Gabriel?"

"Then I look round."

"And that's your RAS, waking up and telling you something important's happening in your immediate environment."

. . .

He sank back behind a tour party of Midwesterners, dressed for the season in voluminous pastel shorts and tops bearing Chicago Bears logos, and called across the street.

"Erin!"

The tourists nearest to him turned round in surprise, but through a gap between their well upholstered frames, he observed something that brought forth a tight-lipped smile from the ex-Special Forces man.

The woman whipped her head round.

"Got you," Gabriel whispered, keeping pace with the waddling tour party and his eyes fixed to Erin Ayers and her bodyguard.

Leaving the party and tagging on behind a group of businesspeople walking towards the southeast corner of the park, Gabriel watched as the woman shook her head to a question from the goon and reached into her handbag for her phone.

Moments later, a bright-red Ferrari Testarossa roared around the corner and stopped beside them with a brief squeal from the fat tyres. A young man in a pale-blue blazer – a valet, Gabriel assumed – jumped out of the driver's seat, was rewarded with a bill, and trotted back the way he'd come.

Ayers slid into the driver's seat, and the goon dropped his bulk, with some difficulty, into the seat to her right. With a louder squeal of tyres and a blast from the exhausts, the strake-sided sports car took off, heading downtown.

Something was seriously interfering with Gabriel's wiring. It felt as if two parts of his brain were arguing with each other, thoughts meshing then spinning apart like a gearbox thrown into neutral.

I know you.I can't know you.

Who are you?I know who you are.

That walk.What walk?

The car.What about it?

. . .

He returned to his bench and closed his eyes, pressing his fingertips to his forehead and frowning with the effort of remembering something that didn't want to be remembered. With an effort, he relaxed, keeping his eyes closed and slowing his heartbeat, searching for that quiet internal space where he could access his subconscious thoughts.

"Excuse me, sir, are you all right?"

Gabriel opened his eyes. He had no idea how long he'd been sitting there.

Looking down at him, her hands on her knees, was a black police officer, a wary smile on her face. He glanced beyond her compact frame to see an NYPD cruiser pulled up, with her male partner leaning across the seats to monitor the situation.

"Yes, officer," he read her name badge, "Harris. I must have just dozed off for a minute."

"Oh, OK. You British?"

"Mm-hmm."

"So, listen, strictly speaking you're not supposed to sleep on the sidewalk. But you're our guest, so I'm just going to suggest maybe you get some rest at your hotel."

He nodded, stood up and turned to go, after giving her a smile and a salute. Identifying Erin Ayers would have to wait. He needed to figure out his next move. Entering the building wouldn't be that difficult, and now he had a visual on his two targets, nor would taking them out. But with Britta still missing, they were his only link to her.

What Gabriel needed more than anything was certainty.

He didn't have long to wait.

78

BAITING THE TRAP

Ayers put her phone back in her bag. She looked at Guy, and smiled.

"That was Sasha. Torossian's people just came through. Falskog is at the house in Ithaca."

"Secure?"

"What do you think? The super-Swede may be ex-Special Forces, but I bet she's never met anyone like Sasha Beck before."

"What now, then?"

Ayers sat in one of the low leather armchairs in the living room, and pushed one of her shoes half off. She enjoyed the way Guy struggled to keep his eyes on hers, and off her legs, which she crossed at the thigh to further discomfort him. She knew all about his stupid crush on her, and it amused her to toy with this big, dumb Dutchman. She angled her right foot to one side, admiring the sheen of the emerald-green snakeskin loafer dangling from her toes.

"I'm going up to Ithaca. I want you to set up at the motel in Scranton. I'll send him to you; you disarm him, then bring him to me. Then the fun begins."

"I'm worried, boss. I know you say Beck is a pro hitter, but I've been with this guy in Kazakhstan. He's tough. Please can't I just do him myself? You can still kill his girlfriend. Get Sasha to video it and send it to him. You'll still get the pleasure of knowing you've destroyed his life."

"No!" Ayers's eyes flashed with anger. "*I'm* going to kill him. *I* am! Not you, not Sasha, not anybody but me."

"Please, boss. It's not a job for a woman."

At his words, Ayers sprang at him and slapped him viciously across the face. Then again, just as hard.

"Don't you ever, EVER patronise me!" she shouted, her face just inches from his, which was now reddening from the two blows as much as the embarrassment at breaking rule number one. "Jesus! I ought to put a bullet in that thick skull of yours."

With amazement, she realised that Guy was crying. Tears were creeping over his cheeks, magnifying the open pores each side of his nose as they rolled towards the corners of his mouth.

"I'm sorry, boss. It won't happen again. I was just, I don't want you to get hurt, that's all."

She sighed, patted his arm and returned to her chair. *Oh, God, please don't tell me I'm feeling sorry for the big ox.*

"I'm sorry, Guy. For hitting you. It's getting close now, and I suppose I might be a teensy bit tense. I'll be careful, I promise. Now, go and get ready to receive our guest. Take the Range Rover."

She watched as Guy left the apartment, swiping a meaty forearm across his eyes.

With Guy gone, she fetched a saddle-tan leather holdall from a closet, placed it on her bed, and began packing for her trip. As she packed, she hummed a tune – "Rule Britannia," her father's favourite little ditty while he was working – then began itemising the objects she was placing into the holdall.

"Jeans, check. T-shirts, check. Undies, check. Socks, check. Fleece, check. Boots, check. Washbag, check. Makeup bag check. Book, check. Walther CCP," – she swung her right arm out and aimed the pistol's ArmaLaser sight at a spot on the wall – "check. Fiocchi nine-millimetre rounds, check." The last item had been a gift from an Italian countess, the great-granddaughter of a friend of Mussolini's.

Before leaving the penthouse, Ayers sent a text to the number Sasha had provided.

* * *

From his balcony, Gabriel kept the binoculars trained on the windows of the penthouse. He could see Ayers inside, speaking to the man he'd known as Carl Mortensen. Then she jumped up from her chair and slapped him twice. Hard blows that moved the man's head sideways both times. An argument? That could be helpful.

The man left, and Ayers disappeared into another room.

His phone rang. It was Kenneth Lao.

After the pleasantries were exchanged, Lao came to his point.

"Zhao's will has been probated. You are now the official owner of his house, investments and property. When you can, please come to see me. I need your signature on a few documents."

Gabriel thanked him and rang off. Shaking his head to clear the memory of Master Zhao's bloodied body, he resumed his surveillance of the apartment building.

Ten minutes later, having seen no further sign of Ayers, his phone vibrated. Thinking it was a follow-up text from Lao, he ignored it for a few more minutes. Eventually tiring of watching an empty apartment, he swiped up the text.

His heart stuttered when he read the message and he felt that old familiar squirm of anxiety curling its way around his insides.

If you want to see your girlfriend alive, be at Liberty Motor Court, Scranton by noon tomorrow. Sound horn twice. She loses a finger for every minute you're late. EA.

He texted back.

Need to know she's alive.

. . .

A few seconds passed. His phone buzzed again.

You're wasting time. Here's a pic.

The photo showed Britta, looking tired but with that familiar hint of defiance in her gaze into the lens. She was holding up a copy of that day's New York Times.

79

WELCOME TO SCRANTON

After paying for a further week, Gabriel left the hotel wearing the black tactical outfit and carrying the camouflage version and all his materiel in his holdall.

He found a car rental place on Columbus and was driving away in a grey metallic Ford Taurus shortly afterwards. The car had a 3.5-litre V6 engine, so plenty of power for any kind of pursuit he might need to engage in.

Inside, he was half-elated, half-terrified. He'd worked on plenty of hostage rescues in The Regiment, and knew that despite the way moviemakers portrayed Special Forces ops, there was always a high risk that the hostage-takers would decide to cut their losses. You'd gain entry to the compound, or hotel, or office building, only to find the perpetrators long-gone and only bullet-riddled, at best, corpses remaining. Britta was alive. Probably. That meant he had a chance to save her.

As he drove down Henry Hudson Parkway heading for the George Washington Bridge, he began working the mission, beginning with how he'd do it from the enemy's side.

"I'd pick up the rescuer at a third location. Not his and not the hostage's. They'd be at a safe house. Take his weapons, blindfold him. Chuck him in the boot and drive him to the safe house. Torture them both in front of each other. Kill the woman. Kill the man. Exfil."

Yes. That was definitely how he'd do it. *So what's the response? How are you going to rescue Britta and kill Ayers, Beck and the goon?*

As the miles rolled under the wheels, Gabriel worked the angles. After three and a half hours' hard driving on I-80, he pulled into a parking spot behind a single-storey, brick-built diner five miles outside Scranton. The car park was screened from the road by trees, which were just coming into leaf. He ordered coffee and a grilled cheese sandwich and ate while consulting a map he'd bought at a gas station further up the Scranton Expressway. Cross-checking with the motel's location on his phone, he plotted a cross-country route from the diner to the motel in Scranton. This wasn't jungle-country, just meadows, woods and tracks, so the going would be good. He saw no obvious geographical features to slow him down; an hour to reach the motel looked perfectly achievable.

He changed in the car, slithering around on the rear seats as he swapped his black tactical outfit for the camouflaged version. The knife and compass went into pockets, the first-aid kit, gollock and gloves went into the backpack, and the HK 45 he seated firmly in his belt holster. Blipping the key fob over his shoulder, he struck out eastwards, planning to tab across the intervening five or so miles of country and be at the motel by 11.30.

Forty-five minutes into the journey, which he alternately walked and jogged, he stopped at a stand of trees. He could see the tall sign of the motel, the word LIBERTY picked out in red-white-and-blue, with a large white star above the *I*, stark against the sharp blue of the sky. The terrain between his position and the motel was a mixture of low scrub and more stands of trees. Excellent cover for a covert approach, even without three more members of a patrol.

The adrenaline was flowing freely in his veins as he reached the two-hundred-yard point. But this was the purposeful flow of the performance-enhancing chemical, not the stomach-churning anxiety-driver. He felt sharper than he had done for days, ready to tackle Mortensen, as he still thought of him. He circled around, crossing both carriageways of I-81, and the stone ramparts to each side, and settling into a patch of scrub.

He scanned the motel through the binoculars, noting the number of cabins extending in two wings from the office in the centre – twenty – and the layout of the parking – chevrons in front of the cabins. Half of the spaces were empty. Of the remaining ten, four held mid-sized sedans of varying makes and colours from shit-brown to the grey of his own Taurus; two had full-size sedans, a white Crown Vic and a silver Lincoln Town Car; one had a cobalt-blue metallic Corvette, an early-eighties model judging from the shark nose; one held a forest-green Ford F150 pickup with a logo for a tree surgery business; one bulged with a black Chevy Suburban, the SUV's massive bulk casting a shadow over the Vette; and one played host to a highly polished Range Rover. In British Racing Green. A British car, in a signature British colour. Why did that make him tense his muscles?

People in the States drive Rangies, don't they? Yes. But how many drive their £160,000 imported luxury SUVS to a crappy motor-court in Scranton, NY?

He heard Don's voice in his head.

Which one would you choose to transport an unwilling guest, Old Sport?

"The Rangie or the Suburban, boss. Both have blacked-out windows and plenty of space for an inert body," he said out loud.

He re-crossed the road, then crept towards the motel through the brush, keeping the peak of his cap well down over his sunglasses. Keeping the cars between himself and the cabins, he slithered over to the Corvette. *No security beyond the locks, boss.*

He opened the blade of the BÖKER and slid it into the gap between the driver's side window and the roof, grateful that the Corvette had frameless windows. Applying steady pressure, he managed to drop the glass enough to get his fingers inside. Then he dragged the glass down through brute strength, feeling the gears of the motor inside the door protesting. With the glass all the way down, he leaned in and opened the door. Slumped in the driver's seat, it took him a minute or so to hotwire the car. With the ignition live, he leaned on the horn button twice. As the twin blasts echoed off the hard surfaces of the cabins, Gabriel scooted away into the ornamental shrubs bordering the car park and waited.

Mortensen emerged from the cabin on the far left of the office: number 1. He strode into the centre of the car park, looking for the new arrival. He was to be disappointed. Gabriel watched from his hide as Mortensen went over to the Range Rover, walked all the way round it, then, frowning, went back inside.

Got you!

80

REPEAT BUSINESS

Once Mortensen was inside his cabin again, Gabriel skirted round the motel and approached the row of cabins from the rough ground behind them. Coming up to the door, he drew the pistol, racked the slide, and banged on the flimsy painted wood with his left fist.

"Police! Open up!" he called, using the tone of command drilled into him first at Sandhurst and then in the Parachute Regiment, coupled to what he hoped was a passable New York accent. He stepped back, keeping the pistol close to his side and aimed at a point corresponding to centre mass for a six foot-plus combatant.

He was ready. Muscles pumped with blood and taut with unspent energy. Eyes flicking up and down, from door handle to a point at head height. Hand gripping the HK45's butt, trigger finger curled and ready to squeeze.

"Coming, I'm coming," the voice from behind the door said, the former generic American accent now replaced by a tone that was softer, less hard to define, but with a definite Dutch catch to it.

The door swung inwards revealing the man Gabriel knew had been tasked with bringing him to Erin Ayers, and death.

Not giving him time to react, Gabriel swung the gun up and smacked it sharply against the man's left temple. Mortensen staggered backwards, clutching his palm to the cut that Gabriel's blow had opened on the side of his head. His other hand was groping at the back of his waistband but Gabriel had anticipated that his man would be armed. As Mortensen's right arm swung round with a pistol, a 1911, Gabriel chopped his own gun down onto the wrist, loosening Mortensen's grip so that he dropped the 1911, which Gabriel kicked away into a corner of the room.

Gabriel kicked out at Mortensen's left knee, eliciting a howl of pain as the leg buckled, throwing Mortensen in a twisting fall to his right. He kicked the door closed behind him, readying himself to beat Britta's location out of Mortensen.

As Mortensen went down, he rolled over and hooked his right boot around Gabriel's ankle, pulling his working knee in and unbalancing Gabriel so he stumbled sideways. The opportunity was fleeting, but Mortensen took it. Rearing up, he swung a massive fist into Gabriel's gun arm, catching him halfway between wrist and elbow.

It was a numbing blow, and Gabriel felt his grip on the pistol loosen, just for a split second. Mortensen was ready and grabbed hold of the barrel, twisting it out of Gabriel's grasp.

Gabriel reacted instinctively, taking a check-step backwards then launching a kick at Mortensen's hand that sent the HK45 flying across the cabin to hit the rear wall and drop behind a sofa upholstered in grimy brown fabric.

Mortensen was on his feet, breathing heavily and grimacing, his lips pulled back from his teeth.

"You fuck!" he growled. "You're a dead man."

He lunged forwards, chopping a blade-like right hand at Gabriel's throat. Gabriel moved to block the incoming blow, but it was a feint, and Mortensen's hand swerved in mid-air to deliver a straight-fingered blow into his gut. The solar plexus was obviously the target but Mortensen's damaged knee had thrown his balance off. The blow connected painfully with Gabriel's stomach, but missed the sweet spot that would drive all the air from his lungs and leave him gasping for air, curled up on the ground, ready to receive a kick or a punch as Mortensen wanted.

Gabriel lashed out at Mortensen's face, hand curled into a claw. He felt his index and middle fingers grab onto the man's eye sockets, and pulled down and clenched his fist simultaneously, dragging a screech of pain from Mortensen. As Mortensen staggered backwards, looking to create space between him and Gabriel, Gabriel pressed forward, trying to gain a fight-ending advantage.

But Mortensen wasn't done yet. As time slowed down for Gabriel, he was able to analyse his opponent's fighting style and concluded this was no hired heavy with all his strength in his biceps. This man had learned how to fight properly.

Mortensen appeared to buckle, and started toppling towards Gabriel, then he thrust upwards from his knees, driving the top of his shaved skull into Gabriel's midsection, winding him.

A balled fist at the end of a massively muscled arm caught Gabriel on the side of the head, dizzying him for a moment, and forcing him back a couple of steps. Mortensen pressed home his advantage, lashing out with his good leg and landing a kick midway up Gabriel's right thigh that felt as if he'd been hit with a round from a Kalashnikov.

Gabriel dropped to his knees, one hand clutching his injured thigh, presenting an easy target for a swinging kick from the man's booted right foot.

Mortensen grunted in triumph and swung his leg back.

Gabriel rammed his left fist into Mortensen's balls.

Off- balance, his right leg still behind him, Mortensen screamed and fell backwards.

Knife drawn, Gabriel was on him before he hit the carpet. With his knees planted on Mortensen's chest he jabbed the point of the knife into the notch of his throat.

His own breath coming in ragged gasps, Gabriel addressed the man who would take him to Britta.

"Where is she?" he hissed.

Mortensen lay still under Gabriel's knees. He sneered up at Gabriel.

"Somewhere you'll never find her, *pokkenlijer*."

Gabriel pushed the knife downwards so the tip disappeared into the depression above Mortensen's collarbone and a runnel of blood trickled away to the right.

"Fuck you!" Mortensen said.

Gabriel brought his face closer to Mortensen's until he could smell the man's breath.

"You're going to tell me. One way or—"

Mortensen convulsed his body. He catapulted Gabriel forwards, and rolled away before the knife could swing round.

Grabbing a table lamp for the nightstand beside the bed, he swung it in a wide arc at Gabriel's head. Gabriel evaded the incoming blow simply by ducking under Mortensen's arm. As he came up, he lunged forward and flicked the knife out under Mortensen's still-swinging arm.

The edge sliced cleanly through Mortensen's shirt and into the soft tissue of his upper arm, opening a deep, six-inch gash.

With a squeal, Mortensen grabbed the wound, from which bright arterial blood was squirting. He looked down, mouth open, absorbing the fact that his lifeblood was being pumped out onto the floor by his own heart.

Gabriel closed with him and delivered a kick to his chest that sent him sprawling onto his back. This time, Gabriel kept his distance.

"That's a bleeder. I hit the brachial artery. You won't survive it. Not on your own. Tell me where she is and I'll save you."

Mortensen was glaring up at Gabriel, his teeth clenched against the pain and what Gabriel saw in his eyes was the fear of his own death. In battle, on manoeuvres, in training, you could sustain a wound like that and survive. One of your mates would tie on a tourniquet, slap on a field dressing or stitch the fucker closed with fishing line if necessary. But in a motel room, with only your assailant for company, well, let's just say now might be a good time to start planning the songs they'll play at your funeral.

"Give me something to tie it off with," Mortensen grunted out, looking from his blood-soaked sleeve to Gabriel and back again.

"Tell me where she is or I'll open one on your thigh as well."

Mortensen clamped his lips shut. Gabriel could feel Britta

slipping away from him. Red spots floated around the edge of his vision and a roaring sound filled his ears. He knelt beside Mortensen and pinched the top edge of his right ear between his thumb and forefinger. With a swift slicing action, he brought the knife back and down in the angle between the ear and the thin, hairless skin behind it.

The ear came away with a tearing sound. Fresh scarlet spattered Gabriel's face as the dozens of tiny arteries jetted blood like miniature firehoses, before adrenaline choked them off. The blood continued to flow, coursing down Mortensen's neck and onto the carpet under his head.

"Location! Now!" Gabriel bellowed into Mortensen's face. "Or I'll do the other one, then your nose, then your eyes."

Something seemed to click in Gabriel's mind as he shouted at Mortensen. He felt as though he was watching himself squatting over the mutilated body of his enemy from a point halfway between the floor and the ceiling. He had time to observe the pattern of blood spreading out over the man's shirt sleeve, and the way the bloody shreds where his ear had been attached to his skull resembled a bullet wound. Only the black hole at the centre was put there by nature, not a rifle round. Mortensen had reached his limit. Everybody had one, even Special Forces soldiers. He was ready to talk. To save his own skin.

"Ithaca," Mortensen said.

Gabriel watched from the ceiling as he shouted another question.

"Where in Ithaca? Tell me now." The blade was pressing against the root of Mortensen's other ear, hard enough to draw blood.

"It's a farmhouse: 15777 Mecklenburg Road."

"Car keys."

"Over there." Mortensen pointed to the desk beside the door. "Hey, my arm, man. I'm bleeding out. You said you'd help me."

Gabriel looked down, felt himself swooping back into his body.

He stood, releasing Mortensen, who had turned pale and was breathing shallowly. He crossed the room to the desk, grabbed the Range Rover's keys, and Mortensen's phone, then tore a strip of fabric from the curtain. He returned to Mortensen, who was clutching his opened triceps muscle with white-knuckled fingers.

"I did, didn't I?" Gabriel said. Then he lunged down, grabbed Mortensen by the cheeks and dug his fingers in hard, forcing his mouth open. He stuffed the fabric strip in and pushed it home with his thumb, wadding the lurid orange patterned fabric down until Mortensen's eyes bulged out.

"But you helped kill my friends," he said.

Then he cut Mortensen's throat.

He retrieved the HK45 from behind the sofa, and Mortensen's 1911 from the spot near the bed, then left, closing the door softly behind him.

Behind the Range Rover's steering wheel, he rechecked the map then tapped the address into the satnav. He gently steered the big car out of the parking space, being careful not to scrape the Chevy Malibu next to it, which looked brand new, and headed for Ithaca.

81

FINDING BRITTA

Close to contact. Engage enemy. Win firefight. Secure and release hostage. Exfiltrate. Extract.

As plans went, it was basic, but Gabriel's rationality was in tatters as he piloted the Range Rover northwest towards Ithaca. Mortensen had installed a radar detector on the dash, but even without it, Gabriel would have maintained the same high speed as he did now, keeping to between 90 and 100 mph.

The satnav screen told him he was just two miles away from his destination. He roared past a white, clapboard house then braked sharply as he saw a sign for a US Forest Service plantation coming up on his right. He slewed the Range Rover off the road, losing traction for a second on the loose surface before the four-wheel-drive system restored order, and then slammed his foot back down on the throttle, powering away from I-81 at a right angle down the forest track.

After insisting he turn around where possible a few times, the satnav gave up and began plotting an alternative route. Finding no official roads, it switched to giving him a dotted line back to I-81 and a chequered flag in an expanse of plain green for the safe house where they were holding Britta. Which was fine. The car was built for exactly this type of driving, even though he imagined 99% of owners spent all their time on metalled roads.

After half a mile, he turned right down an even narrower track. When that dissolved in a swathe of vegetation, he simply slowed down and kept going, checking the satnav from time to time and also relying on his own sense of direction.

With about five hundred yards to the target, he brought the Range Rover to a stop in a small clearing. He killed the engine, collected his gear and got out.

The tree cover was thick, a light mist hanging between the ground and the canopy. Shafts of sunlight arrowed down, illuminating spots of tawny leaf litter and bright-green shoots pushing their way through to the light. As the petrol-scented exhaust fumes drifted away from him, their sharp smell was replaced by a mossy, vegetal smell he'd inhaled in woods, forests and jungles from Belize to Mozambique. The wind had picked up, and the tops of the trees – birch mostly, but also sugar maple and white oak – were swaying gently.

He checked both pistols, even though he'd checked the HK45 before leaving Manhattan. The HK still had its full magazine. He pushed it home with a damped *snick* and moved on to inspect Mortensen's 1911. It was a Kimber Stainless II, a handsome weapon with a satin-silver-finished barrel, slide and frame, and rosewood grips. He dropped the magazine out. Also full: seven Hornady .45 ACP hollow-points. He sniffed the muzzle. Unlike Tall Man's gun, this weapon had recently been fired. As he'd expect from a bodyguard. He replaced the HK in his belt holster, next to the TacMed first-aid kit, and inserted the Kimber into the back of his waistband, next to the gollock in its leather sheath. He stuck the BÖKER down inside his boot.

Time to move.

The undergrowth was thick with fast-growing shrubs and creepers, eager to exploit the spring warmth and spread as far and as fast as possible. Staying as silent as he could in his approach, he observed a "no-cutting" rule, pushing through the stems and foliage rather than using the gollock. It slowed progress, but the tactical advantage was worth it.

A strange, half-human wail away to his left made him freeze in position. It sounded like a child's voice. But rough, and throaty, despite the high pitch. Then a second voice joined the first. He could hear undergrowth being smashed and flattened.

Straining to pinpoint the direction the sound was coming from, he had to stop himself from gasping in shock, as a bear cub came lolloping towards him through the undergrowth, followed a moment later by a second. Their bitter-chocolate-coloured fur stood out in sharp contrast to the greenery. Five yards out, the cubs obviously smelled him. They veered off in alarm, back the way they'd come. Gabriel pressed himself down into the leaf litter, praying that the cubs' mother was nowhere around. After five minutes had passed, and no overprotective, 300-pound mama bear had trampled him, he resumed his approach to the house.

Half an hour later, peering through a gap between some sycamore saplings, he had his first glimpse of the house where Erin Ayers was holding Britta. Two hundred yards away was a large, rambling structure clad in cedar shingles that had silvered with age, curling away from the frame of the house like the scales of a ripe pinecone. Three windows with white-painted wooden frames on the ground floor of the side facing him, three above, plus a dormer in the slate roof.

He brought the binoculars up, grateful for his cap, which kept the sun out of the rubber eye cups. The windows were obscured by net curtains. He began a clockwise circle around the house, crawling on his belly, and checking the structures and windows on each side. The rear of the house had four more windows, all curtained. To the right of a timber outbuilding with a padlocked door was the red Testarossa. Next to the Testarossa was a black Cadillac Escalade with blacked-out windows. *Prisoner transport*, he thought, grimly. The far side of the house was virtually identical to the side he had come at initially, except that one of the upstairs windows was uncurtained. He brought the binoculars to his eyes again and focused on the room beyond. And gasped.

82

ELEMENT OF SURPRISE

Rifle over her shoulder, smiling down at something, or someone, stood Sasha Beck. She was talking, so it was someone, not something. The angle of her head said that the person in there with her was on the floor. So not Erin Ayers. It had to be Britta. *Oh, thank God. You're alive!*

If he'd had a rifle, Gabriel would have taken the shot. He wasn't a trained sniper like Britta, but from that distance, he was confident he could make a centre-mass shot. *If* he'd had a rifle. But the pistols would be useless at that range. He'd have to go in. *Fine, it's time we settled this face to face. No more messages.*

When he'd been fighting battles with the SAS, and the Paras before them, he'd rarely been in a position where overwhelming force was on his side. They were small units of highly trained men working far behind enemy lines. Sometimes just a four-man patrol. Rarely more than thirty. So the element of surprise was a prized strategic and tactical asset in any combat situation. When his total forces amounted to one, surprise wasn't just desirable, it was vital. Crashing in through the back door, guns blazing, would be a surprise while it lasted, but it would be a short-lived victory. Beck, he knew, would be heavily armed and trained to fire without thinking. Ayers was the unknown quantity. She'd probably be armed, but something told him she wasn't a professional. Why hire an assassin to do her dirty work otherwise? Britta would be useful just with her hands and feet, or a kitchen knife, but she'd be bound or handcuffed to a pipe, so no immediate help until he could release her. By then he hoped both Ayers and Beck would be dead.

He looked up at the roof. *Yes. That's the way in.*

Wriggling along the ground like a snake, Gabriel made his way closer to the house. He held the HK in his right hand, a round already chambered and the safety off. If the back door opened, he was ready to shoot from his prone position. But nobody emerged from the house.

It took him fifteen minutes to reach the rear wall of the house. It took two for him to scale the outside; the tangle of drainpipes fixed on the rear wall made the ascent easier than shinning up a climbing wall in a gym.

Flattening himself on the slates, he edged his way over to the dormer. He could see that the casement window had a flimsy latch on the inside. The room beyond was empty of all but a couple of hard chairs, a dressing table, and a single bed, minus its mattress. He inserted the point of the knife into the gap between the loose-fitting window and the frame and flipped the latch open. He removed his rucksack then slithered through the narrow aperture, pulling the bag through after him.

Once inside the little attic room, he drew the 1911 and racked the slide. In a confined space, pistols were easier to wield than rifles. He felt confident he could match Sasha Beck's firepower, especially given the surprise factor.

He checked his watch. Three o'clock. Then Mortensen's phone vibrated in his pocket. He checked it. A text from Ayers, readable on the lock screen.

Where are you?

Maybe you're getting twitchy, Ayers. Your man hasn't turned up yet. With no way of unlocking the phone, Gabriel didn't have the option to send a reply, so disinformation was off the table. That was fine. He was ready to close with the enemy.

83

SILENCE IS GOLDEN

Creeping out of the little bedroom, a pistol gripped in each hand, Gabriel paused on the landing. He could hear women's voices. From the volume, he was sure they were on the ground floor. One was recognisably Sasha Beck's. The other was also an English accent, but with a mid-Atlantic inflection, as if its owner was making an effort to shift her identity from Britain to the US. Something about its tone and its cadences pricked at Gabriel's subconscious mind, but the adrenaline coursing through his bloodstream was blocking all but mission-critical data, and he brushed it aside.

The half-landing floor was bare wooden boards. In a house like this one, Gabriel had no illusions about the quality of the carpentry. Treading on the boards would be like spinning a roulette wheel. Any one of them could have warped enough to pull its brads free of the joists beneath, creating a perfect burglar alarm.

Breathing evenly, he placed his right foot onto the end of a floorboard just at the base of a baluster. He eased his weight over. The board was solid: not even a squeak of protest from the joint. He leaned over the edge of the polished pine handrail, smoothed and discoloured by decades of hands sliding along its length. Beneath him 'was another, longer landing. Off it were four doors. His assessment: three bedrooms and a bathroom. Behind the door nearest to the foot of the staircase was Britta Falskog. Alive at least, if not in the best of health.

He took a deep breath, let it out with a quiet sigh, and began descending the staircase, keeping the toes of his boots to the edges of the treads.

The first-floor landing was soundproofed with a nubbly brown carpet. Maintaining his wide-legged stance, Gabriel holstered the HK. Holding the 1911 in his right hand, he turned to the door at the bottom of the staircase and used his left to grip and then twist the worn brass knob above the keyhole.

He pushed the door open and slid inside, closing it behind him. He took in the room at a glance. Britta, sitting with her back to a silver-painted, cast-iron radiator, her arms behind her. A strip of white cloth was tied across her mouth, tight enough to dent her cheeks. A single bed. A second door.

Britta looked up as he entered the room. Her eyes opened wide, then she looked away from him, jerking her head at the corner of the room.

He put his finger to his lips and came closer. As he worked the gag from her mouth, he spoke in a low murmur.

"Quiet! They don't know I'm here. I came in from the roof."

She still didn't speak. Just jerked her head again at the corner of the room, eyes signalling something to him, forehead furrowed.

He turned and saw what she was nodding at. Sitting on the floor by the bed, in soft shades of pastel blue and green, a stubby antenna protruding from its top, a green light glowing on its side, was a baby monitor.

Fuck!

Footsteps crashed on the stairs. Gabriel whirled round, aiming at the door.

Sasha Beck burst through, firing a pistol directly at Gabriel. Four or five rounds. Lucky or not, her first shot took him in the left arm, clipping his bicep. He fired back with the 1911, three shots in rapid succession, aiming centre mass. But the shock of the bullet wound had messed with his aim. His shots went wide and the .45 rounds tore holes in the plaster to the right of the door instead of through Sasha.

The reports of the unsuppressed pistols were deafening in the confined space of the bedroom. The room filled with blue gun smoke, and the acrid stink of burnt propellant and hot brass filled the air.

Sasha ducked out of the room again, heading to Gabriel's left.

He emptied the rest of the magazine at the wall, chest height, hoping to catch her with at least one round.

"Gabriel, look out!" Britta cried out.

He felt a searing pain in the back of his head then Britta's cry faded, his vision turned black, and he crashed to the floor.

84

RIP BRITTA FALSKOG

The Colombian drug lord was screwing the point of his knife into the back of Gabriel's head. He pushed his stubbled face close to Gabriel's, close enough for Gabriel to smell his garlicky breath.

"You fucked me up, Englishman. Now I'm gonna fuck you up. Real good."

He pulled the blade from Gabriel's skull and inserted the tip into the soft flesh on the right side of his neck. He slashed right to left, pushing the blade deeply into Gabriel's throat. Then he withdrew it, reached through the bloody rent in the flesh, dragged Gabriel's tongue out through the slit and jerked it down so it flopped onto his shirt front.

"How you like your Colombian Necktie, huh? Fuckin' sharp, man."

Then he screeched with laughter and dissolved into the blackness.

Groaning, Gabriel opened his eyes. His wounded arm was hurting, but not too badly. Adrenaline is a wonderful painkiller as well as a performance-enhancer. When he looked down he could see that somebody had bandaged it.

His wrists were strapped to the arms of the chair with cable ties, the go-to bonds for modern criminals and military personnel for whom the bulk and weight of handcuffs weren't worth the trouble. He tried moving his feet – same problem.

Sitting facing him on an identical wooden dining chair was the woman he loved, the woman he had proposed marriage to a few weeks earlier. Britta Falskog, late of Swedish Special Forces and now a permanent employee of MI5. Her freckled complexion was grimy and her normally shiny red hair was lank and greasy. She looked tired, but still had a defiant spark behind her eyes. The gag was gone. She smiled at him, then spoke.

"This is another fine muck you've got us into."

He smiled back, amazed at her ability to go for humour in any tight situation.

"It's 'mess.'"

"I know, idiot. I've been brushing up on my English while I've been here. They let me have books."

"You OK?"

She nodded.

"Yeah, fine. You?"

"Apart from the obvious, yes."

"You should have checked the other door. It's a connecting door to the next room. Ayers smacked you on the back of the head with a pistol."

"Sorry. I was distracted by your dishevelled beauty. Next time I will, I promise."

"Any bright ideas for getting us out of this? Any of that Chinese voodoo shit Master Zhao taught you going to come in useful?"

"He's dead. She killed him in Hong Kong."

"Oh, God. Sorry. I overheard them talking sometimes but I couldn't tell who they were going after. They just used numbers, like off a list or something."

The door burst open.

Erin Ayers walked in, the Walther CCP gripped in her right hand. The ArmaLaser sight was switched on, and she played the red dot over Gabriel's face, making him squeeze his eyes shut as she aimed at each in turn.

She strutted into the space between Gabriel and Britta, forming a shallow triangle so she could look at each of them in turn.

"Well, well, well," she said. "Look what the cat dragged in. The famous freedom fighter, Gabriel Wolfe, MC. Come to rescue his *Swedish girlfriend*." She adopted a hammy Swedish accent for the last two words. "Oh, no, wait. She's not your girlfriend, is she? She's your *fiancée*."

"Who the fuck are you? And why do you call yourself Fury?" Gabriel asked, maintaining an even tone even though he wanted to shout and scream at the woman who had stripped him of almost everything and everyone he cared about.

"Oh, please. Don't tell me your great strategic mind hasn't figured it out yet?"

"I know you hate me. I know you think I committed some sort of crime against authority. You see yourself as an avenging goddess of the underworld"

"Ooh, who's been brushing up on his Greek myths! Yes, you clever boy. I do think all of that about you. You see, by now, I should have been running things across the pond. We were so close. Then you fucked things up for me. Killing Daddy was always part of my plan, but you jumped the gun, pun intended." She came to him and bent down to whisper in his ear. "Now, do you know who I am?"

As he inhaled, he caught her perfume, a fresh, floral scent that took him spinning back to a huge kitchen in a manor house just outside Salisbury. This close, he noticed a fine, silver scar behind her right ear, and another in the corner of her eye.

It all came together. The gait outside the apartment building. The turns of phrase. The coded messages. Lizzie Maitland.

"They shot you! The Home Secretary himself told us."

She patted herself down, then smoothed one hand over her breasts and down to her hips, never taking her eyes off him for a minute.

"I must have got better, then, mustn't I? The woman they couldn't kill. Maybe they'll make a film of my life one day."

"How? The place was crawling with soldiers. You couldn't have just walked away."

"Actually, that's exactly what I did. When Daddy bought Rokeby Manor, I was nine. An only child," she pouted, "and all that space to rattle around in. I used to explore. And guess what? I found a secret passage. It was originally built by a Catholic family who owned the place in the sixteenth century. Oh, yes, I know it looked Georgian, but it was built over the ruins of an Elizabethan place. I told Daddy, and he brought the tunnel out into the garage, under all those lovely cars I showed you, remember? So when the heavy mob arrived, I just climbed down and as you say, just walked away."

Gabriel was trying to formulate another question, mainly to keep her talking, when Sasha Beck entered the room.

"Hello, darling," she said with a smirk.

"How's the side?" he asked, eyes hard.

She looked down to her left. Just above the waist, her white shirt was bloodstained.

"Just a scratch from a splinter you blasted out of the wall with that hand cannon. I'll live." She paused. "Which, I'm sorry to say, is not a prognosis I can offer you and the charming Miss Falskog here." She turned to Lizzie. "Ready when you are, Erin."

She drew a slim, horn-handled lock-knife from her pocket and opened it with a *click*. Standing behind Britta, she placed the edge of the blade against her throat, dividing a triangle of freckles.

She looked down at the top of Britta's head.

"Rest in peace, darling."

85

BRIGHT, WHITE LIGHT

Gabriel stared at Britta, straining with all his strength against the plastic ties, but only succeeding in digging their edges deeper into the flesh of his wrists and ankles.

"No!" he shouted at Lizzie. "Don't kill her. Please. I'll do anything you ask."

She squatted down in front of him, then, and smiled.

"Oh, I know you will. Believe me, by the time I've finished with you, you'll be pleading to make me happy. But I'm afraid the Swede has to be sliced and diced. She was the final item on my list. Not counting you, of course." She sighed. "Poor old Gabriel. Before you betrayed me, I had thought that one day, you know," she lowered her eyelids and looked at him coquettishly, speaking in a breathy voice, "you and I might have formed an alliance. All that power and nobody to share it with would have been so boring." Then she stood, abruptly dropping the little-girl voice. "But you put the kibosh on that, didn't you? So now it's time for your *hubris*, to use another Greek word, to be punished." She looked at Sasha. Then down at Britta. "Goodbye, Miss Falskog. I wish I could say it's been a pleasure, but you're such a cunt, I'll be glad to see the back of you."

Sasha smiled and gripped the knife tighter.

Gabriel closed his eyes.

Felt his heart bumping against his ribs as if trying to burst free.

Then the room exploded. Three bright, white flashes burst into his retinas through his eyelids, and three deafening bangs made his ears sing.

86

SITUATIONAL UNAWARENESS

Gabriel opened his eyes, cautiously. Britta still faced him. Alive, though he saw a one-inch cut had been opened on the side of her neck. She was wide-eyed and shouting, but he couldn't hear her over the ringing in his ears from the flashbangs and the rattle of small arms fire from downstairs. It sounded like an AR15. But it was firing on full auto, so a military-spec weapon. Sasha and Lizzie had both left the room.

Someone downstairs, Sasha presumably, was returning fire, squeezing off pistol rounds in closely-spaced triplets.

Bang-bang-bang.
  Bang-bang-bang.

Another burst of automatic fire and then both weapons fell silent.

Gabriel could just make out footsteps on the stairs. He readied himself. Mouthed, "I love you" at Britta. And waited.

Then he laughed.

He laughed, because standing in the open doorway, a smoking

Colt M4A1 assault rifle resting nonchalantly over his shoulder, was Don Webster.

"Hello, Old Sport. Hello, Britta. Let's get you out of those, shall we?"

He unsheathed a knife and cut the cable ties. Gabriel and Britta leapt towards each other. He hugged her tightly until she squawked in protest.

"You're suffocating me! Let me go!"

Gabriel stepped away from her, then turned to Don.

"Where's Erin, I mean Lizzie?"

"The other woman? No idea. Just thought I'd come in all guns blazing and rescue you. I think I killed the one downstairs. Sasha Beck? Plenty of blood, at any rate."

"Shit! Lizzie's gone. Give me the gun." He reached out for the M4.

"You need to calm down and regroup. You've taken a round in the arm, and you're in no state to start pursuing anyone."

"No! Give it to me or I'll go after her unarmed." He stuck his hand out again, glaring at his commander.

Don unshouldered the assault rifle and handed it over. He pulled a new magazine from the pocket of his jacket.

"You'll need this. I think I emptied that one. Be back here in an hour, whatever happens. That's an order."

Gabriel snatched the M4 from Don's hand, slapped in the new magazine and ran for the stairs.

As he ran through the kitchen, he almost skidded in a wide pool of blood by the back door. *OK. She's not dead. Better be careful.*

Outside, he ran to check on the cars. The Escalade and the Testarossa were slumped on shot-out tyres. He spun around, trying to get a visual on Sasha, or Lizzie. His ears were still buzzing and ringing from the flashbangs Don had lobbed into the bedroom.

He noticed a broken bracken stem between the two cars and a couple more beyond that. One or both of them had run for the safety of the woods. Not a bad move in the circumstances. Pulling the M4's charging lever back, *clack-clack*, he ran for the woods beyond the cars.

The trail was simple to follow. Whichever of his two targets had taken this route had left perfect impressions of her shoes in the soft leaf litter on the ground, and she'd crashed ahead in a dead straight line, flattening and breaking the bracken. Here and there he spotted blood spatters on the pale-green ferns.

So intent was he on his pursuit that Gabriel completely missed the sound of a magazine being slotted home into the butt of a pistol.

87

WOUNDS

Exploding from the tree to his right, the spray of sharp-edged bark splinters threw Gabriel to his side, tripping and tumbling into the bracken. The report from Sasha Beck's M&P Shield echoed around the forest. He poked experimentally at his face and had to suppress a yelp of pain. A flap of skin was hanging away from his cheekbone. He unzipped the TacMed kit, and, holding the flap in place, slapped on the QuikClot combat gauze and secured it with a fat Band-Aid.

Keeping his head below the tops of the fast-growing bracken plants, he called out.

"Is that you, Sasha? Rubbish shooting, by the way."

"Oh, don't be like that, darling," came a roughened version of Sasha Beck's normal, teasing voice, from about twenty-five feet to his right. "I am hurt, you know."

"I saw the blood. Bad?"

"Two in the thigh, one in the side. Your boss has rather put the brakes on my career, I'm afraid."

* * *

Crawling on his belly towards her voice, Gabriel keeps the M4's muzzle aimed about four feet off the ground dead in front of his position. He crawls twelve inches closer.

"You killed innocent people, Sasha. Friends of mine. People I loved." Another foot closer.

"We all kill innocents, Gabriel. You of all people should know that."

Shit! She's right. Philip Agambe was a good man. A decent politician in a corrupt government, and I wiped him off the face of the earth. "Maybe I do." Another foot. The thick, sappy growth bending without crackling as he pushes it aside. "But you made this personal."

"Me? It was Lizzie who made it personal. After all, didn't you kill *Daddy?*"

Another foot. There's a sudden rustle to his left. He looks up. Sasha is on her feet. He sees her drawn face through the fronds at the top of the bracken stems. She's pointing the pistol down at him, holding it unsteadily in her left hand. Her right is clamped over her midriff. His M4 is aimed in completely the wrong direction. Somehow, she's circled around him.

"I'm sorry, darling. I always thought there could have been something for us. Beck & Wolfe, Assassins has a certain ring to it, don't you think?"

His thoughts spiral, lightning fast. Everyone's arrived for the party.

You need an idea, mate. Now! It's Dusty's voice.

Quick, Old Sport. Don.

Love is a strange thing, Gabriel. Fariyah's voice.

Do a trick for me, Gable. Michael.

Gabriel speaks.

"Me, too, Sasha. But Britta was always so possessive."

"Was?"

"Lizzie hit her when the flashbangs went off. She's dead."

He watches as she processes this information. The lips she's tightened against the pain ease upwards.

"I'm hurt, darling. Rather badly."

"We can get you out. To a hospital. Then once you're patched up, you and I can talk, properly. No guns."

She grunts out a sound halfway between a cough and a laugh.

"Then off to a black site in Thailand? I don't think so."

"No. Don wants to talk to you. About joining us. You're very good at killing people. We need those skills in The Department."

Her gun arm is wavering. The colour has left her face again. She is pale from blood loss.

"If you let me up, Sasha, darling, I can help you back to the house. I've got a trauma kit right here on my belt."

He waits, heart racing, eyes glued to the pistol, which is dropping inch by steady inch.

"Hurry, darling," she says, finally. "This is a bad one."

Gabriel stands, keeping the M4 pointed at the ground and a smile on his mouth, and takes a step towards Sasha.

88

LOVE IS BLIND

Smiling wearily, the two assassins stand facing each other, fifteen feet apart.

Neither loves the other.

Sasha, because although she doesn't know it, she is incapable of feeling emotion.

Gabriel, because right now emotion is all he *can* feel: a burning desire to kill Sasha Beck.

This disparity in emotion gives Sasha the trump card.

She sees it. In his eyes. The mouth is lying; the eyes are telling the truth.

"Bastard!" she hisses as she sees, in slow motion, the M4's barrel rising.

Summoning all her strength she takes her right hand away from the wound in her side to steady the pistol.

She screams with pain as she begins firing and the blood floods out from the bullet wound in her abdomen.

Three rounds hurtle towards Gabriel.

Gabriel fires simultaneously: a five-round burst.

Exploding propellant shatters the calm of the forest.

Sasha is bleeding profusely from the wounds to her left thigh and her internal organs. The NATO rounds Don shot her with yaw on contact with soft tissue, and her chances before contact with Gabriel were already slim. Now, standing, and haemorrhaging badly, her balance is gone and her aim is wild. The .40 explosive rounds bury themselves in the soil several feet from Gabriel. If they do explode, the devastation is underground and drowned out by the noise emitted from the muzzles of both guns.

Gabriel's aim is unaffected by the tear in his cheek, or the wound in his left arm. Three of the five rounds hit Sasha, one in the side of her neck, two in the face. At this range, the damage is catastrophic. The shot to her neck tears through the muscle and blood vessels, ripping a chunk of flesh free as it exits, spraying blood into the bracken behind her. The two shots to the head kill her instantly. Her skull bursts outwards in an explosion of bone fragments, bloody flesh tatters and brain tissue.

The body falls backwards into the bracken with a soft *clump*. Sasha Beck, lonely schoolgirl, wide-eyed tourist, reluctant killer, professional assassin, disappointed lover, is dead.

89

URSUS AMERICANUS

Jumping to his feet, Gabriel ran on for two hundred yards, following Lizzie Maitland's trail. He skirted the massive trunk of an oak tree and pulled up in a sharp stop. Dead ahead, in a small clearing bathed in golden sunlight like a stage set, stood Lizzie Maitland. Pistol in hand, she was facing two bear cubs and behind them, rearing up on her stumpy hind legs to a height of seven feet, their mother.

The bear dwarfed the woman. As it towered above her, forepaws clawing the air, it bellowed its rage at this threat to its family.

Lizzie aimed at the bear's exposed chest and fired two-handed: a rapid sequence of five shots. Her 9mm rounds were man-stoppers. But not bear-stoppers. Gabriel saw bright spurts of blood as the bullets found their target, but the damage was clearly superficial and only enraged the bear further. It launched itself forward and down, swiping at Lizzie with one massive paw, the long, steel-grey claws raking across her torso.

She went down with a scream, emptying the magazine into the bear.

Gabriel looked on in horror as the mother bear bellowed with pain and rage, exposing massive fangs. She reared back and came down again with both front paws, smashing them over and over onto Lizzie Maitland's head and body.

He sighted on the bear, then changed his mind. He raised the rifle's muzzle and aimed at a spot above her blocky head and fired a burst into the trees behind her.

It was enough. The bear stopped her attack and stared at him, panting and grunting. He backed off a few paces, keeping the M4's muzzle pointing at her head. Then, from the edge of the clearing where it had been cowering, one of the cubs cried – a sound almost like that of a human baby. The sound distracted the mother. Gabriel kept still, watching as she weighed up her options. Then she decided. She called to the two cubs, roared a final time at Gabriel, then turned and trotted away into the forest, her offspring gambolling behind her, perfectly in step as they disappeared into the greenery.

Gabriel came out into the centre of the clearing and knelt beside Lizzie's body. She was almost unrecognisable. Her face was gone. The blows from the bear's front paws had fractured her skull. Her chest and abdomen were bleeding heavily from multiple closely-spaced sets of gashes, and he could see a glistening coil of silvery-purple intestine through a gaping wound in her belly.

"Help me, Gabriel."

He jumped back in shock as her mangled jaw and torn lips struggled to form words.

"There's nothing I can do. You're too badly wounded."

"I know," she whispered. "Help me."

Her eyelids fluttered, and he took one final look at her.

He took the bloodstained pistol from her unresisting hand.

Stood and took a couple of paces back.

Turned.

Aimed.

And fired.

A double-tap between her closed and bloodied eyes.

The head jerked upwards, then flopped back into the leaf litter.

Lizzie Maitland AKA Erin Ayers AKA Fury, was dead.

90

BACK TOGETHER AGAIN

After propping the M4 in the corner of the kitchen, Gabriel sat down at the table next to Britta and opposite Don.

"Any more coffee?" he asked.

Don got up, poured a mug from the drip machine on the countertop and handed it to Gabriel.

"Everything OK?" Don asked.

Gabriel nodded. "They're both dead. You hit Sasha three times; she wasn't going to live long anyway."

"And the other one, Fury?"

"Her name was Lizzie Maitland. Daughter of Sir Toby Maitland. Dead, too."

Don took a sip of his own coffee. "Ah. Well I suppose that makes sense. I thought you'd dealt with her in that business at Rokeby Manor."

"There was a tunnel. Built by the original owners."

"I'll have to make a few calls. Get a clean-up team out here."

"I'm sorry for causing a scene in the US. I know you said not to."

Don smiled. "That's OK, Old Sport. Worse things happen at

sea, eh?" Then he nodded at the M4. "Incidentally, next time you shout at me like that, I may not take it so kindly."

Gabriel grinned. "Sorry, boss. Must have been shock."

He turned to Britta.

"How are you? Did they mistreat you?"

He noticed a momentary cloud flit across her face.

"Did they 'mistreat' me? What are you, the police? No, it was fine. Nothing I wasn't trained for. The worst bit was getting shipped over here like a fucking dog in the cargo hold of some plane."

"You two can catch up properly once we're out of here," Don interrupted. "But I think we really should exfiltrate before the local constabulary arrive."

"I couldn't see a third car," Gabriel said.

"Well, that's because I tabbed my way here, presumably the same as you did. D'you know, I wondered if my shooting war days were behind me, but it appears I can still handle a search and destroy mission, even at my advanced age."

Gabriel laughed then, a genuine expression mixing relief at being reunited with Britta with the pleasure of being ribbed by his old commander again.

"Before we go, boss, can I just ask you one question?"

"How did I know where to find you?"

"Yes. I mean I know you have all sorts of high-level contacts over here, but I was acting on my own."

Don smiled.

"Remember that little drink you had with Eli after you left me last time?"

"Yes. In a tourist trap in Trafalgar Square, why?"

"She give you anything? A little keepsake, maybe?"

Gabriel felt in his pocket, already knowing how his boss had found him with such ease. His fingers closed around the silver insignia Eli had given to him in the pub and brought it into the light.

"You bugged me," he said.

"Yes, I did. You always were a headstrong so-and-so, and you had a look in your eye when you promised to obey my order that was about as hard to decode as a ten-foot neon sign."

"I didn't say I'd obey it. I said I understood it."

Don chuckled. "So you did. Now drink up. We need to go. I left my car about a mile up the road. Then we're leaving the US on a military flight on which I have managed to secure three seats."

91

LIKE A WOMAN SCORNED

YEREVAN, ARMENIA

Tashkend Street was quiet, and the mid-afternoon sun bathed the Soviet-era buildings each side of the roadway in a soft light that relieved some of their ugliness. Very few cars passed along the dusty tarmac, and the pavements were free of pedestrians. Starlings were cackling and calling to each other from the telegraph wires stretching across the street, jostling for position and occasionally flying up in small flocks of ten or twenty birds before settling back down to continue their morning convocation.

In a circle of grey rocks in the centre of the road, three flowering cherry trees blazed with pink. The soft clouds of blossom weighed the thin outer branches down to the ground, where the slight crosswind blew them back and forth as though urging them to sweep the street clean of rubbish. Britta Falskog raised her eyes to the horizon. She could see the four snow-capped peaks of Mount Aragats to the northeast of the city. She looked both ways out of habit before jogging across the road and entering the cool, dim lobby of the red-brick apartment building.

Once inside, she removed her sunglasses and zipped them into a pocket of her jacket. She bent down and slid a couple of fingers into the side of her right boot. The Fallkniven F1 survival knife she'd been issued during her service in Swedish Special Forces was snug in its leather sheath. The holster under her left armpit was strapped around her ribcage. Not so tight as to hamper her breathing, but tight enough to avoid any possibility of its slipping as she drew her firearm. Thanks to a contact of Eli's, Britta had a pistol fitted with a suppressor. A brown-skinned kid on a moped had sped up beside her at the agreed location, handed her a white plastic carrier bag, and disappeared into the traffic. The SIG Sauer P229 Nitron Compact pistol was chambered for .357 SIG rounds. She screwed on the suppressor.

Torossian's apartment was on the top floor of the block. Britta glanced at the graffiti-smeared steel door of the lift and shook her head. She took the stairs to the tenth floor two at a time for twenty flights without slowing. She kept her weight on her toes, but her lightweight boots still scraped and scuffed on the bare concrete of the steps.

Outside the apartment door, which, she noticed, was protected by an unpainted sheet of three-millimetre steel screwed to its face, she paused for a few moments. Once her breathing had slowed, she rapped on the steel with the knuckles of her gloved left hand. Three hard, determined blows. She waited.

"Who is it?" a deep male voice called from the other side. Not Torossian's.

"Pizza!" she yelled back.

She heard muffled male voices beyond the steel. Arguing about who ordered takeout, she assumed.

The door opened wide.

Standing in the opening was a six-foot-six giant: swarthy; short, black beard and matching moustache; suspicious expression on his face; Glock 17 in hand.

A black hole, rimmed with scarlet, appeared between his eyes, and he fell backwards, blood fountaining from the entry wound in an arc that painted the ceiling with spatters of red.

The suppressor damped the explosion as the round travelled the six inches from the SIG to the man's forehead. But the sound was still loud in the cramped confines of the hallway and it bounced flatly off the bare concrete walls. It also drew a second heavy from the interior of the apartment.

This man was carrying a Mini Uzi machine pistol. As he took the corner into the hallway, he tripped over the corpse of his former crewmate. The stumble hampered his aim, but even without the obstacle, he was a dead man.

By the time he brought the gun up, three rounds from Britta's pistol were smashing into his chest cavity and bursting his heart. He died without firing, collapsing into a bloody heap on the hall carpet.

Two down, one to go.

She entered the flat, stepping over the two bodies, careful to avoid standing in the blood. She kicked open the three doors leading off the narrow hallway. The first two rooms were empty.

The third contained Dmitri Torossian.

He was standing by a window. His pistol, a chromed Walther PPK, was aimed at the doorway. As she entered the room, he began firing at head height, burning through the eight rounds in the magazine in a couple of seconds and filling the air with acrid gun smoke.

If she'd been standing, he might have scored a hit.

If.

She got to her feet.

Aimed at his groin.

Shot him twice.

With his screams ringing out, she bent to relieve him of his pistol.

"I told you I'd find you, didn't I, *kuksugare?*"

Torossian's eyes were rolling wildly in their sockets. His breath was coming in frantic gasps through bared teeth.

"Don't kill me," he managed to rasp out. "I have money. Name your price."

She smiled down at him, watching the way the pool of blood spreading out beneath him was soaking into the carpet.

"How about all those women and girls? The ones who learned to call you *Le Démon Blanc?* Can you bring them back here from whatever Godforsaken life you sold them into? *Hej?* Can you do that, motherfucker?" She stood over him, then, straddling his torso and pointed the pistol at his face. "I didn't think so. This is my price."

"No!" he screamed.

"Yes! This is for them."

She shifted her aim from his head to his torso, and shot him three times in the stomach.

"And this," she leaned down and pulled the F1 from her boot, "is for me."

She swept the four-inch blade from left to right, so deeply that she exposed his spinal cord, and jumped back to avoid a soaking from the bright-red jets of arterial blood carrying the white demon's life force away and sending him to hell.

92

A PROMISE, BROKEN

LONDON

Scratching at the dressing on his left arm, Gabriel stood hip to hip with Britta. They were looking down from a stone bridge at a family of ducks paddling around on the surface of an ornamental lake. On this late-May Saturday morning, the grounds of Chiswick House were swarming with families and couples enjoying the sunshine. A child's squeal made Gabriel look up. On the grassy slope leading down to the lake, a little girl, maybe three or four, was running by the water's edge, trailing a tiny blue and green kite behind her. Her parents looked on from twenty feet away. They seem unconcerned by the danger she was in. His stomach clenched with anxiety as she ran closer and closer to the water. Then she turned away and ran back towards her parents, and Gabriel let his breath out as her father scooped her up into his arms, laughing and tickling her under the arms, making her squeal even louder.

He tapped Britta on the shoulder and then nodded towards the family.

"So that could be us in a few years. How weird would that be?"

Britta looked briefly at the retreating backs of the parents and child, now swinging from their outstretched hands. She turned back to Gabriel and as she did so, he saw a look of sadness flitter across her face.

"I heard from my old CO. In Stockholm. They're putting together a new unit. Counterterror. He's asked me to lead it."

Gabriel frowned, then smiled.

"That's excellent! Kudos to you. So I guess that settles it. We're moving to Sweden."

She sighed and reached for his hand, pulling him round to face her and then taking his other hand in hers.

"We're not. Just me."

"What? But you said you'd marry me. That you just needed time to think through the practicalities."

"I know, I know, and I feel such a shit for doing this to you. But I can't. It just wouldn't work."

"Yes it would!" Gabriel said, his voice getting louder. "Of course it would. If anything, it would work better. You'd be in a command role, so fewer crazy foreign outings."

"Oh, Gabriel, can't you see? You know what I call you? *Riddare i skinande rustning.* The knight in shining armour. Always galloping off on your white horse to rescue some damsel in distress, or slay a dragon. I had a lot of thinking time in that house in Ithaca. And I realised something. That description fits me at least as well as it fits you. I'm just not the settling down kind. I mean, can you really see me bouncing a fat baby on my knee and baking cakes all week? I'd go crazy inside a month. The new job is a command role, but it's an active role, too. Travel, undercover work, everything."

Gabriel felt a hollow void open in his stomach, worse than when he'd heard about Julia, or Dusty, or Daisy, or even Zhao Xi. He wanted to argue, wanted to hold her tightly until she relented.

"Please Britta," he said, realising even as the words left his lips how pathetic he sounded. "Take the job. But let me come with you. We'll get married and then figure out the practicalities later."

She smiled, but Gabriel saw no happiness in it.

"Come on, Gabriel. You and me were never going to be settled down with babies and dogs and family holidays at the beach. I'll always love you, but you're not going to settle for a desk job, are you? Well, nor am I. I have to keep doing what *I* love, too."

He just looked into her eyes, then, not speaking, not crying, not feeling. The silence lengthened from seconds to minutes to what felt like hours. Time enough to register the strand of copper-coloured hair that had escaped the plait at the back of her head and was now blowing across her face. To notice, once more, the triangle of freckles on the side of her neck, where he'd often kissed her and where, so recently, Sasha Beck had held the blade of a knife. To remember the day she'd walked back into his life, driven, really, behind the wheel of a Range Rover, chasing him out of his village and skidding to a stop in front of his car to pull him back into a world of violence.

"So that's it, then," he said, finally. "When are you leaving?"

"I have until next Friday to wind things up here, then I leave for Stockholm. I'll send for my things later. You can stay in my flat for as long as you like. I've put it on the market, so until it sells, it's yours. You know our paths are bound to keep crossing." She stretched up to kiss him on the lips. "And perhaps we'll settle down when we're in our 70s."

Gabriel turned away from her. The hollow in his stomach had ballooned upwards into his chest cavity and his skull. He felt like he might float away at any moment, up into the clear blue skies above London and keep ascending until the thin air ran out, the sky turned black, and he simply ceased to breathe.

93

A LIFE OF EASE?

HONG KONG

Compared to the clamour, and the crowds, and the smells of the city, the house on the hill was an oasis of calm. The only sounds were the *clock-clock-clock* of bamboo stems knocking against each other in the breeze and the twittering of sparrows coming from a bright-pink flowering shrub.

Kneeling in the centre of the moss lawn, wearing simple white cotton trousers and a white jacket belted at the waist, Gabriel settled his weight onto his heels and looked down at the harbour. Sailing boats scudded between larger pleasure cruisers, heeling over into the wind and leaving frothy white trails on the blue-green surface of the water.

Behind him, the glass doors of the dojo were open. He'd just completed a two-hour training drill: yoga, kendo, and karate.

A year earlier, he'd presented himself at Kenneth Lao's offices, where he'd signed half a dozen documents that gave him legal title to the estate of his former mentor and surrogate father, Zhao Xi.

He was, as the lawyer said, rich. Three million dollars, give or take, in US bearer bonds secure in a Zurich bank vault. Zhao Xi's investments and his priceless collection of jade. And the insurance settlement from his own car and house, together with the proceeds of the sale of the plot of land on which it had stood. Gabriel enjoyed a position many men of his age would envy. He had no need to work for a living anymore. He could spend the rest of his life travelling the world, or staying right here in Hong Kong, reading, learning to paint watercolours, visiting museums and historical sites, or mastering new martial arts, as he had been doing for the previous twelve months.

He *could* do that.

But he wouldn't.

He picked up his phone.

Swiped the screen to unlock it.

And read again the short message that had arrived five minutes earlier.

Vinnie's gone. Remember your promise? T.

Gabriel closed his eyes, raised his hands above his head and pressed his palms together, breathing deeply and clearing his mind of everything but his own will.

"I do," he whispered.

Thirty minutes later, Gabriel lowered his arms, stood, and went inside to pack.

NEWSLETTER

Join my no-spam newsletter for new book news, competitions, offers and more…

Follow Andy Maslen

Bookbub has a New release Alert. You can check out the latest book deals and get news of every new book I publish by following me here.

Website www.andymaslen.com.
Email andy@andymaslen.com.
Facebook group, The Wolfe Pack.

Read on for the opening chapter of *Rattlesnake*, the next book in this series …

FALLING MAN

The man was whistling as he fell to earth. It wasn't a tuneful sound. As it came from a neat nine-millimetre-diameter hole in his chest wall, that was forgivable. The air pressure in his collapsing lungs was higher than that of the surrounding atmosphere. So he whistled.

The F-15 Silent Eagle, from whose starboard conformal weapons bay the dead man had so recently been ejected, roared away to the east, climbing from thirty to fifty thousand feet. The pilot was singing "Somewhere over the Rainbow," interrupting himself to laugh hysterically every few lines.

From the ground, the jet's contrail appeared pink in the rays of the sun setting over the Sonoran Desert in Arizona. The man's bare skin shone like burnished copper in the slanting light.

After twelve seconds, when the forces of gravity and wind resistance reached an accord to stop fighting each other, he achieved terminal velocity: one hundred and twenty-two miles per hour. The whistling had stopped by this point, another result of equalising forces.

Had he been able to see, the man would have marvelled at the beauty of the landscape rushing up to greet him. A spine of mountains, in shades of petrol-blue and steel-grey, ran north-south beneath him. Low, thorny shrubs and cacti punctuated the hard-baked earth, throwing shadows far longer than their own height, in grey stripes.

Sixty seconds after being ejected from the bomb bay, the man had travelled a little over nine thousand feet. His limbs flailed in the uprushing air, and as he fell into the path of a powerful crosswind, he slid sideways like a wheeling bird.

Ninety seconds after that, face up, he made landfall.

Although his body stopped instantaneously, his internal organs continued their downward travel at the same speed he'd been falling, crashing into the back of his ribcage, his spine and the thick sheets of his back muscles. Liver, heart, lungs, kidneys, spleen, pancreas, intestines: all ruptured and split as they slammed into the buffers.

His brain was pulped as it bounced around inside his skull, before spilling from the smashed head into the sandy earth.

From the moment the nine-millimetre full metal jacket round stole his life away, the man's body had begun to decompose. The hot, dry air of the desert slowed the process and began to mummify the soft tissue. But Mother Nature abhors waste, and, in the absence of any cover or protection, the man's destiny was to become part of the food chain.

The flies came first.

Then the beetles.

The first large scavenger, an adult male turkey vulture, arrived after fifteen minutes. Circling in a thermal, 20,000 feet above the ground, the vulture had seen and smelled the corpse. Mantling its wings over the man's broken body from ankles to collar bones, like a pair of black capes, it raked its beak and claws at the soft skin of the torso. Then it plunged its boiled-looking head into the belly and began to eat.

Five minutes later, the first bird was jostling for elbow room with half a dozen more of his species, and a clutch of black vultures, all eager for a share of the carrion, hissing at each other in irritation as they tore at the carcass.

Fifteen minutes after the vultures, the apex predators appeared.

First was a female mountain lion, ribs visible on her flanks, with three hungry cubs to feed. The vultures flapped away in an untidy mass of black wings like tarpaulins blown free of a car by the wind. She wrenched away a portion of one arm, trotted back to her cubs with it, then returned to the fray.

Finally, the coyotes arrived. A tawny trio, three brothers, who bossed their way in, yipped and growled at the mountain lion until she fled, and began squabbling over what remained of the body.

COP SUICIDE

Dylan Frasier was forty-two, a veteran of the second Iraq war and the war in Afghanistan, a decorated trooper with the Arizona Highway Patrol, a father of two, an alcoholic, occasional coke user, and a man with a serious gambling problem. He was into a local poker player – a man with connections in the Arizona gang scene – for thirty-two thousand dollars. As a result of his addictions, he'd emptied his children's college fund, run up debts on his credit cards, borrowed money from colleagues and bowling buddies, and missed his last three mortgage payments. He hadn't told his wife.

Seeing no way out of his troubles, suffering from depression, and figuring his life insurance, on which he had kept up the payments and specifically included cover for death by suicide, would help his family out of the jam he'd created, Dylan had decided that this was the day to resolve everything.

He woke early, 5.55, dressed in his uniform, kissed his wife and children, all sleeping, and left the house in Glendale. By eight, he was pulling away from the precinct house in a Ford F-150 truck painted in the AHP's blue and copper livery, heading for the desert. Traffic heading towards Tucson on I-10 was light, and after an hour, he pulled off onto West Battaglia Drive. The name made the street sound like some chichi suburban avenue, but actually denoted an arrow-straight, dusty, two-lane blacktop with nothing but thousands of square miles of the Sonoran Desert to the north and south.

Turning left onto South San Simon Road, little more than a concrete track edged with low growing weeds and the odd flowering shrub, he drove on for a couple of miles before swinging the wheel right and pulling onto the desert itself. After another mile, he killed the truck's engine. He put it into park and climbed out, grabbing a quart of Wild Turkey from the glovebox.

He walked away from the truck, heading for a boulder he thought might make a decent resting place for a man at the end of his miserable life.

With his back to the hot rock, he cracked the seal on the bourbon, took a long pull, then a second, then stood the bottle by his right hip.

He pulled his Smith & Wesson M&P 9mm pistol from his belt holster. The pistol was an older model and didn't have the optional thumb safety. He shrugged and took another pull on the bourbon. Then he laughed.

"Doesn't really matter, now, does it?" he asked a little brown lizard scuttling up to his right boot.

He racked the slide, tilted the gun and opened his mouth to receive the muzzle.

He tried not to think of his children as he tightened his trigger finger.

He squeezed his eyes shut.

Then he opened them again.

A chorus of yowls, yips, grunts and guttural hisses had erupted from somewhere behind him. It sounded like a bar fight, if the drinkers were all doing animal impressions at the same time as throwing punches and swinging pool cues.

He stood, uncertainly, and walked round to the other side of the boulder. Two hundred yards to the southwest he could see the source of the commotion. A gang of vultures were getting into it with a handful of coyotes, and on the edge of the brawl he could make out the sandy fur of a mountain lion.

"Hell, might as well have one last look-see before I go," he said, walking towards the animals. When he got to the fifty-yard mark, he fired a couple of shots into the air over the heads of the scrapping scavengers. The lion and the coyotes fled at the sound of the gunfire.

"Hey! Scram! Get lost!" he yelled at the vultures, which had risen into the air in an ungainly crowd, then settled again. He fired three more shots, not taking so much care to aim high this time.

He hit one of the vultures, which flopped around on the ground, its wing torn off by the Speer Gold Dot Hollow Point round. The other birds took to the air, hissing and cawing in anger at this intrusion.

Dylan reached the site of the scrimmage, shot the wounded vulture dead, then let out a sound halfway between a groan and a sigh.

"Oh, man. I guess this ain't my time after all."

He was looking down at the remains of a human body. Most of the flesh had been removed and what remained was a bloody skeleton, minus an arm, the rest hung with scraps and tatters of muscle, skin and sinew.

PROMISES

Terri-Ann Calder packed her books and her students' assignments into her tote bag and left school for the week. She loved her job at the University of Texas at San Antonio almost as much as her husband.

Outside, on her way to the staff carpark, one of her students called out to her.

"Hey, Mrs Calder? You going to be supporting us tomorrow? We're playing Texas State."

She smiled and called back to the student, a rangy black kid with his hair cut short, bulked up under his bright orange UTSA basketball polo shirt.

"You bet! I'll bring my husband too. He's back tonight. We'll make a day of it. Good luck, David."

"You promise?"

She laughed.

"I promise! Go Roadrunners!"

Still smiling, she climbed into her car, a three-year-old VW Jetta, white to reflect the sun's heat, switched on the ignition, cranked up the air and hit play on the stereo. With George Strait singing "All My Ex's Live in Texas," she pulled out onto the road and headed for home. Vincent had been away working up north for a couple of weeks, and she was looking forward to snuggling up with him on the sofa with a bottle of wine and a movie, then a long, delicious night in bed with the man she'd married at seventeen and still loved like a giddy schoolgirl.

After changing into a simple white cotton dress that showed off her figure, she laid the table for two, placing tall, red candles in the sterling silver candlesticks her mother and father had given them as a wedding present. In the kitchen, she tied on an apron and tended to the meal she was cooking: rack of lamb, new potatoes and French beans.

At ten to seven, she opened a bottle of Californian Merlot, poured herself a glass and lit the candles.

At half-past seven, she called Vincent's cell phone. It went straight to voicemail.

"Hey, honey. Everything OK? I've got dinner waiting for you and I picked up something special for dessert. From Victoria's Secret."

Vincent's plane would have gotten in at three thirty that afternoon. She went online and checked the airline's site. Then the airport. The plane had landed on schedule.

A little flicker of anxiety raced around her bloodstream. She took a swig of the merlot and called Vincent's secretary on her cell.

"Hey, Kristin. It's Terri-Ann. Did Vincent make his flight OK?"

"Oh, hi, Terri-Ann. I guess so. He didn't come in to work this morning, but I just assumed he finished up with Clark yesterday and then went straight from his hotel to the airport. Why? He's not home yet?"

"No. I'm kinda worried. The flight landed fine, but he's not home yet."

"Look, honey, he probably stopped off on the way home to buy you flowers or a gift or something. You know what he's like. Such a romantic." She sighed. "I should be so lucky."

"OK, thanks, Kristin. I gotta go."

At eleven, Terri-Ann called the San Antonio Police Department. The officer who answered the phone told Terri-Ann not to worry and to call again in the morning if her husband hadn't appeared by then.

The weekend passed in a fever of worry. Terri-Ann called her father, and they spent the two days together at her house, praying, calling the SAPD and everyone they could think of, and drinking. He returned home on the Sunday evening, leaving Terri-Ann to try and get some sleep before the week ahead. Vincent hadn't returned by the morning so she called the English department's secretaries and explained she wouldn't be coming in that day, then called the SAPD once again. This time she insisted on talking to a detective and eventually found herself talking to a female detective called Perez. The detective sympathised, took a note of her husband's name, then took her name, address and cell phone number and asked her to come in and complete a missing persons report.

Terri-Ann arrived at the substation at ten. She presented herself at the reception desk and asked for Detective Perez.

Five minutes later, a tall woman with pale-coffee-coloured skin and a heart-shaped face approached Terri-Ann's chair. She bent down and spoke in a quiet voice.

"Mrs Calder?"

"Yes," Terri-Ann said. "Are you Detective Perez?"

"I am. Please call me Val, though. It's short for Valentina."

Terri-Ann's heart fluttered in her ribcage. Why was this police officer being so friendly? Somehow, maybe it was a wife's intuition, she knew Vincent was dead.

"Val, has something happened to Vincent?"

Val put a hand on Terri-Ann's shoulder.

"Why don't you come with me?"

Sitting opposite each other in a room furnished with a pale-blue sofa and two matching armchairs, the two women stared at each other. Terri-Ann's face was taut, pale. Val's was softer but creased with worry lines.

"Mrs Calder, I'm afraid I have bad news. On Friday, an Arizona State Trooper out of Phoenix found a body in the desert. We got the preliminary DNA results back a half hour ago. They were a match to the information held in your husband's service record. I am so sorry for your loss."

Terri-Ann heard her voice echoing around inside her head.

"That was too quick. For DNA results. You guys never have enough money for rush jobs, everybody knows that."

"Normally, that's right. But they found a tattoo. The Army Rangers and a service number. So they contacted their regimental commanding officer. After that, they fast-tracked the DNA test. The Rangers came back with your husband's service number, and it all matched. I'm really sorry."

After the funeral guests had all left, Terri-Ann poured herself another glass of wine and slumped in Vincent's battered old La-Z-Boy. Now the tears did come. As she cried, and drank, she thought of a man she hadn't spoken to for five years. A British guy Vincent had brought home for dinner one time on leave. She knew his name. Gabriel Wolfe. She knew he was Special Forces, like Vinnie. And she knew that he and her husband had taken a blood oath to investigate if either of them should die anywhere except in bed.

She pulled out her cell phone and sent a text.

Vinnie's gone. Remember your promise? T.

***

Order your copy of Rattlesnake now on Amazon.

COPYRIGHT

ACKNOWLEDGEMENTS

With each new book I write, I find I am indebted to a growing number of people who help me make these stories live and breathe.

I would like to single out for thanks the following kind, patient and talented souls for their time, expertise and understanding this time round: Karen Allonby, Giles Bassett, Darren Bennett, Mike Dempsey, Dickie Gittins, Christina Larsson, Michelle Lowery, Jo Maslen, Sean Memory, Cheryl Torricer, Anouchka Towner-Coston, Crystal Watanabe

Andy Maslen
    Salisbury, 2017

ABOUT THE AUTHOR

Andy Maslen was born in Nottingham, in the UK, home of legendary bowman Robin Hood. Andy once won a medal for archery, although he has never been locked up by the sheriff.

He has worked in a record shop, as a barman, as a door-to-door DIY products salesman and a cook in an Italian restaurant.

As well as the Stella Cole and Gabriel Wolfe thrillers, Andy has published five works of non-fiction, on copywriting and freelancing, with Marshall Cavendish and Kogan Page. They are all available online and in bookshops.

He lives in Wiltshire with his wife, two sons and a whippet named Merlin.

ALSO BY ANDY MASLEN
THE GABRIEL WOLFE SERIES

Trigger Point

Reversal of Fortune (short story)

Blind Impact

Condor

First Casualty

Fury

Rattlesnake

Minefield (novella)

No Further

Torpedo

Three Kingdoms

Ivory Nation (coming soon)

The DI Stella Cole series

Hit and Run

Hit Back Harder

Hit and Done

Let the Bones be Charred

Other fiction

Blood Loss - a Vampire Story

Non-fiction

Write to Sell

100 Great Copywriting Ideas

The Copywriting Sourcebook

Write Copy, Make Money

Persuasive Copywriting

Made in United States
Orlando, FL
14 June 2023

34143660R00272